WENDELL BERRY

WENDELL BERRY

Three Short Novels

Nathan Coulter

Remembering

A World Lost

COUNTERPOINT
WASHINGTON, D.C.

A CIP catalog record for this book is available
from the Library of Congress.
ISBN 1-58243-178-7

FIRST PRINTING

Jacket and text design by David Bullen Design

COUNTERPOINT
P.O. Box 65793
Washington, D.C. 20035-5793

Counterpoint is a member of the Perseus Books Group.

10   9   8   7   6   5   4   3   2   1

Contents

Nathan Coulter

For John

1

Dark. The light went out the door when she pulled it to. And then everything came in close around me, the way it was in the daylight, only all close. Because in the dark I could remember and not see. The sun was first, going over the hill behind our barn. Then the river was covered with the shadows of the hills. Then the hills went behind their shadows, and just the house and the barn and the other buildings were left, standing black against the sky where it was still white in the west.

After supper it was only the inside of the house, lighted where we moved from the kitchen to the living room and upstairs to bed. Until the last of the light went out the door; and it was all there in the room, close enough to touch if I didn't reach out my hand. The dark broke them loose and let them in. The memory was closer than the sight of them. What was left outside was the way it had been before anybody had come there to see anything.

I lay awake listening to the wind blow. It was the beginning of the dream, I knew, even if I was still awake listening. The wind came hard against the back of the house and rattled the weatherboarding and whooped around the corners; and went on through the woods on the hillside, bending the trees and cracking the limbs together; and on with a lonely, hollow sound into the river bottoms; and on over the country, over the farms and roads and towns and cities. It seemed that I could hear the sounds the wind made in all the places it was, all at the same time.

I never knew when I began to dream the wind and quit listening to it. But after a while the bed rose off the floor and floated out of the house. It flew up high over the roof and sailed down again to the hillside above the river. The wind pulled at the bedclothes and I had to hold them around my neck to keep them from blowing away.

Standing at the edge of the woods was a lion, looking up at the house, with the valley and the river lying in the dark behind him. I could see every muscle in his body rolled up smooth under his hide. The wind blew through his mane. His eyes reminded me of Grandpa's, they were so fierce and blue.

While I watched he lifted his head and roared toward the house, his white teeth showing and his tongue curled under the sound. I knew then it wasn't the wind I'd heard, but the lion's voice, lonely and like a wind. The muscles in his belly hardened and heaved the voice out of his mouth; and he stood quiet while the sound went on and on over the country. I held the covers around my neck and watched him, and heard his voice go through the woods and into the valley and against the walls of the houses where the people were asleep.

Late in the night the bed floated into the house again. And it was quiet until the roosters began to crow in the dark where the voice of the lion had been. While the roosters crowed I dreamed of them, their voices crying in the barns and henhouses, close and far away under the dark. In my dream their combs were red, and their feathers black as coal. And while I slept they crowed the dark away.

⁂

Sunlight came red into my sleep and I nearly woke until I turned over and slept again in the shadow of my face. Then the light brightened and hardened in the room and I couldn't sleep any longer. But I kept my eyes closed, remembering what I'd dreamed.

I heard Mother walk across the kitchen floor and shove the teakettle to the back of the stove. I listened to her clear away the dishes that she and Daddy had used for their breakfast and begin cooking breakfast for Brother and me. The sounds separated me from the night, and I let my eyes come open.

Brother was still asleep on the other side of the room. He'd thrown the sheet off and was lying on his back with one foot sticking over the edge of the bed. I watched his ribs fold and unfold over his breathing. The sun hit the mirror on top of the bureau and glanced off against the ceiling. Beside my bed my pants and shirt were piled on my shoes where I'd taken them off the night before. My clothes were hand-me-downs that Brother had outgrown and passed on to me. His clothes were newer, not so faded as mine.

I pushed the sheet back and sat up on the side of the bed. Out the window I could see Daddy harnessing the mules in the driveway of the barn. He took the gear off the pegs in front of their stalls and swung it over their backs and buckled it on. Then he led them out into the lot and shook out the checklines and snapped them to the bits. I was too far away to hear the sounds he made. One of the mules kicked at a fly and I waited for the harness to rattle, but there wasn't any sound. He backed the mules into their places on each side of the wagon tongue and hitched them up. I could hear the wheels joggle when he started out of the lot. Mother went to the back porch, letting the screen door slam, and called something to him. He stopped and answered her, and drove on through the gate.

Across the hollow that divided our place from Grandpa's I could see his house and the two barns white in the sun. The back door slammed over there and Grandma crossed the yard and emptied a pan of dishwater over the fence. Grandpa's hogs came up to see if she'd given them something to eat, and smelled around where she'd thrown the water.

Grandpa and Uncle Burley were walking out toward the top of the ridge to meet Daddy and the wagon. Uncle Burley's two coon hounds trotted along at his heels, sad-looking and quiet because they knew he was going to work and not hunting. Grandpa walked in front; he and Uncle Burley weren't talking to each other. They got to the top of the ridge and stopped. Uncle Burley turned his back to the wind and rolled a cigarette. When Daddy came up they climbed on the wagon and rode out of sight down the other side of the ridge.

Grandpa's farm had belonged to our people ever since there had been a farm in that place, or people to own a farm. Grandpa's father had left it to Grandpa and his other sons and daughters. But Grandpa had borrowed money and bought their shares. He had to have it whole hog or none, root hog or die, or he wouldn't have it at all. Uncle Burley said that was the reason Daddy had bought our farm instead of staying on Grandpa's. They were the sort of men who couldn't get along owning the same place.

Our farm was the old Ellis Place. Daddy had bought it before Brother and I were born, and we still owed money on it; but Daddy said it wouldn't be long before we'd have it all paid. If he lived we'd own every inch of it, and he said he planned to live. He said that when we finally did get the farm paid for we could tell everybody to go to hell. That was what he lived for, to own his farm without having to say please or thank you to a living soul.

Uncle Burley didn't own any land at all. He didn't own anything to speak of; just his dogs and a couple of guns. In a way he owned an old camp house at the river, but it was Uncle Burley's only because nobody else wanted it. He'd never let Grandpa or Daddy even talk to him about buying a farm. He said land was worse than a wife; it tied you down, and he didn't want to be in any place he couldn't leave. He never did go any-place much, except fishing and hunting, and sometimes to town on Sat-urday. But he wanted to feel that he could leave if he took the notion.

I stood in the patch of sun in front of the window and began putting on my clothes. The day was already hot. Hens were cackling, and a few sparrows fluttered their wings in the dust in front of the barn. I watched our milk cows wade into the pond to drink. Over Grandpa's ridge I could see where the road came up from the river and went into Port William. At the top of the hill a gravel lane branched off to come back past Grandpa's gate to our place. On the other side of town the road went down into the bottoms again and followed the river on to the Ohio. I couldn't see the houses at town, but the white steeple of the church pointed up over the trees and I could make out the weather vane on top. On Sunday morn-ings we could hear the church bell ringing all the way to our house. And we heard it on Wednesday nights when it rang for prayer meeting.

Between the hills white fog covered the river and bottoms, and trailed off into the woods along the bluffs. Grandpa remembered when steam-boats were on the river, carrying tobacco and passengers and livestock down to the Ohio and on to Louisville. But now there were only a few towboats pushing bargeloads of sand. The hills on our side of the river were green, and on the other side they were blue. They got bluer farther away.

Uncle Burley said hills always looked blue when you were far away from them. That was a pretty color for hills; the little houses and barns and fields looked so neat and quiet tucked against them. It made you want to be close to them. But he said that when you got close they were like the hills you'd left, and when you looked back your own hills were blue and you wanted to go back again. He said he reckoned a man could wear himself out going back and forth.

Mother came to the foot of the stairs and called us to breakfast. I shook Brother awake and waited for him to dress, and then we went down to the kitchen.

❧

Our mother was sick, and in the afternoons when she'd washed the dinner dishes she had to lie down to rest. Daddy made Brother and me stay out of the house then so it would be quiet. When the weather was good we'd go to the field with Daddy or Uncle Burley, or go swimming, or just wander around looking for things to do. And even though we worried about our mother's sickness it was good to have the whole afternoon to ourselves without anybody to bother us.

We went down the hill and into the woods that grew along the hollow between our farm and Grandpa's. Just enough air was stirring to tilt the leaves without rustling them together, and except for our feet rattling dry leaves on the ground the woods was quiet. We climbed the fence and started on toward the dry streambed at the bottom of the hollow.

When we'd gone about ten feet on Grandpa's side of the fence we came to Aunt Mary's grave. The grave was a shallow trough in the hillside, filled with sticks and leaves. There was no stone to mark it.

Our Aunt Mary had been buried there a long time ago. It was the first thing anybody remembered about our family, and nobody could remember anything else for a good while after that; we didn't know how many years it had been since she died.

Aunt Mary was our great-great-grandfather's youngest daughter. His name was Jonas Thomasson Coulter. And about the time Aunt Mary was grown he got into an argument with a man named Jeff Ellis who was living on our place then. Jonas thought the line fence between their farms should be built on Jeff Ellis's side of the hollow, and Jeff Ellis thought it ought to go on Jonas's side. They squabbled over it for several years, and there was some shooting done by both sides before it was settled.

While they were in the worst of this fight Aunt Mary took scarlet fever and died. Jonas Thomasson Coulter went down to the hollow and dug a grave where he thought the fence ought to run, and he made the rest of the family bury her in it. His wife never would speak to him or even look at him after that; but it settled the argument over the fence.

Jeff Ellis was afraid of the dead, and he wouldn't come close to the grave. So they built the fence ten feet on his side of it. That made Jonas's farm ten feet wider than even he thought it should have been.

It didn't really matter much, because the land in that hollow was steep and ill-natured anyway, and nothing ever grew there but trees and buck bushes. But Uncle Burley said that wouldn't have bothered Jonas Thomasson Coulter. What he wanted was to own land; it didn't matter a damn whether it was flat or straight up and down, or whether it would grow tobacco or buck bushes.

That was all we knew about Grandpa's grandfather—his name, and how he'd made certain that Grandpa's line would run where it did. We didn't know where he came from, or even where he was buried.

It wasn't long after they buried Aunt Mary there in the hollow until one of the Ellises saw her ghost. She walked back and forth across her grave on dark nights, carrying a dishpan in one hand and shaking a dishrag with the other one, the way she'd always looked coming back to the house after she'd emptied the dirty water over the yard fence. From then on a lot of people saw her, our people and different ones of the Ellises. Grandpa said he saw her once when he was a boy. And I thought I'd seen her a time or two, but I wasn't sure enough to tell anybody but Brother.

Her ghost walked because she wanted to be buried in the graveyard with the rest of the dead people in our family. But nobody had ever taken the time to dig her up and bury her there. We never even put flowers on her grave.

The top of the grave was caved in where the dirt had fallen into the hollow places between her bones. I thought her bones had probably rotted too. It would have been hard to dig her up and take her anyplace.

We'd waited too long. A big hickory grew up beside the grave, and she was just some earth tangled in the roots. It was strange to think of Aunt Mary being a part of Grandpa's farm, or maybe a hickory tree.

We climbed out of the hollow and walked along the edge of the big woods on the river bluff, then crossed the point of the ridge and went down again until we came to the hollow where Grandpa's spring was. Old Oscar was standing in the shade of the oak trees below the spring.

Grandpa had raised and trained saddle horses once until he went broke at it. And old Oscar had been his stud. He was a dark chestnut with a narrow white blaze on his face. He'd been beautiful when he was young, and high-spirited. When they were breaking him he kicked Grandpa in the face and left a long, jagged scar across his cheek. But now he was gentle. He was twenty-five years old, and he stayed thin because his teeth were bad. Uncle Burley said he'd finally starve to death because he wouldn't have enough teeth to eat with. He was blind too, and his eyes were as white as milk. It was as if he'd turned his eyes back into his head to look at whatever it was he thought about.

Brother and I spoke to him and walked toward his head. He rattled his breath through his nose and trembled until we let him smell our hands and he recognized us. Brother caught him by a hank of his mane and led him over to the spring wall. I broke a switch off a tree and stripped the leaves; we climbed up on the wall and onto Oscar's back. We guided him with the switch; when we wanted him to go to the right we jiggled the switch against the left side of his face, and against the right side of his face when we wanted him to go to the left.

Daddy and Grandpa always said that Oscar would fall down someday and cripple us. But he hardly ever stumbled. Uncle Burley said Oscar knew his way around the farm as well as he knew the inside of his skin. He had it all in his head. He didn't need to see it. In a way, Oscar walked and grazed and drank in his own mind.

Brother guided him around the spring and along the side of the hill to the Coulter Branch hollow, and then turned down toward the river. Oscar didn't like walking in a strange place, but we spoke to him and encouraged him, and before long he got used to the slant of the hill. He walked slower, though, than he did when he was in the pasture, as if afraid the road might drop out from under him or a tree grow up in his way.

We followed the old wagon road down Coulter Branch to the bottom of the hill and turned upriver past the old Billy Hole landing where Beriah Easterly had his store. The river ran close to the road there. We took the path down through a woods of water maples and elms and sycamores to where Uncle Burley's fishing shack stood overlooking the river.

Once the shack had been painted green, but the paint had weathered to a color that was as much blue as green. The trees grew up close around it, and vines had grown over the walls and out along the eaves.

We got off old Oscar at the camp house and walked the rest of the way to the river. He stood still where we'd stopped him, as if he'd run against a wall and didn't know how to get around it.

We walked upstream along the top of the riverbank. Behind us the trees closed around the camp house and Oscar; and then we went into a patch of horseweeds and out of sight. The horseweeds grew high over our heads, and so thick we had to bend them out of our way.

"This is a jungle," Brother said. "Nobody ever was here before."

All we could see was horseweeds. We had to look straight up to see the sky. But we knew where we were, and we went on, turning the bend of the river.

Brother stopped and broke off two dead weed stalks and handed one of them to me. "Here's a gun," he said.

"We'll kill a lion," I told him.

Before long we crossed a gully filled with tin cans and bottles, and followed a path into the open place that Jig Pendleton had cleared on the bank above his shanty boat. From there we could look down into the bend and see Uncle Burley's camp. Oscar stood there with his head turned toward the river.

In the middle of the open place was a table where Jig cleaned his fish. Above the table an old set of grocery scales hung from a tree limb. A few worn-out nets were strewn around on the ground, and one of Jig's trotlines was stretched between two trees to dry.

The path went to the edge of the bank, and then stair-stepped to the water. We went down the steps and crossed the plank to the shanty boat.

Jig Pendleton lived there alone and fished for a living. He was crazy on religion, and when he wasn't busy fishing he'd fasten himself in the shanty and read the Bible from cover to cover over and over again. He worried all the time about the sins of the flesh, and believed that if he could purify himself the Lord would send down a chariot of fire and take him to Heaven. But he never could quite purify himself enough. Sooner or later he always gave it up and got on a drunk, and then he'd have to start all over again.

He'd invited Uncle Burley and Brother and me in to see him several times, and the inside of his shanty was a sight. He'd found an old Singer sewing machine, and thrown the sewing part of it away, and fastened the iron frame with the wheel and treadle to the floor. Then he'd wired a lot of spools to the walls and run strings between them, zigzagging and crisscrossing from one end of the shanty to the other. This contraption of strings and pulleys was hooked to the wheel and treadle. It worked like a charm, but Jig never had been able to decide what it was for. He just kept adding spools and string until it was more complicated than a spider web. The whole inside of his house was a machine that couldn't do anything but run. When he was drinking Jig would sit and treadle the machine and sing and shout and pray for the Lord to purify him. One night when he came home drunk he got tangled up in it and nearly choked to death before Gander Loyd came along and found him the next morning. Some of the missionary society women in town saved string and spools to give to him because they felt sorry for him. He had a wife and daughter living somewhere, but they hadn't had anything to do with him since he'd got so crazy.

A couple of times Jig had taken his boat out of the river and left the country. He stayed away a year both times, and nobody knew much about where he went or what he did. Once he told Uncle Burley that he just wandered around, looking at the mountains and rivers and oceans that the Lord had made. Since the Lord had gone to all the trouble of making them, he thought the least a man could do was go and look at them. He was as crazy as a June bug, but he was a good fisherman and didn't bother anybody, and he was Uncle Burley's friend.

Jig was busy loading bait and tackle into his rowboat, and we sat down to watch him.

"Hello, Jig," Brother said.

"Hello there, Tom and Nathan," Jig said. "How're you little children?"

"Fine," I said.

"We hunted for a lion up there in the horseweeds," Brother said, "but we couldn't find one."

"The lion and the lamb shall lie down together," Jig said, "and a little child shall lead them."

"You wouldn't lead the lion that lives in that horseweed patch," Brother said. "He'd bite your durned arm off."

"You oughtn't to cuss," Jig said. "It makes Jesus sad."

Brother was ashamed of himself then, and he hushed. Jig began to bail out the rowboat.

"What're you fixing to do?" I asked him.

"Fixing to run my lines," Jig said.

"We'll go with you," Brother said.

Jig shook his head. "No, honey. You might drown. It's awful easy to drown in this river."

"We can swim," Brother said. "We won't drown."

"Listen," Jig said. "If the Lord's planning for one of you all to drown, that's His business. But He don't want me to get messed up in it."

He untied the boat and began rowing up the river. Brother and I went back to the bank.

"Let's go swimming," Brother said.

He started upstream again toward the sandbar, and I went with him, feeling a little guilty as if Jig might tell the Lord on us. But when we got to the sandbar Brother began to take his clothes off, running to the water; and I ran too, trying to beat him.

I kicked my clothes off and ran out into the river, letting the weight of it against my legs trip me under. I felt the water slap over my head, and I swam down the slope of the rock bottom until the deep cold made my ears ache. I rolled over and looked up into the blackness. The current carried me along. I loosened myself in it, and held still in the movement of the water. I couldn't tell whether my head was up or down; I felt as if I could swim forever in any direction. My lungs tightened, wanting to breathe, and I kicked the bottom away from me and swam up until I saw a patch of light floating on the surface. I broke through it into the air again.

I shook the water out of my eyes and floated. The sky seemed a deeper blue after my eyes had been in the dark. Over my head a white cloud unraveled in the wind. The sky widened to the tops of the hills that circled around the valley. Inside the ring of hilltops trees grew along both banks of the river. They leaned toward me — willow and maple and sycamore.

I watched them, letting myself float in the slow current. I thought if I floated to the mouth of the river I'd always be at the center of a ring of trees and a ring of hills and a ring where the sky touched. I said, "I'm Nathan Coulter." It seemed strange.

Brother swam up behind me and threw water in my face. We raced back to the shallow water, and waded out onto the bar.

I found a flat rock and stretched out to let the sun dry me. It was warm and I felt clean and tired. Across the river a hawk held his wings to the wind and circled. The sky was empty except for the hawk and the cloud. I cupped my hands around my eyes. And then there were three of us — the hawk and the cloud and me.

✻

When we got back to Grandpa's place we turned old Oscar loose; he wandered off down the hill toward his shade trees at the spring. We went on to the top of the ridge and back toward our place where Grandpa and Daddy and Uncle Burley were digging postholes. The ground was shallow along that part of the fence row; they were digging to the rock and blasting the rest of the way down with dynamite. When we got there Uncle Burley was sitting at the edge of a hole, guiding the rock drill, and Daddy was driving it down with a sledge hammer. Grandpa was working at the post pile, facing the posts with an axe. We sat behind Uncle Burley and watched.

Daddy glanced at us between swings. "Have you all been riding that old horse again?" He had to interrupt himself to say "Ah" when the hammer came down. The sun was beaming hot, and he was sweating through his shirt.

"No," Brother said.

Daddy looked at Brother and then at me, and swung the hammer down. "If I see you on that horse one more time, I'm going to skin both of you. It looks like you can't hear when I tell you something."

Then he said, "Get out of the way, now, before you get hurt. You don't have any business up here."

He dropped the hammer and went to find the water jug. As soon as he was out of earshot Uncle Burley winked at us. "You'd better do what he tells you, boys. It's a bad day."

"What's he mad at us for?" Brother said. "We weren't bothering him."

"That's just his way, " Uncle Burley said. "He loves you boys."

Several sticks of dynamite and a coil of fuse and a box of caps were lying on the ground behind us. When Uncle Burley turned his head and began working the drill back and forth in the hole, Brother picked up a scrap of fuse and took a cap out of the box.

We went out the ridge again and took the road to town. A few patches of red clover were blooming along the sides of the road, and daisies and sweet clover. Big dusty-looking grasshoppers flew up ahead of us, their wings clicking, and dropped back into the weeds, and flew again when we caught up with them. Finally we moved out to the middle of the road to be rid of them.

The road went slanting over the top of our ridge past Big Ellis's pond and his house, then it made a sharp turn and ran straight on to where the town's ridge pointed off on the river bluff. Beriah Easterly's house set on the outside of the turn, and we stopped to see if his boy, Calvin, was at home. We knocked on the door, but nobody came. We guessed Mrs. Easterly and Calvin had gone down to the store with Beriah. Their old bird dog was asleep under the porch swing, but he just raised his head and looked at us and went to sleep again.

"It looks like somebody ought to be at home," Brother said.

I knocked again. We could hear a clock ticking somewhere inside the house, and that was all. Things had quit working right. Daddy wouldn't let us stay with him, and now Calvin was gone. All of a sudden it got lonesome. We went back to the road and didn't stop again until we got to town.

The town strung out along the road for maybe half a mile — a few houses and other buildings and the bank and the church. Except for the preacher and the banker and the storekeepers, about everybody who lived there worked on the farms. There was one side road but no houses were built on it. We went past the poolroom and on up the street to where the drugstore and grocery store and harness shop stood in a row along the sidewalk across from the church. The harness shop had been closed a long time. The harnessmaker died and the town didn't need another store, so it had been left empty. The door and windows had been boarded up and covered with political posters and cigarette advertisements, and Calvin Easterly said that bats lived inside. In the daytime the bats hung together like a curtain down the back wall. It was a scary place when we thought about it, especially at night. But it had been shut up for so long that we hardly noticed it was there.

Aside from the harness shop it was a pretty town. Most of the buildings were painted white, and tall locust and maple trees grew in the yards along the road.

Big Ellis and Gander Loyd and the Montgomery twins were squatting in front of the drugstore, leaning back into the shade of the wall. The Montgomerys didn't look at us when we came up, and we didn't speak to them. Grandpa had thrashed their father one time for calling Uncle Burley a drunkard, and none of them had ever got over it. They were always shamefaced and hangdog when even Brother and I were around, as if they expected one of us to walk over and kick them in the shins. Their names were Len and Lemuel, but everybody called them Mushmouth and Chicken Little. We walked past them to where Big Ellis and Gander were.

"How're you boys?" Big Ellis said.

"All right," I said. "How're you, Big Ellis?"

"Hot. Too hot to work. What're they doing over at your place?"

"Digging postholes."

"Whoo," Big Ellis said. "They're feeling the heat." He squinted his eyes and giggled.

We spoke to Gander and sat down. Gander turned his head and looked at us with his one eye. He was chewing on the end of a matchstick. "Hello," he said. He wiped the matchstick on the bib of his overalls and began picking his teeth. Gander never had much to say. He'd killed a man and lost an eye in the fight, and it always took me a while to get used to his one-sided face. He stayed quiet, even when he was in town, keeping what he knew to himself.

"Could you boys use a chocolate ice cream cone?" Big Ellis asked us.

"We had dinner a while ago," Brother said. "Thank you just the same."

"Aw hell, you can eat a chocolate ice cream cone anytime. Let's have one."

We got up and went into the drugstore.

"Three chocolate ice cream cones," Big Ellis said. The girl behind the counter scooped them up for us. Big Ellis gave her three nickels and we went out and sat down again.

"You boys ever get in a fight?" Big Ellis asked me.

"No," I said.

"If we ever did I'd win," Brother told him.

Big Ellis looked around at Gander and giggled. But Gander wasn't paying any attention. Big Ellis let it go, and ate his ice cream without talking anymore. He wasn't likely to stir any conversation out of Gander — or the Montgomerys, either, as long as we were there. It wasn't very good company. After we finished the ice cream we stayed a while to show Big Ellis that we appreciated his buying it for us, then we thanked him and left.

Up the street from the harness shop was the hotel. It was a long, two-story frame building with a porch running all the way across the front of it. Salesmen and travelers used to spend the night there, but now the rooms were rented out by the month, to old people mostly. Some of them were sitting in rocking chairs on the front porch when we went by. An old woman nodded her head to us. "Good afternoon, young gentlemen." She turned to the others and said, "Such fine young men."

An old man leaned toward her and said, "Whose boys are they?"

"Why, they're Dave Coulter's grandchildren."

"Well, God damn," he said. "Are they old Dave's boys?"

"Grandchildren," she said.

On a rise at the far end of town was the graveyard. In a way it was the prettiest part of the town — with its white headstones and green grass and flowers, shady under the gray-trunked cedars. From there you could see a long stretch of the river valley. Grandma said it was a restful place, and it was. But it was hard to forget all the dead people buried underneath it. In the summer it was easier to forget them than it was in the winter. In the winter you felt they must be cold.

We went through the gate and up the driveway. Toward the top of the rise, jutting up even taller than most of the cedars, was the Coulter family monument. It was made of granite — a square base, then a long shaft like a candle with an angel standing on top of it. Grandpa's mother had bought it from a traveling salesman when she was old and childish. Grandpa said she must have been crazy too. It had taken twenty mules to pull the base of it seven miles from the railroad station. And the old woman had been dead about five years before Grandpa was able to pay for it. On the front of the monument was written:

FATHER —— *MOTHER*

George W. Coulter *Parthenia B. Coulter*
1826–1889 *1835–1917*

Beneath this monument
the mortal remains
of George and Parthenia
parted by death
wait to be rejoined
in Glory

George and Parthenia were Grandpa's mother and father. On the other side of the monument was Grandpa's name:

THEIR SON
David Coulter
1860–

Grandpa was the only one of Parthenia's children left at home when she bought the monument, and she'd left the other names off — had forgotten about them, or was mad at them for leaving. But Grandpa wasn't flattered that she'd remembered him. The last thing he wanted was to have his name carved in four-inch letters on a tombstone. The monument had been enough trouble to him without that. He still got mad every time he thought about it. It was as if she'd expected him to write his other date up there and die right away to balance things.

It had finally bothered him so much that he'd sent Daddy to buy a new lot for the family. He said he'd be damned if anybody was going to tell him where to be buried. The new lot was way off on the far side of the graveyard. Nobody was buried there yet, and it was all grown up in weeds.

The angel on top of the monument had his wings spread as if he were about to fly down and write the rest of our names in the blank spaces. Parthenia B. Coulter had left plenty of room for whoever might come along. Uncle Burley said the angel probably would fly on Judgment Day. That kind of talk always disturbed Grandma; she thought it was sacrilegious. And so he'd usually mention it when the subject of graveyards came up. He said he could just see that old angel flying up out of the smoke and cinders and tearing out for Heaven like a chicken out of a henhouse fire.

A little past the graveyard gate was the Crandel Place. When we passed there Mrs. Crandel's grandson, who had come to visit her from Louisville, was sitting in the front yard playing with a pet crow. Old man Crandel had caught the crow for him before it was big enough to fly. The boy was cleaned up and dressed as if it were Sunday.

He walked over to the fence and looked at us. "Hi," he said.

We told him hello.

"What's your name?" he asked Brother.

"Puddin-tame," Brother said.

"Would you like to come over and play with me?" the boy asked. "I'll let you ride my bicycle if you will."

Brother and I climbed over the fence.

"Where's the bicycle?" Brother asked him.

"On the porch."

We followed him up to the porch. The bicycle was a new one. And he had a new air rifle too.

He brought the bicycle down the steps and rode it around in the yard. It was painted red and the sun shone on the spokes of the wheels. I wished Brother and I had one.

In a little while the boy got off and gave the bicycle to Brother. But Brother couldn't ride it, and it turned over with him. Then I got on it and it turned over with me. Mrs. Crandel came out on the porch and told the boy not to let us tear up his bicycle.

When she went back inside Brother said, "Let me try it one more time."

The boy said, "No, you can't. You might break it."

He caught the pet crow again and we went over to the corner of the yard and sat down under a locust tree.

"That's a mighty fine crow you've got there," Brother said. "Can I look at him?"

The boy said, "You can if you'll be careful not to hurt him. Grandfather's going to let me take him home with me."

"Sure. I won't bother him." Brother put the crow on his shoulder and smoothed its feathers. "Say," he said, "I'll bet you don't know much about crows."

"Not much. Grandfather says they'll eat about anything, and if you split their tongues they'll talk."

"I can show you a little trick about crows. You want to see it?"

"Yes," the boy said.

Brother motioned to me to come and help him. I held the crow while he got the dynamite cap and the piece of fuse out of his pocket. The boy came up and watched Brother put the fuse into the cap and crimp the cap against a rock.

"Here," Brother told me. "Hold his tail feathers up."

I held the tail feathers up and he poked the cap into the crow's bunghole. I gave him a match and he struck it on his shoe.

"Now you watch," Brother said. "You'll learn something about crows." He lit the fuse and pitched the crow up in the air.

The crow flew around over our heads for a minute, and Brother and I got out of the way. Then he looked around and saw that little ball of fire following him, spitting like a mad tomcat. He really got down to business then. He planned to fly right off and leave that fire. But it caught up with him over old man Crandel's barn. *BLAM!* And feathers and guts went every which way. Where the crow had been was a little piece of blue sky with a ring of smoke and black feathers around it.

Brother and I took off over the fence. When we looked back the boy was still standing there with his mouth open, staring up at the place where the crow had exploded. He started to cry. I felt sorry for him when I saw that, but there was nothing to do but run.

When we got back to the graveyard we were out of sight of the Crandels' house and we stopped running. The angel on top of the monument was looking in the direction of town. I could still hear the explosion going off.

Brother said, "He thought a lot of that crow."

"He was crying," I said.

It was late; but we wouldn't have supper until dark, after Daddy quit work, and we didn't hurry.

"Do you think Mrs. Crandel heard the explosion?" I asked.

"If she wasn't dead she did."

"If she didn't he'll tell her."

"Whoo," Brother said.

Big Ellis and Gander Loyd had gone home by the time we got to town. Mushmouth and Chicken Little Montgomery were sitting by themselves in front of the drugstore, and we walked down the other side of the street to keep them from seeing us. If one of them had pointed at us and said, "There go Tom and Nathan Coulter, and they just blew up a poor old boy's crow," we couldn't have said a word. The sun had gone down and the nighthawks were flying. I was glad Brother and I were together.

When we were outside town again Brother said, "We'll tell Uncle Burley about it when we get home. He'll get a kick out of it."

That made us feel a little better. But Uncle Burley was still at the fence row with Grandpa and Daddy when we got there. They were busy, and we didn't go where they were.

⁂

By the time we got home that evening Mrs. Crandel had telephoned our mother and told on us. Mother made us stay at the house until Daddy came in from work. We sat on the back porch and waited for him.

When he came Mother told him what we'd done, and he cut a switch and whipped us. He was already mad at us for riding old Oscar, and he whipped us for that too while he was at it.

"Now I know what that crow felt like, " I told Brother.

"That crow never felt it," Brother said. "He was dead before he heard the explosion."

The next morning Daddy said that if we didn't stay out of trouble he'd take up where he left off the night before. After he went out of the house Mother told us not to feel bad because he was mad at us. He was just tired, she said.

It started raining that afternoon, and rained off and on for a couple of days. The wet weather kept Daddy from working in the field; that gave him a chance to rest and he got into a better humor. He let us stay with him while he did odd jobs around the barn, and we enjoyed each other's company.

On the morning after the ground had dried Daddy hitched the team to the cultivator and drove to the tobacco patch. We watched him leave; and then we fed Mother's chickens for her because she wasn't feeling good.

After a while we saw Grandpa riding his saddle mare across the field toward our house, and we ran to open the lot gate for him.

"Where's your daddy?" he asked us.

"Plowing tobacco," Brother said.

He turned the mare around and rode back through the gate. Brother and I watched him go up the ridge. When he rode the mare he kept his walking cane hooked over his arm. Mother said he carried the cane because he was old, but mostly he used it as a riding whip. He could walk almost as fast as Daddy, poking the cane straight out in front of him as if to get the air and everything out of the way so he could move faster. He always hurried, even across a room, setting his feet down hard. You could never imagine him turning around and going the other way. When he walked through the house he made the dishes rattle in the kitchen cabinet, and you half expected to find his tracks sunk into the floor. He was tall and lean, his face crossed with wrinkles. His hair was white and it hung in his eyes most of the time when he wasn't wearing a hat, because he didn't use a comb for anything but to scratch his head. His nose crooked like a hawk's and his eyes were pale and blue.

Before long he came over the ridge again, and Daddy came with him. Daddy had unhitched the team and the wind blew the sound of the loose trace chains down into the lot. Grandpa rode through the gate ahead of him and unsaddled the mare and put her in a stall, and then helped unharness the mules.

"Did you get done, Daddy?" Brother said.

"No," Daddy said. He sounded mad again.

I was going to ask him why he'd quit, but Grandpa told me to get out of the way before one of the mules kicked my head off.

"They won't kick me," I said. "I feed them all the time."

He looked at me and snorted. "Shit," he said.

When they got the mules unhitched Daddy went to the house, and Grandpa led the mules to the barn to put them in their stalls. Brother and I followed him into the driveway. "Didn't I tell you to stay away from these mules?" he said. "Go to the house."

Daddy was in the kitchen talking to Mother when we came in.

"What's going on?" Brother asked.

Daddy didn't answer. He went out and started the car, and he and Grandpa drove off toward town.

In about half an hour they came back. Uncle Burley was slouched between them in the front seat. Grandpa got out and hooked his cane around Uncle Burley's arm and told him to come on out of there. Uncle Burley crawled out and stood up, holding on to his head with one hand and on to the car door with the other one. He hadn't shaved for two or three days, and his whiskers were matted with blood and dirt.

There was a knot on the left side of his head, starting above the ear and ending in a cut an inch long across his cheekbone.

"Hello, Uncle Burley," I said.

"Well now," he said, "good morning boys." He let go the door to wave to us and fell down in a pile.

"For God's sake, look at Uncle Burley," Brother said.

Daddy and Grandpa picked him up between them and helped him into the house. Mother filled a pan with hot water and got the iodine out of the medicine cabinet and followed them to the living room. They stretched Uncle Burley out on the sofa and Mother began washing the blood off his face. She was gentle with him, and washed carefully around the cut so it wouldn't hurt.

"What did he hit you with, Burley?" Daddy asked.

"Jack handle. Surely must have been a jack handle."

"It's a damned shame he didn't use the jack," Grandpa said.

Mother finished washing Uncle Burley's face, and then poured some iodine into the cut. He whooped and sat up.

Grandpa jobbed the cane into his ribs. "Lay down there, God damn it."

Uncle Burley lay down again and let Mother bandage his face. Then they got him up and led him out to the kitchen. Brother and I kept out of the way and watched them set him down at the table. Mother poured him a cup of coffee, and she and Daddy and Grandpa went out on the back porch and began talking.

Uncle Burley's hands shook so much that he splashed some of the coffee out into his saucer; he tried to drink it out of the saucer and shook it all over his shirt.

He saw Brother and me watching him and grinned at us. "Now boys," he said, "let Uncle Burley tell you something. Don't ever drink. It's bad for you." Then he said, "But if you ever do drink be sure to get to hell away from home to do it." He set the coffee cup down and touched the side of his head with his fingers. "If you ever drink, and you ever get in a fight, always try to make an honorable show." He laid his right hand on the table so we could see it. It was skinned up across the knuckles and the middle finger was out of joint. "Boys," he said, "I was after him just like a hay rake."

He finished the cup of coffee and Brother got the pot and poured him another one. He put an arm around each of us and said, "Don't let on to the rest of them, but Uncle Burley was drunk."

He told us to keep it to ourselves, because there were some things that were a man's own business. We said we'd be quiet about it.

"It don't pay to talk too much about your business," he said.

When he'd finished the second cup of coffee Grandpa and Daddy loaded him back into the car and started home with him. Mother told us to stay in the kitchen and help her, but she had to leave the room for something and we ducked out the back door.

We cut across the field and got to Grandpa's house just as they were helping Uncle Burley out of the car again. Grandma was in the kitchen cooking dinner. When she saw them coming across the back porch with Uncle Burley, she dropped a pot full of green beans on the floor, and stood there saying, "Oh Lord, oh Lord."

Then she hurried to help them bring Uncle Burley in. Grandpa told her to get out of the way; Uncle Burley wasn't dead yet, he said. Grandma's old yellow cat started rubbing against Grandpa's leg and purring. He took a cut at it with his cane, but missed.

"Scat, damn you."

The cat backed off a little, and then followed them into the house and up the stairs. Grandma fixed Uncle Burley's bed and they undressed him and put him under the covers. He really did look sick then. Under the whiskers his face was as white as the pillow. Grandma leaned over him and smoothed the covers and asked if there was anything he wanted.

"That's right, by God," Grandpa said. "You coddle him."

They looked at each other for a minute; and Grandpa turned around and started out of the room, the cat weaving in and out between his feet. He took another swing at it with his cane as he went out the door, but missed again.

Grandma looked at Uncle Burley and said, "Lord help us. I don't know what's going to become of us."

"Shhhh," Uncle Burley said. "It don't pay to talk too much."

She sat down beside him on the edge of the bed, rolling her hands into her apron. "Oh, Burley. Why do you have to be so bad, Burley?"

Daddy took Brother and me down the stairs.

"Is everything all right?" I asked him.

"It's going to be."

When we went out on the back porch Grandma's cat was hanging by a piece of string from a limb of the peach tree. It didn't look as if it ever had been alive. The wind swung it back and forth just a little.

"Look at that old cat," Brother said.

2

Our mother had been sick since I was born, Daddy told us. And she began to get worse. She had to spend more and more time in bed, until finally she didn't get up at all. Grandma came every day and cooked our meals for us and did the housework, and took care of Mother while Daddy was in the field.

Daddy got short-tempered with us, and stayed that way longer than he ever had before. He took us to the field with him every morning to keep us out of the house and we stayed with him all day. It was hard to have to be with him so much. Brother and I were careful not to aggravate him, but scarcely a day passed that we didn't get at least a tongue-lashing from him. He was worrying a lot and working hard, and the least thing could set him off. The worst times were when we came to the house at noon and at night. He wouldn't let us make a sound then.

I quit having the dream about the lion, and began dreaming things that woke me up in the middle of the night. I came awake sweating and afraid, but I could never remember what I'd dreamed. It always took a long time to get used to the room and the darkness again and go back to sleep.

On one of those nights when I woke up I heard Daddy talking on the telephone. I couldn't hear what he said, and I dozed off again until I heard a car come in the driveway and stop beside the house. The door of the car opened and slammed; and I heard Daddy's voice and then the doctor's on the front porch. They came inside and their footsteps went down the hall and into the room where Mother and Daddy slept. Before long the back door opened and I heard Grandma talking to Daddy in the kitchen. "I saw the light burning and thought I'd better come over," she said.

They went into the bedroom and it was quiet again for a while. I went back to sleep finally. But I woke again several times before morning, and each time I'd hear them talking quietly downstairs and tiptoeing over the floors. The last time I woke the sky was turning gray. I heard the doctor's car leaving.

Nobody called Brother and me to wake up, and we slept a little past the regular time. When we got dressed and went downstairs Daddy was standing in the living room looking out the window. He didn't speak to us, and we crossed the room and started down the hall to the kitchen. Grandma opened the bedroom door and came out, shutting it quickly behind her. Her face looked tired, and her eyes were red.

"Boys, your mother's dead," she told us.

She stood there watching us. I nodded my head, and Brother said, "Yes mam."

She walked down the hall. "Come with me. I'll fix your breakfast."

We followed her into the kitchen and sat down in our chairs at the table. The sun wasn't up far; the light came in at the windows and stretched halfway across the room before it touched the floor. Off in the distance I could hear somebody calling his cattle.

Grandma took the lids off the stove and kindled a fire. When it had caught she added wood and set the lids back in place. She put the skillet on and got out the bacon and eggs while the stove warmed and ticked in the quiet.

Daddy came into the kitchen while she was filling our plates.

"Here's some breakfast for you," Grandma told him. "Eat. You'll need it."

He didn't answer her. He went on out the back door. After a minute we heard his axe at the woodpile.

We weren't long eating. When we'd finished we went out where he was. He didn't notice us. We sat down on a log at the edge of the woodpile and watched him. He took a chunk of sawed wood from the pile and propped it against the chopping block. He swung the axe over his head, sinking the blade, and drew it out and swung again. The chunk split clean, down the middle. Then he split each of the halves and threw them into another pile. Every time the axe came down he said "Ah!"—the keen sound of it ready to turn into crying, until the bite of the axe stopped it; and he tightened his mouth and swung again.

The undertaker came in his black hearse and took our mother's body away. Then some of the neighbors began coming. Big Ellis and his wife came, and the preacher and Gander Loyd and Beriah Easterly and his wife and Mrs. Crandel. As they came in they looked at Daddy working there at the woodpile, then stood on the back porch with the others and watched him, wondering when he'd quit and come to the house and allow them to speak to him.

Grandpa came, riding his mare into the lot, and stopped on the other side of the woodpile. He looked at Daddy for a minute, as if he wanted to tell him to quit or say something to comfort him. He looked away finally and sat still, only jerking the bridle reins a little when the mare got restless and began to paw and toss her head. Daddy never looked up from his work. The axe blade glinted in the sun and came down. Grandpa spoke to the mare and rode home again.

When Daddy had split all the wood, he stuck the axe into the block and started to the house. The people watched him cross the yard; when he came to the porch they turned away from him, embarrassed because they'd come to say they were sorry and the look of him didn't allow it.

They backed away from the door to let him through. He went into the bedroom and cleaned up. When he came into the living room he stood at the window again, not speaking to any of them.

The preacher told Brother and me that we should go upstairs and put on clean clothes. "You must be quiet," he said. "Your mother has gone up to Heaven."

"We know it," Brother said. "We knew it before you did."

As we were going up the stairs Mrs. Crandel came to the living room door and said, "Do you boys want me to help you get dressed?"

Brother said, "No mam."

"Do you know where to find everything?"

"Yes mam."

We went upstairs to our room and poured some water into the wash-pan. The sun came through the window curtains and made their shadows on the floor. When the wind waved the curtains the shadows on the floor waved.

"Let's both wash at the same time," Brother said.

I said all right. We put the pan between us on the floor and began washing. Brother squeezed the soap and it flew out of his hands and splashed water on me. I splashed back at him; both of us laughed. He started snapping at me with the towel and I caught the end of it, trying to pull it away from him.

I heard a step behind me, and when I looked around there was Daddy. He grabbed me by the shoulders and held me clear off the floor and shook me. Then he put me down and caught Brother and shook him. He went out the door without saying a word to us.

I sat on the floor and kept from crying until I started to feel better.

"Did he hurt you?" Brother asked me.

"No," I said.

I got up and we put our dirty clothes back on; we slipped down the stairs and out of the house.

"If Mother was alive he wouldn't pick on us," I said.

"She wouldn't let him," Brother said.

I felt like crying again, and I could see that Brother was holding it back too. We started across the hollow toward Grandpa's place.

"I'm not going to stay here any longer," I said. "He doesn't have any right to treat us that way."

Brother kept quiet.

"Are you coming with me?"

"We'll both go," he said.

We heard one of the cars start at our house, and Big Ellis and his wife drove out the lane.

"We'll go and live with Big Ellis."

"All right," I said.

We found old Oscar at the spring and rode him out the gate and up the road toward Big Ellis's place.

"As long as we've got Oscar we're all right," Brother said. "If Big Ellis won't let us stay with him we can go as far as we need to."

"We can stay at Big Ellis's," I said. "He'll be glad to have us."

When we got to his house Big Ellis was sitting out on the front steps. He still had on his black suit; but he'd loosened his tie and taken his shoes off to rest his feet, and his shirttail had come out.

We rode through the gate and into the yard.

"We've come to live with you, Big Ellis," Brother said.

Big Ellis got up and tramped barefoot across the grass. He forgot old Oscar was blind and couldn't see him coming. "Hello, boys," he said.

When Oscar heard that, he snorted and shied and ran backwards into a flower bed. He hit a wagon wheel that Annie May Ellis had put there for a morning glory to climb on, and sat down on his haunches like a dog. Brother and I fell off.

"Whoa, boy," Big Ellis said.

Annie May ran out on the porch waving her hands in the air. If Oscar hadn't been blind he'd have run off then for sure. But he just sat there trying to figure out what had happened to him.

"Get that old horse and them boys out of my flowers," Annie May said.

Oscar got up and shook himself, and Big Ellis caught him by his forelock and quieted him. "Never mind about your flowers," he said. "Go on inside and be still." He led Oscar out of the flowers.

Annie May waited until she was certain that Oscar was going to behave himself, and then she did what he'd told her.

Big Ellis looked at us and giggled. "That old horse can't see any better going backwards than he can going forwards, can he?"

"He can't see either way," Brother said. "We thought we'd stay at your house for a while, Big Ellis, if you don't mind."

"What do you want to stay here for? We haven't got any more to eat than anybody else," Big Ellis said. He was still holding on to Oscar's forelock.

"Daddy's mad at us," I said.

"Aw hell, he ain't mad at you all."

"We'll work for you," Brother said.

"Well, I could use a couple of boys all right. But we'd better think about it first. Annie May's nearly got dinner ready, so you boys just as well come in and have a bite to eat while we think."

We heard a horse coming up the road, and Grandpa turned his mare into the driveway. He had a halter and a lead rope over his arm.

"Don't tell him about old Oscar falling down," I said.

"I won't," Big Ellis said.

Grandpa kept the mare in a stiff rack right up to the gate, then he slowed her down and walked her into the yard. I was afraid he was going to whip us, he came in such a hurry. But he only nodded to Big Ellis and told us that Grandma had our dinner ready.

Big Ellis took the halter and slipped it over Oscar's head and handed the lead rein to Grandpa. "I was about to feed them some dinner here," he said. He came around and helped Brother and me onto Oscar's back.

"I'm much obliged to you," Grandpa told him. He turned the mare and led us out of the yard. When we were going down the driveway he said, "Damn it, your daddy's told you to stay off of that old horse." After a minute he said, "And damn it, I've told you."

But he kept his face turned away from us, and he let us ride old Oscar home.

※

For three days they kept our mother's body in a coffin in the living room. They kept the lid of the coffin open so people could look at her. They kept flowers around her coffin, and a lamp always burning at her head. The lights never went out in our house during those three days.

Grandma began staying with us even at night. She told Brother and me to stay in the yard or in the kitchen with her, and not to go in the room where our mother's body was. Once or twice we looked through the windows at the coffin and the people talking in the living room. But most of the time we stayed away. We'd see Daddy now and then walking around in the house or in the yard, but when he saw us he always turned around and went the other way. He'd changed and we didn't try to talk to him.

Everybody brought food to us when they came to sit by the coffin, until the kitchen was fairly stacked with cakes and pies and ham and fried chicken. Brother and I enjoyed looking at all the things they brought, but we didn't enjoy eating them. Mealtime always reminded us of Mother. It seemed strange to be sitting at the table eating while her dead body was there in the house with us.

Once while we were eating breakfast Brother looked at me and said, "Many's dead."

I said, "Minnie who?"

"Many people," he said.

We laughed. Grandma turned away from the stove and said, "Oh Lord, boys, you never will see her any more." And she cried, holding the dish towel against her face.

We cried too, and then she hugged us and told us not to grieve. She said our mother was in Heaven with all the angels, and she was happy there and never would have to suffer any more.

"Why, she's probably up there right now, singing with the blessed angels," Grandma said. She wiped her eyes on the towel and went back to the stove. "Oh, it's a pretty place up there, boys."

At night a few of the neighbors always came and sat up by the coffin. We could hear them talking and the chair rockers creaking for a long time before we went to sleep, and it seemed that we still heard them while we slept. We felt as if we never had lived in that house before.

For the first two days there were always cars parked in the yard, and people coming in and out. But on the morning of the funeral it got quiet. Big Ellis and Annie May and Uncle Burley had spent the night by the coffin, but they left early, and nobody else came. Grandma worked until noon, getting the house ready for the funeral, and then she warmed some leftovers for our dinner.

After we finished eating Brother and I went out on the back porch. Daddy and Grandma were sitting in the swing, talking. When we came out they hushed.

Grandma stood up and smiled at us. "Well, the boys can come and help me," she said. She leaned over and laid her hand on Daddy's arm. "It'll be time now before long." She went into the house and up the stairs.

Daddy sat there looking down at his hands, handling them, running the fingers of one hand across the palm and out over the fingers of the other one. His hands were heavy and big, with white scars on them that never sunburned. His hands never quit moving. Even when he went to sleep sometimes at night sitting in his rocking chair in the living room his hands stirred on the chair arms as if they could never find a place to rest.

Finally he looked up at us. "You'd better go help your grandma, boys."

We went upstairs and found her in our room. She had the bureau drawers open and was packing our clothes into a big pasteboard box.

"What're you doing that for?" Brother asked her.

"You'll have to come over and live with us for a while. Your Uncle Burley'll bring the wagon to get you."

We started helping her pack the clothes.

"How long are we going to live at your house?"

"Oh, a while."

"Why do we have to leave?" I asked.

"Your daddy's not going to be able to take care of you. He's going to
be by himself now."

I saw that she was about to cry again. I didn't want her to do that, and
so I laughed and said what a good time Brother and I'd have with Uncle
Burley.

We packed all the clothes that were in the drawers, and then took our
Sunday clothes off the hooks in the closet and folded them on top of the
rest and closed the box. Grandma left to get ready for the funeral.

Brother and I went out in the back yard and waited for Uncle Burley.
And before long he came, driving the team and wagon down the ridge
toward our house, sitting dangle-legged on the edge of the hay frame.

He left the team standing in front of the barn and came on into the
yard. "Hello, boys," he said.

It didn't come out the way it usually did when he said it. It had the
same sound as everything that had been said to us for three days, as if it
were embarrassing to be around people whose mother was dead. So all
we said to him was hello.

Grandma came to the back door. "Burley, take Tom and Nathan in to
see their mother before you go." She went back inside, and we didn't see
her any more until that night.

Uncle Burley put his hands on our shoulders and went with us into the
house and down the hall to the living room. When we went through the
door I realized that Grandma had forgotten to make us dress up.

The people quit talking when they saw us. It made me uneasy to have
them quiet and watching, and I looked down at the floor while we crossed
the room to the coffin.

Big Ellis and Annie May were there ahead of us, and we stopped to
wait for them to get out of the way.

"Ain't she the beautifullest corpse!" Annie May said. And she started
crying.

Big Ellis looked around at us and grinned. "Howdy, boys," he said. His shirttail was half out, and he'd sweated until his collar had rolled up around his neck like a piece of rope. Seeing him made me feel better. I told him hello.

Annie May finished crying and we went up to the coffin. Our mother had on a blue dress, and her head made a little dent in the pillow. Her hands were folded together, and her eyes were closed. But she didn't look really comfortable. She looked the way people do when they pretend to be asleep and try too hard and give it away. I touched her face; it felt stiff and strange, like touching your own hand when it's asleep and can't feel.

The inside of the coffin looked snug and soft, but when they shut the lid it would be dark. When they shut the lid and carried her to the grave it would be like walking on a cloudy dark night when you can't see where you're going or what's in front of you. And after they put her in the ground and covered her up she'd turn with the world in the little dark box in the grave, and the days and nights would all be the same.

We went up to our room to get our clothes. The wind blew the window curtains out over the corner of the bureau where the empty drawers were, and I could see the barn out the window with the sun shining on it. It seemed awful to go. I felt like crying, but I held it down and it knotted hard in my throat. I took the pillow off my bed and crooked my arm around it.

"You'd better leave the pillow, boy," Uncle Burley said. "We've got plenty of them."

"It's mine, God damn it." I said it loud to get it over the knot.

Uncle Burley laughed. "Well, take it then, old pup."

Brother and I laughed too, and it wasn't so bad to leave then.

Uncle Burley picked up the box and we went down the stairs. As we walked out the back door they started singing in the living room. I listened to them, while we crossed the yard and went through the lot gate:

> *There's a land that is fairer than day,*
> *And by faith we can see it afar;*
> *For the Father waits over the way,*
> *To prepare us a dwelling place there.*

Uncle Burley set the box on the wagon and we climbed on and started out of the lot. I heard them singing again:

> *We shall sing on that beautiful shore*
> *The melodious songs of the blest,*
> *And our spirits shall sorrow no more,*
> *Not a sigh for the blessing of rest.*

My mother's soul was going up through the sky to be joyful with the angels in Heaven, so beautiful and far away that you couldn't think about it. And we were riding on a wagon behind Grandpa's team of black mules, going to live with Grandma and Grandpa and Uncle Burley, leaving the place where they were singing over her body. The sun was bright on the green grass up the ridge and glossy on the slick rumps of the mules. When we were driving away from the lot gate the people at the house were singing:

> *In the sweet by and by,*
> *We shall meet on that beautiful shore;*
> *In the sweet by and by,*
> *We shall meet on that beautiful shore.*

It was pretty; and sad to think of people always ending up so far from each other. We could hear Annie May Ellis's high, clear voice singing over all the rest of them.

"That Annie May's got a voice on her," Uncle Burley said.

He let the mules into a brisk trot, and we went up the ridge and around the head of the hollow where Aunt Mary was buried, and down the next ridge toward Grandpa's house.

❧

It was strange at first to wake up in the mornings and remember that I wasn't at home any more, and to see Daddy go away every night and leave us at Grandpa's. But before long we got used to the way things were and began to feel like a family again. Brother and I began calling Grandpa's house our home.

Things got pretty jolty there sometimes. Once in a while Grandpa would get mad at Brother and me and swat us with his cane, and then he and Grandma would get mad at each other because she always took up for us. The two of them didn't agree on much. Grandma said you didn't live with a man like Grandpa; you lived around him. And that was pretty much the way things were between them. Grandpa didn't feel at home in the house, and when he wasn't at work he spent most of his time at the barn. When he was in the house they lived around each other.

Both of them were usually aggravated at Uncle Burley. Grandpa thought Uncle Burley was a disgrace because he'd rather hunt or fish than work. Grandma didn't mind that so much, but she was always grieving because he was so sinful. He never was very sorry for his sins, and that got her worse than anything. But he hardly ever paid attention to their haggling. When they started on him he'd grin and ask them if they didn't think it was going to rain, and that usually put a stop to it. When it got to be more than he could stand, he'd leave and spend a few days in his camp house at the river. Brother and I stayed with him whenever we could, and when the three of us were together we had a good time.

We'd been living at Grandpa's for a little more than a year when Mrs. Crandel died. And the next day Kate Helen Branch had a baby. Uncle Burley said that was just the way things were. They put one in and pull another one out.

Mrs. Crandel's funeral was the day after that. Grandma tried to get Grandpa to go, but he wouldn't. He said the Crandels needed thinning out anyway. Uncle Burley and Brother and I laughed until Grandma made us shut up. After dinner was over and Grandpa had gone out she cautioned Brother and me about laughing at the sinful things Grandpa said. She told us it was an awful thing to speak that way of the dead, and that it was written down against Grandpa in the Great Book of the Judgment. Uncle Burley said he imagined Grandpa had been giving the bookkeeper about all he could handle for a good while now. Grandma told him to hush his mouth. She said that he and Grandpa were doing all they could to make sinners out of Brother and me.

"Tom and Nathan want to be good boys," she said, "so they can go up to Heaven where their mother is."

Brother was going to the funeral with her, and she'd said that I could go too. But I'd never liked Mrs. Crandel much, and I didn't like funerals, so I was going to stay at home with Uncle Burley.

While they got ready to go I went out on the front porch to talk to him. He was propped against one of the porch posts, whittling on a piece of yellow poplar two-by-four. The sun was shining straight down and hot beyond the shade of the porch roof. Down in the yard the locusts were singing. First one would start and then the rest would take it up, until it seemed they made the air and the sky rattle. When they stopped I could feel the quiet muffling down into my ears.

"Plague of Egypt," Uncle Burley said.

"What're you whittling?" I asked him.

"A piece of wood."

"What're you going to make out of it?"

"Be right quiet," he said.

I sat down beside him on the edge of the porch and watched.

He split off four chips as thin as a ruler and laid them in a neat pile between us. Then he started scraping them smooth, whistling "Molly Darling" through his teeth. He frowned as if he were taking pains to do everything just right.

Daddy came in the car to take Grandma and Brother to the funeral. Uncle Burley watched them leave, and went back to his whittling.

"When will they be back?" I asked.

He held one of the chips up to the sun and squinted at it with one eye. "Shhhh. Be awful quiet, boy."

He went on shaving and scraping at the pieces of wood. After he got them all shaved down fine enough to suit him, he split a thicker piece off the two-by-four and began trimming on it. The shavings curled all the way from one end of the piece to the other without breaking. He didn't let on that I was there at all. When he caught me looking at him he'd gaze off across the river and start whistling again. He shaved on that stick until it was round, then tapered the ends and cut four notches longways down the center of it.

"What's it going to be?" I asked.

Without looking at me he gathered up the pieces and lined them in a row on the porch. "Boy," he said, "I just can't think with you doing all that talking."

He got out his whetrock and walked down in the yard, sharpening his knife. There was a big maple by the fence and he walked around it a time or two and finally cut two forked branches. I waited on the porch while he trimmed them, afraid that if I bothered him again he wouldn't finish what he was making.

He came back and squatted down by the steps and started putting the pieces together. He stuck the little blades of wood into the notches he'd made in the round piece. Then he looked at me under the brim of his hat and grinned.

"Well, I'll be dogged," he said. "It turned out to be a water wheel."

We stuck the maple branches in the ground and laid the axle of the water wheel in the forks. Uncle Burley flipped one of the blades with his finger and twirled it around.

After he'd watched me twirl it for a minute he got up and started into the house. "Well, put it away now, Nathan. You can set it up at the spring tomorrow."

I took the water wheel upstairs and put it away. When I came down Uncle Burley was waiting for me in the living room. He'd put on a clean shirt and his newest pair of shoes.

"Are we going someplace?" I asked him.

"Well, since everybody else is gone, I figured we might as well go and see Kate Helen Branch's new baby. How'd that suit you?"

"All right."

"We'll just keep it to ourselves around your Grandma and the others. It's not any of their business where we go."

I said it wasn't. We went back to the kitchen and Uncle Burley got enough matches to last him the rest of the afternoon and stuck them in the band of his hat.

"It won't do to talk too much about your business," he said.

We took the road to Port William, and stopped at the grocery store. Uncle Burley bought a sack of Bull Durham and a box of snuff, and a candy bar for me. We went on through town toward the house where Kate Helen and her mother lived.

There were a lot of cars parked at the church, where Mrs. Crandel's funeral was being held; and when we went past the graveyard we saw the fresh dirt mounded beside her grave.

Uncle Burley pointed to the angel on top of the Coulter monument. "Chairman of the welcoming committee," he said.

"Uncle Burley," I said, "do you think Mrs. Crandel was good enough to get to Heaven?"

"Beats me. It's hard to tell what happens after they get them planted."

"Planted?" I said.

"Planted in the skull orchard."

That was odd to think about. It sounded as if people's bodies were like seeds and could grow up into trees after they were dead, and maybe those trees had skulls on them instead of apples or pears.

I thought how my mother was dead. But I didn't think of her growing up into a tree. Her body had to stay in the ground, but her soul was in Heaven because she'd been good. Grandma said she was happy up there with the angels. I thought it would be a bad thing to be dead anyway. I figured it was probably darker there than it was on Earth. And maybe she missed Brother and me.

I said, "Uncle Burley, there's not any way to find out how many times they've got your name in that book, is there?"

"I reckon not." Then he pointed his finger down the road. "Well, boy, if there's not the prettiest little walnut tree you ever saw."

I looked, and it was, sure enough.

When we got down to Kate Helen's house, old Mrs. Branch was sitting on the porch. The shadow of the roof had moved until it ran in a straight line down the middle of her face.

Uncle Burley tipped his hat to her and said, "Good evening, Mrs. Branch."

She squinted the eye that was in the sun and looked at us. "Howdy," she said. "Is that you, Burley?"

"Yes mam," Uncle Burley said. He asked her how her rheumatism was.

"Well, it's summer now and it's better. But before long it'll be winter again and the cold'll cripple me. I just live from one summer to the next one." She laughed as if she'd told a joke.

Uncle Burley laughed a little too, and said that she looked mighty spry to him. He took the box of snuff out of his pocket and handed it to her. "Thought you might be needing some."

She said it was good of Uncle Burley to be so thoughtful of an old woman.

"We thought we'd come over to see the baby," Uncle Burley said.

"Kate Helen's yonder in the bed," Mrs. Branch told him. "You all go right in."

Uncle Burley took his hat off when we went through the door and said, "Well, hello there, Kate Helen."

She smiled and held the baby up so we could look at it.

"Well, I'll be dogged," Uncle Burley said. "It's a boy, ain't it, Kate Helen?"

She said yes, it was a boy. Uncle Burley wanted to know what his name was, and she said it was Daniel.

"That's a fine name." Uncle Burley laid his hat on the foot of the bed. Kate Helen let him hold the baby and he sat down with it in a rocking chair.

"Well, I'll declare," he said. "If that's not a fine-looking baby."

The baby stuck one of its fists up in the air and started crying. But Uncle Burley rocked it a little and whistled to it, and it settled down and went back to sleep.

Uncle Burley looked at Kate Helen and looked at the baby again and said, "Well, I'll be switched."

He motioned for me to come and look too. And I did.

"Now ain't that a pretty baby, Nathan?"

It didn't look like much to me. But I could tell that Uncle Burley thought a lot of it, so I said it was the prettiest baby I ever did see.

"Little Daniel," Uncle Burley said.

I went across the room and sat down in a chair by the window. And then Uncle Burley began telling Kate Helen how we were getting along with our work. He told her how most of the tobacco crop had ripened early, and how we'd already cut all of it that was ripe. He said we were planning to cut the rest of it in about a week. And then he talked about how many young squirrels he'd seen that year, and promised to bring Kate Helen and her mother a couple of fat ones as soon as he got time to do a little hunting. After that he said he looked for an early frost, because the katydids had been singing for about three weeks already. Kate Helen took a little nap while he was talking.

After a while she woke up and said it was time for the baby to eat. I looked out the window while she fed him, and Uncle Burley got busy and rolled a cigarette.

The baby finished its supper and went to sleep again. It was late and we got up to leave. Mrs. Branch came hobbling in from the porch and asked us to have supper with them.

Uncle Burley said we'd like to, but we had to get on home and fire up the coke stoves in our tobacco barn. He told her that the tobacco had a lot of sap in it that year, and we had to keep the fires under it so it wouldn't rot in the barn.

He leaned over the bed to look at the baby again. It was smiling in its sleep. "Look at him. He's seeing the angels," Uncle Burley said. "Well, I'll swear." He put his hat on and started backing toward the door. "Well now, Kate Helen, don't take no wooden nickels."

We walked home and went to the tobacco barn to fire up the coke stoves. Uncle Burley shook the ashes out, and then we took a bucket apiece and started carrying fresh coke to the fires. There was enough trash in the coke to make the stoves smoke a little at first, and it made my eyes smart. It was already dark in the barn, and the row of stoves glowed red-hot down the driveway. I could see Uncle Burley's legs passing back and forth in front of them under the smoke. I imagined that Hell looked like that. It was hot enough too when I leaned over the stoves to empty my bucket. My eyes watered when I looked at the blue flames crawling over the coals. It would be a bad place to stay forever, I thought.

When we came out of the barn it was dark, except for a thin red cloud stretched along the edge of the sky. A cool breeze was blowing and it was fine to be outside again. I thought it would be better to sprout into a tree than to stay down there in the fire.

"Uncle Burley," I said, "it's a bad thing to be dead, ain't it?"

He lit a cigarette and flipped the match out. "Well, this world and one more and then the fireworks."

3

For a week before the Fourth of July, Brother and I worked at Big Ellis's place, cleaning out a fence row. The fence was a good half a mile long, running all the way down one side of the farm, and we contracted to clean it out for five dollars apiece so we'd have plenty of spending money for the Fourth. We worked from daylight to dark every day except Sunday, axing out the sassafras and locust and thorn and scything down the briars, with the sun as hot as it could get at that time of year.

Early on the morning of the Fourth, Grandpa hitched his team to the mowing machine and went to help Daddy mow a field of hay. After he'd gone the day began to feel like a Sunday because we weren't going to work and it was so quiet around the house. The sun wasn't up far, but already you could hear the heat ticking down like a flock of sparrows on the back porch roof.

In a little while Uncle Burley came out and asked Brother and me to help him with a little work before we left for the Fourth of July picnic. We followed him to the smokehouse. He went inside and came out with a long-handled dip net.

"What're you going to do?" I asked him.

"It would be bad for a man to pass up a chance to make some money, wouldn't it?"

"I suppose it would," I said.

He sent me to the corncrib to get an ear of corn, and when I came

back we went down to the pond. Grandma's ducks were swimming single file close to the bank, dabbling their bills into the water. Uncle Burley
shelled the corn and scattered it along the bank. When the ducks came
to eat he dipped up five of them in the dip net. We tied their bills shut
with pieces of fishing line to keep Grandma from hearing them quack
and carried them to the barn. We found an old wire chicken coop and
loaded it on the wagon and put the ducks in it. Then we got the long gal-
vanized tank that Grandpa kept shelled corn in, and loaded it on the
wagon with the coop.

Uncle Burley sat down and looked at the tank. "Well, all we need now
is water." After a minute or so he said, "Well, we can fix that."

He got up and brought two buckets from the barn and pitched them
into the tank. And we loaded two water barrels.

"What're you going to do with all this?" Brother asked.

"Did you ever hear why they call a duck a duck?"

Brother looked at me and laughed, and we gave up asking him questions. We harnessed a team of mules and hitched them to the wagon, and
went back to the house to wash and put on clean clothes.

When we were leaving the house Uncle Burley swiped three of
Grandma's embroidery hoops and stuck them into the crown of his hat.
On the road to town he whistled to himself, letting the mules trot on the
downgrades. Once or twice he winked at Brother and me and said, "A
duck is a duck." That always seemed to please him, and he'd grin and
start whistling again.

Before we'd gone halfway to the picnic we caught up with a man who
was walking in the same direction we were going. Uncle Burley stopped
and asked him if he wanted a ride.

"God bless you, brother," the man said. And he climbed on the
wagon.

"Where you going?" Uncle Burley asked him.

"Wherever the Lord's fixing to send me."

"You a preacher?"

"I am, brother."

He looked as if he'd been a long time going wherever the Lord was
sending him.

"I am one of them it has pleased the Lord to send to the four corners of the world to preach the gospel," he said.

He began to talk about unbelievers and the sin of the world, and who was going to Hell and who wasn't. The Lord had appointed him to be a witness, he said, to all the people he met. Uncle Burley whistled and spoke to the team, trying not to pay any attention. But I could see that he was getting aggravated. After a while he handed the reins to Brother and rolled a cigarette.

"A cigarette is as much of an abomination in the sight of the Lord as a bottle of whiskey," the preacher said.

Uncle Burley lit the cigarette and smoked, looking straight down the road.

The preacher said, "If the Lord had wanted you to smoke He'd have give you a smokestack, brother."

Uncle Burley took the reins again and stopped the team. He looked at the preacher. "If He'd wanted you to ride, you'd have wheels," he said. "Now you get off."

The preacher got off and stood in the ditch looking up at us. He raised his hand and said, " 'Blessed are ye, when men shall revile you, and persecute you.' Matthew, five-eleven."

We drove off and left him standing there preaching in the ditch.

"If he's going to Heaven I want him to have to walk every foot of the way," Uncle Burley said.

A couple of miles from Hargrave, we turned out the side road toward the picnic ground. Just before we got there we went by a pond, and Uncle Burley pulled the wagon off the road. We took the buckets and made a line between the pond and the wagon and filled the barrels with water. Then we drove on into the grounds.

The picnic ground was a fifty-acre field, and when we drove through the gate we could see automobiles parked everywhere, looking hot and shiny with the sun baking down on them. In the center of the field was a grove of tall oaks; people stood under them talking and laughing. Here and there a woman sat by herself in the shade beside a dinner basket. A carnival was set up outside the grove, the tents of the side shows in a double line, facing each other across a kind of street like the houses of a town. At one end of the carnival was a Ferris wheel, and at the other end was the dance hall where the Odd Fellows held a dance on the night of the Fourth.

Uncle Burley drove around the carnival and pulled in by the dance hall on the far end of the rows of tents. We unloaded the tank and set it on the ground with the long side parallel to the street of the carnival, about twenty-five feet from the tent next to us. That tent was a shooting gallery, and we could hear the rifles cracking and a bell ringing when somebody hit a bull's-eye. When we got the tank leveled to suit Uncle Burley we filled it with water from the barrels. We found five good-sized rocks and tied pieces of fishing line to them, and then used them to anchor the ducks in the tank of water. Uncle Burley scratched a line in the dirt in front of the tank and looped the embroidery hoops over his hand.

Brother and I drove the wagon out of the way and hitched the mules to a tree. When we came back Uncle Burley was walking up and down in front of the tank, twirling the hoops around his finger. Before long a big pimply-faced boy came over from the shooting gallery and looked at the ducks. He was wearing a little hat that he'd won at one of the carnival booths, with a red felt ribbon that said I'M HOT STUFF pinned to the top of it.

Uncle Burley twirled the hoops. "Boy, do you think you can ring one of them ducks?"

"Hell yes," the boy said. "How much?"

"Three rings for a dime."

The boy looked at the ducks and then at the hoops in Uncle Burley's hand. "What do I get if I ring one?"

"Five dollars cash money, plus the satisfaction of it."

The boy handed Uncle Burley a dime and took the hoops. He aimed a long time before he made a throw, and I was afraid he was going to win on the first try. But when the duck saw the hoop coming she stuck her head under the water. He made three tries and every time the duck ducked her head.

"Takes a lot of skill," Uncle Burley said.

"Hell," the boy said. He paid another dime and tried it again. He spent seventy cents standing there throwing those embroidery hoops at the ducks, throwing at whichever duck wasn't looking at him. But they always ducked in time. The boy gave up finally and went away.

"That's why they call a duck a duck," Uncle Burley told us.

A fat man in a wrinkled brown suit, who'd been watching the boy, staggered up to Uncle Burley. "Give me a try on them ducks."

Uncle Burley looked him up and down and shook his head. "Fellow, don't you reckon you're too drunk to throw straight?"

The man pointed his finger at Uncle Burley. "You're a liar if you say I'm drunk. I can ring one of them ducks left-handed."

"I'm willing to bet you can't ring one right-handed," Uncle Burley said.

The man took two dollars out of his pocket and laid them on the ground.

Uncle Burley laid two more on top of them. "Three rings for a dime," he said.

The man had the same luck the boy had, only he spent a dollar. After the first ten throws he got mad and started throwing hard, trying to kill the ducks. He never even hit the tank after that. The more he missed the harder he threw, and the harder he threw the more he missed.

Finally he turned around and hollered, "I quit!"

Uncle Burley picked up the money and put it in his pocket. The man watched him, swelling up and getting red in the face.

Then he shook his fist at Uncle Burley and hollered, "I'm a mean son of a bitch!"

Uncle Burley caught him by the necktie and tightened the knot until you could see the veins pumping in his neck. He said, "You don't look so mean to me, son of a bitch."

The man walked off, loosening his tie and cursing to himself, down the tent rows.

Pretty soon Uncle Burley had as many customers as he could handle. A crowd was gathering and some of the men knew him. They laughed and asked him when he went into the carnival business. He grinned and kept quiet, taking their dimes and gathering the hoops after they finished throwing. One or another of the ducks was always looking over the back of the tank, and that gave them something to try for.

Brother and I stood around and watched until it got tiresome. Nobody ever managed to ring a duck. After the first dozen or so customers had tried and failed, we went to see the carnival.

One of the side show tents had a sign on it that said THE WONDERS OF THE WORLD in red and gold letters. An old woman stood out in front with a loudspeaker, telling what they had inside.

"See the two-headed baby," she said. "See the big jungle rat. It ain't like the rats you got around here — ain't got no tail — all spotted and striped like a tiger."

Another show had a fire-eating cannibal and a woman who weighed eight hundred pounds and a turtle with two tails. We didn't go into either tent. It was bad enough to know such things as eight-hundred-pound women and two-headed babies could be in the world without paying a quarter for it.

In the middle of the carnival was a tent with pictures of half-naked women on the front, and a sign that said BUBBLES: BEWITCHING ENCHANTRESS OF THE FAR EAST. A crowd of men and boys had gathered around a ticket stand where a big-nosed man in a derby hat was making a speech.

"Starting right now with one of them old bloodboilers," he said. "Hottest — fastest — meanest little burlesque show you ever saw. The show starts in ten seconds, gentlemen. Only a few seats left."

He stood there a minute, looking over the crowd, then started again. "Gentlemen, it's as hot as a billy goat in a pepper patch. It shakes — it bumps — it bounces like a Model T Ford on plowed ground. Only fifty cents to see Bubbles unveil the secrets of the East. Gentlemen, if you suffer from heart trouble, high blood pressure or dizzy spells I beg you not to come in here. You won't be able to stand it."

He wound up again and told how Bubbles was the Crown Princess of Mesopotamia, and had been kidnapped and carried on a camel through the enchanted deserts of the Far East, and how she had spent six years in the harem of the Sheik of Araby.

While he was in the middle of this somebody piped up in the crowd and asked him if she'd take it all off.

He said, "Gentlemen, you will see Bubbles as fully clothed as she came into this world. That is, you will see her in the garment which the good Lord give her — her naked hide. Come in, gentlemen. We only got a few seats left. It'll cost you only fifty cents, one half of one dollar, to see what you can't afford to miss for any price."

A few of the men crowded up to buy tickets.

"Let's go in," Brother said. He looked at me and grinned. "Come on."

I wanted to ride the Ferris wheel, but I let him go in front and we got into the line at the ticket stand. When we bought our tickets the man said, "Now here are two young men seeking to further their education. Go right in, gentlemen. You'll never be the same again." That got him a big laugh from the crowd. I felt silly then with everybody looking at us and laughing, but we'd already paid our money and there was nothing to do but keep going.

It was so dark inside the tent after we'd been out in the sun that we could hardly see. But our eyes got used to it, and we stood around waiting for the show to start. There weren't any seats. About a third of the tent was roped off to give Bubbles room to put on her show. In a corner of the roped off part was a kind of booth made of old carpets, and beneath the front flap we could see a woman's bare feet with red polish on the toenails.

We waited a good while, hearing the man making his speech again in front of the tent, and now and then another bunch of men and boys came in. The tent filled up. Mushmouth and Chicken Little Montgomery came in with one of the last bunches, but they were the only ones we knew. I'd seen most of the others before, but I didn't know their names.

Mushmouth and Chicken Little were ashamed to be seen in such a place. While we waited they stood together on the edge of the crowd, pretending they were the only ones there. They were both a little drunk, and when somebody happened to look at them they'd grin and back up.

Finally the man in the derby hat quit talking and followed the last bunch through the door. Everybody crowded up to the rope, thinking the show was about to start. But he went into the booth where Bubbles was and came out with a little table and a deck of cards. He set the table up on our side of the rope.

"Gentlemen," he said, "we still have a few minutes before show time." He shuffled the cards and made them rattle down in a pile on the table. "There's nothing to ease the body, clear the mind, and settle the soul like a friendly card game." He shuffled the cards again, but that time he made a mislick and they fell out of his hands. "Excuse me, gentlemen. I've had a little too much of your good Kentucky whiskey, I'm afraid." He picked up the cards and shuffled them again, then thumbed three cards off the top of the deck and held them up. "I have here the queen of spades, the nine of diamonds and the four of clubs." He laid the three cards face down on the table and switched them around.

Then he looked at Mushmouth and Chicken Little, who were standing on the other side of the table. "Now, can one of you gentlemen pick the queen?"

The queen card had a bent corner and it was easy to pick out. Chicken Little looked around the tent and grinned, then he turned the card. It was the queen.

"You have a fine eye, sir," the man in the derby hat said. "A wonderful eye."

He turned the card over and began switching them again. "And now for a dollar, sir, can you tell me the queen?"

Chicken Little laid a dollar on the table and turned the card with the bent corner. He had it right again, and the man in the derby hat paid off. It seemed he'd had too much whiskey to keep straight on what he was doing.

Mushmouth and two or three others laid down dollar bills and the man lost again. On the next round about a dozen of the men laid down dollar bills, and Brother and I laid down a dollar apiece. He asked which was the queen. Somebody turned the card with the bent corner, but it was the nine of diamonds. The next time it was the nine of diamonds. And the next time it was the four of clubs. Before we realized what had happened the man had crossed the rope and was in the booth. Everybody was awfully quiet, feeling too foolish even to be mad.

The man in the derby came out again and said that Bubbles would now dance for us. Some thumpy music began playing, and he pulled back the flap and let Bubbles out. We crowded up to the rope.

She was a tall black-haired woman who looked hardmouthed and tired until she faced us and began to smile and sway back and forth to the music. Her eyebrows were painted black and curled around on the ends; where she'd sweated the paint had run down the sides of her face. Her clothes were made of a gauzy red material that you could see through, except for a skimpy brassiere and pants. She was decked out in feathers and jewels, and a silky tassle was fastened to each of her breasts. Mushmouth and Chicken Little were standing next to me. I kept my head turned away from them so they wouldn't recognize me.

Bubbles danced back and forth across the tent a time or two, and then she stopped midway of the rope and stood there smiling, looking at us under her eyebrows. She started the tassle on her right breast twirling around. She stopped that tassle and twirled the other one. After that she twirled both of them at the same time. Everybody whistled and cheered.

"I'm going to teach my old lady to do that," somebody said.

When Bubbles got both tassles going she began to wiggle her hips. Mushmouth looked as if somebody had hit him in the face with a big grin and it had stuck there. He leaned over the rope and started grabbing at Bubbles, and the man in the derby had to come and tell him to behave himself. Chicken Little looked the other way, trying to act like somebody else's twin brother.

Bubbles sashayed across the tent again and went back into her booth. The man in the derby walked out and told us that for fifty cents more we could see Bubbles reveal other secrets of the mysterious East. Nobody liked that, and there was a good deal of cursing and grumbling. But they all shelled out. Brother and I did too. It seemed a shame to leave after we'd all stared at Bubbles and let her begin her show, even if it was wrong to make us pay a dollar for what they'd told us was worth fifty cents.

The music started and Bubbles came back. She wiggled and danced and took off her clothes until she was as naked as a jaybird. With all the jewels and feathers gone she looked the way any ordinary person would look naked, except for the eyebrow paint streaked down the sides of her face. She wasn't as pretty as I'd thought she'd be. It was hard to think of her as the Princess of Mesopotamia, or even somebody named Bubbles. I felt sorry for her then, standing there without her clothes in front of a crowd of men who'd paid a dollar to look at her. It was a cheap thing, and she couldn't grin enough to change it.

Then before anybody could catch him Mushmouth had climbed over the rope and was trying to catch Bubbles. She never did quit dancing. She just skipped from one place to another as nimble as a cat, keeping out of his way, with Mushmouth slobbering and floundering after her, smacking his mouth like a blind dog in a meathouse.

"You come out of there, Mushmouth," Chicken Little said.

Half of the men were whooping for him to get away and leave her alone, and the other half were whooping for him to catch her.

"Go to it, Mushmouth," somebody said.

Chicken Little said, "Mushmouth, you quit that now."

Then the man in the derby caught him and threw him out over the rope. He and Chicken Little went out the door together, hanging their heads. They seemed to get the worst of everything.

The show was over then, and we were happy to get out. It was dinnertime by then and we were hungry. We found a tent where they were selling hamburgers and ate three apiece. Then we went to another tent where a man was selling watermelons and ate four slices apiece for dessert. After that we decided to go and ride the Ferris wheel.

But on the way to the Ferris wheel we passed a tent where some gypsy women were telling fortunes. Three of them were standing in front of the tent, calling to the crowd. One pointed to Brother and me. "You boys are brothers. You let us tell your fortune."

Brother said he didn't want his fortune told and kept walking toward the Ferris wheel. But the youngest of the women ran out and caught my hand.

"You got nice things in your future, handsome boy. Let me tell you about it. For a quarter I will tell you all that will happen to you."

She was pretty, and she sounded like she really needed the money. I gave her a quarter and followed her into the tent. The inside was divided into rooms and we went into one of them. She took my hand and looked into the palm. There was a mole under her left eye and she was wearing a scarf and bright gold earrings.

"I see you will have happiness," she said, "and sorrow, but not as much sorrow as happiness. I see you will have a beautiful wife. I see you will have a lot of money before you are old."

She looked down into my hand again. "I see you will travel. You will see strange parts of the world."

I didn't believe in fortunetelling, but I couldn't help feeling uncomfortable, as if she saw how I looked without my clothes on.

She traced her finger across my hand and said, "From this line I see that you will have a very long life."

That line was a scar from a barbed-wire cut, but I didn't tell her that.

"You are a nice boy," she said. "If you will let me I will bless your money for you. For free. Because I like you." She held out her hand and smiled at me.

I never had heard of that, but I didn't want to hurt her feelings. I got out my pocketbook and handed it to her.

"Now," she said. "You must put your hand on my heart."

She took my hand and put it down inside her dress. She didn't have on any underwear at all. The feeling of her went all through me. I couldn't look at her. She spoke some sort of conjure over my pocketbook and handed it back to me.

After I got away from the tent I looked to see what she'd done to my money when she blessed it. It was gone. Two dollars. She'd stolen it all. And there wasn't a thing to do about it.

I started looking for Brother, edging through the carnival and watching in front of the tents. The crowd was thick. The afternoon was hot and close, and the carnival had begun to have the smell of sweat and cotton candy. Everybody had been there long enough to be tired and badtempered. It was miserable. I wished I was at home, a long way from that crowd and the gypsies and the two-headed babies and the Sheik of Araby's wife.

I found Brother playing some sort of game with a mean-looking little man in a checkered shirt. There was a circle of nails driven into the counter of the man's booth, and in the center a wooden arm set on an axle. You bought a red washer for a quarter and put it on one of the nails. The man spun the arm, and if it stopped on your nail you won a dollar. If you bought two washers you stood to win two dollars. When I came up Brother had just laid down a quarter.

"Have you got any money?" I asked him.

"I will have just as soon as he spins this thing again," Brother said. He had eight washers stuck around on the nails.

The man spun the arm and it stopped on a nail that Brother didn't have a washer on.

"That was my last quarter," Brother said.

I had two quarters left and I gave him those. He bought two more washers and tried it again. If he'd won he'd have had eighteen dollars. But he lost. He had a nickel left, but that wasn't enough to buy any more chances, and I was glad of it. We never did get to the Ferris wheel, and I didn't mind that either. I guessed that if we'd paid the dime or quarter or whatever it cost to get on, somebody would have made us pay a dollar to get off.

"Come on," I said. "Let's see how Uncle Burley's doing."

We went back through the crowd to where Uncle Burley had his tank of ducks. People were still waiting to try their luck with the embroidery hoops. Uncle Burley winked at us. His pockets were crammed with the dimes he'd taken in.

We went off to the side and sat under a tree to watch the people try to ring a duck and wait for Uncle Burley to be ready to go home.

It wasn't long until the ducks began to get tired. They'd had a hard day of it, and one after another they quit ducking when the hoops came at them. They just sat there, looking fretful and disgusted and let the people win Uncle Burley's profit. He'd made the throwing line only a few feet from the tank, and everybody began ringing ducks. The people who'd lost in the morning heard what was going on and came back. Uncle Burley's pockets were flattening out fast. He looked more fretful and disgusted than the ducks.

Finally he called Brother and me. He was down to six or seven dollars, and he gave us all but one of them. "Take care of things until I get back," he said. "I won't be a minute."

After Uncle Burley left, Brother stood by the tank to pick the hoops up, and I handled the money. Our first customer was the man in the brown suit who'd lost the bet to Uncle Burley that morning. I could see that he'd come back to get even, and I was afraid he'd make trouble, but he won five dollars on his second throw; that seemed to satisfy him, and he left. But then I was really in a mess; Uncle Burley hadn't come back and I only had eighty cents.

I was wondering what in the world I'd do if somebody else won and found out that I didn't have money enough to pay him, when I saw the head fly off one of the ducks. It couldn't have been done any neater with a butcher knife, but nobody was even close to the tank. I looked over at the shooting gallery, and there was Uncle Burley popping away at the target and ringing the bell every time. Then I saw him lead off toward the ducks as if he were making a wing shot; and another duck flopped in the tank.

When he'd killed all the ducks Uncle Burley walked off toward the other end of the carnival without looking back. He was carrying a big red plaster frog that he'd won at the shooting gallery. Everybody stood around, looking at us and looking at the ducks and looking at Uncle Burley going off through the crowd, with their mouths open. Then they all laughed a little and began to straggle back into the carnival.

I put Uncle Burley's eighty cents in my pocket, and Brother and I started after him.

We caught up with him in front of Bubbles' tent. He and Big Ellis were listening to the man in the derby hat make his speech. We stood with them, listening a while, then Uncle Burley said, "Let's go."

We elbowed our way out of the crowd and Big Ellis went with us.

"I'd like to have a little something to drink," he said to Uncle Burley.

Uncle Burley just carried his red frog and didn't say anything.

Big Ellis said, "I got a little something." He looked at Brother and me and then at Uncle Burley. "It's all right, ain't it?"

"I imagine," Uncle Burley said.

He let Big Ellis take the lead, and we followed him across the grounds to where he'd parked his car. When we got there Big Ellis opened the door and rammed his hand into a hole in the driver's seat and pulled out a pint of whiskey. He said that was the first Fourth of July he'd ever been able to hide it where Annie May couldn't find it.

"She can smell it before it's even uncorked," he said.

He opened the bottle and passed it to Uncle Burley. Uncle Burley set the frog on the seat of the car and drank.

"She couldn't track it inside that seat," Big Ellis said. He giggled and drank out of the bottle when Uncle Burley passed it back to him.

They sat down and leaned against the side of the car, handing the bottle back and forth. Every time Big Ellis took a drink he'd giggle and say something about Annie May's nose not being as good as it used to be.

And the happier Big Ellis got the sadder Uncle Burley got. Those ducks had hurt his feelings and he couldn't get over it.

"God Almighty, women are awful," Big Ellis said, and giggled and wiped the whiskey off his chin.

He hadn't any more than said it before Annie May came around the car, mad as a sow and screeching like a catamount. She told Big Ellis to get himself in that car and take her home. They left with Uncle Burley's red frog sitting bug-eyed on the seat between them.

Uncle Burley stood there with the bottle in his hand and watched them go. Then he drank the rest of the whiskey and threw the bottle down. He swayed back and forth, looking down at it.

"Well," he said, "around and around she goes."

It was dark by the time we got the tank emptied and loaded on the wagon and started home. Brother drove, and Uncle Burley sat on the back of the wagon leaning against the tank. He was quiet all the way.

The moon was up when we turned into Grandpa's gate, shining nearly as bright as day. The river bottom was white and quiet below us, and away off somewhere we could hear a dog barking. It seemed a long time since the Fourth of July.

❧

The next morning Annie May Ellis came over to bring the red frog home, and told Grandma about Uncle Burley's day at the picnic. Grandma told Grandpa and Daddy, and from then on Uncle Burley had no peace. Grandma lit into him about his sinful behavior every chance she got. Grandpa ignored him, but he ignored him in a way that kept all of us from being comfortable when the two of them were together. Even Daddy was aggravated, and that was unusual because he and Uncle Burley had always allowed each other to be the way they were and had got along.

Nobody knew what to do with the red frog. Uncle Burley was too proud to claim it, and Grandpa was too proud to throw it away. Annie May had set it on the mantelpiece in the living room when she came in that morning, and it stayed there. Grandma said she'd just leave it as a reminder to Uncle Burley. But it was a better reminder to her and Grandpa and Daddy than it was to Uncle Burley. He never looked at it.

He was used to that sort of trouble and he stood it well enough. He stayed in a quiet good humor that kept him always a little beyond their reach. But it was intentional good humor; there were times when it was too quiet and too pleasant, and although it spared him a lot of his trouble it could be as insulting as the red frog. He wouldn't say he was sorry and he wouldn't let them make him mad. That kept them after him.

During the week he worked hard. He stood the work the same way he stood everything else, laughing when he could, saying no more than he had to. The work sheltered him; he didn't give them a chance to find fault with him in that. When it was over on Saturday night he ate his supper and left. He'd go to the camp house at the river and stay until Monday morning, avoiding Sunday when Grandma had sin on her mind and Grandpa and Daddy had time enough to be quarrelsome.

While this was going on Brother and I quit being as good friends as we'd always been. I didn't know when it started, but things gradually began to change between us. He started running around with boys who were older than I was, and he went to town every Saturday night. Sometimes I noticed that I called him Tom instead of Brother. I was sorry, but he never gave me a chance to talk about it, and it just kept happening. I spent more time with Uncle Burley; and once in a while I'd walk to the Easterlys' and talk to Calvin. I didn't like Calvin much, but he was about my age, and he was better than nobody.

One Saturday at the end of July, while we were at work in the hay, Big Ellis and Gander Loyd began riding Brother about having a girl in town. I didn't pay much attention to it then. But that evening, after we'd done the chores and Brother had gone upstairs to get ready for town, Grandma said, "Tom's got a girl, hasn't he?"

"I don't know," I said.

"Well, I don't know either. But he's getting old enough. And if I know the signs he's got a girl." She shook her head. "Lord, it seems just yesterday when he was a baby."

She finished straining the milk and went into the kitchen to start supper, and I went to the front porch and sat in the swing. I could hear Uncle

Burley calling his hounds. He whistled and called each one by its name. In the field by the house Grandpa's mules were grazing along the side of the hill. I could see the sweaty marks of the harness on their backs and shoulders. They looked naked and strange without the harness. The day had come apart. After the week of hard work Sunday would feel awkward and too quiet, and even though we were glad of the rest we'd be a little relieved when it was Monday again. I heard the hounds come up to be fed, barking around Uncle Burley until he pitched the food to them, then quiet. A few swifts circled up into the sky and down again over the tops of the chimneys. The mules grazed side by side on the hill, walking together as if they were still at work.

In a little while Brother came around the corner of the house. He'd already eaten his supper and was dressed up, ready to go. His hair was shiny and black from the oil he'd put on it, and I could smell shaving lotion.

"You going to town?" I asked him.

"You got any objections?"

"What're you going to town for?"

He grinned at me, feeling the part in his hair with the ends of his fingers. "You don't know, do you?"

I watched him walk down the driveway and turn toward town. Uncle Burley came up and leaned against the post at the corner of the porch. He'd hunted me up to stay with me until supper was ready; he wouldn't risk being alone with Grandpa even that long. I scooted over and made room for him.

But he stood there, watching Brother walk out the lane. "Where's he going?"

"To town."

"He's courting a little, I expect."

"I don't know," I said.

Uncle Burley sat down. He leaned his head back and yawned and then closed his eyes. "There's one good thing about work," he said.

"What?"

"Stopping."

Grandma called us to supper. We went inside and washed our hands and sat down at the table. It was hot and stuffy in the kitchen, and with

Brother gone the meal was quieter than usual. As long as Uncle Burley was there Grandma and Grandpa wouldn't allow themselves to say anything pleasant, and they seemed too tired to be in a bad humor.

When Grandpa had cleaned his plate he turned his chair to the window and looked out at the sky. "We'll get a rain," he said. "It's been too hot."

He got up after a minute and left the room, and before the rest of us were finished eating we heard him going up the stairs.

"He's gone to roost," Uncle Burley said.

"You've got no respect, Burley," Grandma said.

She'd meant to say more, but held it back. She looked down at her plate, and then got up and began clearing the table.

Uncle Burley and I went to the porch again. He lit a cigarette and sharpened the end of the match to pick his teeth. Neither of us said anything. The day had been hot, and it was still hot. No air was stirring.

Uncle Burley flipped the butt of his cigarette out into the yard. He laughed then — quietly and to himself, as if it were the laughter he'd had ready for whatever Grandma had intended to say to him; and now he used it up, wasted it on himself, to be rid of it.

He got up and stood on the edge of the porch, looking out in the direction of the road. He held his hands open in front of him and looked at them, then rubbed them together. "Well," he said. He stepped off the porch and walked slowly across the yard. Halfway down the driveway he looked back and waved at me. After that he walked faster, on down the driveway and out the lane.

When he was out of sight I called to Grandma that I was going over to see Calvin, and I started through the field toward the Easterlys'. It was nearly dark, but when I looked back the swifts still circled above the house. They dived at the chimney tops, and swerved away as if they couldn't bear for the day to end. Finally, I knew, they'd give up the light and go down for good.

When I got to the Easterlys' I called Calvin from the back door. He came out and we sat down on the step.

"What you been doing?" he asked me.

"Working mostly."

"Where's Tom?"

"Gone to town."

"He's got a girl out there, ain't he?"

"They say he has."

"He has," Calvin said. He took a sack of peppermint sticks out of his pocket and took one and gave one to me.

"Maybe he has," I said.

"What we ought to do," Calvin said, "is slip out to town and watch him."

"It's his business," I said.

"Come on. It won't hurt anything. You'll have something to tell on Tom when you go to work Monday morning."

"All right," I said.

Calvin laughed and stomped his foot. "God durn, I wish I could be there when you tell it on him."

There was a crowd in town. Groups of men squatted on the sidewalk in front of the stores, talking and greeting each other. Up the street beyond the store lights the small children played tag, running and laughing around the parked automobiles. Women collected in the stores and talked while they shopped, and carried out armloads of groceries. A few of them were already standing at the edge of the sidewalk, holding their babies, waiting for their men to be ready to go home. Above the rest of the noise you could hear the jukebox playing in the poolroom.

Brother and four or five other boys were standing with two girls in the light of the drugstore window. He was talking and the others leaned toward him, listening to what he said. The prettiest one of the girls stood next to Brother, smiling at him while he talked, and he spoke mostly to her. She was his girl, I imagined, and I was proud of him for having one so pretty. While I watched him standing there with the other boys it seemed to me that he was the best of them, and I began to be ashamed of what I'd come to town for.

When he finished talking all of them laughed. The girl swung away from him, holding to his hand, and he pulled her back and put his arm around her.

I stood with Calvin, pretending to look in the grocery store window, hoping Brother wouldn't see me. But then the whole bunch of them started up the street past us. I didn't want Brother to know I'd sneaked on him, and I turned toward him to make the best of it.

"Hello," he said. "What're you doing here?"

For a minute I couldn't think what to say. Then I said, "Let's go down to the river and talk to Uncle Burley for a while."

They laughed, looking at Brother and then at me.

"Go ahead," Brother told me. "Who's stopping you?"

The way he said it made me mad. "I reckon you'd rather stay here and fool around with a damn girl," I said.

Brother's face got red and he took a step toward me, but the girl pulled at his arm. "Come on," she said.

He looked at me and laughed, then he turned around and they went past me and on up the street.

I stood still for a minute, feeling my own face red and knowing I'd made a fool of myself. There was no other way to see it. What I'd said had been wrong. Brother ought to have slapped my face for saying it. And I thought I should have knocked Calvin's teeth out for suggesting that we come to town in the first place. I turned to tell him so, but he was gone. I looked around for him and saw him going into the drugstore. He was ashamed of me too.

I started back down the street. The game had moved down in front of the stores, the children chasing each other in and out of the crowd. As I walked away I heard a woman's voice telling them, "Get someplace else if you want to play."

I went out the road toward home, feeling lonesome and stupid and ashamed. For a while I could hear the noise of the town, the music and talking and laughter, more quietly and more quietly as I got farther away. The frogs were singing in Big Ellis's pond when I passed, the sounds getting louder and then quieting too. I turned into our lane, but I didn't feel like going to bed and I went on past the house and down Coulter Branch toward the river. Now and then I'd hear a screech owl calling, and now and then a dog barked down in the bottom.

When I got to Uncle Burley's shack a light was burning in the window. I opened the door and went through the dark kitchen and into the other room where Uncle Burley and Big Ellis were sitting with a bottle of whiskey and a lighted lamp on the table between them. Their backs were turned to the kitchen door, and Uncle Burley had pulled one of the cots away from the wall and propped his feet on it. When Big Ellis looked around and saw me he started to hide the bottle, but Uncle Burley caught his arm and stopped him.

"It's all right."

"He's a good boy, that boy is," Big Ellis said.

Uncle Burley grinned at me. "The more the merrier," he said. "Have a seat."

I crossed the room and sat down on the other cot.

"Where you been, boy?" Uncle Burley asked me.

"I went to town a while," I said, "and then I came down here."

"I'm glad you came," Uncle Burley said.

"He's a pretty damn good boy, I tell you," Big Ellis said.

Neither of them could think of anything else to say. They just smoked, and passed the bottle once in a while, looking at the wall.

Finally Uncle Burley said, "It's hot."

"It's too hot," Big Ellis said. "We're bound to get some rain."

They were quiet again for a minute or two, and then Uncle Burley looked at Big Ellis and grinned as if he'd just thought of something that made him happy.

"I wonder if old Jig's at home," he said.

Big Ellis leaned toward the window and looked up the river toward Jig Pendleton's shanty boat. "No light up there. I expect he's asleep."

"The more the merrier," Uncle Burley said. He got up and went out the door.

Big Ellis and I followed him onto the porch. Jig's boat was dark and quiet. We could barely make out the shape of it through the trees.

"Call him," Big Ellis said.

Uncle Burley cupped his hands around his mouth and called, "Jig!"

There was no answer.

"Call him again," Big Ellis said; and Uncle Burley called again.

"What?" Jig said.

"Come on down," Uncle Burley said. "We're having a little social event here."

Jig didn't answer, but before long he came out with a lantern and untied his rowboat. We heard the knock and creak of his oarlocks as he came down the river toward us.

Jig tied the boat to a tree and climbed the bank. When he came onto the porch we went back inside and he followed us.

"How're you, Jig?" Uncle Burley asked.

Jig blew out his lantern and hung it on a nail over the door, and then he shook our hands. I'd never seen anybody look so sad in my life.

"No man's strength is equal to his wickedness," he said. "God has to forgive us before he can love us. Surely the people is grass."

"The more the merrier, Jig," Uncle Burley said. "Have a seat."

Jig sat down. Big Ellis handed him the bottle and he drank.

"That's an evil thing, Burley," he said. He looked at the bottle and handed it to Uncle Burley.

"But ain't it a mellow-ripe sample of it?" Uncle Burley said.

Jig shook his head. "Mellow as sin, Burley, and ripe."

Uncle Burley looked at him and then patted his shoulder. "You'll feel better when it's morning, old Jig."

Uncle Burley and Big Ellis sat down and began drinking again. But Jig had made them sad and they were even quieter than they'd been before. The three of them passed the bottle back and forth, drinking as if it were a chore they'd be glad to be done with.

Their seriousness and quietness began to bother me. I was more in the dumps than I'd been when I got there. I wished I'd gone on home to bed.

"I'd just as soon it was morning," Uncle Burley said.

"I'd just as soon it was," Big Ellis said.

"What time is it?"

Big Ellis got out his watch and held it to the light. "Half past eleven."

"She's a slow one, ain't she?" Uncle Burley said. Then he said, "Wind that thing."

Big Ellis wound the watch and put it back in his pocket.

Jig got up and wobbled out the door, and I heard him take his boots off and lie down on the porch. Uncle Burley and Big Ellis didn't seem to notice he was gone. I leaned back against the wall and dozed off. But I couldn't get all the way to sleep; every little sound woke me. Sometimes

I'd hear Jig turning over on the porch. He'd grunt and say, "Oh me," and then be quiet again. And Uncle Burley and Big Ellis sat on, drinking at the table.

Finally I heard Big Ellis say, "Where's Jig?"

"I don't know," Uncle Burley said. "We ought to get him to come and talk to us."

"Tell him to," Big Ellis said.

Uncle Burley stood up, and then he got down on his hands and knees and began crawling toward the door.

Big Ellis giggled. "What're you crawling for?"

"You got to watch this floor," Uncle Burley said. "It's a booger."

He got to the door and called, "Oh, Jig!"

Jig stirred and grunted. "What?"

"Come on down, Jig. We got a little social event going on here."

"All right," Jig said.

Uncle Burley cocked his ear up the river and listened.

"Is he coming?" Big Ellis asked.

"No," Uncle Burley said. "I can't even see a light."

"He'll come," Big Ellis said. "Call him again."

Uncle Burley called, "Jig!"

I heard one of Jig's elbows thump on the porch.

"What?"

"Come on."

"All right."

Uncle Burley listened again.

"You hear him yet?" Big Ellis asked.

"Aw, he ain't coming," Uncle Burley said. "He's scared of the dark." He stretched out across the doorway and folded his hands over his chest. "We'll see him in the morning, I reckon."

When I looked back at Big Ellis he was asleep, his head resting against the tabletop. They seemed to have settled down for the night. I was too sleepy to go home, so I took off my shoes and stretched out on the cot, thinking I'd take a nap and then get home before daylight to keep from worrying Grandma.

When I woke it was thundering. A strong wind had come up, fluttering the lamp flame until the whole house seemed to sway and jiggle in the wind. The rest of them were still asleep. Big Ellis hadn't moved since I'd lain down. The light bobbled his shadow over the wall behind him, and when the lightning flashes came his shadow jumped to the other wall and flickered there. It was like waking up on Judgment Day.

I was trying to untangle the blanket to pull it over my head when the rain came — a few big drops spattered the roof, and then a sheet of water blew into the door where Uncle Burley was sleeping.

He rolled over. "Quit," he said. He wiped the water out of his eyes and scrambled into the room. Jig followed him in and slammed the door.

Big Ellis sat up and rubbed his eyes. "It's raining," he said.

"You ought to been a prophet," Uncle Burley said. He sat down at the table again.

The lightning got worse. Jig stood in the middle of the floor and watched it, as wild-eyed as a ghost.

"Burley," he said, "He could strike us down with one of them."

"I reckon so," Uncle Burley said.

"He could strike you down just like a rabbit."

"He can shoot 'em like a rifle," Uncle Burley said.

It lightened again; the thunder clapped down, jarring the house.

"Oh," Jig said. He fell on the floor with his hands over his face.

"Bull's-eye," Uncle Burley said.

The thunder bumbled away over the top of the hill.

"Burley, that one struck something," Big Ellis said.

"It must have," Uncle Burley said.

We went to the windows and looked out, but it was raining too hard to see anything. Jig was still on the floor hiding his face.

"Get up, Jig," Uncle Burley said. "You're not dead."

He and Big Ellis helped Jig onto his feet.

"He ain't even wounded," Big Ellis said.

Jig sat down on one of the cots and put his hands over his face again. "Burley, He let me live. And He didn't have to do it. He didn't have any reason to do it. It was out of his goodness. He don't have to stand for any such foolishness, Burley."

The rain didn't last long. When it was over we went out on the porch to see if we could tell what the lightning had struck. The stars were shining where the cloud had passed, and everything was cool and fresh-smelling. I felt as wide awake as if I'd slept all night.

Big Ellis went around the corner of the house, and then we heard him say, "Burley, yonder's a fire."

"Where?" Uncle Burley asked him. He went around the house, and Jig and I hurried after him.

Big Ellis pointed. "Right up there."

We saw the smoke beginning to roll up over the top of the hill, and under it the dim red shimmer of the fire.

"It's at our place," I said.

"It could be," Uncle Burley said.

He started toward the road and Big Ellis went with him. Jig had gone back to the porch to put his boots on, and I ran into the house to get my shoes. Jig waited for me at the door, and then we started after the others. We ran hard and caught up with them a little past Beriah Easterly's store.

The trees hid the smoke from us, but by the time we were halfway up the hill we heard a bell ringing.

"That's the dinner bell," Uncle Burley said.

He broke into a run, and the rest of us strung out behind him. I could hear Jig's rubber boots bumping and stumbling behind me.

We were out of breath when we got up on the ridge and we slowed to a walk. But by that time we could see that the fire was in Daddy's barn, and we only walked a few steps before we started running again.

When we went past Grandpa's house Grandma was standing in the yard in her nightgown, ringing the dinner bell. She waved and called something to us.

Uncle Burley slowed down. "What?"

"Buckets!" she said. "Get some buckets."

We ran to the back porch and got the milk bucket and the slop bucket and the two water buckets. When we ran back into the yard she was ringing the bell again. She called something else to us when we went past her, but we didn't stop to hear what she said. She was barefooted, the firelight red on her face and gown.

Daddy's team had been in the barn, and he and Grandpa had got them out and turned them loose in the lot. The two mules stood together in the farthest corner, their heads up, turning to face the fire, then snorting and whirling away.

Daddy and Grandpa were dipping water out of the trough at the well and carrying it into the driveway where part of the loft had broken through. The fire had started in the far end of the barn, and the wind seemed to be holding it back a little.

When we got into the lot Jig stopped and pointed at the fire. "That's what it's like," he said. "The fire of Hell, my brothers in sin." Then he grabbed the pump handle and began pumping.

We stood in line to fill our buckets, and carried them into the barn and emptied them. Grandpa and Daddy had set the pace, and we kept it up, running from the well to the fire and back again. The driveway was so full of smoke that we could hardly breathe or see. I held my breath and ran in until I could see the light of the fire, and flung the bucket of water at it and ran out again, coughing and wiping my eyes while I waited in line at the well.

"It's got too much of a start," Uncle Burley said. "We'll never stop it."

I knew he told the truth. It had been hopeless when we got there. But he never stopped or slowed down, and none of the rest of us did either.

A crowd had gathered at the yard fence. The red light flickered and waved on their faces, and shone on the roofs of the automobiles behind them. Their faces looked calm and strange turned up into the light of the fire, like the faces of people around a lion's cage, separate from it, only seeing.

And once when I came back to the well with my empty bucket I saw that Brother was standing in the line ahead of me. Gander Loyd and Beriah Easterly and Mr. Feltner had come to help us too. But it was hopeless. Nothing was there to save, only a thing to look at. Grandma still rang the dinner bell, but we couldn't hear it now above the sound of the fire. Jig worked at the pump.

For a few minutes we managed to hold the fire at the back of the driveway. But it was spreading into the loft, and there was nothing we could do about that. Finally the heat drove us outside. The driveway ticked and cracked like an oven, and then the whole barn blazed up at once. Flames shot over the well top and we dropped our buckets and ran. We stood in the center of the lot, watching the fire and getting our breath.

"You all haven't got any barn," Gander said. "You've just got a fire." He turned around and walked toward the crowd at the fence.

Beriah stood with us for another minute or two, and then shook his head. "It's gone now." He followed Gander away.

Daddy never looked at them, nor at any of us. He watched the fire die down after the first big blaze; and when the wind turned the flames back from the well he moved toward the barn again, without looking back or asking us to go with him, and without any hope, but going anyway. Grandpa started after him, hurrying to catch up. Uncle Burley and Big Ellis and Mr. Feltner and Brother and Jig and I followed them.

Jig ran past us and splashed water on the pump handle to cool it, and pumped again. We filled our buckets and began dowsing the wall nearest the pump. Daddy wet his clothes so he could get closer to the fire, and we passed our buckets to him. He was furious, throwing water at the fire as if he were trying to bruise it. We worked to keep the fire away from the pump, and to save the crib and the granary and the wagon shed. Cinders dropped on our faces and hands, and scorched our clothes; we brushed them off and kept going. Jig worked the pump with his whole body, rattling the handle up and down as if he were doing some kind of dance.

Big Ellis yelled, "Look out!" and we ran again.

We ran to the fence and turned around in time to see the whole barn cave in—loft and roof and walls—like logs in a fireplace. Red ashes spewed around it on the ground; sparks from the hay spiraled and wound into the smoke.

We went back to the well again. From then on we worked more slowly, but we never stopped. Daddy and Grandpa kept us going. They hated the fire and they had to fight it, and none of us would leave them to fight it alone. We stayed with them, and we saved the outbuildings.

By morning the fire was out. We left our buckets at the well and went into the lot and sat down. We were too worn out to try to talk. We were blackened and parched and blistered, our eyes bloodshot and stinging from the smoke.

While daylight came we sat and looked at the black pile of ashes. We hadn't accepted the fire; we'd been able to fight that as long as it burned. But now, in the daylight, in our tiredness, as if we'd fought all night in a dream, we accepted the ashes.

It was quiet. The crowd had gone soon after the barn caved in, and Grandma had long ago quit ringing the bell. At the far end of the lot the two mules grazed on the short grass. After a while they walked over to the trough at the well, and Jig got up and pumped water for them.

"Bless you, God's creatures," he said.

They drank, and then Daddy opened the gate and turned them out on the hillside.

Uncle Burley found the drinking cup where it had been kicked into the ashes. Jig rinsed it and filled it for each of us and we drank. Daddy was the last to drink; when he finished he turned the cup upside down and set it carefully beside the base of the pump. After that there seemed to be nothing to do.

After the fire Uncle Burley quit leaving home on the weekends. He could be free with his own troubles but not with Daddy's. He did his best to be agreeable; and with the loss of the barn to worry about, everybody seemed to have forgotten how he'd misbehaved on the Fourth of July.

One day he carried the red frog to Big Ellis's house and asked Annie May to accept it as a gift from a friend. There was nothing she could do but take it and thank him.

Several weeks went by before we cleaned up the ruins of the barn. The black pile of ruck and cinders was too dismal. Daddy hated the sight of it; and I knew it was hard for him to think of cleaning it up, as if that would only finish what the fire had begun. After the swiftness of the fire I felt the ashes would stay forever.

But finally one Friday morning all of us went to work and hauled away the leavings. Once we'd got beyond our dread of the job we were anxious to be rid of every trace of the fire.

Brother stayed mad at me for what I'd said to him in town the night the barn burned. I'd been in the wrong, and he never gave me a chance to forget it.

On the Saturday night after we'd cleared away the remainders of the old barn Calvin came over to our house. I hadn't seen him since he'd slipped away from me in town, and I didn't care if I never saw him again. But when I went out of the house that night, after we'd finished supper and Brother had left for town, Calvin was coming across the yard.

He grinned at me, sucking on a peppermint stick. "What're you doing?"

I didn't go to meet him. "I'm standing here looking at you," I said.

He came on across the yard and sat down. I walked away toward the barn, and he got up again and followed me.

"Want some candy?" he asked.

"No thanks."

"Let's do something."

He trailed along behind me. I heard him close the sack and put it back in his pocket.

"I'm walking out to the barn," I said, "and I don't need your help."

"Let's go down to the river and talk to Uncle Burley for a while," he said, mocking the way I'd said it to Brother.

I turned on him and he dodged. I waited until he looked at me, and then I grinned. "Give me a stick of candy," I said.

He held the sack out and I helped myself.

"Let's go and see how Brother's getting along with his courting," I said.

He looked away. "We'd better not do that."

"Come on," I told him.

I started toward the road. He stood there a minute and then hurried after me. When we got to the road he caught up and walked beside me into town.

Brother and his girl were drinking Cokes at one of the tables in the back of the drugstore. We stood in front and watched them through the window until they got up and started out.

"We'd better get out of sight," Calvin said.

We crossed the street to the churchyard and watched them leave the drugstore. The moon had come up, but the trees around the church made shadow enough to hide us.

"Let's follow them," I said.

"We oughtn't to do that."

I told him to quit being such a chicken, and he didn't say any more.

We let them get a long way off, then followed. They went along the road toward the river, walking slowly with their arms around each other. When we'd got beyond the noise of the town we could hear Brother talking—the rising and falling of his voice, too quiet for us to make out the words. And now and then the girl laughed. Sometimes when she laughed she laid her head on Brother's shoulder.

Calvin nudged me in the ribs. "Look at that. Wait till you tell Tom you saw that." He had another peppermint stick in his mouth.

We passed the graveyard and I could see the angel on the Coulter monument standing up black over the tops of the trees. Brother and the girl walked close together. The moon threw their shadows behind them on the road.

They turned off where the road started down to the river and went along a path to a level place on the hillside. We stopped behind a bush at a bend in the path where we could look down on them.

"God durn if this ain't some fun," Calvin said.

The girl sat down and held her hand out to Brother, and he sat down beside her. She took the scarf off and put it in her purse, then ran her fingers through her hair and let it fall back over her shoulders. She reached and touched Brother's face. The light on her hair moved when she moved. Brother put his arms around her and kissed her. I looked at Calvin. He was standing there with his mouth open, watching them as if it were happening in a picture show. I jerked his sleeve to tell him to come on, and went up to the road again.

Before long Calvin came up opening the sack of peppermint sticks. He was grinning. "We've sure got a good one on old Tom now. You wait till we tell it on him."

"You'd better not," I said.

He looked at me. "Why?"

I caught him by the collar and shoved him backward. The peppermint sticks shook out all over the road.

"God damn you, go home."

I shoved him again, and he ran until he was out of sight over the hill.

I went on toward home then, and where our lane turned off I stopped and waited. There was nobody on the road. All the houses I'd passed were dark and quiet.

I heard Brother's footsteps. And then I could see him. When he saw me he took his hands out of his pockets and walked faster.

"What're you doing here?" His voice sounded peaceful and friendly.

"Just messing around."

"Well, let's go home." He started into the lane.

"Tom," I said. "I saw you."

He turned around. "Saw who?"

"You and that girl. Down there on the hillside."

He hit me square in the face and I fell. My head hit the road.

His footsteps went away and it got quiet again. I felt the blood running out of my mouth.

❊

Brother never mentioned what had happened that Saturday night, and he was peaceable enough afterwards. But he wasn't friendly. He kept his distance. We got along better than I'd expected we would. I had to be grateful for the distance. If we'd been any closer, or tried to be brothers the way we'd always been, we'd have had to keep fighting each other. But we'd quit being brothers, and it was my fault.

When the work let up early in September and Uncle Burley suggested that he and I go fishing for a few days, I was glad of the chance to get away.

We'd been busier than usual during the last part of the summer, and all of us were tired. The weather had been wet, and Daddy and Grandpa hadn't been able to plan work more than a day ahead. That had kept them on edge and hurrying, and Grandpa's patience had worn out.

When we sat down to breakfast that morning Grandpa noticed one of the kitchen windows was shut. He told Grandma to open it.

"It's stuck," she said. "The damp weather made it swell."

"Get up and open the window," Grandpa told Brother.

Brother got up and tried to open it, but it wouldn't budge. Grandma came to help him. But it was stuck tight, and they only got in each other's way.

Grandpa watched them fumbling at the sash for a minute; and then without saying a word he unhooked his cane from the back of his chair and knocked out the glass.

Grandma and Brother dodged the splinters, and Brother sat down again. Grandma stood still for a minute looking at Grandpa, her eyes snapping. But he'd turned his back to her and begun eating. She went to the stove then and took the biscuits out of the oven. We ate without talking or looking at each other.

Grandpa finished in a hurry and went to the barn. Uncle Burley looked at the broken window and the pieces of glass on the floor and began laughing. He looked up at the ceiling and rocked back and forth in his chair, whooping and howling with laughter until Grandpa must have heard it at the barn. He'd stop for a second to get his breath, then he'd look at the window and say "Oh my God" and start laughing again.

"You're a fine one to be laughing," Grandma told him. "It's no funnier than some of the things you do."

He looked at her, still laughing, and said, "Oh my God."

She left the room then, and Uncle Burley quit laughing. He looked across the table at me and said, "Let's go fishing, for God's sake."

I said that suited me but I was afraid Grandpa had work for me to do, and I didn't want to ask him because of the mood he was in.

"I'll take care of that," Uncle Burley said.

Grandpa was harnessing his team in the driveway of the barn. He hadn't told us what he was going to do that day, but nearly always when we had a break in our regular work he'd slip away from us and spend a day or two at odd jobs around the farm — mowing weeds or mending a fence. He liked to work by himself, and he was always resentful if we asked where he was going or offered to help him.

Uncle Burley went into the barn and squatted in the middle of the driveway so that Grandpa had to walk around him. "What're you fixing to do?" he asked.

Grandpa didn't pay any attention to him. He threw the harness over the back of the second mule and buckled it on. He picked up his cane and led the mules out into the lot and began hitching them to the wagon. Uncle Burley got up and followed him.

"You've got the lead mule hitched too short."

"I was working mules before you were born," Grandpa said.

"Well," Uncle Burley said, "Nathan and I think we'll go fishing for a few days."

Grandpa said he didn't give a damn if we fished the rest of the year, and Uncle Burley said he hadn't thought about that but we might do it.

He sent me to the house to tell Grandma we were going. Then we went to the smokehouse and got a side of bacon and a tin can full of salt.

It was a fine brisk morning, cool and bright, the wind in the north. The leaves on some of the bushes beside the road had begun to turn yellow. I knew we wouldn't think of summer again; it was easier to imagine cold and fire in the stoves and snow.

When we came over the brow of the hill we stopped and looked down at the river. The corn in the bottoms had ripened and turned brown; the tobacco patches were naked now that the crop had been put in. The river lay green and quiet between the rows of trees.

"Poor old Chicken Little," Uncle Burley said.

I turned to look at him; he stood there watching the river as if he didn't realize he'd spoken aloud.

Chicken Little Montgomery had fallen out of a boat and drowned the week before, but this was the first time I'd heard any of our family mention it. None of us had ever been friends with the Montgomerys, and we'd never spoken of them. But now that Chicken Little was dead you noticed the silence. All of us felt uneasy about his drowning. He stayed on our minds as if our dislike for him while he was alive had somehow made us guilty of his death.

"Wonder if they've ever found his body," Uncle Burley said.

"I don't know," I said.

We went on down the hill, and up the bottom to Beriah Easterly's store.

Beriah and Gander Loyd were sitting on nail kegs in front of the store, looking up toward the top of the hill. Beriah saw us coming and called, "Morning, Burley."

"Morning, Beriah," Uncle Burley said. "Morning, Gander. I hear you got married."

"It's a fact," Gander said.

Beriah pointed up at the top of the hill. "A lot of buzzards up there this morning. Must be something dead."

We looked at the buzzards for a minute. Then Uncle Burley and I went into the store and Beriah got up and came in after us. He went behind the counter and propped his elbows on it, waiting to hear what we wanted.

Uncle Burley ordered two pounds of line and a hundred hooks, five pounds of meal and three sacks of Bull Durham.

"Going to do some fishing, are you, Burley?" Beriah said when he came back with the line and hooks.

"Thinking about it," Uncle Burley told him.

"Pity about Chicken Little, wasn't it?" Beriah said.

"It was," Uncle Burley said.

"You know they never found his body. They gave him up."

Beriah sacked up the things we'd bought and handed the sack across the counter to me. "Looks like we're going to have some more fishing weather."

"Could be," Uncle Burley said.

"Well, I hope you all have luck."

Gander was still sitting on the nail keg when we came out. Uncle Burley nodded to him. "Give my respects to your wife, Gander."

"Thank you, Burley," Gander said. He got up and went into the store.

When we were on the road again Uncle Burley said, "Gander's out awfully bright and early for a bridegroom."

"I didn't know he was married," I said. "Who did he marry?"

"Old Gander outdid himself, from what I hear. They say he married a young woman. And a pretty one too. Her name was Mandy something or other."

When we got to the camp house Uncle Burley shoved the door open and we went inside. "Well, here we are," he said.

He told me to open the windows, and he got a broom and swept the floors. We took the bedding down and spread it over the beds. After we got everything clean and in order we sat outside to talk and look at the river. There was a breeze blowing and a few spots of sunlight came through the leaves onto the porch; it was quiet and comfortable. We'd gone a few days without rain and the river had cleared, although there was still some current. It felt good to have nothing to do but be there.

"I don't see how Gander ever persuaded a pretty woman to marry him," Uncle Burley said. "That one-eyed old pup. She must be blind in both eyes. I wonder if she's looked at him yet."

"He's not very pretty, " I said.

Uncle Burley laughed. "His face would stop an eight-day clock and run it backwards two weeks."

He lay down on his back and pulled his hat over his eyes. After a minute he laughed again. "Your grandpa sure did ventilate the kitchen," he said. "Damned if he can't be outrageous sometimes."

"It's hard on Grandma," I said.

"And everybody else," Uncle Burley said. He sat up and put his hat back on, folding his arms across his knees. "But I tell you, there's no give in him. And no quit. You've got to admire that. He's been a wheel horse in his time. He's worked like the world was on fire and nobody but him to put it out. It's a shame to see him getting old."

I nodded. Grandpa had been hard on all of us. He'd kept himself stubborn and lonely, not allowing any of us to know him; we saw him and he saw us through his loneliness. But his loneliness and stubborness humbled us too. We had to admire him.

At dinnertime Uncle Burley lit the coal oil stove, and I filled the water bucket at the spring behind the house. We fried some bacon and a pile of corn bread and sat down to eat.

Uncle Burley raised his hat and said,

> *Oh Lord, make us able*
> *To eat all that's on this table,*
> *And if there's some we haven't got*
> *Bring it to us while it's hot."*

After dinner we found the boat where Uncle Burley had hidden it in a patch of horseweeds and turned it over and slid it down the bank to the river. And then we got the bait box and the fish box from under the porch and tied them in the river by the boat.

We climbed the bank again and sat on the edge of the porch to rest.

"Well," Uncle Burley said, "we got her fixed. We're in business."

When we'd rested Uncle Burley said we'd better be thinking about catching some bait if we were going to fish. He said there ought to be plenty of perch up in the creek, and we could try them for a start. He found the minnow seine and I got a five-gallon bucket from under the stove in the kitchen. We started upstream toward the mouth of the creek.

Uncle Burley carried the seine on his shoulder, whistling a tune and watching the river.

"Do you think we'll catch any fish?" I asked him.

"The river's full of them," he said. "We ought to. If we get another rain to stir the water and freshen it a little, we ought to have good fishing."

We caught a bucketful of perch up in the creek and carried them back and put them in the bait box at the river. It was getting late by then. Uncle Burley said there wasn't much use in trying to fish that day, so we made another meal off the bacon and corn bread.

As soon as supper was over we set a lantern on the table in the bedroom and started getting our fishing gear in shape. We rolled the hanks of line into balls so they'd run out without tangling when we put them in the river. Uncle Burley got out a ball of lighter line and we snooded the hooks, cutting the line into pieces about a foot and a half long and tying the hooks to them.

It was comfortable work to do after supper. We were full and a little sleepy. A couple of owls called in the woods. Frogs were singing.

The next morning we finished breakfast by sunup. We loaded the lines and hooks and a baiting of perch into the boat and started up the river. Uncle Burley rowed. The red sunlight slanted through the trees on the bank and down to the water. A soft wind was coming up the river, rippling it, and the reflections of the trees were speckled and pointed in the water like big fish. Two or three herons flew from one snag to another, keeping ahead of us. We went past Jig's boat, but it was quiet and we didn't call him.

When we got to the bend where Uncle Burley wanted to fish I tied the end of one of the lines to a willow, and let it unwind as Uncle Burley rowed across to the other bank. We found another willow on that side and fastened the line, then tied on the weights — a small rock near each shore and one in the middle. We pulled ourselves back across on the line, and I tied on the hooks and Uncle Burley baited them.

The sun was getting hot when we finished putting the lines out. Uncle Burley said it would save a lot of rowing if we stayed there for the rest of the morning; we'd run the lines at noon and maybe get a mess of fish, and then go in. He pulled the boat into the shade along the bank and we tied up to a snag.

We made ourselves comfortable and watched the river, talking about how many fish we might catch and what kind and how big. Uncle Burley remembered all the good ones he'd ever caught and what he'd caught them on and what time of year it had been. Finally we ran out of talk, and he lay down in the bottom of the boat and went to sleep.

I watched the sun climb up toward the top of the sky. A few birds were singing, and I could see a mud turtle sunning himself on a log. King-fishers flew over the willows, calling, tilting down to the water after min-nows. After a while it got hotter and the river quieted down. The only things moving then were the clouds and the water.

The surface of the river was still. You could see every leaf of the trees reflected in it. The white glare of the sun glanced so brightly it hurt your eyes; and in the shade where we rested the water darkened, rippling a little as it passed the boat. The whole calm of the river moved down and past us and on, as if it slept and remembered its direction in its sleep. And somewhere below the thin reflections of the trees was Chicken Little, hidden in that dark so quietly nobody would ever find him.

After a while I propped my back against the side of the boat and went to sleep too.

It was nearly noon when Uncle Burley woke me. We ran the lines and took off four or five little catfish, and then rowed back to the house to cook them for dinner.

That afternoon we caught another bucketful of perch, and ran the lines again after it began to cool off. We took six nice channel cats on that run and baited the lines up fresh. Three of the fish made enough for our supper, and we put the other three in the fish box to keep them alive.

It began to rain at supper time, a slow drizzle at first, then hard and steady against the roof and windowpanes. It sounded as if it had set in for the night. When supper was over we sat in the bedroom and talked and listened to the rain fall.

I'd about made up my mind to go to bed when Uncle Burley picked up the lantern and put his hat on. "I feel my luck working," he said. "Let's go see what we've caught."

"At this time of night?" I said.

We waited until the rain slacked up a little, and went down to the boat. It was dark. The rain fell out of the black sky and splattered our clothes and sizzled on the lantern globe. Uncle Burley set the lantern in the front of the boat and we shoved off. We stayed in close under the trees. The lower branches caught in our light and we guided by them.

We ran the first line and took off two white cats and three channel cats, all of a good size. I rowed to the other line and Uncle Burley began raising it. We went about fifteen feet from the bank and I saw the line jerk in his hands. It pulled him off balance and he turned the line loose and caught himself on the other side of the boat.

He wiped his hands on his pants and looked at me. "We got a fish, boy."

"Can you tell how big?"

"Pretty near too big."

I rowed to the bank. He caught the line again, and I held the lantern up so he could see. The line tightened in his hands, cutting back and forth through the water. It was still raining, and pitch-dark beyond the light of the lantern. Uncle Burley knelt in the front of the boat, working us slowly toward the fish. He had his underlip in his teeth, being careful.

We heard the fish roll up on top of the water, his big tail splashing out in the dark toward the middle of the river. He went down then, and Uncle Burley had to turn the line loose. We played the fish for what seemed an hour, running out, losing the line, and rowing back to the bank to start all over again.

Finally we wore him out. He came to the top of the water, and Uncle Burley held him there and pulled the boat out to him. He was a white cat, the biggest I'd ever seen. Uncle Burley hooked his thumb into the fish's mouth and ran the fingers of his other hand into the gills. I caught the tail and we hauled him over the side of the boat. He flopped down at our feet and lay there with his big red gills heaving open and shut. Uncle Burley was breathing hard, and the thumb he'd hooked in the fish's mouth was bleeding. He sat down and looked at the fish while he got his breath, then he grinned at me. "He's a horse, ain't he?"

We were drenched with rain, and by the time we got back to the house our teeth were chattering. We stripped off our clothes and hung them on the chairs to dry. Uncle Burley lit the stove and we stood in front of it until we were warm. When we went to bed the rain was still coming down, rustling through the trees and rapping the tin roof. We lay snug and awake for a long time, remembering everything that had happened.

❦

After breakfast the next morning we went down to the river. We'd tied the fish to the back of the boat with a piece of strong line, doubled and looped through one of his gills. Uncle Burley lifted him out of the water. We were surprised again to see how big he was.

"What're we going to do with him?" I asked.

"We'll get Beriah to put him on ice for us so he'll keep," Uncle Burley said. "You can cut slabs of meat off of him as big as steaks, and just as white as snow."

When we'd finished looking at the fish Uncle Burley let him back into the water so he could breathe. He jerked his head against the line like a horse jerking against a hitch rein.

"There'll be a lot of fine eating on that fish," Uncle Burley said. "We ought to have a fish fry. We'll get Big Ellis and Jig and Gander to come down tonight and have a feast. We'll have to let Beriah in on it too, so he'll be willing to furnish some ice."

As soon as we'd baited the lines we took the fish out of the water again. We tied him to one of the oars and started up the road, carrying him between us, holding him high to keep his tail from dragging.

"We'll cook plenty of corn bread," Uncle Burley said, "and maybe get hold of a watermelon. It'll be a supper they won't forget for a while."

Beriah was sitting in front of the store again, and when he saw us he came out to meet us. "Lord amercy," he said. "Look what a fish."

"We're going to use him for bait," Uncle Burley said. "We're going to try to catch one big enough to eat."

Beriah held the door open for us and we carried the fish inside and stretched him out on the floor in front of the counter.

"Lord amercy," Beriah said. "You've caught the granddaddy of them all." He knelt down beside the fish and patted its head as if it were a dog. "You don't see a fish like this more than once in a lifetime, Burley."

When I saw how Beriah admired our fish I was prouder than ever and so was Uncle Burley.

"Don't it make your mouth water just to look at him?" Uncle Burley said.

"There's some fine eating on him, all right," Beriah said.

"I'll tell you what," Uncle Burley said. "We'll clean him and you can put him on ice for us, and then we'll all get together tonight and have a big fish fry."

"Nothing could suit me any better," Beriah said. "But, Burley, you all don't want to dress that fish yet. Keep him a while so people can see him."

They looked at the fish. Uncle Burley leaned over and picked up the line again and held it, as if he were going to lead the fish out of the store. "He'll spoil."

"No, he won't. We'll keep him alive. Hell, Burley, you don't want to treat him like an ordinary fish. People don't get a chance to see a fish like that every day."

Beriah went to the back of the store and opened the cooler. "Bring a couple of those crates," he said.

He began to take the bottles out of the cooler and we brought the crates and helped him.

"Now, what's the matter with that, Burley? He'll stay alive a long time in that cold water."

"I reckon he will," Uncle Burley said.

Beriah picked up the fish. "Lord amercy," he said.

We helped him lift the fish into the cooler, and then we stood there looking in.

"Why, that's a regular aquarium," Beriah said. "I just wish it had glass sides on it."

Uncle Burley laughed. "Well, we could caulk up the candy counter and put him in that."

Beriah and I laughed too, and we looked at the fish again.

"Well, he looks comfortable enough," Uncle Burley said. He shut the lid and turned around. "We'll be seeing you, Beriah."

Beriah sat down on the bench beside the cooler. "Aw, stick around a while, Burley."

Uncle Burley didn't say whether he'd stay or not, but I could see that he was relieved when Beriah asked him to. He opened the screen door and started out.

"When did you all catch him, Burley?"

Uncle Burley stopped and turned around. "Last night." He stepped back inside and let the door close behind him.

"Last night?" Beriah said. "You all caught a fish like that in the dark?"

"Well," Uncle Burley said, "it wasn't a lot of trouble."

Beriah kept asking questions; and while Uncle Burley answered them he moved back into the store. He walked to the counter, and to the cooler again, and finally sat down on the bench with Beriah and propped up his feet. He'd tell only as much as Beriah asked for, and then he'd wait for another question.

"And what did you do then?" Beriah would ask. And when Uncle Burley told him, he'd let his hands drop onto his knees and say, "Well, I'll swear."

When Uncle Burley began to tell how we'd fought the fish out in the dark and the rain his voice got tight and excited in spite of all he could do. He sounded like somebody was tickling his feet.

Before he got it all told Gander Loyd came in.

"Gander, go look there in the cooler," Beriah said.

"What for?"

"Just go look in it."

Uncle Burley straightened up and Beriah rubbed his hands together and patted his feet while Gander opened the lid and looked in.

"Nice fish," Gander said. "Who caught him?"

"Burley and Nathan here."

I was glad Beriah included me, but he was about to turn the fish and Uncle Burley and me into some sort of freak show. He'd got to be as proud of the fish as we were and I was sorry we'd let it get out of our hands.

"How'd you catch him, Burley?" Gander asked.

"Caught him last night in the dark," Beriah said. "Ain't that right, Burley?"

Uncle Burley nodded, and Beriah began asking him the same questions he'd asked before, making him tell the story again from the beginning.

He got it all told that time, and after he finished everybody was quiet for a while. Beriah and Uncle Burley had used up all of their talk, and Gander wouldn't help them any. Now and then Beriah slapped his knees and said, "Uhhhhhhh-uh!"

After a while Big Ellis's car pulled up in front of the store and stopped.

Beriah yawned and stretched. "Customers," he said. He went behind the counter and set his elbow on the top of the cash register.

Annie May came in and began ordering groceries. Big Ellis and two other men followed her through the door and walked on back where we were.

"This is J.D.," Big Ellis told us, pointing to one of the men. "He's my brother-in-law. And this other one is William."

J.D. and William stepped up and shook hands with Uncle Burley and Gander and me.

"They work at the same place in Louisville," Big Ellis said. "This is their vacation."

"Well, I'll declare," Uncle Burley said.

Big Ellis sat down on the bench between Uncle Burley and Gander; J.D. and William stood in front of them, shifting their feet and looking around the store.

Finally Big Ellis said, "J.D. hasn't been here for thirty years."

"I grew up around here," J.D. said.

Everybody kept quiet. Uncle Burley was studying J.D.'s face, but I saw that he couldn't recognize him. Gander had turned his blind side to them and was looking at the toe of his shoe.

"Yep, this is where I was raised," J.D. said. He looked at Gander and then at Uncle Burley. "I expect you all remember me."

Uncle Burley got embarrassed then and looked away, and so did Big Ellis. I began to feel sorry for J.D. He stood there waiting for somebody to remember him and be glad to see him now that he'd come back home after thirty years. But he was a stranger to us. I knew Big Ellis had relatives who'd moved away, but he never talked about them.

J.D. looked at Uncle Burley. "You're Burley Coulter, aren't you?"

Uncle Burley nodded.

"And I remember you had a brother."

"That's his boy there."

J.D. turned to me and said, "Is that so? Well, I'll declare. How're your folks, son?"

"Fine," I said.

Uncle Burley looked down at his hands for a minute, and then he said, "Why, I believe I remember you."

J.D. nodded. He looked grateful enough to have paid money for that. I knew Uncle Burley was lying, but I was glad for J.D.'s sake.

"You married Big Ellis's sister," Uncle Burley said.

J.D. nodded again. "That's right."

Uncle Burley laced his fingers around his knees and leaned back. "I was just a boy when you left here."

"That's right, Burley."

After that all Uncle Burley had to do was listen. J.D. talked about his boyhood; and told why he'd left home and how he'd got to be a foreman where he worked and was doing well for an old country boy. He told it all to Uncle Burley, looking at him while he talked. Uncle Burley had said he remembered who J.D. was, and J.D. was Uncle Burley's friend.

"Burley," J.D. said, "it don't seem like more than a few days since I was a boy here, and it's been half a lifetime. I tell you, time goes in a hurry."

"That's right," Uncle Burley said.

Beriah hustled around, waiting on Annie May. He filled a box with groceries and pushed it across the counter, and then we heard him say, "Right there in the cooler, Annie May. Just help yourself."

He looked at us and winked. And we watched her walk to the cooler and open it.

"Ouch!" she said, and slammed the lid down.

Beriah's belly shook with laughter, but he kept his face straight.

"What's the matter, mam?"

Annie May backed out into the middle of the floor. "A stinking catfish!" she said.

As soon as they heard her say catfish, Big Ellis and J.D. and William went to the cooler and looked in. Uncle Burley and Gander and I got up and followed them. And then Beriah came, forgetting all about Annie May.

"Who caught that one?" Big Ellis asked.

"Burley and Nathan," Beriah said.

"You might know it would be Burley's," Annie May said. But when she saw that nobody was going to pay any more attention to her she picked up her box of groceries and started to the door. "I'm going home," she said. "If you all don't want to come now, you can walk."

"Well," Big Ellis said. He never looked up when she slammed the door.

"That's a pretty good fish," William said, "for a river fish."

"That's about as good a fish as you'll ever see caught," Beriah said.

William ignored him. "Of course now, you can catch them plenty bigger than that in the ocean." And he began telling us that he'd lived near the ocean once and used to go fishing clear out of sight of land. I figured he was going to tell how he'd caught a bigger fish than we had, and I didn't want to hear it; but he finally noticed that nobody had turned away from the cooler to listen to him. He slowed down then; and Beriah horned in and started telling how Uncle Burley and I had caught our fish.

Beriah stretched the truth in some places and added to it in others. Every time he got beyond the facts he'd say, "Ain't that right, Burley? Ain't I telling them just what you told me?"

Uncle Burley only nodded his head, without looking at anybody. It seemed to me that if he talked much longer Beriah would believe he'd caught the fish himself. William walked around the store, looking at the merchandise, being as uninterested in our story as we'd been in his.

The door opened and shut quietly; when we turned around there was Mushmouth Montgomery wandering up to the counter. Looking as much like Chicken Little as he did, and so lonesome-faced and grieved, it was as if a corpse or a ghost had come in. All of us stood still for a minute, and then Beriah closed the cooler and hurried behind the counter.

"What can I do for you, Mushmouth?"

Uncle Burley went back to the bench, and Big Ellis and Gander and I went with him. Mushmouth's coming made the fish seem unimportant — as out of place there as it would have been at a funeral. We kept quiet, each one dreading the chance that one of the others might mention it.

Mushmouth bought smoking tobacco and a candy bar. We watched him walk toward the door, hoping he'd leave. But he sat down by himself in the front of the store and began to eat the candy. J.D. and William leaned against the cooler, waiting for one of us to say something.

Beriah stayed at the counter, shuffling through a handful of bills. Once in a while he'd thumb one out and look at it, then shake his head and lay it on top of the cash register.

Finally J.D. lost his patience and walked up to Mushmouth. "Say," he said, "you ought to see what a fish Burley's caught. I imagine it's as fine a fish as was ever caught in this river." He said it proudly, as if he and Uncle Burley had been friends all their lives.

Uncle Burley got up and headed for the door. "Well, I reckon we'll get on back."

I went with him, trying not to seem in a hurry, past Mushmouth and out to the road. It was the middle of the morning and the sun had turned warm.

"Boy, we've let it all turn into talk," Uncle Burley said.

Big Ellis called to us; and we stopped and waited while he and J.D. and William caught up with us.

"It's too solemn to stay at the store," Big Ellis said, "as long as Mushmouth's there."

"That Mushmouth's a one-man funeral procession," Uncle Burley said.

We walked to the shack and sat on the porch in the shade.

Big Ellis got Uncle Burley to tell him where we'd caught the fish; and then he wanted to know what size hooks we'd used and what kind of bait. William started in again to tell how he'd fished in the ocean. But Big Ellis had catfish on his mind, and William didn't get any farther than he had before.

Big Ellis said he knew where there was a fish nearly as big as the one we'd caught, and he and J.D. started planning how Uncle Burley could catch that one. William walked over to the edge of the porch and sat down by himself. It looked like he'd never get a chance to tell his story, and I could see that it was beginning to sour on him. He and J.D. had both been strangers when they'd come to the store, but now that J.D. thought Uncle Burley remembered him he'd changed sides. William had been left out. I wished Uncle Burley would pay some attention to him, but he was fed up with all the talk about fish. Big Ellis and J.D. spoke to him and he listened, staring past them at the river.

Jig Pendleton came in sight, rowing his boat down toward the store, and Big Ellis called, "Come up, Jig."

Jig waved and pulled in to the bank. When he came up on the porch he nodded his head to us and sat down.

"We haven't seen much of you, Jig," Uncle Burley said.

"I haven't been getting out much, Burley. But I've noticed you and the boy fishing."

Big Ellis introduced J.D. and William. William only looked at Jig and said hello, but J.D. got up and shook hands.

"I used to live here once," he said. "I expect you remember me."

"Not a single sparrow falls without He knows about it," Jig said. "No sir, I don't remember you. But that don't make any difference."

J.D. looked puzzled, but then he said, "Yes sir," and sat down again.

William stared at Jig for a minute and began laughing.

"What's funny?" Uncle Burley asked him.

William looked at Uncle Burley and then down at the ground. "Nothing," he said.

"You all had any luck fishing?" Jig asked.

"Burley caught one as long as from here to the door," Big Ellis said.

It was about ten feet from where Big Ellis was sitting to the door. Uncle Burley winked at me, but he didn't say anything.

"Burley, if you caught one that big I'm glad you caught it," Jig said.

William got up all of a sudden and started off the porch. "Hell," he said, "I'll show you all how to catch fish."

We watched him go up the path toward the road.

"He's kind of odd," Big Ellis said, "ain't he, J.D.?"

"Kind of odd," J.D. said.

Before long William came back, carrying a paper sack in his hand.

"Where you been?" J.D. asked him.

"To the store," William said.

He put the sack on the porch and took out a half stick of dynamite with a piece of fuse already set in it. He started down the bank, carrying the dynamite by the fuse, holding it away from him as if he were carrying a live wildcat by the tail. Before anybody could say anything to stop him he lit the fuse and flung the dynamite into the river.

After the explosion we sat there, watching the dead fish float up to the surface.

William turned toward us and grinned, without looking at any of us as if he grinned at the empty house. He was already ashamed of what he'd done, but he wasn't going to back down.

"How's that for fish?" he asked.

Big Ellis said, "Burley, do you want some of them fish?"

"No," Uncle Burley said. "Help yourselves."

Big Ellis asked to borrow our boat, and he and J.D. and William rowed out to pick up the fish.

"Jig," Uncle Burley said, "they've got enough fishes to feed a multitude."

Jig shook his head. "It's unblessed, Burley, and no loaves."

"Maybe they'll blow up a bakery," Uncle Burley said.

When they'd gathered the fish and strung them they came up the bank again. Big Ellis went by the porch without stopping; J.D. and William followed him, neither of them looking at us.

"Thanks, Burley," Big Ellis called back.

Uncle Burley raised his hand. "Don't mention it."

After they'd gone Jig said, "That kind of doings is what ruins fishing, Burley."

"It don't help any."

I looked in the sack that William had left on the porch and there was another half stick of dynamite and a fuse. I held it up for Uncle Burley to see.

"Well," he said, "it's good bait."

Jig left then, and Uncle Burley and I went inside and fixed dinner.

In the afternoon we were sitting on the porch again, talking and letting our dinner settle, when we heard a car stop out on the road and the door open and slam. We went around the house to see if somebody else was coming to visit us. Before long we saw a tall, heavy-set man walking down the path through the trees. Uncle Burley touched my arm and whispered that he was the game warden.

"Do you know him?" I asked.

"I know him all right. But he don't know me." Uncle Burley watched the game warden for a minute, and then he said, "He thinks we did that dynamiting."

The game warden came on down the path. "Howdy," he said.

Uncle Burley told him good evening.

The game warden said he was from out of the county, just driving through, and had heard we might have some fish for sale.

"We don't sell fish," Uncle Burley said.

But the game warden wouldn't stop at that. He'd laid his trap for us, and he had to try to catch us in it. "I'm sure this is the right place," he said. "The fellow at the store directed me here. He said you'd been catching a lot of fish."

Uncle Burley frowned when he heard that, and I began to get scared. If the game warden had been to the store there was no telling what Beriah had said to him. And Big Ellis had borrowed our boat to bring in the fish William killed. I was afraid we were half caught already.

"We do all our fishing for fun," Uncle Burley said.

"Well," the game warden said, "if you've got more fish than you can use, I'd like to buy a few pounds."

Uncle Burley looked down at the boat, scratching his cheek. "How many fish do you need?"

"About fifteen pounds."

Uncle Burley thought a minute and said, "Well, we'll have to go get some then."

The game warden turned his head and coughed. "Do you mind if I go along?" he asked.

"Help yourself," Uncle Burley said. He went to the porch and picked up the other half stick of William's dynamite.

The three of us got into the boat and rowed out to the middle of the river.

Uncle Burley looked at the game warden. "About fifteen pounds, you say?"

The game warden said yes, that would be plenty.

Uncle Burley lit the fuse and watched it splutter for a second or two, then he dropped it under the game warden's feet.

The game warden jerked back and stared at Uncle Burley. He couldn't believe it. But Uncle Burley didn't give him any help. He just smiled, as if we had all the time in the world. The game warden snatched the dynamite and threw it down the river. He shut his eyes until the blast went off.

We picked up the fish we'd killed and rowed to the bank.

Uncle Burley said he judged we had at least fifty pounds of fish, and he offered them all to the game warden for ten cents a pound.

The game warden didn't say anything. We strung the fish and he helped us carry them to the road and put them in the trunk of his car.

When we got the fish loaded he took out his billfold and handed Uncle Burley three dollar bills. He said that was all the money he had with him, and he wondered if we'd trust him to pay the rest of it when he came through that way again. Uncle Burley told him that would be fine.

We stood in the road and watched him drive away.

"It's a shame we had to mistreat him," Uncle Burley said.

I knew how he felt. There was no reason for what we'd done, except that we'd all wound up together in the same mess. We'd been having a good time, and now we'd ruined it. "It takes the pleasure out of fishing," I said.

"It sure does." He folded the money and put it in his pocket. "Well, let's go home. We've stayed a day too long already."

"What about the fish fry?" I asked.

"It's called off," he said. "I'm tired of fish."

We put things in order at the house and took the lines up and pulled the boat out of the river. It was getting late. We strung what fish we had left and started home.

When we came to the store we saw that Beriah had hung our fish outside the door so everybody could see it. Flies were swarming over it, and several men were standing there looking and talking.

As we passed one of them called, "Is this your fish, Burley?"

"It's Beriah's fish," Uncle Burley said.

4

There were six of us in the tobacco harvest — Grandpa and Daddy and Uncle Burley and Gander Loyd and Brother and I — swapping back and forth from Grandpa's crop to Daddy's to Gander's, taking tobacco from each as it got ripe from one day to the next; hurrying, because it was a late season and everybody was anxious and on the lookout for frost or rain.

The weather had changed a little toward fall at the end of the first five or six days — the mornings cool and brisk and clear, baking-hot in the middle of the day, and cool again late in the afternoons. Morning was the best part of the day, when we worked the sleep and stiffness off, and joked and laughed around the wagons, loading what we'd cut the day before and left in the patch overnight to wilt, and riding the loaded wagons down the ridges to the barns. The heat built up toward noon, and we stopped a half hour or so for dinner. Then the long hot afternoon when we just stood it, driving ourselves to quitting time. After supper was over we sat and talked around the table until we couldn't put off sleep any longer, then slept to daylight, when Grandpa called us out of bed. After the first days, when our tiredness had got to be more than a night's rest could cure, we dreamed of work, moving through the ripe and golden rows in our sleep until morning. During the day we'd begun to notice the little whirlwinds full of dust and dried tobacco leaves that were a sure sign it was getting close to fall.

We'd worked almost an hour past dinnertime, Daddy pushing us, trying to make up the time we'd lost when he let his team jerk a load off the wagon early in the morning. He stood on the wagon, cursing, mad at himself and at us and at the team, and grieved because what he'd done could have been avoided and because the sun wouldn't stop to let him make up the time, building the load again and calling on us to move faster than we could move. And he pushed us through the rest of the morning, until we quit and ate green beans and potatoes and fried ham and corn bread at the big table in Grandma's kitchen.

Daddy finished eating before any of us and slammed out of the house again, and Grandpa picked up his hat and followed him, hurrying to catch up. Grandpa had been like Daddy once; and now he was old and could only do a boy's work—drive a team or carry water or do the other odds and ends of jobs that saved time for the men who were stronger, cursing the walking cane that he had to depend on a little more every year. He hated to be old and was ashamed of his weakness, because he was work-brittle; what had driven him to work all his life had used up his strength and outlasted it. And even though he was proud of Daddy for taking his place as well as he had, you could tell sometimes that he grieved.

He sat on the edge of the wagon bed while we drove back up the ridge to the tobacco patch, holding his hat in his lap, looking out over the river valley.

We stopped the wagon under a walnut tree at the edge of the patch, and sat down in the shade to sharpen the cutting tools. Uncle Burley used the file and handed it to Gander, then he rolled a smoke and sat looking at the sun beat through the hot air outside the shade.

"You know," he said, "when the first fellow that owned this cut the trees off of it and dragged the logs and brush away and grubbed out the stumps and plowed it and planted a crop on it and an Indian came along and shot him, that son of a bitch was better off."

Gander stopped filing and snickered, his whole face tilting up in the direction of the eye that was out. He filed again, saying over to himself what Uncle Burley had said, and passed the file on to Daddy.

Daddy set the blade against his knee and ran the file across it carefully, stopping to feel the edge with his thumb. "Well," he said, "you work on this damned old dirt and sweat over it and worry about it, and then one day they'll shovel it in your face, and that'll be the end of it."

Grandpa prodded the cane into the ground between his feet, looking out at the sun. "Ah Lord," he said.

Brother used the file and passed it to me, and I used it while the rest of them stood up and began to move out of the shade toward the patch.

Daddy turned around and looked at me. "Come on, Nathan. You'll file the damned thing right down to the handle." He was half joking, wanting the others to hear too, wanting to make it up to us for losing his temper that morning; but still not able to spare any of us.

I laid the file on the wagon and followed them.

Daddy picked up the first stick in his row and stuck it in the ground. "Take a row, boys. Move fast, but be careful." He leaned and cut a stalk and speared it, then another one. "Do your damnedest. That's all a mule can do. I wouldn't ask a man to do more."

He warmed to it, talking himself and us into the work, talking against the dread of heat and sweat and tiredness that always came after dinner and that he felt too. We took a row apiece and followed him toward the other side of the patch.

"Show it to me, boys," he was saying. "Make me know it."

I watched him out the corner of my eye, working himself into the motion of it, his shoulders swaying in the row ahead of us. He worked without waste or strain, bending over his movement.

"Ah boys, when the sweat runs it quits hurting." The sound of his voice had changed — not talking to us anymore, but a kind of singing his own skill and speed and endurance.

I quit watching him and let myself into the work. Sweat stuck my shirt to my back. And a wide swath opened behind us to the edge of the patch.

The afternoon went on, hot and clear, the ground soaking up the heat and throwing it back in our faces. We cut one row and went back and started another. When we ran out of water Grandpa took the jug to the house and filled it. We stopped to drink, and worked again. The rows were long, and the tiredness wore down into our shoulders and backs and legs.

It was lonely to work that way, bending over your own shadow, without energy enough to talk or listen or do anything but push yourself into the row. Uncle Burley and Gander and Brother and I worked along together, not to talk, but for what little comfort it was to hear somebody working next to us, and so we could walk back together to the starting end and joke a little at the water jug.

And Daddy led us. He gained a row, and passed us again, not stopping to drink as often as we did, and not saying much. Only now and then he'd sing out to us, "Follow me, boys — you'll wear diamonds," or, "It won't be as long as it has been."

By five o'clock we could see it was the best day's work we'd done since we started. That made us feel good, and we worked faster, looking forward to quitting time when we could talk about what we'd done and brag on ourselves a little.

Daddy finished a row ahead of the rest of us and came back to where we were. He stood there with his hands on his hips, grinning at us and watching us work.

"Well," he said, "the old man's laying right in there, right there in front all day long. When the sun comes up in the morning and when it goes down at night he's right there, laying 'em in the shade."

It was a challenge, not so much to Gander and Uncle Burley because they had their pace and stuck to it and wouldn't pay any attention to him, but to Brother and me.

He joked sometimes about how one day we'd be able to do more than he could. "One of these days they'll go by the old man," he'd say. "They won't even look at him. They'll say, 'We're coming, old man,' and there won't be a thing for me to do but get over." And he usually wound up, "But, by God, they'll have to have the wind in their shirttails when they do it. I'll tell them that. When they go past me they'll look back and know they've been someplace."

And Brother and I had thought about it and talked about it between ourselves. In a way passing him would be the finest thing we could do, and the thing we could be proudest of. But in another way it would be bad, because it would kill him to have to get out of the way for anybody. We'd told each other that we might never do it, even when we were able, because of that. And both of us knew that if the time ever came it would be a hard thing to do, and a risky one. Once we'd passed him we could never be behind again. We'd have to stay in front, and it was a lonely and a troublesome place.

But once or twice a year, and nearly always during tobacco cutting, he'd have to challenge us. He'd tease us into it. He'd stop and wait for us to get close to him, the way an old fox will sometimes stop to wait on the dogs; then race with us for the love of it, and beat us for the love of it. He had to have somebody pushing him to really feel himself ahead. And always one of us would have to try him. After the race started we forgot what we'd thought about it and went after him for all we were worth; and he'd hold his lead, working as if he had to stay in front forever.

He stood there grinning, waiting to see if one of us would answer him. Then he looked at Brother and said, "Did you notice how that gap between us keeps widening?"

"You'd better go on back to work and be quiet," Uncle Burley told him. "One of these days you'll ask for it and they'll give it to you."

Daddy said, "They've got to move faster than they're moving now if they do it." As he started away he looked back and said, "When the old man's dead and gone I want you all to walk in front of the coffin so you'll know what the country looks like out in front of him."

He went on to the other side of the patch then and got a drink out of the water jug and sat there smoking, watching us.

Brother led us to the end, and when we started back Daddy got up and took the next row. Uncle Burley and Gander and I went to get a drink, and by the time we got to the jug, Brother was already in the row next to Daddy's, starting after him.

Uncle Burley unscrewed the top of the jug and handed it to Gander to drink first, then squatted on his heels watching Daddy and Brother. "There they go," he said.

"It's bad enough to have to work," Gander said, "without trying to kill each other at it."

Daddy glanced over his shoulder and saw that Brother was after him. "Well, look who's coming. If it's not old Tom. Going to put it on the old man today. Look at him come."

It was an old song. We'd been hearing it ever since we'd been big enough to threaten him. Sometimes when we raced with him he'd talk us into a mistake, and then just loaf along in front of us, talking and laughing at us, until finally we'd have to quit. But it didn't seem to be bothering Brother. He was holding his own.

"Brother's staying with him," I said.

"He's getting more apt to beat him every year," Uncle Burley said. "And it'll never stop until he finally does. It was the same way between your daddy and grandpa. For a while there it got to be a race between them just to be breathing."

"Look at the boy coming on," Daddy said. "Look at him lay it on the stick. He don't talk about it, but he's thinking it. Thinking, 'Go ahead and talk, old man. Your day is done. I'm coming after you. Just go ahead and talk while I'm coming on.' Ah, the old man knows. And the old man's going on. The boy may be coming. But the old man's going. Right out in front where he always is. Nobody been to the end of the row ahead of him. And damn few can get there very soon afterwards."

I put the top back on the jug and followed Uncle Burley and Gander into the next rows. We worked along behind them, watching them in the corners of our eyes. They held together, the distance between them strained tight, until sooner or later it would have to break and go one way or the other.

The strain of it suited Daddy. He was happy in it, as if he'd just made the world over to suit himself, feeling the demand on his strength and endurance close to him, and feeling himself good enough. He'd had to work hard for so long, pushed by creditors and seasons and weather, until now it was a habit. That had made him what he was. That was the way he knew himself, and he needed it.

We could hear him, working up the row ahead of us:

> *"He ain't the boss, he's the boss's son,*
> *But he's going to be boss when the boss is done.*

"But I tell you, boys, it's going to be a long time yet. The old man's going through the middle of a lot of days yet with the whole pack behind him. I tell you, boys, when he's dead and gone they'll be standing in line to see what the country looks like without him wheeling and dealing in the middle of it. And it'll be a sight they never saw before."

They finished their rows and went back and started again. Brother couldn't gain any ground, but he wasn't losing any either. That was beginning to bother Daddy, and he quit talking so much. Brother was just coming up to the pace that Daddy had been working in since noon, and that was in his favor. But watching from where we were, it didn't look as if Daddy was even hurrying. He'd made every movement so many times that he could do it almost without thinking about it, as naturally as he walked. It was like watching a machine that could go on at the same speed until it got dark and the lights went out in the houses at bedtime, and on through the night until the lights came on again before sunup. The race had lasted longer than it ever had before, and I began to dread the finish of it.

Uncle Burley straightened up and watched them for a minute, wiping his face with his sleeve. "They're getting serious about it, ain't they? I've seen friendlier dogfights."

"I wish they'd quit," I said.

He laughed. "The last one to drop dead is the winner."

It was getting on toward sundown, and turning cooler. The sun slanted red across the green and gold of the tobacco, filling the spaces between rows with shadows.

Then I heard Brother cursing. He'd made a mislick and it took him three tries to fix it.

"That looks like the end of it," Uncle Burley said. "He's let himself get flustered."

Daddy took up his song again. "Some people just can't work without floundering and falling around at it. But there's always one who can do it all day long and never miss a lick." He kept talking and kept working, and we could see that he was beginning to move away from Brother.

And before long Brother made another mistake.

"Yes sir," Daddy said, "these little boys just barely weaned come out and try the old man. And they want to put it on him so bad, and they work at it so hard. But they just can't quite make it."

Brother threw down his tools and went for Daddy. Daddy turned and met him. We heard them come together, the thump of bone and muscle that sounded as if they'd already half killed each other; and then they went down, gripped together and rolling in the dirt. We could hear Brother cursing, nearly crying, he was so mad and hurt over losing. And Daddy was laughing; from the sound of it I knew that he was in a mood to fight everybody in the world one at a time and would enjoy doing it.

We laid our tools down and started to them. But Grandpa was nearer them than we were. He was in the middle of the patch, counting the rows we'd cut. And he got there first. He waded into the dust they were raising and tried to prod them apart with his cane, but they rolled under him and knocked him down. He sat there with his hat twisted around on the side of his head, cursing and flailing at them with the cane.

We hurried to him and picked him up. Gander brushed some of the dirt off his clothes and led him down the ridge toward the house. By that time Daddy had Brother down on his back and was straddling him, slapping him in the face. He was laughing, his teeth gritted and his face caked with sweat and dust, breathing hard.

Uncle Burley locked his arms around Daddy's shoulders and dragged him away, and I helped Brother up. Daddy stood there with Uncle Burley still holding him, laughing in Brother's face.

"You God-damned baby," he said.

"Go to hell," Brother said. And he turned around and followed Grandpa and Gander down the ridge.

Uncle Burley let go his hold on Daddy, and the three of us walked back across the patch to where we'd left the team and wagon. We didn't say anything. We tried to act as if we'd just quit work and were going home.

When we got to the other side, Uncle Burley picked up the water jug and he and I climbed on the wagon. Daddy started across the hollow to his house.

"Good night," he said.

We said we'd see him in the morning.

Uncle Burley and I didn't talk after that either. It had got quiet all of a sudden, and there was only the jolt and rattle of the wagon and the knowledge of what had happened. Daddy and Brother had fought. It had happened, and it was over. We couldn't think of anything to say.

I felt sorry for both of them. Brother had been beaten and insulted until it would be a long time before he'd know what to think of himself. And I knew that in the night, when he was by himself in his house, Daddy would lie awake thinking about it, and be sorry.

While we drove home the sun went down.

Uncle Burley and I unharnessed the mules and put them in their stalls and did the feeding and milking. It took us until nearly dark. When we finished the work and started to the house, Brother was coming out the yard gate. His face was cut up a little and his lower lip was swollen. He had a bundle of clothes under his arm.

"Boy, are you going?" Uncle Burley asked him.

"I guess I am."

"You're going to let us know about you?"

"I will."

Uncle Burley took some money out of his pocket and put it in Brother's hand. And then we told him good-bye.

A few stars were out. We stood in the gate a long time after Brother was out of sight, dreading to believe that he was gone.

※

We worked on through the tobacco cutting. Daddy was easier to get along with after Brother left. He joked with us more, trying to make himself pleasant; and even though we were shorthanded he started giving us time to rest before we went back to work in the afternoons. Nobody talked about Brother's leaving when Daddy was around, but we could tell that it was on his mind and that he hated what he'd done. He didn't push us so hard anymore, but he drove himself harder than ever. There were a good many days when he worked in the field by himself until it was too dark to see, after the rest of us had quit and gone home.

Brother's leaving was harder on Grandma and Grandpa than it was on any of the rest of us. They grieved over him most of the time, and it made them seem older. We hadn't heard from him; and every morning Grandma talked about how she expected to get a letter from him that day, and at night when no letter had come she wondered where he was and if he was well and why he hadn't written to us. Sometimes at the supper table she'd remember things he said and did when he was little, and then she'd cry and have to get up and leave.

Grandpa never talked about it when she did. Her grief made him ashamed of his own. And he never mentioned the fight in the tobacco patch, because he was ashamed of that too, and embarrassed that he hadn't been able to stop it. But Brother had been a satisfaction to him, and now and then he'd mention to Uncle Burley or me that Brother promised to have a better head on him than anybody in the family, saying it as if Brother was dead.

After we finished the tobacco harvest we harrowed the ground and sowed it in grain. Then we cut the fall hay crop and put it in the barn. In a day or two after that the first hard frost came. The good brittle days began. The trees turned brown and red and yellow and dropped their leaves, and wild geese flew over the house at night. Uncle Burley and I went out in the early mornings to hunt squirrels in the woods. If Brother had been there it would have been perfect. Uncle Burley and I talked about him a lot, remembering the other years when we'd hunted together.

We spent two weeks mending fences and doing other work that had to be done before the weather got cold. And after that we began the corn harvest. There was no letup in the work, and I was glad of it for Daddy's sake. It kept him from worrying too much about Brother, and as long as he was busy he could take some pleasure in himself. He and Uncle Burley and I worked together, or swapped work with Gander or Big Ellis, watching the season change and planning the winter's work. The cool weather made us feel good, and it was a pleasant time.

Winter set in. The first snow fell and melted, then it turned cold again and the ground froze hard and stayed frozen. We scooped the last of the corn into the crib on a Wednesday, and then slacked off work to rest before we started stripping the tobacco and getting it ready for market. And that Saturday, for the first time in a couple of months, Uncle Burley and I cleaned up after dinner and walked into town. It was clear and bright and beginning to thaw a little. We cut across the fields to the road, taking our time and looking at things. It hadn't been winter long enough for us to be tired of it, and it felt good to be outside with the whole afternoon ahead of us. On the tops of the ridges the wind stung our faces and hummed in our ears, and when we went down into the hollows we could feel the warmth of the sun and it was quiet.

The grass on the hillside was brown, and the trees in the hollows were bare and black except for a few green patches of cedars. Now and then a rabbit jumped up ahead of us, and we'd find his snug nesting place in a clump of grass.

"It'll be Christmas before we know it," Uncle Burley said.

All at once I had the feeling I used to have when I was little, enjoying the newness of the winter and waiting for Christmas. Then I thought about Mother being dead and Brother gone away, and I lost the feeling.

"We'll have to go coon hunting before long," Uncle Burley said. "It's getting about that time."

I knew by the way he said it that the notion excited him. He always started hunting at about that time of year, and hunted almost every favorable night from then until the end of the winter. In the mornings when we went to work he'd talk about what a fool a man was to hunt half the night when he had to work the next day, and he'd swear he'd never go on a weeknight again. But by four o'clock in the afternoon he'd have the fever to hunt; and he'd usually go, by himself if the rest of us were too tired to go with him.

"If this thaw keeps up we'll have good tracking for the dogs," he said.

We walked the rest of the way to the road, planning what night we'd hunt. When we got to the road we saw Jig Pendleton coming up the hill toward us, and we stopped to wait for him.

Uncle Burley called, "Come on, Jig. We'll walk in with you."

Jig came up and said hello to us, and we went on toward town.

"You see that hand, Burley?" Jig said. He held his hand out for Uncle Burley to see.

"I see it, Jig."

"It's putrefied," Jig said. He flapped along with his head tilted up sideways, as sober and dead serious as an undertaker.

"Well, it might be, Jig."

Jig held out his other hand. "There now, Burley, can't you tell the difference? That one ain't. One of them's good and the other one's evil. One of them's blessed and the other one's damned."

"You're in a fix," Uncle Burley said. "You tried a poultice on that bad one?"

"Now Burley, there ain't but one poultice that'll heal her. There ain't but one poultice that'll draw the corruption out of that hand. And that's the poultice of the Holy Spirit."

He'd stopped in the middle of the road and was beating the palm of the putrefied hand with the fist of the sound one. We saw that he was about to start into a sermon, so Uncle Burley said, "Got any nets in the river, Jig?"

Jig hushed and caught up with us. "Aw now, Burley, the water ain't right. The water's got to be right first."

We kept him on fishing for a while, then he asked Uncle Burley how everybody was getting along at our house.

"All fine. We're getting ready to start stripping tobacco the first of the week."

"Tobacco," Jig said. "I used to raise tobacco once. But I quit. I was plowing one morning, and the Lord said, 'Jig, how'd you like for your daughter to smoke?' And I said, 'I wouldn't like it, Lord. It's a sin for a woman to smoke.' And I unhitched the mule right there in the middle of the row, and I left."

"You say you left?"

"Left," Jig said. "I went to fishing then. You know that's where He called them from. From fishing. One of these mornings He'll come and stand on the riverbank and He'll say, 'Jig.' And I'll say, 'Yes, Lord?' And He'll say, 'Follow me, Jig.' And I will arise and follow Him. Aw, He ain't come yet. But He's coming. He's got to get my mansion ready first, but He'll be here."

Then Jig told us about Heaven. He said it was a million miles square and a million miles high, and every street was gold and every house was a mansion. And at night every star was brighter than the sun.

"Do you know why He made the stars?"

Uncle Burley said he didn't know.

"He liked to hear them sing," Jig said.

When we got to town Uncle Burley and I went into the poolroom, and Jig went on up the street to the grocery store. Inside the poolroom it was dark, except for the three green tables in a row down the middle of the floor with lights shining on them. We went past the counter and on to the center of the room, where half a dozen men were standing in a circle around the stove. Big Ellis and Gander Loyd were there, and they made room for us between them.

"Good afternoon, gentlemen," Uncle Burley said. He held his hands over the top of the stove and rubbed them together. "That wind's kind of brittle around the edges, ain't she?"

"We haven't seen you for a while, Burley," Gander said. "Where you been keeping yourself?"

Big Ellis giggled. "We heard you were dead, Burley."

"So did I," Uncle Burley said. "But I knew it was a lie as soon as I heard it."

They laughed, and then drifted into a conversation about who had started stripping tobacco and who hadn't. They talked about what kind of season it promised to be for that work; and from there they went into an argument about the prospects for a good market that year.

After we got warmed up Uncle Burley and Big Ellis and I played two games of straight pool, and Uncle Burley won both of them. The games lasted a long time. All three of us were out of practice, and we were missing easy shots; but after he won the second game Uncle Burley said he guessed he might as well quit since the competition was so poor.

We went back to the stove and talked again. You couldn't remember how the conversation started, or figure out why it should have got to where it was from the last subject you could remember. Now and then somebody buttoned his coat and left. And others came in, letting a cold draft through the door with them, and stood with us at the stove and smoked and talked. The talk shifted from weather to jokes to crops. The wind muffled at the corners of the building. The sound of the fire whipped in the stove like a flag.

Mushmouth Montgomery came in and stood by himself at the counter, eating cheese and crackers; the conversation slowed and hesitated as we turned to look at him and looked away. Since Chicken Little's drowning Mushmouth's face had changed—had turned hollow and blank as if his eyes had given up seeing. And in my memory of him Chicken Little's face had changed the same way; I couldn't remember how he'd looked when he was alive. Mushmouth's face burdened us and quieted us as if we were seeing Chicken Little's ghost. He didn't stay in the poolroom long, and when he left the talk hurried again.

After a while we heard laughter and commotion in the street, and we went out to see what was happening. A crowd of men and boys had gathered at the edge of the sidewalk. They'd caught a stray dog and were tying a roman candle to his tail.

One of them lit the fuse and they turned him loose. The dog ran up the street with the roman candle fizzing behind him, shooting red and yellow and blue balls of fire under his tail. He stopped two or three times before he was out of sight and tried to catch his tail in his teeth, but then another ball of fire would hit him and send him howling off again. Everybody stood there on the sidewalk and laughed. I hated to think of anything being treated that way, and I was sorry I saw it. But every time one of those colored balls of fire flew out and hit the dog under the tail I had to laugh too. The idea of it was funny, and if it hadn't hurt the dog it would have been all right.

As the crowd began to break up and go back into the stores we saw Brother coming across the street.

"Well, I'll swear," Uncle Burley said. "Look who's here."

We shook hands and laughed and clapped each other on the back. Uncle Burley caught Brother in his arms and held him off the ground, hugging him.

I hadn't realized until then how much I'd missed him. I couldn't think of anything glad enough to say.

Uncle Burley put Brother down. "How're you doing, old boy?"

"All right," Brother said.

We went into the poolroom and drank a Coke together while Brother told us about himself. Since he left home he'd been working for a man named Whitlow who owned a farm on the other side of the county. He said that Mr. Whitlow and his wife had treated him kindly, and they had fixed a room in their house for him. Mr. Whitlow had hired him to work by day through the fall and winter and had promised a crop of his own for the next year.

"Well, you've got a good place," Uncle Burley said. "I'm glad to hear it."

When we'd finished our Cokes we sat on a bench behind the stove and talked some more. Uncle Burley and I were relieved to have found Brother and to know he was all right. It felt familiar and good to be there with him, and I hated for the afternoon to pass.

We spoke of Daddy, and Brother didn't seem to be mad at him anymore; but he said that he didn't intend to come back to live with us. He wanted to stay on his own. He was saving his money and planning to buy a farm for himself.

He asked how Grandma and Grandpa were, and we talked about them

for a while. And Uncle Burley and I told him how we were getting along
in our work.

Finally Brother said it was time for him to start home. We walked along
with him to where Mr. Whitlow's car was parked. The sun was nearly
down and there was more chill to the wind.

Uncle Burley turned his collar up and looked at the sky. "It's going to
be a coon hunting night," he said.

Mr. Whitlow was standing beside his car when we got there; Brother
introduced us and we stood around and talked a while with him. He told
us that he thought he was lucky to find as good a hand as Brother, and
that we'd be welcome at his house any time we wanted to come and visit.
We promised we'd be over before long and we made Brother promise to
come to see us.

"Write to your grandma," Uncle Burley said.

They got into the car and drove away, and we were sad to see them go.

On our way home we went around by Daddy's house to tell him our
news. Nobody had mentioned Brother to him since their fight, and I felt
embarrassed about it now. I dreaded it a little.

It was dark when we came into his yard, and a light was on in the
kitchen. We went around the house and called to him from the back
door. He answered us and we went in. He was sitting at the table with his
supper dishes empty in front of him, eating a piece of corn bread. We
pulled out chairs and sat down; and Uncle Burley began telling him
about Brother, where he was and what he was doing and what his plans
were and what kind of people he was living with. Daddy didn't say anything while Uncle Burley was talking. He sat there looking at his plate
and taking a bite off the corn bread now and then.

When Uncle Burley had finished I said, "He's not mad at you anymore."

And then Daddy cried. He didn't say that he was glad Brother wasn't
mad at him, or that he was sorry for their fight. He just sat there, looking
at his plate and chewing on a bite of corn bread, with tears running down
his cheeks.

I could have cried myself. Brother was gone, and he wouldn't be back.
And things that had been so before never would be so again. We were the

way we were; nothing could make us any different, and we suffered because of it. Things happened to us the way they did because we were ourselves. And if we'd been other people it wouldn't have mattered. If we'd been Mushmouth or Jig Pendleton or that dog with the roman candle tied to his tail, it would have been the same; we'd have had to suffer whatever it was that they suffered because they were themselves. And there was nothing anybody could do but let it happen.

We left Daddy sitting at the table and started home.

"It's bad," Uncle Burley said. "It's bad." After a minute he said, "We're going to have a fair night. Let's you and me hunt a while."

⁊

We hurried through our chores and went to the house. Grandma had supper waiting for us when we came into the kitchen, and Grandpa had already finished eating and turned his chair to the stove. We ate, and Uncle Burley told them we'd seen Brother. They listened while he told them all that Brother had told us.

When he quit talking Grandma said, "And he's not coming home?"

"No," Uncle Burley said.

Grandpa got up then and went into the living room. And Grandma filled the dishpan with water and set it on the stove.

"We thought we'd hunt tonight," Uncle Burley told her.

She nodded, keeping her face turned away from us.

Uncle Burley went upstairs and got his rifle and flashlight and I lit the lantern. We went out the back door and called the dogs. They came, wagging their tails and whining, knowing when they saw the rifle in Uncle Burley's hands that we were going to hunt. There were two of them — Sawbuck and Joe. Uncle Burley let them rear against him. He rubbed their faces and spoke their names.

We walked down the hill toward the woods on the river bluff. Behind us the walls of the house were dark; the lighted windows shone as if they were floating and might twist or slant or change places. On the next ridge a light was still burning in Daddy's house.

When we came to the brow of the hill and saw the house lights scattered through the river bottoms, it wasn't the place of daytime or our memories, but only a distance filled up with night where a few lights burned, the woods and the hunt dividing us from them.

"Well," Uncle Burley said, "they'll grieve in this old land until you'd think they were going to live on it forever, then grieve some more because they know damn well they're not going to live on it forever. And nothing'll stop them but a six-foot hole."

When we went into the woods the dogs trotted off ahead of us, and we walked in the room of light the lantern made, our shadows striding tall against the trunks of the trees. The light was an island, drifting until the dogs would strike a track and give us a direction.

We walked slowly, stopping now and then to listen, moving along the face of the bluff toward the creek valley. After a while Joe bayed a time or two down near the creek. And then the quietness settled around us again and we heard the wind in the tops of the trees. We climbed higher on the bluff so we could hear better, and went on toward the point where the creek valley came into the valley of the river. We crossed the point and climbed down to the edge of the woods on the other side, then squatted on our heels by the lantern and listened to the dogs.

First one of them and then the other crossed the trail and bayed, then lost it, and the quiet came down into the valley again.

Uncle Burley shifted his feet a little, and his hunched shadow swayed against the trees behind him. "They may finally straighten it out."

The dogs worked the trail until it got warm, and then they bayed up the hillside across the valley, running fast and mouthing at every jump, their voices hacking through the dark.

"That sounds more like it," Uncle Burley said.

We started down the hill, taking our time and listening. When we got to the creek bottom the dogs had gone almost out of earshot. We stood still for a few minutes, straining to hear them above the sound of our breath.

"They're treed, aren't they?" I said.

"If they're not they're good liars," Uncle Burley said.

They'd followed a draw out of the bottom all the way to the top of the bluff; and we went up after them, climbing where the streambed stair-stepped down the hill.

We found them treed at a thick-trunked old hickory on the side of the draw. Uncle Burley leaned the rifle against a stump and turned the flashlight up into the branches. We walked around the tree, searching until we saw the coon sitting humpbacked in the fork of a long limb, his eyes glowing in the light.

"There's plenty of limbs all the way up," Uncle Burley said. "You can climb up and shake him out, and we'll let one of the dogs have him."

I set the lantern down and climbed, feeling my way up in the dark while Uncle Burley held the light on the coon. The dogs whined and barked, trotting back and forth under the tree.

I got to the limb where the coon was and eased out on it, holding to the limb above my head. Uncle Burley caught Sawbuck by the collar and moved down the hill. He called Joe into the place where the coon would fall, and I shook the limb.

Joe was on the coon by the time he hit the ground, and they went growling and snarling down the slope toward Uncle Burley. He held the light on them, following them where they rolled and fought in the leaves. The ground was too steep for Joe to get a foothold, and the coon was having a fairly easy time of it. He'd wrapped himself around Joe's head, and Joe couldn't stand up long enough to shake him loose. Sawbuck howled and reared against the collar, trying to get into the fight; and Uncle Burley slid and plunged after him, trying to hold him out of it. The coon kept his hold on Joe's head as if he'd decided to spend the night there; and Joe bucked and rolled and somersaulted through the underbrush, the leaves flying up around them. Sawbuck jerked Uncle Burley off balance, and the two of them scrambled in with Joe and the coon. I saw Uncle Burley's hat fly off, and then the beam of his flashlight began switching around so fast that I couldn't tell what was happening. I could only hear them crashing farther down the hillside, Uncle Burley yelling, and the dogs growling, and the coon hissing and snarling—the beam of light flickering and darting this way and that through the trees like lightning flashes.

Then the light steadied and I saw Uncle Burley dragging Sawbuck out of the fight. Joe caught the coon behind the forelegs and held. That was all of it.

"Whoo," Uncle Burley said.

He picked up the coon and found his hat, then turned the light up into the tree to help me down. The dogs trotted off into the woods again. Uncle Burley slung the coon over his shoulder and I took the rifle and lantern; we climbed to the top of the bluff and started across the ridge.

We were walking parallel to the river again, the valley dark on our left, and three or four miles behind us a few lights were still burning in town. It was easier walking on the ridge, and there were a lot of stars. But the wind was strong up there, and cold. We could hear it moving through the grass and rattling in the woods below us.

At the top of the ridge we went through an old graveyard. When we'd gone halfway across it Uncle Burley stopped and told me to bring the lantern closer. He pointed to a set of false teeth lying on the edge of a groundhog hole that ran down into one of the graves. "God Almighty," he said.

He picked up the teeth and we looked at them. They were covered with dirt and one of the eyeteeth was broken off. "I wonder who these belonged to." He took the flashlight out of his coat and turned it on the headstone, but it was so badly weathered we couldn't read the name. He dropped the teeth back into the hole and kicked some dirt in after them, and we went on toward the woods on the far side of the ridge.

"We're all dying to get there," Uncle Burley said.

After we killed the first coon things were slow for a long time. We went into the woods again and sat down. Once in a while we'd hear the dogs, their voices flaring up as they fumbled at a cold trail, then quiet again while we waited and talked beside the lantern. Finally we got cold and built a fire, and Uncle Burley lay down beside it and slept. He woke up every time one of the dogs mouthed; but when they lost the trail and hushed, he turned his cold side to the fire and went back to sleep. I watched the flames crawl along the sticks until they glowed red and crumbled into the ashes, then piled on more. It was quiet. The country was dark and filled with wind. And in the houses on the ridges behind us and below us in the river bottoms the people were asleep.

About midnight the dogs started a hot track and ran it down the hillside, and treed finally out in the direction of the river. We went to them.

They were treed at a white oak that was too tall and too big around to climb. So I held the flashlight over Uncle Burley's rifle sights and on the coon, and he shot it.

After that he said he was ready to call it a night if I was, and I said I was. We were a long way from home, and since Jig Pendleton's shanty boat was tied up just across the bottom we decided to go and spend the rest of the night with him.

The boat was dark when we got there. We stopped at the top of the bank and quieted the dogs.

Uncle Burley called, "Oh, Jig."

"I'm coming, Lord," Jig said.

We heard him scuffling and clattering around trying to get a lamp lighted.

"It's Burley and Nathan," Uncle Burley said.

The shanty windows lighted up and Jig came out the door in his long underwear and rubber boots, carrying a lamp in his hand.

Uncle Burley laughed. "Jig, if the Lord ever comes and sees you in that outfit, He'll turn around and go back."

"Aw, no He won't, Burley. The Lord looketh on the heart." Jig stood there shivering with the wind blowing through his hair. "You all come on down."

We went down to the boat, the dogs trotting after us across the plank.

"We thought we'd spend the night with you, Jig," Uncle Burley said, "if you don't mind."

"Why, God bless you, Burley, of course you can," Jig said. He asked us if we'd like some hot coffee.

Uncle Burley said we sure would if he didn't mind fixing it. Jig built up the fire in his stove and put the coffee on to boil, and Uncle Burley and I sat down on the side of the boat to skin the coons.

When we finished the skinning, we cut one of the carcasses in two and gave a half of it to each of the dogs. They ate and then curled up beside the door and licked themselves and slept. The coffee was ready by that time. We washed our hands in the river and went inside, ducking under the strings of Jig's machine.

The coffee was black and strong; we sat at the table drinking out of the thick white cups and feeling it warm us. Jig asked how our hunt had been, and Uncle Burley told him about it, Jig nodding his head as he listened and then asking exactly where the dogs had treed. When Uncle Burley named the place he'd nod his head again. "The big white oak. I know that tree. I know the one you're talking about, Burley."

Then Jig mentioned that ducks had been coming in on the slue for the last couple of days. They talked about duck hunting for a while, and Uncle Burley said we'd cross the river early in the morning and try our luck.

Jig gave us a quilt apiece when we'd finished our coffee. We filled the stove with wood and stretched out on the floor beside it. Jig sat at the table reading the Bible for a few minutes, then he blew out the lamp, and we slept.

Uncle Burley woke me the next morning while it was still dark. The lamp was burning on the table again, and Jig was making us another pot of coffee. It seemed darker and quieter outside the windows than it had been when we went to sleep. While we drank the coffee a towboat passed down the river, its engine humming and pounding under the darkness.

Uncle Burley borrowed Jig's shotgun and a pocketful of shells.

"There ought to be plenty of ducks up there," Jig said. "I expect you'll have luck, Burley."

We led the dogs up the bank and tied them to trees, and went over to the slue. The air was cold and brittle, the sky still full of stars. A heavy frost had fallen toward morning; the ground was white with it, and our breath hung white around our heads. When we got away from the trees that grew along the riverbank the wind hit us in the face, making our eyes water. We buttoned our collars and walked fast, hurrying the sleep out of our bones.

We got to the slue and made ourselves as comfortable as we could in a thick patch of willows near the water. Uncle Burley smoked, and we waited, hearing the roosters crow in the barns and henhouses across the bottoms. The sky brightened a little in the east; and we could make out the shape of the slue, the water turning gray as the sky turned, the air above it threaded with mist. While it was still too dark to shoot, four or five ducks came in. Their wings whistled over our heads, and we saw the splashes they made as they hit the water.

The sun came up, the day-color sliding over the tops of the hills; and we heard Gander Loyd calling his milk cows. Then a big flock of mallards circled over our heads and came down.

Uncle Burley raised the gun and waited, and when they flew into range he shot. His shoulder jerked with the kick of the gun, and one of the ducks folded up and fell, spinning down into the shallow water in front of us. Uncle Burley grinned. "That's the way to do it," he said.

He reloaded the gun and we waited again, watching the sky. The rest of the morning the flocks came in, their wings whistling, wheeling in the sunlight down to the water. And the only thing equal to them was their death.

5

After Uncle Burley and I saw Brother in town at the beginning of the winter, he came home every two or three Sundays to eat dinner and spend the afternoon with us. When we'd finished eating all of us sat around the table and talked a while, then Uncle Burley and Brother and I usually went out to hunt rabbits or wander around together and look at things. We always enjoyed ourselves when Brother was there, and we began to think of him as part of the family again.

When Daddy and Brother were together they were friendly, but they never had much to say to each other. In the months that had gone by since their fight Brother had got to be his own man. He wasn't asking any of us for anything, and that made a difference. While he'd been a boy living with us at home he and Daddy had known how to think about each other. They had known themselves in Daddy's authority. But their fight had ended that; and the old feeling had been too strong and had lasted too many years to allow them ever to know each other in a different way. They were always a little uncomfortable when they tried to talk to each other. Still I could see that both of them were relieved when they were on speaking terms again.

We finished stripping the tobacco crop in the first week of January and shipped the last truckload to the market. And from then until the last of February the cold days came one after another without a thaw. Grandpa said it was the hardest winter he'd ever seen. And for him it was.

It seemed to us that every day of the cold left him older and weaker. He could never get warm enough. While we kept ourselves busy feeding the stock and cutting and hauling wood to burn on the plant beds in the spring, he sat in the house bundled up in a sheepskin coat, throwing coal into the stove and poking the fire with his cane until it roared.

When spring came and the warm days began he didn't get stronger as we'd thought he would. Daddy and Uncle Burley and I put out the crops and plowed them and looked after them through the spring and early summer, but Grandpa didn't go to the field with us as often as he always had. He still got up every morning before daylight, but more and more often when we went to work we'd find him asleep again, sitting in the sun in front of the barn. And he began talking about his death.

One day he told Daddy, "I reckon another twenty years'll see me out." That got to be a kind of byword with us. Daddy or Uncle Burley would repeat it while we were at work, and we'd laugh.

Another day when the four of us were sitting in the door of the barn watching it rain, he pointed toward a corner of the lot and said, "When I die I want you to bury me there."

Uncle Burley laughed and told him, "You've got to go farther away from here than that."

He never mentioned it often, and he tried to keep from showing that he grieved about it. But talking about his own death was a new thing for him, and it saddened us.

It seemed to us that we'd never thought of him before as a man who would die. He never had thought of himself in that way. Until that year, although he'd cursed his weakness and his age, he'd either ignored the idea of his death or had refused to believe in it. He'd only thought of himself as living. But now that he finally admitted that he would die we thought about it too. We couldn't get used to the feeling it gave us to go to work in the mornings without him. He stayed in our minds, and on the days when we left him sleeping at the barn we talked about him more than anything else. We wished he could have enjoyed his sleep now that he was old and nobody expected him to be at work. But he always woke up bewildered and ashamed of himself, and we felt sorry for him.

Uncle Burley was more troubled by the change in Grandpa than any of us. Daddy and Grandpa had argued and fallen out at times, but that had happened because the two of them were alike. They had fought when their minds crossed because they were stubborn and proud, and because they couldn't have respected themselves if they hadn't fought. And Daddy had made himself respectable on Grandpa's terms. But Grandpa and Uncle Burley were as different as he and Daddy were alike. They never had been at peace with each other, and there never had been any chance that they would be. Their lives had run in opposite directions from the day Uncle Burley was born. Grandpa's life had been spent in owning his land and in working on it, the same way Daddy was spending his. But Uncle Burley had refused to own anything. When he was young he worked only because he had to, and Grandpa never had forgiven him for it. They'd been able to live together in the same place mostly by being quiet, and because Grandma and Daddy had stood between them. And although Uncle Burley was a kind man and had as much need to be sorry for Grandpa as Daddy and I, he didn't have a right to. That embarrassed him, and when he wasn't able to joke about it he didn't say anything.

One morning toward the end of July Grandpa rode with us on the wagon to help Gander Loyd put in a field of hay. We'd been held up nearly a week by wet weather; and when it had cleared off two days before, Daddy had helped Gander mow the field. The air was still fresh and clear from the rain, and as we started down to Gander's place we could hear other wagons all around us rattling out to the fields — everybody behind in his work and hurrying.

A heavy dew had fallen, covering the trees and bushes along the sides of the road, and the sun glittered on the wet leaves. The mules were skittish and Daddy leaned back against the lines. They set their heads high and pranced sideways.

"I'll cure you of that nonsense when I get a load behind you," Daddy told them.

Uncle Burley stood up, slack-kneed against the jolt of the wagon, and rolled a cigarette, singing,

> *"Down along the woodland, through the hills and by the shore,*
> *You can hear the rattle, the rumble and the roar . . ."*

After he rolled the cigarette he lit it and sat down again, dangling his feet over the edge of the hay frame.

Grandpa sat beside us, watching the land open in front of the wagon and close behind it, his eyes on it as if it had some movement that only he knew about and could see. The land was what he knew, and it comforted him to look at it. Since he'd been too old to work we'd noticed that he spent more and more of his time watching it, forgetting what was going on around him. Now and then he turned away from it to speak to us of his death, as if hearing himself talk about it could make it real, and turned back to his watching again to be comforted. His hands held the cane across his lap, the skin brown and thin over the knuckles and blue veins.

When we pulled into the hayfield Gander was already there with his team hitched to the rake. "It's too wet," he called to us when we stopped. "We'll have to wait for the dew to dry off."

He and Daddy walked across the field together, picking up wisps of hay and twisting them in their hands to test the moisture. After they came back we sat on the wagon and talked. Once in a while Gander or Daddy got up to see if the hay had dried, but it was past ten o'clock before we could begin work.

Gander drove the rake, putting the hay in windrows. And Daddy and Uncle Burley and I followed him with pitchforks, shocking it. We sweated; the wind blew dust and chaff into our faces and down our necks, and it stuck to the sweat and stung. Now and then we'd see a meadowlark fly up and whistle — a clear cool sound, like water — and drop back into the stubble.

Before long Uncle Burley began to sing. He'd gather a fork load of hay and as he lifted it onto the shock sing, "Ohhhhhhh, 'down along the woodland . . .'" And as he strained at the fork again: "Ohhhhhhh, 'through the hills and by the shore . . .'"

"You must be happy," Daddy said.

"I was thinking about the good old days," Uncle Burley said, "when I was a teamster for Barnum and Bailey's circus. You didn't know about that, did you?"

"Never heard of it before," Daddy said.

Uncle Burley had invented the story about driving a team for Barnum and Bailey to tell to Brother and me when we were little, and all of us had heard it a hundred times. But when the work got hard he'd usually tell it again to make us laugh, and because he enjoyed hearing it himself. He said he'd driven a team of eight black horses with silver harness and red plumes on their bridles. His team had drawn the calliope at the head of all the parades, and it had been a glorious sight. He told about the girl bareback riders on their white horses and the tightrope walkers and the trapeze men and the lion tamers. Finally he got fired, he said, because he whipped one of the elephants singlehanded in a fair fight. He tied the elephant's trunk to his tail and ran him around in a circle until he passed out from dizziness. Barnum and Bailey told him that he was the best teamster they'd ever had, but they just couldn't stand for him mistreating their elephants.

Daddy said he supposed it must make Uncle Burley awfully sad at times to have such fine memories of his past.

Uncle Burley shook his head. "I tell you, back in those days when I had three flunkies to polish my black boots and brush my red forked-tail coat, I never would have believed that I'd end up here, sweating on the handle of a pitchfork. It's enough to make a grown man cry."

While we worked Grandpa sat in the shade at the edge of the field, nodding off to sleep, and waking up to carry us a fresh jug of water when we needed one.

"Look at him sleep," Uncle Burley said. "He's living the good life, ain't he? When I get that old I want somebody to wake me up every once in a while just so I can go back to sleep again."

"I reckon so," Daddy said.

"I reckon so. Sleep and fish. That's all I'll do. I'll switch back and forth from maple shade to sycamore shade. And when it's chilly I'll sleep in the sun."

Gander called dinnertime. We fed and watered the teams and went to the house. Gander filled the washpans with water and we washed our hands, then sat at the kitchen table while Mandy Loyd brought the food to us. She was young enough to have been Gander's daughter — slender and well made, and always smiling though she never talked much when we were there. It seemed strange to me that she could have married anybody as old and ugly and one-eyed as Gander. And he must have wondered about it too, because he was jealous of her and he kept her at home most of the time. It made him uncomfortable to have other men in his house; when we ate dinner with him he always clammed up, and nobody ever felt free to joke or laugh. We ate without talking except to ask for the food, feeling as uncomfortable as Gander, and hurrying to finish the meal. Only Grandpa felt free enough to compliment Mandy on her cooking. And she smiled and thanked him.

We went back to work, and Grandpa sat in the shade again, and slept, and woke up to bring us water.

"I wish he'd stay awake," Uncle Burley said. "It makes the shade look too cool and good when I see him sleeping in it."

In the middle of the afternoon when Grandpa was bringing the jug from the well we saw him stagger a little. He steadied himself with the cane and came on; but when he handed the jug to us and Daddy asked him if he was all right he said he'd had a dizzy spell. He looked pale, and it would be a long time before we could quit for the day, so Daddy told me to walk home with him.

He told Grandpa that Uncle Burley had broken the handle out of his pitchfork and he was sending me to get another one. "Do you want to go along with Nathan? You'll feel better when you get home and rest a while."

Grandpa said he'd go with me, and we started up the hill, stopping every couple of hundred yards for him to rest. Once when we stopped he said, "An old man's not worth a damn. He might as well be knocked in the head."

He rested, and we went on again. He climbed the hill almost as fast as a young man, ashamed that I had to wait on him, until the tiredness caught up with him and he had to stop to rest.

When we came up out of the woods, the bottom spread out below us, and I could look back into Gander's hayfield where they were loading one of the wagons. From that distance the three men looked like dolls, but I could tell them apart: Daddy on top of the load, taking the hay as they pitched it to him, placing it and tramping on it; Gander leaning backward against the weight of his loaded fork, his head tilted, favoring the good eye; Uncle Burley making the whole thing into as much of a joke as the heat and strain of the work would allow, the joke ready in the set of his shoulders and in the way he walked from one shock to another as the wagon moved across the field. On the other side of the river the hills were blue, as if the sky came down in front of them.

When we got to Grandpa's spring we stopped to drink.

The water of the spring came from a notch in the rock just under the brow of the hill, and the land sloped steeply around it. The grove of oaks that stood there made the hollow a kind of room where it was always shady and cool in summer, filled with the sound of water running.

Grandpa sat on a ledge of the rock, and I dipped the drinking cup full of water and carried it to him. He drank, then held the cup in his hands, looking at the spring.

"That's a good vein of water," he said. "Nobody ever knew it to go dry."

I thought of the spring running there all the time, while the Indians hunted the country and while our people came and took the land and cleared it; and still running while Grandpa's grandfather and his father got old and died. And running while Grandpa drank its water and waited his turn. When I thought of it that way I knew I was waiting my turn too. But that didn't seem real. It was too far away to think about. And I saw how it would have been unreal to Grandpa for so long, and how it must have grieved him when it had finally come close enough to be known.

Grandpa had owned his land and worked on it and taken his pride from it for so long that we knew him, and he knew himself, in the same way that we knew the spring. His life couldn't be divided from the days he'd spent at work in his fields. Daddy had told us we didn't know what the country would look like without him at work in the middle of it; and that was as true of Grandpa as it was of Daddy. We wouldn't recognize the country when he was dead.

After he rested we started toward the house again. We got to the top of the slope above the spring, and Grandpa stopped, holding the cane off the ground, his mouth open, staring off in the direction of the house.

"What's the matter?" I asked him.

Then he fell. He hit the ground limp, and the wind caught his hat and rolled it down the hill.

I straightened him out and knelt beside him, rubbing his hands and speaking to him. But I couldn't bring him to. The wind whistled through the grass, and the sky was hot and blue, too quiet and lonely to let him die.

I called his name, but he didn't stir. I picked him up in my arms and I carried him home.

Remembering

For Ed McClanahan and Cia White

... to him that is joined to
all the living there is hope ...

Ecclesiastes 9:4

Let the fragments of love be reassembled in
you. Only then will you have true courage.

Hayden Carruth

Heavenly Muse, Spirit who brooded on
The world and raised it shapely out of nothing,
Touch my lips with fire and burn away
All dross of speech, so that I keep in mind
The truth and end to which my words now move
In hope. Keep my mind within that Mind
Of which it is a part, whose wholeness is
The hope of sense in what I tell. And though
I go among the scatterings of that sense,
The members of its worldly body broken,
Rule my sight by vision of the parts
Rejoined. And in my exile's journey far
From home, be with me, so I may return.

1. Darkness Visible

It is dark. He does not know where he is. And then he sees pale light from the street soaking in above the drawn drapes. It is not a light to see by, but only makes the darkness visible. He has slept, to his surprise, but has wakened in the same unease that kept him sleepless long after he went to bed and that remained with him in dream.

In his dream a great causeway had been built across the creek valley where he lives, the heavy roadbed and its supports a materialized obliviousness to his house and barn that stood belittled nearby, as if great Distance itself had come to occupy that place. Bulldozers pushed and trampled the loosened, disformed, denuded earth, working it like dough toward some new shape entirely human-conceived. The place was already unrecognizable except for the small house and barn destined to be enrubbled with all the rest that had been there. Watching, Andy knew that all the last remnants of old forest, the chief beauty and dignity of that place, were now fallen and gone. The flowers that had bloomed in the shade of the standing groves in the spring were gone. The birds were gone. The fields and their names, the farmsteads and the neighbors were gone; the graveyards and the names of the dead, all gone.

So near to the causeway as to be almost under it stood a concrete building of long, windowless, humming corridors, in which workers were passing. In the depths of the building, in a blank-walled, whitely lighted room, a fat man sat behind a desk, eating the living flesh of his

own forearm, all the while making a speech in a tone of pleading reasonableness:

"I *have* to do this. I am *starving*. Three meals a day are *not* enough. To
get more, it would be necessary to contract unsavory foreign alliances. I
cannot *afford* to quit. I realize that this is not ideal. But I am not an ideal-
ist. I am not a naive dreamer. I am constrained by my circumstances to be
a hard-headed realist. Neighbors? I have no neighbors. Friends? I have no
friends. This is my independence. This is my victory."

The causeway, the labyrinthine building, the house and barn, all the
diminished, naked valley were dim in midday dusk, the dingy light too
weak to cast a shadow.

An old terror, learned long ago from his time, returned to Andy now
and shook him — not the terror of the end of the world, but of the end,
simply, of all he knew and loved, which would then exist only in his
knowing, the little creature of his memory, and so he would be forced to
collaborate willy-nilly in the dominance of human intention over the
world.

But he knew that he was already implicated, already one of the guilty,
for as he looked upon that destroyed place, which once had been his
home, he realized that even as he mourned it he could not remember it
as it was; he could find in his spirit no vision of anything it ever was that
it ever might be again. For he himself had been diminished. He himself
was disformed and naked, a mere physical quantity, its existence verifi-
able by an ache. That is what woke him.

※

As he lies in bed in the dark room, only his mind is awake, his body feel-
ingless and still. Leaving the dream, as a place to which it may return
again, his mind resumes a thoughtless, exhausted wakefulness, dumbly
pained. The unhanded, healed stump of his right wrist lies in the dark
beside him. For the time, he is refusing to think about it, though that
refusal costs him all thought.

But thought comes. His body twitches and stirs on its own, alerts itself
to the strangeness of bed and room, and absence lives again at the end of
his arm.

The feel of the bed, the smell of the room seem compounded of the strangeness of all the strangers who have slept there: salesmen, company officers, solitary travelers, who have entered, shut the door, set down their bags, and stood, weary and silent, afraid to speak, even to themselves, their own names. A man could go so far from home, he thinks, that his own name would become unspeakable by him, unanswerable by anyone, so that if he dared to speak it, it would escape him utterly, a bird out an open window, leaving him untongued in some boundless amplitude of mere absence.

It is as though his name is now a secret, a small vital organ pulsing its life away. For now he has come to a place where no one knows his name but himself, where nobody but himself knows where he is. He is still going away on the far side of the boundary he crossed when he came up the ramp at the airport and saw the young woman whose name and description he carried in a letter in his pocket. She stood amid the crowd, looking for him this way and that around the heads and shoulders of the unloading passengers who hurried past, dividing around her. She saw him and smiled, anxiety leaving her face. She was from the college where, in two hours, he was to speak.

"Pardon me. Are you Andrew Catlett?"

He looked at her as if surprised to be so accosted, and stepped past. "No mam."

❧

He had come to San Francisco from an agriculture conference held that day at a great university of the Midwest. The meeting had taken place in a low building of cast concrete, of which the second story was much wider than the first, as if an architect unable to draw a curve had attempted to design a large mushroom. The walls inside were also of concrete, left unfinished. In contrast to the rude walls, all the appointments of the interior were luxurious: the stair rails of polished mahogany, the draperies richly woven, the carpets so bright and soft that the conferees moving over them made no sound, as if treading on clouds. The second-floor lobby, surrounded by meeting rooms, was furnished with deep-cushioned chairs and sofas; a table with a white cloth bore a coffee urn and an assortment of pastries. The effect of these rich furnishings, the silence of the carpet, and the correspondingly hushed voices of the conferees standing in groups was that of bated anticipation; the room seemed not to have accepted those who were in it, but to remain expectant of someone more important who perhaps was not going to attend.

As the time of the meeting drew near, the conferees moved to the white-clothed table, set down their empty cups, and singly and in groups straggled into the meeting room. Andy, who did not know anyone, took a seat high up in the back. The room was a large theater, with many rows of seats steeply pitched toward a dais at the front. On the dais was a lectern with a microphone in front of a huge blank screen. The room was windowless, lighted with bright, cold light. The fan of a distant air conditioner whispered through the walls.

Having come in just at starting time from the clear warm morning outdoors, Andy felt suddenly submerged, as if he were sitting on the bottom of an aquarium. That his ears were still tightly stopped from his plane flight seemed to corroborate this impression with physical evidence. It was as though he had changed, not only elements, but worlds. Where was he only this morning?

❧

He got up in the dark, the whole country asleep around him in the stillness at four o'clock. He went to the barn, did the feeding and milking, and returned to the house where Flora had his breakfast waiting. He went in sheepishly, for they had quarreled the night before and he had not succeeded in shedding the blame for it, not even in his own eyes. But she said "Good morning" brightly, and took the milk bucket from him with a smile.

He wanted impulsively to tell her how slow and awkward he still felt, choring with one hand, but he held himself back. He had told her, Heaven knew, often enough, for much of his thought now had to do with the comparison of times, as if he were condemned forever to measure the difference between his life when he was whole and his life now. He told her, instead, "Good morning," and then, reaching toward her as she turned away, "Listen, Flora, I *hate* to quarrel with you."

She turned back, smiling, determined, he saw, to be superior to the possibility of yet another quarrel. "Then why do you do it?"

He had hoped, vaguely, for some reconciliation between them. And so he did not say as he might have said, not in justice, but to prolong the contest, the contact, "Well, why do you quarrel with me?" There was not time for that, and he felt hollowed out by his anger of the night before. He said, "Wait. Listen. Are the children up?"

"No."

"Well, listen. I don't like to leave, feeling the way I do."

She answered him in the lighthearted, practical tone that always infuriated him, as she undoubtedly knew. "When the time comes to leave you have to leave, I suppose, and how you feel doesn't matter. How *do* you feel?"

Again the anger flashed in him that would leave him burnt and empty in his soul. "You know goddamned well how I feel."

He had the satisfaction of seeing her lips tighten. She was straining the milk, not looking at him.

"Oh," she said. "Well, if you say so. It's lovely that you understand me so well."

"I feel like I'm no account to anybody."

"Well, unfortunately, that's not for you to decide. Have you asked me? Have you asked the children? Have you asked Nathan or Henry or Wheeler or your mother?"

He started to raise his right forearm in a gesture, as if the hand were still attached, and then caught himself and put the hook behind him. "*Why* should you want to live with me?"

Even in his anger he knew that he was pleading with her, hoping to be surprised by a better reason than he knew.

"Oh, I guess because I'm used to you. Sort of."

She had put the strained milk into the refrigerator and now was at the sink, rinsing the bucket, wiping it out with the dishrag.

"Flora, you don't love me. You never have."

She stood looking at him, holding the dishrag in her hand. And then she flung it hard into his face. He can still feel the lick, as if it is burned onto his skin. Lying in the strange room in the dark, he can feel it. And he can see the look she gave him afterwards, surprised at herself, perhaps, as he certainly had been, but determined too. He saw that he had met finality in her, and he understood it. She was *done* with him as he had become. There was nothing for him to do but change his clothes and go.

She did not look at him again. She did not leave the kitchen. She did not call out to him any word at all. And he said nothing to her. When he shut the door behind him, the children were not awake.

His anger flickers in him again. She will not have him as he is, and he will not crawl back to her through the needle's eye of her demand.

Now he is outside whatever held them together. He feels the vastness of that exterior, but it does not excite him as he wishes. Would there be in all the boundlessness of it another woman, perhaps more than one other, another kind of life, for such a man as himself?

It does not excite him. It is only where he is.

❧

A man with somewhat disheveled hair and a worried look came to the rostrum, removed the worried look from his face as if suddenly aware that he stood in public, and smiled warmly at the clock on the back wall of the room.

"We appear at last to have reached the beginning of our conference, 'The Future of the American Food System.'"

He introduced himself as a member of the Department of Agricultural Economics and one of the organizers of the conference. He expressed his deep conviction of the importance of the conference in this our Bicentennial Year, quoting, in support, words of a high agricultural official to the effect that "man can live without petroleum, but not without food." He said that he supposed we had to have *some* petroleum in order to produce food but that, anyhow, we could not eat petroleum. He said that he was an old farm boy himself, and understood from firsthand experience the problems of America's food producers and also their indispensable contribution to the economy of our country and indeed of the world.

He then said that he felt highly honored to present the first speaker of the day, the high agricultural official just quoted, in fact, who was an old farm boy who had made good, by becoming, first, a professor of agriculture, and then a great administrator in a great college of agriculture, and then the chairman of the board of a great agribusiness firm, and then an agricultural official, and then a high agricultural official.

The professor sat down. The high official stood and, amid much respectful applause, made his way to the rostrum. His dark suit was as unwrinkled as if made of steel. He was faultlessly groomed. He was a man completely in charge of his face, on which not the slightest smile or frown might appear without his permission. Or he was completely in charge of his face except for his left eye, which, while his right eye looked at his notes or the audience, gazed about on its own.

"Thank you," he said. "I have thought that perhaps it is inappropriate for me to speak at the beginning of this conference, the title of which implies that there may be some question or problem about the future of the American food system, and I can only reassure you: The American food system is going to continue to be, because it is, one of the wonders of the modern world."

Andy, sitting in the back row with Flora's lick angry on his face, shrugged it away in response to pain from another adversary. He took from his jacket pocket a small notebook, opened it, and wrote, "Am Fd Syst. Wndr of mdrn wrld." After months of enforced practice, his left hand was finally learning to write at moderate speed a script that was moderately legible. But it was still a child's script that he wrote, bearing not much resemblance to the work of his late right hand. That had flowed like flight almost, looping and turning without his consciousness, as if by intelligence innate in itself. This goes by rude twists and angles, with unexpected jerks, the hand responding grudgingly to his orders, seized with little fits of reluctance.

"I thank my stars," the high official said, "that I grew up a farm boy, and had the opportunity to work closely with my father. I learned some things then that I have never forgotten, and that have stood me in good stead.

"But let's face it. Those days are gone, and their passing is not to be regretted. A lot of you here are old farm boys, and you know what I mean. You knew what it was to look all day at the north end of a south-bound horse. You knew what it was to walk that outhouse path on a zero night. Your mothers and sisters knew what it was to stand over a hot woodstove when it was a hundred degrees, and no air conditioning.

"I, for one, don't want to go back to those days. I'm glad you can't turn back the clock. I want to live in a changing, growing, dynamic society. I want to go forward with progress into a better future."

Andy wrote, "Lvd wrk. No rtrn. Lvs ftr."

"When I was a boy," the high official said, "forty-five percent of our people were on the farm. Now we have reduced that to about four percent. Millions of people have been released from farmwork to make automobiles and TV sets and plumbing fixtures—in other words, to make this the greatest industrial nation the world has ever seen. Millions of people have been freed from groveling in the earth so that they can now pursue the finer things of life.

"And the four percent left on the farm live better than the forty-five percent ever hoped to live. This four percent we may think of as the permanent staff of this great food production machine that is the farms and fields of America. These people have adapted to the fact that American agriculture is big business. They are as savvy financially as bankers. And they are enjoying the amenities of life—color TV, automobiles, indoor toilets, vacations in Florida or Arizona.

"Oh, I know there are some trade-offs involved in this. There is some breakdown in the old family unit we used to have. The communities are not what they were. I see some small businesses closing down. Farmers have fewer neighbors than they used to have. We have some problems with soil erosion and water shortages and chemical pollution. But that's the price of progress.

"Let me tell you something. This is economics we're talking about. And the basic law of economics is: Adapt or die. Get big or get out. Sure, not everybody is going to make it. But then, not everybody is *supposed* to make it. This is the way a dynamic free-market economy *works*. This is the American system.

"I'm telling you one of the greatest success stories you have ever listened to. The American farmer is now feeding himself and seventy other people. And he can feed the world. He has put in the hands of our government the most powerful weapon it has ever held. I am talking about food."

Andy wrote: "4%. Grvlng in rth. Big biz. Amnty of lf: TV. Trd-offs: fam, cmmnty, nghbrs, soil, wtr. Prc of prg. Adpt or die. Gt bg or gt out. Fr mkt. 1 to 70. Fd wrld. Weapon."

The audience sat submerged in the bright sea-space of the room, the air conditioner pulsing in the walls, the high official's confident, dryly intoned sentences riding over them, wave after wave.

Andy thought, "Why did they invite me?" But he guessed he knew: because he had achieved a certain notoriety for contrary opinions. He was there to inject a note of controversy into the proceedings.

⚘

He is a man, he thinks, of contrary opinions — a man the size of a few contrary opinions. In the simple darkness, far away, he no longer feels the uneasiness, the fear indeed, that tightened him in that meeting room. He is afraid, but not of the rostrum, not of any answer anyone might make to anything he might say. What he is afraid of now has not answered.

He raises his right forearm, its lightness still residing in it as if by permanent surprise. The memory comes to him, rising out of the flesh of his arm, of how it felt to flex and then extend the fingers of his right hand. He longs for the release of that movement. As sometimes happens, his hand seems now not to be gone, but to be caught, unable to move, as if inside an iron glove.

In October they had been helping Jack Penn harvest his corn: Andy and Nathan Coulter and Danny Branch. Jack's father, Elton, had died in March, and Jack, who was twenty-two, had never farmed on his own apart from his father's experience and judgment. And so the three of them, his father's friends, and his, had gone through the whole crop year with him, accepting his help in return for theirs. Now the harvest was almost over. If they could keep everything going until night, they would finish the field. Andy was running the picker, the other three hauling the loaded wagons to the crib and unloading them. They had, in fact, more help than they needed; it was brilliant warmish fall weather, ideal for the job; and today, with the end in sight, they had worked with an ease of mind that they all had enjoyed. Still, because it was getting on in the day with plenty left to do, there was some pressure on the tractor driver to hurry.

The picker became fouled as it had been doing off and on all afternoon, and Andy stopped to clear it, leaving it running. He began pulling the crammed stalks out of the machine, irritated by the delay. He pulled them out one at a time, shucked the ears that were on them, and threw the stalks aside. And then something happened that he thought he had imagined but, as it turned out, had not imagined at all: The machine took his hand. Of course, he knew he must have given the hand, but it was so quickly caught he could almost believe that the machine had leapt for it. While his mind halted, unable to come to the fact, his body fended for itself, braced against the pull, and held. When intelligence lighted in him again, he saw that only the hand was involved, and he carefully shifted his feet so as to give himself more leverage against the rollers; he did not want his jacket sleeve to be caught. And he was already yelling — *Hey! Hey!* — trying to pitch his voice above the noise of the machine.

There is no way for him to know how long he held out against the pull of the rollers, which soon pulled with less force, for they were lubricated with his blood. He was there long enough, anyhow, for the horror of his predicament to become steady, almost habitual, in his mind, although it retained the shock and force of its sudden onset. He heard the long persistence of the noise of the machine that did not know the difference between a cornstalk and a man's arm. He felt its relentless effort to pull him into itself, while the bloodied rollers wore against flesh and crushed bone, and the oblivious metal rattled and shook. He heard his cries to the other men go out time and again.

Finally they must have heard him, for he saw them coming, not with the tractor and empty wagon, but in Nathan's truck. He saw them coming along not too fast, until they saw him and suddenly sped up, the old truck leaping and swaying across the harvested rows.

He saw Jack leap out of the truck before it stopped, run to the tractor, and turn the ignition off. He heard the silence coming slowly down, and Nathan, running, saying to Danny, "Get my toolbox!"

And then they were with him, Danny holding him, his arms around him, while Jack and Nathan tied a tourniquet above his wrist and then worked to loosen the rollers. When what was left of the hand was ready to come free, Danny clamped his own hand over Andy's eyes.

"Andy," Nathan said, "we've got to get you into the truck now. Don't look at that hand, do you hear? Just keep your eyes shut. We're going to help you."

"All right," Andy said. His voice breaking, he said, "Shoo!" He began to shake. The silence around him rang, the air traveled by flashes and whirls, the day outside him, beyond him, uncannily bright.

By the time he was ready for the operating room, Flora was there. She smiled and picked up his left hand in hers and patted it. She seemed still to be living in that other time, before. "What have you done to yourself?"

Bitterness and fear and shame rushing upon him then, he said, "I've ruined my hand."

⁂

His foream raised as if to lift his open hand to the air, to learn the temperature of it, he lies in the dark, listening. The city around him has subsided to a remote hum, constant and unregarded as the breath of a sleeper. Only once in a while there is the sound of a solitary car moving in the street below.

He is long past sleep now. His mind has begun to work on the agenda that it sets for itself, and he knows that he will not be able to stop it. It is hunting, as if for a way out, and yet is fascinated by every obstacle. He offers it one of his contrary opinions, as he might offer a bone to a dog, and his mind, like a disobedient dog, takes it, tastes it, lets it fall, and continues with its own business. It intends to sniff its way through the Future of the American Food System until it finds the ache in it.

After the high official's speech there was a bustle while he made his exit from the meeting, surrounded by handshakers and thankers. The audience drew its attention back to itself in vague underwater stirring and murmuring until the door to the lobby shut upon the official exit and the organizer of the conference returned to the rostrum to introduce the next speaker: an old farm boy who had become one of the most astute agricultural economists in the world today, whose accomplishments had been universally recognized, and whose services had been found useful by many governments both domestic and foreign.

The great agricultural economist then gravely assumed the rostrum. Like his predecessor, he was impeccably clad, a tall man in a dark brown suit, with a face prepared to be consulted by the government. He beamed upon the audience a moment by way of greeting, adjusted his spectacles, and began to read statistics from a paper:

In the slightly more than a quarter century from 1950 to the present bicentennial year, the tonnage of fertilizer used on American farms increased by 500 percent. During the same period, work hours required in farming decreased by 69 percent, tractor horsepower increased by 149 percent, and the number of tractors by 30 percent. Simultaneously, the farm population declined from 23 million to 7.8 million, a difference of 15.2 million. The number of farms decreased to about half the number in 1950 (from 5.4 to 2.7 million), whereas the average farm size had doubled (from 200 to 400 acres).

These figures, the economist said, were causing concern in some quarters that the family farm might disappear, along with the family's traditional role in farming and other traditions of American agriculture. On the other hand, larger and more efficient farms would provide a larger volume of farm commodities at lower prices and, at the same time, provide a higher standard of living for the remaining farmers.

Obviously, he said, we have a choice to make — or, perhaps, a choice that we have already made. In order to facilitate this choosing, or this acceptance of a choice, as the case might be, the economist and his colleagues had developed a quantimetric model of the American food system.

"The model," he said, "has pre-input, input, and output divisions for each of its fifteen crop submodels." The economist read in a detached monotone, as if thinking of something else.

Andy wrote: "15.2 mlln gone. Qntmtrc mdl. Pre-inpt, inpt, outpt. Submdl." He could see bubbles rising from the great economist's mouth, breaking, high up, in the wash of the light. The economist looked almost as far away as he sounded, far off through the water, his words popping out of the bubbles and sinking back into the room:

"A model will be recursive in structure when two conditions prevail: the matrix of coefficients of endogenous variables must be triangular, and the variance-covariance matrix of structural equation disturbances must be diagonal."

The pencil fell out of Andy's hand, and he leaned and picked it up. His mind was coming loose from his body, beginning to float. It soared upward slowly and, looking down, saw a large green fish give the economist a kiss just under his right eye.

Andy's head fell forward and he woke. He sat up and shook his head. He felt like a sentinel on watch, a mourner at a wake — aggrieved, endangered, and falling asleep.

He wiggled his toes and bit the knuckle of his forefinger and looked around at the people in the room: an audience of professors, mostly, so far as he could tell. A few students. He wondered if any farmers were there and knew that it would be surprising if any were. Plenty of old farm boys, no doubt, but no farmers. Only sons and a few daughters of farmers, their parents' delegates to the Future of the American Food System.

He thought of Elton Penn, that accurate man, in his year-old grave.

The economist said, "The aggregate submodel collects the preinput and input variables and adds to them the exogenously derived pre-input and input variables for the American food system as a whole."

What would Elton have said about that? He would have said, "If you're going to talk to me, fellow, you'll have to walk."

That was what Old Jack Beechum once said to Andy's grandfather, Mat Feltner, when Mat was trying to impress him with something learned in college. Old Jack stopped and regarded him, his smart nephew, and went on to the barn. "If you're going to talk to me, Mat, you'll have to walk."

Mat had never forgotten it, and neither had any of the rest of the company of friends who inherited the memories of Old Jack and Mat. It had become one of Elton's bywords, one of the many that he kept stored up for emergent occasions. He had said it to Andy a thousand times. When Andy got his mouth running on what Elton classified as a Big Idea and there was work to be done, Elton would give him a look that made Andy remember the words even before Elton said them. And then Elton would say them: "If you're going to talk to me, Andy, you'll have to walk."

Elton's mind had been, in part, a convocation of the voices of predecessors saying appropriate things at appropriate times, talk-shortening sentences or phrases that he spoke to turn attention back to the job or the place or the concern at hand or for the pure pleasure he took in some propriety of remembrance; and he was a good enough mimic that when he recalled a saying its history would come with it. When he would tell Andy, "If you're going to talk to me, you'll have to walk," it would not be just the two of them talking and listening, but Old Jack would be saying it again to Mat, and Mat to his son-in-law, Wheeler, Andy's father, and Wheeler to Elton, and Elton to Andy all the times before; and an old understanding and an old laughter would renew itself then, and be with them.

"And now may we have the lights out and the first slide, please?" the economist said, and the light obediently subdued itself and departed from the room. The great screen came alight with Table I of the Quantimetric Model of the American Food System, dense with numbers.

❧

In the dark Andy saw what he never actually did see, but had seen in his mind many times as clearly as if he had seen it with his eyes.

Elton had not been well, something he pretended nobody knew. But they did know it. His wife, Mary, knew it. Wheeler knew it. Andy and his brother, Henry, knew it. Arthur and Martin Rowanberry knew it. They knew that he needed help with jobs he never had needed help with before. And they knew he was worried about himself.

"If you don't feel good, Elton, go to the doctor," Mary told him.

And he said, "I feel all right."

"Go to the doctor," Andy said. "I'll go with you."

"No."

"Why?"

"Because I'm not going to do it."

"Why?"

"Because I'm not sick."

"And you're not stubborn, either."

"That's right," Elton said, grinning big. "I'm not."

But they knew he was sick. And he knew it, though he made a principle of not knowing it.

"You all come over to supper," Mary said to Sarah, Henry's wife. "Elton's down in the dumps and I am too. Come over and cheer us up."

So they went. And it *was* a cheerful meal. They ate, and then sat at the table afterwards, talking about the times, beginning nearly thirty years before, when Henry and Andy had worked sometimes as Elton's hands. They had gone through some hard days together. The work had been complicated always, and sometimes impeded, by the youth and greenness of the boys, by the brotherhood of the brothers, by the friendship of them all. Most of their workdays had ended in simple weariness, but some had ended in coon hunts, some in fish fries, some in furious arguments, one or two in fights.

Among the results were a lot of funny stories, and that night Elton had been telling them, Henry egging him on.

Elton told about Henry and the bumblebees. They had been cleaning the toolshed, and there was a bundle of old grain sacks hanging from a rafter.

"Cut it down," Elton said.

"Sounds like I hear something humming in there," Henry said.

"Ahhhh, take your knife and cut it down!" Elton said. "There's nothing in there."

"I swear I didn't think there was," he said, for the hundredth time, laughing and looking at Henry, who laughed and looked back, for the hundredth time not believing him.

"So I loaned him my knife. He didn't have a knife, of course. Never did have one. Hasn't got one yet. And he cut it down.

"It fell right on his feet. 'Ow!' he said. 'Ow!' He did a little dance, and then ran right out from under his hat. His clothes were just sizzling."

Elton was laughing while he told it, and they all laughed.

"I reckon it's a lot funnier now than it was then."

"A lot," Henry said. "You were running before I even cut the string."

"*Naw*, I wasn't! No *sir*! I was just as surprised as you."

That had been a long time ago, when Henry was about fourteen and Elton not yet thirty. Probably neither of them any longer knew whether Elton had known about the bees or not. But they played out their old game of accusation and denial once more, both enjoying it, both grateful to be in the same story.

Elton pushed back his chair and got up as if to lead the way into the living room.

"Well," he said, "we've had some good times, haven't we?"

He staggered, reached to catch himself, failed. And all that was left of him fell to the floor.

※

To Andy, Elton's absence became a commanding presence. He was haunted by things he might have said to Elton that would not be sayable again in this world.

That absence is with him now, but only as a weary fact, known but no longer felt, as if by some displacement of mind or heart he is growing absent from it.

It is the absence of everything he knows, and is known by, that surrounds him now.

He is absent himself, perfectly absent. Only he knows where he is, and he is no place that he knows. His flesh feels its removal from other flesh that would recognize it or respond to its touch; it is numb with exile. He is present in his body, but his body is absent.

He does not know what time it is. Nothing has changed since he woke. The darkness is not different, nor is the faint blur of light above the curtained window, nor are the muted night sounds of the streets.

For a long time he has not moved. He lies with his unhanded right forearm upright in the air in the darkness, his body bemused at its own stillness, as if waiting patiently to see how long his strayed mind will take to notice it again.

And now the anger he felt at the conference starts up in him again, for after his fear and grief and boredom it was anger that finally woke him and hardened him against that room. He did not belong there. He did not know anybody who did belong there.

He listened to a paper on "Suggestible Parameters in the Creation of Agricultural Meaning," read by a long-haired man with a weary face, who had never been consulted by a government and who read his paper diffidently, with oddly placed fits of haste, as if aware of the audience's impending boredom or his own; and then another paper on "The Ontology and Epistemology of Agriculture as a Self-Correcting System," read by a woman whose chief business was to keep anyone from viewing the inside of her mouth.

It was endless, Andy thought, a place of eternal hopelessness, where people were condemned to talk forever of what they could not feel or see, old farm boys and old farm girls in the spell of an occult science, speaking in the absence of the living and the dead a language forever unintelligible to anyone but themselves.

And then—it was nearly noon, and a number of the auditors were leaving—he heard himself introduced as "an agricultural journalist who could hardly be said to be complacent about the Future of the American Food System, but whose ideas had attracted some attention — Mr. Andrew Catlett of Fort William, Kentucky."

Andy, getting to his feet, said loudly, "Port!"

The organizer of the conference bent to the microphone again. "I'm sorry. Yes, of course, Mr. Andrew Catlett of *Port* William, Kentucky." He smiled, and the audience laughed, with sympathy for the organizer and in discomfort at Andy's unseemly chauvinism.

Having made one mistake, and knowing it, Andy proceeded directly to another. Instead of the text of the speech he had prepared, he spread on the rostrum the notes he had made on the speeches preceding his.

"What we have heard discussed here this morning," he said, "is an agriculture of the mind. No farmer is here. No farmer has been mentioned. No one who has spoken this morning has worked a day on an actual farm in twenty years, and the reason for that is that none of the speakers *wants* to work on a farm or to be a farmer. The real interest of this meeting is in the academic careerism and the politics and the business of agriculture, and I daresay that most people here, like the first speaker, are proud to have escaped the life and work of farmers, whom they do not admire.

"This room," he said, "it's an image of the minds of the professional careerists of agriculture — a room without windows, filled with artificial light and artificial air, where everything reducible has been reduced to numbers, and the rest ignored. Nothing that you are talking about, and influencing by your talk, is present here, or can be seen from here."

He knew that he was showing his anger, and perhaps the fear under the anger, and perhaps the grief and confusion under the fear. He looked down to steady himself, feeling some blunder, as yet obscure to him, in everything he had said. He looked up at the audience again.

"I don't believe it is well understood how influence flows from enclosures like this to the fields and farms and farmers themselves. We've been sitting here this morning, hearing about the American food system and the American food producer, the free market, quantimetric models, preinputs, inputs, and outputs, about the matrix of coefficients of endogenous variables, about epistemology and parameters — while actual fields and farms and actual human lives are being damaged. The damage has been going on a long time. The fifteen million people who have left the farms since 1950 left because of damage. There was pain in that departure, not shown in any of the figures we have seen. Not felt in this room. And the pain and the damage began a long time before 1950. I want to tell you a story."

He told them how, after the death of Dorie Catlett, his father's mother, he had sorted through all the belongings that she had kept stored in the closets and the dresser drawers of the old house where she had lived as wife and widow for more than sixty years. He went through the old clothes, the quilt pieces, the boxes of buttons, the little coils and balls of saved string. And old papers—he found letters, canceled checks, canceled notes and mortgages, bills and receipts, all neatly tied in bundles with strips of rag. Among these things he found a bill on which the ink had turned brown, stating that in 1906 Marce Catlett's crop had lacked $3.57 of paying the warehouse commission on its own sale.

Neither Andy nor his father had ever seen the bill before, but it was nevertheless familiar to them, for it had been one of the motives of Wheeler Catlett's life, and it would be one of the motives of Andy's. Wheeler remembered the night his father had brought that bill home. His parents tried to disguise their feelings, and Wheeler and his brother pretended not to notice. But they did notice, and they learned, over a long time, what the bill meant. Marce Catlett had carried his year's work to the warehouse and had come home *owing* the warehouse $3.57. And that meant difficulty, it meant discouragement, it meant grief, it meant shame before creditors. And it might have meant ruin. It was a long time before they knew that it did not mean ruin.

On the back of the bill, in some moment of desperation, Dorie Catlett had written, "Oh, Lord, whatever is to become of us?" And then, beneath, as if to correct what she had written already, she wrote: "Out of the depths have I cried unto thee, O Lord."

"I think that bill came out of a room like this," Andy said, "where a family's life and work can be converted to numbers and to somebody else's profit, but the family cannot be seen and its suffering cannot be felt."

He knew then that he had damaged himself. As he had spoken of his grandmother in that room, she had departed from him. He was sweating. His legs had begun to tremble. And yet he still stood at the rostrum, in the harsh light, in his anger, sounding to himself as if he spoke at the bottom of a well.

"I say damn your systems and your numbers and your ideas. I speak for Dorie Catlett and Marce Catlett. I speak for Mat and Margaret Feltner, for Jack Beechum, for Jarrat and Burley Coulter, for Nathan Coulter and Hannah, for Danny and Lyda Branch, for Martin and Arthur Rowanberry, for Elton and Mary and Jack Penn."

As he named them, the dead and the living, they departed from him, leaving him empty, shaking, wet with sweat. The audience, embarrassed, had begun to shift and murmur. He had to get down, away, out of that light and that room.

"In conclusion," he said, "I would like to say that what I have had to say is no more, and is probably less, than what I have had to say."

He hears himself cry out — "Ah!" — and he is standing in the dark.

2. An Unknown Room

He is standing in the dark, the sound of his outcry so present to him as to be almost palpable, as if he might reach out and put it back in his mouth. Slowly the memory of the meeting room drifts away from him, and the remembered panic of yesterday becomes, without changing, the panic of today.

He cannot see himself. He reaches into the darkness with his left hand, feeling for the lamp. His fingers encounter loudly the shade, and fumble over it and down over the unfamiliar shape of the stem and base, feeling for the switch, and find it. The room, as strange to him as if he had just entered, assembles itself around him: the disheveled bed, the low stands on either side with identical lamps, and over the lamps identical pastel prints of large tulips, identically framed. Against the wall opposite the bed there is a long sideboard with empty drawers, and over it a mirror that reduplicates the duplicate lamps and pictures, the bed, and himself, his right arm stumped off at the wrist, his left hand still on the lamp switch, his hair and underclothes as mussed as the bed.

He stands, looking at himself in the room in the mirror as though he is his own disembodied soul. When he'd answered, "No mam," to the young woman waiting to meet him at the airport gate, he had felt the sudden swing and stagger of disembodiment, as though a profound divorce had occurred, casting his body off to do what it would on its own, to be watched as from a distance, without premonition of what it might do. And what of that young woman? He is going to be sorry for his lie to her. He is standing so still that he might be looking at himself, stuffed, behind glass: "*Homo Americanus,* c. 1976, perhaps from a border state." And then he sees the image grimace in dismissal of itself or its onlooker and turn away.

He turns away into his singularity in 1976 itself, the twenty-first of June thereof. In the light the room reasserts its smell of stale smoke and perfumed disinfectant. It is a little before three o'clock.

In Port William now it is a little before six. Daylight, he imagines, is reddening the sky over the wooded slopes of the little valley of Harford Run, which falls away eastward from his house; the treetops are misty in the damp morning air, a few stars and the waning moon still bright in the sky. And he would be going out, if he were there, with the milk bucket on his arm, calling the cows. Flora would be starting breakfast, the children putting on their shoes, half asleep, getting ready to go out to their own chores.

He is outside that, the air and light of that place filling his absence, the disturbance of his departure subsided. He looks back on it as from somewhere far off in the sky. In the quieted place where yesterday he went out, the children are now going out to do the work that he went out to do, Flora going with them, probably, to help them. He knows that she is being cheerful with them. Even if she does not feel cheerful, she will be cheerful. She will be looking for reasons to be cheerful, showing the children the slender moon high up over the colored clouds of the dawn. She is saying, "Look, Virgie, how the mist is hanging in the trees."

He would not have that grace himself. If he were going out into the morning aggrieved, he would be the embodiment of his grievance, and the day could be as bright as it pleased, yet it could not prevail upon him to be cheerful.

His right hand had been the one with which he reached out to the world and attached himself to it. When he lost his hand he lost his hold. It was as though his hand still clutched all that was dear to him — and was gone. All the world then became to him a steep slope, and he a man descending, staggering and falling, unable to reach out to tree trunk or branch or root to catch and hold on.

When he did reach out with his clumsy, hesitant, uneducated left hand, he would be maddened by its ineptitude. It went out as if fearful that it would displease him, and it did displease him. As he watched it groping at his buttons or trying to drive a nail or fumbling by itself with one of the two-handed tools that he now hated to use but would not give up, he could have torn it off and beaten it on the ground.

He remembered with longing the events of his body's wholeness, grieving over them, as Adam remembered Paradise. He remembered how his body had dressed itself, while his mind thought of something else; how he had shifted burdens from hand to hand; how his right hand had danced with its awkward partner and made it graceful; how his right hand had been as deft and nervous as a bird. He remembered his poise as a two-handed lover, when he reached out to Flora and held and touched her, until the smooths and swells of her ached in his palm and fingers, and his hand knew her as a man knows his homeland. Now the hand that joined him to her had been cast away, and he mourned over it as over a priceless map or manual forever lost.

One day Flora came to where he was sitting in the barn and he was crying. She put her arm around him. "It's going to be all right."

And he said, "What did they do with my hand?" For it had occurred to him that he did not know what they had done with it. Had they burned it or buried it or just indifferently thrown it away?—when they should have given it back to him to bring home and lay properly to rest.

"What?" Flora said.

"What did they do with my hand? The goddamned sons of bitches!"

Flora took her arm away. "*What* is the *matter* with you?"

"Just leave me alone."

Alone was the way she left him. Alone was the way he was, as cast away there in his place as his hand was, wherever it was.

It is three o'clock. It is a little after three. He thinks of the lighted, night-filled, shadowy streets. He has no purpose at all. There is now simply nothing in the world that he intends. He looks at the opened, rumpled bed. He intends at least not to go back there. He would as soon lie down in his grave as in that bed.

He goes to the window, parts the heavy curtains, and looks down into the empty street that seems to sleep and dream in the undisturbed fall of its shadows and weak lights. And he could be anybody in the world awake in the night, looking out. "How much longer?" he thinks. "When shall I arise, and the night be gone?"

❧

They passed the winter alone, he and Flora, alone to each other, he alone to all others. He lay awake to no purpose, as he would have slept to no purpose, angry, sore, and baffled, willing to die if he could have died, tossing to and fro unto the dawning of the day. That he was alone was his own fault, he knew. He was wrong. And yet he could not escape the fault and the wrong. He clutched them to himself as he was clutched by them. He made no difference.

Nor did he work to any purpose, it seemed to him, except survival and the slow coming of dexterity to his left hand. The hand learned with the slowness of a tree growing, as if it had time and patience that he did not have.

And he was learning just as slowly to use the mechanical hook that he now wore on the stump of his right forearm, a stiff, frictionless, feeling-less claw that would do some of the things he needed done and would not do others. It fitted his arm clumsily and fitted his work clumsily. The only thing pertaining to it that was fitting was the curse upon it that was shaped and ready in his mouth the moment he put it on.

He now had a left hand and something less good than a left hand, less good than a shod foot: an awkward primitive claw. And the two, the poor hand and the poor claw, did not cooperate, meeting together in the air, dancing together, as his two hands had done, but for the simplest task required all of his mind, all of his deliberation and will, so that he wearied of them and cursed them. There was the problem of balance. He repeatedly set and braced himself, addressing his right hand to some task, only to discover again that the hand was gone.

He continued by the help of time alone. He went on, not because he would not have stopped, but because nothing else would stop. Through the winter he tended to his animals and kept the little farm alive. Flora helped him and so did the children, watchful of him, always apprehensive of his anger, but giving him patience and kindness that he knew he had not earned and did not repay. He knew that Flora talked to the children about him. He knew, as well as if he had overheard, what she had said. "Well, now, listen. This is a hard time for your daddy. You'll have to understand and be patient with him. He'll be better after a while." This was what she said to the children, he knew, because it was what she said to herself. And he could see them watching him, Virgie and Betty, as if for confirmation of what she had told them. That he was a trouble to them he knew, and regretted, and the knowledge only deepened his anger at himself and turned him harder against them.

At the edge of his anger at everything else was always his anger at himself. He was ashamed of himself. He had betrayed his hand. He had put his precious hand into a machine that had obliged him by continuing to do what he had started it doing, as if he had not changed his mind. His hand had been given to him for a helpmeet, to love and to cherish, until he died, and he had been unfaithful to it. He was guilty and he was angry at himself. And yet he turned away. The place of his guilt and shame was like the unknown ocean of the early maps, full of monsters. He knew it was there, but he did not go there.

He could not yet drive a team. He did not trust himself to try that, and for good reason: His left hand had not yet come up to the job; it was strong enough, but not discriminating enough; it had not yet taken responsibility for being the only hand he had. His son, Virgil, could drive the team, was good at it for a boy, but Virgie was only twelve years old. He wanted to do more, and undoubtedly was capable of doing more, than Andy would allow him to do. For Andy was afraid. Catastrophe lived at the end of his arm. Whatever Virgie did, Andy could see how he could be hurt or killed, how the world might simply shrug him off, as a big horse would shrug off a fly. And so Virgie did not do the jobs with the team that he would have had to do alone, but only those at which Andy could be with him, ready to instruct or caution or help.

"We add up to pretty near a man," he said to Virgie, and Virgie gave him a look.

"No," Andy said. "You're pretty near a man youself."

He was moved by Virgie, who was so able a boy and so willing to help, whatever it cost him, and often it cost him a great deal. The words of Andy's bitterness were always prepared; he uttered them before he thought them. Virgie did the best he could, and he did well, and yet in moments of stress or difficulty Andy imposed a demand that it seemed to him he did not even will: He wanted the boy to be as answerable to his thought as his right hand had been. He wanted the boy to *be* his right hand.

"*Come* on, Virgie!" he would say. "Come on! Come on!"

Or he would say, "*No,* damn it! Hit it *there!*"

Virgie, half crying with indignation, would say, "I'm *trying,* Dad!"

And Andy would say, "Try *harder.*"

He was wrong, and knew it. He yearned toward the boy. His anger revealed his love, and yet removed him from it. He seemed to himself far away from all that he loved, too far away to help or to be helped. The pain he gave to Virgie, he saw, stood between him and Flora, and was his shame, and could not be helped. There were days when he could not bear the eyes of his daughter Betty, who saw everything, and loved him, and was hurt by him, and could not be helped.

"Daddy," she said, "are you all right?" And then, correcting herself, "Are you going to be all right?"

"Sure," he said.

He went as an exile into his own house and barn and fields. His wound had shown him the world and, at the same time, his estrangement from it. It was as though he continued to speak to his hand, which did not answer. And this was a loss of speech that could not be spoken of to anyone still whole and alive.

He felt his father watching him, worried about him, and he shied away.

His mother gave him no chance to shy away. "Come sit here," she said, reminding him for the first time of her mother.

"Andy, I'm sorry for what's happened. I can't tell you how sorry. But you must learn something from it."

"Learn!"

"What you don't know, you'll have to learn."

"What?"

"I don't know. But you must accept this as given to you to learn from, or it will hurt you worse than it already has."

He knew that she had missed nothing. He sat under her words with his head down as he had sat, when he was a boy, under a scolding. But she was not scolding.

"Given!" he said.

"You haven't listened," she said, reminding him again of his grandmother. "But don't forget."

He had become a special case, and he knew what he thought of that. He raged, and he raged at his rage, and nothing that he had was what he wanted. He remained devoted to his lost hand, to his body as it had been, to his life as he had wanted it to be; he could not give them up. That he had lost them and they were gone did not persuade him. The fact had no power with him. The powerlessness of the fact made him lonely, and he held to his loneliness to protect his absurdity. But it was as though his soul had withdrawn from his life, refusing any longer to live in it.

He was out of control. He *is* out of control. For months now he has not had the use of his best reasons. He is where he is, two thousand miles from home, where nobody knows where he is, in a room he has never seen before, because of a schedule that he made once and did not especially want to make when he made it. For months he has merely fallen from one day to another, with no more intention than any other creature or object that is falling, only seeing afterwards, too late, what his intention might have been, but by then fallen farther.

And this fall of his involved or revealed or caused the fall of appearances. He no longer trusted the look or sound of anything. He no longer believed that anything was what it appeared to be. He began to ask what had been secretly meant or ignorantly meant or unconsciously meant. And once his trust had failed there was no limit to his distrust; he saw that the world of his distrust was bottomless and forever dark, it was his fall itself, but he could not stop it.

He had long known that his quarrels with Flora proceeded along a line of complaints that they were, in fact, not about — or this had been true of their quarrels in the old days, before he had given his hand to the machine. Then their quarrels, as he knew or would know sooner or later in the course of them, were about duality: They were two longing to be one, or one dividing relentlessly into two. Their marriage seemed to live according to no logic at all, or none that he could see. It was the origin of the quarrel that divided them, and the selfsame quarrel, having consumed whatever fuel occasion may have offered it, would join them together again, and they met in an ease and joy that Andy knew they did not make, and that he at least did not deserve. It was as though grace and peace were bestowed on them out of the sanctity of marriage itself, which simply furnished them to one another, free and sufficient as rain to leaf. It was as if they were not making marriage but being made by it, and, while it held them, time and their lives flowed over them, like swift water over stones, rubbing them together, grinding off their edges, making them fit together, fit to be together, in the only way that fragments can be rejoined. And though Andy did not understand this, and though he suffered from it, he trusted it and rejoiced in it.

And then his trust failed, because his trust in himself failed. He had no faith in himself, and he had no faith in her faith in him, or in his faith in her. Now their quarrels did not end their difference and bring them together, but were all one quarrel that had no end. It changed subjects, but it did not end. It was no longer about duality, but about division, an infinite cold space that opened between them. It fascinated him and held him, even as he feared and hated it. Always there was something that he burned to say about it.

At times, in their quarreling, he knew he was crying out to her across that abyss, and he knew she heard him but would not pretend it was a call she could answer. Sometimes he knew he was crying for her to pity him for his dissatisfaction with her. He knew there was no door leading out from that. If he wanted to be free of it, he must stop it himself, and receive no congratulation from her for stopping it. He knew he was living the life history of a fraction, and that the fraction was growing smaller. He saw no help for it.

"Do you know what you need?" she said to him one day.

"What?"

"Forgiveness. And I want to forgive you. All of us do. And you need more than ours. But you must forgive yourself."

She was crying, and he pitied her. And he knew she had told the truth, and it made him furious.

He did not trust her to love him. He did not trust himself to trust her to love him.

"You don't love me."

He made her furious, and was glad of it, and was sorry he was glad.

He could not win his quarrel with her and he could not quit it. Nothing in his life had ever so exhausted him. He would sit in the kitchen at night, after the children were asleep, and argue with her. All his effort would be to keep his anger and his distrust, the real subjects of the quarrel, in the dark or in disguise.

She would meet his attacks bravely, hopelessly, often in tears. "It's *you* you're talking about. It's not me. You're mad at me because I can't stop you from being mad at yourself."

He would change the line of his attack, returning to his little trove of complaints against her, and she would check him.

"That's true. But it's not what you mean. You don't trust me. Or yourself. You have no faith."

She was right, and he could not win. But he knew nevertheless how to wound her. He would perform another flanking movement and attack again. He was ingenious. He was never at a loss. The agility of his maneuvers surprised him, and he took a mean pleasure in them. He persisted toward a cessation and a peace that he could not achieve. And finally he mystified himself. At some point in the quarrel he would realize that he could not remember how it had started or how it had proceeded or what it was about, that he was lost in its mere presence. And through it all he felt inside him the small, hard knot of his guilt.

Only exhaustion stopped him. Finally, worn and emptied by his hopeless anger and Flora's hopeless resistance, he would have barely the strength to walk to bed. In bed, her back turned to him, he would lie awake. And then he would sleep, but only to dream a dream that would wake him and keep him awake in fear.

He dreamed that it became necessary to set fire to his house, and he set it afire, only to realize, as the flames altogether enveloped it, that his family was inside.

He dreamed that he was in a battle, about to throw a hand grenade. He hesitated, thinking of the humanity of those he meant to destroy, and the grenade exploded in his hand.

He was walking up the creek road. A woman with snaky hair was standing on the roadside, looking down at the water. He meant to pass by her and not be seen. As he drew even with her, she turned and with her stony eyes looked him full in the face. At his outcry the room returned.

"What?" Flora said.

"Nothing."

He heard a heavy engine approaching. He ran around the house and stood beside Flora. A spotlight, surprisingly near, shone directly on them. He cried out, *"Hey!"* and woke.

❧

He picks up the hook where he left it on the floor, too strange to belong anywhere, incomplete in itself, helpless to complete any other thing, and begins putting it on. His hand fumbles at the fastenings. He labors under the balking impulse to use his right hand to install the hook on his right arm. Finally he is taken again by rage at the oddity of his handless arm and the hook and his incompetent left hand. He flings the hook into the waste basket, pleased by the sound of the heavy fall of it. "Lie there where you belong, you rattledy bastard!"

He goes into the bathroom and without turning on the light fills the basin with cold water and lifts it to his face, handful after handful, grateful for the coldness and wetness of it, and dries his face and hand. He feels in his shaving kit for his comb and combs his hair, and stands still again in the twilit little cubicle, waiting for a new intention to move him.

He is coming near to the end of a long labor of self-exhaustion. He is almost empty now. The world is almost absent from him. It is as though he still stands, emptied and shaking, behind the rostrum in his last moments at the conference. The conference was about, and was meant to promote, the abstractions by which things and lives are transformed into money. It was meant, as if by some voiceless will within the speaking voices, to seize upon actual lives and cause them to disappear into something such as the Future of the American Food System. He is oppressed by all that has oppressed him for months, but now also by the memory of his voice and of all the other voices at the conference, abstraction welling up into them, a great black cloud of forgetfulness. Soon they would not remember who or where they were, their dear homeland drawn up into the Future of the American Food System to be seen no more, forever destroyed by schemes, by numbers, by deadly means, all its springs poisoned. For years Andy has been moved by the possibility of acting in opposition to this, but he does not feel it now. It has gone away. He feels himself strangely fixed, cut off, unable to want either to stand or to move.

And yet there is a memory flickering in the stump of his arm, and it is not that of the clasp of the hooks' fastenings. It is the imprint of the thumb and fingers of a man's hand, hard, forthright, and friendly.

When his first crop of alfalfa was ready to harvest in mid May, they came to help him — Nathan and Danny and Jack, and Martin and Arthur Rowanberry. Or, rather, they came and harvested his hay, he helping them, and doing it poorly enough in his own opinion, with embarrassment, half resenting their charitable presumption, embarrassing them by his self-apology.

Nathan, who ran the crew — because Andy was useless to do it, and somebody had to do it — mainly ignored him, except to give him orders in the form of polite questions: "Don't you think it'll do to go up this afternoon?" "What about you running the rake?"

When they were finished, Andy, speaking as he knew out of the worst of his character, said, "I don't know how to thank you. I don't know how I can ever repay you."

And speaking out of the best of his, Nathan said, "Help *us*." So saying, he looked straight at Andy, grinned, took hold of his right forearm, and gave just a little tug.

❦

That was in another world. That memory in the flesh of his arm could not be stranger if it were some spirit's parting touch that he had borne with him into the womb.

The incident gave him no ease. It placed an expectation on him that he could not refuse and did not want. He did go to help them, but only as a nuisance, he felt, to them and to himself. He had little belief that they needed him or that he could help them. And, faced with his uncertainty, they seemed not to know what to ask of him. Except, that is, for Nathan. Nathan ignored him as he was, and treated him as if he were a stranger who required an extraordinary nicety of manners, speaking to him almost exclusively in polite questions. How would he feel about doing this? Would he mind doing that?

And all of this was characteristic of Nathan, who had known a war that was his country's and his time's, and who had made a peace that was his own. He entirely lacked the strenuous dissatisfactions with self and circumstance and other people that had been so much a part of the bond between Andy and Elton. He was Andy's third cousin on Andy's father's side, and he was, in a fashion, the son-in-law of Andy's mother's father, Mat Feltner. He was a good, quiet man, as if he were Mat's blood son as well as the husband of his onetime daughter-in-law. There was an accuracy of generosity in Nathan that Andy wondered at, and no nonsense. He said little and spoke well. And Andy began to live in a kind of fear of him. That clamp of Nathan's hand, by which Nathan had meant to include him, excluded him. Because he could not answer it, it lived upon his flesh like a burn, the brand of his exile.

As though Nathan is standing beside him now in the little dark room, Andy turns away. He begins to dress, avoiding the mirror now, fearfully, as if, looking in, he might see himself with the head of a toad. He does not think, but only feels. He does not think of the origin of the pain he feels, or of the anger hollow and dry in his heart.

And now, dressing, he hurries to get out. He has begun to hear again the night noises of the city. He has known the city since his first travels, nearly twenty years ago, and he feels it around him now, standing stepped and graceful on its heights, and around it the always arriving sea, the sea and the sky reaching westward, past the land's edge, out of sight.

He darkens the room and goes out into the dim hallway and the interior quiet of the building, away from the street sounds. The long hall is carpeted, and he goes silently past the shut doors of rooms where people are sleeping or absent, who would know which? There is an almost palpable unwaking around him as he goes past the blank doors, intent upon his own silence, as though, his presence known to nobody, he is not there himself.

At the elevator he stops and looks at the button saying "Down." But he does not push it. He does not want to hear the jolt of machinery as the elevator begins to rise, or the long groan of its rising, or the jolt of its stopping, the doors clanking open. He does not want to enter that little box and see it close upon him and be carried passively downward in it.

He goes on along the corridor and lets himself out into the stairwell. He has made no noise, but now his steps echo around him as he descends the rightward turning stairs, five floors, to the lobby, where the carpet silences them again.

The lobby is deserted. The empty chairs sit in conversational groups of two or three, their cushions dented. There is no one behind the desk. The clock over the desk says twenty after four.

What have I done with the time?

Remembering as if far back, he knows what he did with it. He stood up there in the room like a graven image of himself, telling over the catalogue of his complaints. There is a country inside him where his complaints live and do their work, where they invite him to come, offering their enticements and tidbits, the self-justifications of anger, the self-justifications of self-humiliation, the coddled griefs.

When he looks at the clock again, it is almost four-thirty. *This is happening to my soul. This is a part of the life history of my soul.* Outside in the street a car passes, stops for the light at the corner, its engine idling, and then turns and goes on. He must go. He must get outside. He is filled suddenly with panic, as though the doors have begun to grow rapidly smaller.

3. Remembering

In the street the wind comes fresh against him, smelling a little of the sea. He stands outside the hotel entrance, the street all his own for the moment. Off in the distance he can hear a siren baying, and then another joining it. A taxi eases up to the intersection nearby, waits for the light, and eases on. Two or three blocks away a garbage compressor utters a loud yawn followed by something like a swallow. And underneath the noises there is a silence as of the sleep of almost everybody, and beside or within the silence a low mechanical hum.

A frail-looking woman passes by, drunk and walking unsteadily but with an attempt anyway at dignity, holding her jacket closed at the throat as if she is cold. Watching her, he feels his silence. An unknown world would have to be crossed for him to speak to her. And yet something in him for which he has no word cries out toward her, for the world between them fails in their silence, who are alone and heavy laden and without rest. *This is the history of souls. This is the earthly history of immortal souls.* He begins to walk slowly past the deserted entries, the darkened windows. A truck passes, shifting into a lower gear as the grade steepens. Somewhere there is an outcry, a man's voice, distressed and urgent, unintelligible. A car engine starts. The garbage truck again raises its wail.

Other night walkers appear, meet him and pass and go on, or go by on the cross streets. They are far between, alone. He can hear their steps, each one, echoing in the spaces around him. It is the time of night, he thinks, when the dying die — *O greens, and fields, and trees, farewell, farewell!* — and the dead lie stillest in their graves, when the dying who are not yet to die begin again to live.

A man overtakes and passes him, carrying a lunch box, walking fast. He meets a woman with long blonde hair, dressed in leotards, spike heels, and a zebra-striped cloth coat. He sees a couple crossing an intersection ahead of him, young and beautiful, their arms around each other, going home. He imagines them risen from their fallen clothes like resurrected souls, stepping toward each other open-armed.

The city at night, he thinks, is like the forest at night, when most creatures have no need to stay awake, but some do, and that is well, for the place itself must never sleep. Some must carry wakefulness through the sleep of others.

He is walking northward, along Mason, toward Aquatic Park. He wants to reach the city's edge. He longs for the verge and immensity of the continent's meeting with the sea. Stopping now and then to listen and to turn and look down into the street behind him, he climbs slowly up the steepening hill. It is shadowy and dim between the streetlights; above him, above the building tops, the sky is dark, its still spaces measured out by stars and the dwindling moon. He pauses by a tiny garden behind a wall, dusky and still amid the buildings; it contains a few dark shrubs and flowers whose pale blossoms seem to float in the shadows. A bird is singing there, and another somewhere toward the top of the hill. The dawn must be beginning now; there must be a little paling in the eastern sky, invisible yet within the city's bright horizon. But at the next cross street, looking eastward across the bay, he sees a cloud with just the first suggestion of daylight touching its underside.

At the top of the hill the Fairmont is brightly lighted. The pavement in front has just been washed, and the lights shine in the wet. Andy stops on the corner to look. He would like to go into the lobby and see it, opulent and empty so early in the morning. He almost does so, and then stops, remembering himself: a one-handed man, unshaven and carelessly dressed. He does not want some elegant-mannered doorman or clerk to ask him, "May I *help* you?" He stands and looks and goes by, and on across the hilltop and onto the downward slant of the street. Behind him a robin is singing in the foliage of one of the cropped sycamores in front of the Pacific Union, and he can hear a street sweeper whistling prettily over the harsh strokes of his broom.

There are trees now, here and there along the street, their crowns dark. As he passes under one of them a bird begins to sing in it, a complex lyric sung as if forgotten all through the night and now remembered. Now wherever trees are, singing is in them. Where the buildings are the city is, and is quiet. Where the trees are the world is, and a sweet worldsong is singing itself in the dark.

He is a walker in the dark, excluded from the songs around him.

🌿

Taxis are creeping along the empty streets almost silently, like beasts of prey. A baby cries, and high in a dark wall to his left a window is suddenly lighted. At the corner of Jackson Street he stops while a noisy Volkswagen bus pauses at the intersection, but when the bus shifts gears and goes on, Andy continues to stand still, looking down Jackson at the bay. He can see the lights of the Bay Bridge stepping out into the air above the dark water. He can hear the cable car machinery humming under the street. A man in a hooded shirt, walking a dog, crosses Jackson and goes on up the hill, his steps echoing in the quiet. Andy is filled with a yearning toward this place. He imagines himself living here. He would have a small apartment up here on the hillside, a cliff dwelling, looking out over the bay. He would live alone, and slowly he would come to know a peacefulness and gentleness in his own character, having nobody to quarrel with. He would have a job that he could walk to in the morning and walk home from in the evening. It would be a job that would pay him well and give him nothing to worry about before he went to it or after he left it. In his spare time he would visit the museums. He would dress well and eat well. He would learn Japanese and spend his vacations in Japan. He would become a student of Japanese culture and art. He would bring back pottery and paintings. His apartment would be a place of refuge, quiet and orderly, full of beautiful things. In his travels he would meet beautiful, indolent, slow-speaking women as solitary and independent as himself, who would not wish to know him well.

But he reminds himself of himself. Something else in him is raging at him: "Damn you! Damn you!" And he says then lucidly to his mind, "Yes, you sorry fool, be still!" For the flaw in all that dream is himself, the little hell of himself alone.

You fool. You sorry fool.

The cable hums under the street. The bridge swings its great stride out into the dark. Now the city parcels itself out in his hearing: the hum of the cable almost underfoot, and in the distance the hum of the night-waking of the whole city. Except for those sounds near and far, for the moment it is quiet, and he can hear the birds singing wherever there are trees. The birds brood or dream over their song, as if the song knows of the coming light that the birds have not yet suspected. The time is neither night nor morning.

He reminds himself of himself.

❦

He walks again, crossing on Jackson to Powell, and turning again northward. The names on windows and awnings are in Chinese now. The street reeks with the smell of yesterday's fish.

A figure lurches upright out of a doorway ahead of him. The man is bearded, long-haired, his head bound with a rolled bandanna. He wears a fringed buckskin coat.

"Hey, man!"

"Hello!"

"Say, brother, could you spare me a buck for a little breakfast?"

Andy feels in his pocket, finding, if he is not mistaken, two nickels and a quarter. "I thought the toll was a dime."

"This ain't 1930, man."

"Well, when is it?"

"How would *I* know? Later?"

Am I going to show this fellow my wallet?

Holding his wallet in his one hand, he will be disarmed.

"I mean, a good breakfast, man, that's a good start on a good day." The man is chanting, dancing a little, as if to a rhythm independent of himself that might carry him abruptly up the street, empty-handed.

Do I even have a dollar bill? Is this charity or madness?

Madness or charity, he holds his wallet against his waist with his right forearm, and with his left hand plucks out a bill, and it is a five, and another, and it is a one; on impulse, he gives them both.

"Oh, wow! Far out! Thanks, Tex. You a man of a better time."

So would I hope, if I hoped, to pray to be.

❦

When he has crossed Broadway he can see the lights of the westward tower of the Bay Bridge centered in the opening of the street, the lights of its cables swaying down symmetrically on either side. Above a dark cloudbank in the east, a pale light is in the sky. The traffic along Broadway is thin but constant, its sound established, the day begun.

A walker in the dark, he feels the touch of the light of the sky around him, but he is not in it. He reminds himself of himself.

In Washington Square, the trees are loud with the cries of sparrows. The little park is an island, green, tree-shaded under the lights; on the far side is the lighted pale front of the church of Peter and Paul. Andy sits down on a bench in the shadows near the firemen's monument. The sparrows clamor overhead. Lighted buses go by, the people inside them sleepy and quiet, on their way to work; as the buses move and stop, the people sway in unison in their seats, unresisting as underwater weeds. Joggers pass, striding long, their breathing loud over their footfalls. A dog passes slowly, his short legs trotting fast. A fat Chinese woman walks by, swinging her arms vigorously. Behind her comes a Chinese man slowly rotating his extended arms as if he is a sluggish seabird preparing to fly.

Now Andy can see daylight in all the sky, brighter to the east, although, below, the lights of the streets are still strong and the shadows dark. He sits and watches. He watches the slow waking of the streets, the gentle people exercising in the park, their movements as fluent and quiet as if dreamed. He watches the lights around the square become weak as the sky brightens. On the bench next to him a man is lying asleep under a blanket. In all the stirring in the square, they two are the only ones who are still. When the daylight has come well into the shadows and the night has entirely gone, he gets up; he stands in front of the church and reads the legend engraved across its face: LA GLORIA DI COLUI CHE TUTTO MUOVE PER L'UNIVERSO PENETRA E RISPLENDE.

GOOD EARTH REALTY, INC., and all the rest of the businesses along Columbus Avenue are still shut, dreaming perhaps of opportunities to come later. In their dreams their mouths are open, and people are rushing in with their pockets full of money. There is nothing like a crowd yet in the gray light of the street. The walkers, some going to work, some going to breakfast, some led by little dogs, appear one at a time, widely dispersed, moved along by singular and undetectable purposes.

What draws him to the sleeper in the doorway, he does not know. He sees the man lying there, his knees drawn up beneath a short piece of blanket that does not cover his feet, and he stops. He stops, perhaps, because of some suggestion of the power of his awareness over the man sleeping unaware. The man, Andy sees, is young, his face unlined under his three days' growth of beard. His hair is blond, his beard red. His head is resting on his extended right arm, the forearm propped at the wrist against the kick plate of the door, the hand relaxed and drooping like the bloom of a nodding flower. The hand, like the blanket, is dirty. The young man's mouth is slightly open. He has the innocent look of a sleeping child. And what can have brought him here?

Andy leans, looking at the young man face-to-face. The young man is loosened and easy in his sleep, in his vulnerability unaware, as if in some absolute trust that to Andy is not imaginable. The sleeper has entrusted himself to his defenseless sleep as confidently as a little child to his own bed at home. As if not with his mind but with his shoulder and breastbone, Andy recalls his grandfather's old fingers prodding him through the covers. "Boy? The sun's up." And then, in pity and sorrow: "And you still a-laying in the bed with the daylight in your face." And Andy thinks of himself leaning over his own sleeping son. For a moment he is almost breathless with the thought that if he reached out and touched this man, he would move; he would stir and wake out of his dark sleep to live in this new day that has come.

But now singing is in the street, and Andy moves away. A man is coming up the street, singing an aria in a fine, strong tenor. As he moves along he is inspecting the interiors of garbage cans, as unfailing in his attentions as a postman. As they meet and pass, the man does not look at Andy. He seems to be aware of nothing in the world but his quest from garbage can to garbage can. He seems not to hear himself singing.

"No," Andy thinks. "Maybe it was not absolute trust. Maybe it was absolute despair. Maybe when he lay down he didn't care if he slept or died." Andy lays his hand on his breastbone as a chill or an ache passes through him and shakes him. He reminds himself of himself.

He is down in the flat now, close to the bay. At intersections he can see Alcatraz with its walls, its lighthouse flashing. A nice gentle-faced woman is waiting at a bus stop alone. Andy says before he thinks, as if in Port William, "Morning!" The woman quickly looks away. Her fear and accusation are in the air around her, leaving him hardly room to pass.

But momentum is going with him now. He is almost outside the network of the streets. And then, at the foot of Hyde Street, he *is* out of it and is standing in the great fall of dawnlight over the bay and its islands, the Golden Gate, the Marin hills and Mount Tamalpais beyond. To the east, beyond the Berkeley hills, the whiteness of the sky has begun to show a faint stain of pink. The air opens and lightens around him, freshening, bearing the cold pungence of the ocean. Seagulls, crying hungrily, circle on spread wings in the unobstructed day.

❧

In Aquatic Park a little lilting surf is running up the beach, the tide going out, and gulls are walking with strange terrestrial flat-footedness among the windrows of drift and trash and seaweed. Andy goes along the curved walk above the harbor into the lee of the high ground of Fort Mason where the air is still and he can smell the eucalyptus trees.

The long pier curves out ahead of him into the bay. He is going over water now. A few fishermen are already leaning on the parapet, watching their lines, which disappear beneath the little waves. The fishermen are already dazzled with expectation and the motion of the water. As Andy stands and watches, a rod tip suddenly vibrates and gestures downward.

A little farther out he encounters suddenly the wind off the sea, pressing in massively and steadily past the bridge. The gulls go against it, and turn, their wings spread to it in overmastering grace; their voices skitter and quarrel over tidbits of garbage or the possible future occurance of tidbits of garbage. Out toward Alcatraz seven pelicans are flying in stately single file. Westward, the great bridge stands aloof, its tower tops hidden in fog, and out beyond it the immense tremor of the ocean. Fishing boats are coming in from the night. Gulls standing on the parapets of the pier call softly, and then for no apparent reason break into laughter.

Andy walks and stands and walks until he comes to the outermost arc of the pier. There, with the whole continent at his back, nothing between him and Asia but water, he stands again, leaning on the parapet, looking westward into the wind. The air has cleared beyond the bridge now; he can see ships there, waiting to come in; a tug is on its way out to meet one of them.

And now almost at Andy's feet, silently and with no disturbance at all, a head appears among the waves. One moment it was not there, and the next it is. It is a head so black and slick that Andy at first thinks it is the head of a man wearing a bathing cap. But it is the head of a sea lion who looks around with the intelligent gaze of a man, and then is gone so quickly and with so little disturbance that Andy, who was looking at it, cannot be sure when it went. So sudden, brief, and silent was its appearance, so intelligent its glossy eye, so perfect its absence, that when it rises again, Andy thinks, it may rise into a day two hundred years ago.

A gray freighter comes into sight, going out. So far away as it is, it is silent, moving steadily along, already submitted to the long pulse of its engines that will drive it out under the bridge, past the headlands, into the wild ocean. Going where?

Where might he not go? Who knows where he is? He feels the simplicity and lightness of his solitude. Other lives, other possible lives swarm around him.

Distance comes upon him. Nobody in thousands of miles, nobody who knows him, knows where he is. If Flora wanted him now, how would she find him? How would a call or letter find him with news of any death or grief? All distance is around him, and he wants nothing that he has. All choice is around him, and he knows nothing that he wants.

I've come to another of thy limits, Lord. Is this the end?

✴

Out of the depths have I cried unto thee, O Lord.

Though he did not think of her, the words come to him in his grand-mother's voice. They breathe themselves out of him in her voice and leave him empty, empty as if of his very soul. As though some corrosive light has flashed around him, he stands naked to time and distance, empty; and he has no thought.

He hears the sound of hoofbeats approaching on a gravel road. It is dusk. He sees a little boy standing barefoot on the stones of a driveway leading up to the paintless walls of an old house, about which the air seems tense with the memory of loss and dying not long past, of weeping and gnashing of teeth. The swifts, oblivious, circle in long sweeps over the roof of the house and hover over its chimneys. The boy watches the swifts, thinking of the sounds of rifle fire and of cannon, of the running of many horses, and of the dead sons of the house, so much older than he, so long gone, that he will think of them always as his father's sons, not as his brothers. He hears the nearer hoofbeats too, and he waits.

They turn in at the gate; he turns to look now, and sees that it is a good high-headed bay horse. The man riding the horse is square-built and has a large beard. The boy likes the man's eyes because they look straight at him and do not change and do not look away. The man stops beside the boy and crosses his hands over the pommel of the saddle.

"My boy, might your sister be home?"

"She ain't ever anyplace else, hardly."

"I see." The man thinks while he talks, and before, and after. "Well, can you show me where to put my horse?"

"Yessir."

"Do you want to ride?"

"Yessir." He does want to ride, for he loves the horse, and perhaps the man too.

The man reaches down with his hand. "Well, take a hold and give a jump."

The boy does as he is told, and is swung up behind the saddle.

"I'm Ben Feltner. Who are you?"

"Jack Beechum."

"That's what I thought."

Ben Feltner clucks to the horse.

"You came to see my sister?"

"Your sister is Nancy Beechum?"

"Yessir."

"Well, I came to see her."

That would have been 1868, and then and thus was the shuttle flung, for the first time in Andy's knowledge, through the web of his making. Beyond that meeting, Mat, his grandfather, wakens, crying, in his cradle, and Bess, Andy's mother, in hers, and Andy in his, and Andy's own children in theirs: Betty, named Elizabeth for his mother, and Virgie, named Virgil for his mother's brother, missing in action, presumed dead, in the Pacific in 1945.

❦

Though the light is still gray on the pier and over the water, a few windows are shining on the hill above Sausalito. Weak sunlight, while Andy watches, begins to color the slopes of other hills north of the bridge, whitening the drifts of fog that lie in their hollows.

A gull is walking on the parapet nearby, crying loudly, "Ahhh! Ahhh!" It comes so close that Andy can see its bright eye and the clear bead of seawater quivering on its beak.

"What?" Andy says.

The gull says, "Ahhh!"

A sailboat passes, its sail unraised, its engine running slowly and quietly. The tug has met its ship and they are starting in.

Again hoofbeats approach him over gravel, and he sees an old man coming on horseback through the same gate through the mist and slow rain of a morning in early March. Except for the strength of the light, the warming air, and a certain confidence in the surrounding birdsong, it still looks like the dead of winter. The pastures are brown, the trees bare. The house, though, is painted, and the whole place, which in 1868 looked almost forgotten, has obviously been remembered again and for a long time kept carefully in mind. It is seventy-seven years later. The old man on the horse is a little past seventy-five. He wears neatly a canvas hunting coat frayed at the cuffs and a felt hat creased in the crown by long wear and darkened by the rain. The horse is a rangy sorrel gelding, who, by the look of his eye, requires a master, which, by his gait and deportment, is what he has on his back. As he rides, the old man is looking around.

He goes up beside the house and through the gate into the barn lot and into the barn.

"Whoa," he says. "Hello."

"Hello," a voice says from the hayloft.

There are footsteps on the loft floor and then a scrape, and a large forkful of hay drops onto the barn floor.

The horse snorts and lunges backward. The old man sits him straight up and unsurprised. "Whoa," he says, and with hand and heel forces the horse back up into the tracks he stood in before. With a little white showing in his eye, breathing loud, the horse stands in them, quivering. He does not offer to move again.

A young man comes down the loft ladder. "I'm sorry. I didn't hear your horse."

"It's all right."

The old man waits, and the young man comes up by the horse's left shoulder, laying a hand on his neck. "Whoa, boy."

"I'm Marce Catlett. I'm your neighbor. I've come to make your acquaintance."

The old man reaches down his hand and the young man reaches up and takes it.

"I'm Elton Penn, Mr. Catlett."

Each knows the other by reputation, and each looks for the marks of what he has heard.

The old man sees that the young man's clothes are old, well mended, and well worn. He sees that he has a straight, clear look in his eye. He sees the good team of horses standing in their stalls, and their harness properly hung up.

The young man sees the respect the sorrel horse has for his rider, and vice versa, the excellent fettle of the horse, the old saddle and bridle well attended, and he recognizes the exacting workman, the man of careful satisfactions whom he has heard about.

"I think you know Wheeler Catlett," Marce says. "He's my boy. He thinks a lot of you."

"Yessir. I think a lot of him."

Elton stands with his hand on the horse's neck. Marce sits looking over Elton's and the horse's heads into the barn.

"Well, Jack Beechum was my neighbor all my life."

He looks back down at Elton and considers and says, "Jack Beechum is a good man. He's been a good one. None better."

"That's what I hear." Elton says, "I haven't met Mr. Beechum yet."

"Well, when you do, you'll know him for what he is. You'll see it in him."

Now, as by agreement, they turn and look out across the lot at the house, Elton no longer touching the horse.

"I've got two grandboys. Wheeler's. They'll be over to bother you, I expect, now that the weather's changing. You won't offend me if you make 'em mind."

"Yessir."

Elton's wife, Mary, comes out the kitchen door with a dishpan of water, crosses the yard, and flings the dirty water over the pasture fence. She comes back, stepping in a hurry, waves to the two of them, smiles, and goes back into the kitchen. Marce has watched her attentively, going out and coming back, and out of the corner of his eye Elton has watched him watching.

"Son, you've got a good woman yonder. She'll cook a man a meal of vittles before you know it."

"Thank you, sir."

They are again silent a moment, and then Marce says, "Well, you'll do all right. Go ahead."

Without any signal from Marce that Elton sees or hears, the horse steps back into the swift, easy stride that brought him.

"Come back, Mr. Catlett."

"I will that."

※

"Old man Marce Catlett will neighbor with you, if you treat him right," Elton had been told before he moved. It proved true. Marce and Dorie Catlett and Elton and Mary Penn were neighbors, and in that neighborhood, Andy and Henry grew familiar and learned much.

It did not last long as it was. It was the end of something old and long that Andy was born barely in time to know. Old Jack Beechum was already gone from his place. In two years Marce was dead, the horse and mule teams were going, the tractors and other large machines were coming, the old ways were ending.

After Marce's death, Andy came to stay with his grandmother, to help her and to be company for her. He was a restless boy, and to keep him occupied, she gave him all the eggs that her dominicker hens laid outside the henhouse. After school, he searched out the hidden nests in the barns and outbuildings, and put the eggs a few at a time into a basket in a closet. Through that early spring of Marce's death, the grieved old woman and the eager boy talked of his project. He would save the eggs until he had enough, and then sell them, and with the money buy a setting of eggs of another kind from a neighbor. "Buff Orpingtons," Dorie said. "They're fine chickens. You can raise them to frying size and sell them, and then you'll have some money to put in the bank."

"And next year we'll raise some more."

"Maybe we will."

The evening comes when they put the eggs under a setting hen in the henhouse. He is holding the marked eggs in a basket, and Dorie is taking them out one by one and putting them under the hen.

"You know, you can just order the chickens from a factory now, and they send them to you through the mail."

"But this is the *best* way, ain't it?" He hopes it is, for he loves it.

"It's the cheapest. And the oldest. It's been done this way a long time."

"How long, do you reckon?"

"Oh, forever."

She puts the last egg under the hen, and strokes her back as she would have stroked a baby to sleep. Out the door he can see the red sky in the west. And he loves it there in the quiet with her, doing what has been done forever.

"I hope we always do it forever," he says.

She looks down at him, and smiles, and then suddenly pulls his head against her. "Oh, my boy, how far away will you be sometime, remembering this?"

The wind blows his tears back like the earpieces of a pair of spectacles. The bridge has begun to shine. He turns and sees that the sun has risen and is making a path toward him across the water.

He is held, though he does not hold. He is caught up again in the old pattern of entrances: of minds into minds, minds into place, places into minds. The pattern limits and complicates him, singling him out in his own flesh. Out of the multitude of possible lives that have surrounded and beckoned to him like a crowd around a star, he returns now to himself, a mere meteorite, scorched, small, and fallen. He has met again his one life and one death, and he takes them back. It is as though, leaving, he has met himself already returning, pushing in front of him a barn seventy-five feet by forty, and a hundred acres of land, six generations of his own history, partly failed, and a few dead and living whose love has claimed him forever. He will be partial, and he will die; he will live out the truth of that. Though he does not hold, he is held. He is grieving, and he is full of joy. What is that Egypt but his Promised Land?

※

Word of death and grief *has* reached him, and it is word of his own death and grief, which are his life too, his remembering and his joy.

"Boys," Mat says, "it was a *hot* day. There wasn't a breeze anywhere in that bottom that would have moved a cobweb. It was punishing." He is telling Elton and Andy.

It was a long time ago. Mat was only a boy yet, though he was nearly grown. His Uncle Jack hired him to help chop out a field of tall corn in a creek bottom. It was hot and still, and the heat stood close around them as they worked. They felt they needed to tiptoe to get enough air.

Mat thought he could not stand it any longer, and then he stood it a little longer, and they reached the end of the row.

"Let's go sink ourselves in the creek," Jack said.

They did. They hung their sweated clothes on willows in the sun to dry, and sank themselves in the cool stream up to their noses. It was a good hole, deep and shady, with the sound of the riffles above and below, and a kingfisher flying in and seeing them and flying away. All that afternoon when they got too hot, they went there.

"Well sir," Mat says, "it made that hard day good. I thought of all the times I'd worked in that field, hurrying to get through, to get to a better place, and it had been there all the time. I can't say I've always lived by what I learned that day — I wish I had — but I've never forgot."

"What?" Andy says.

"That it was there all the time."

"What?"

"Redemption," Mat says, and laughs. "A little flowing stream."

Beside Andy, the city stands on its hills, beyond the last dry pull across the rocks, the last dead mule and broken wheel. He can hear it, all its voices and engines washed together in the long murmur of its waking.

Once, years ago, he and Flora and their friend Hal Jimson stood on Tamalpais, all the world below them covered with fog, and heard that murmur, low and far away, as of a country remembered. The sea of fog, white to the horizons, gleamed below them, and, in the draws of the mountain, swallows swung and dived in their hunting flights as though they moved in the paths of some unutterable song.

And that was on the way. He is not going there.

All the Marin peninsula is in sunlight. So far away, so bright, it might be the shining land, the land beyond, which many travelers have seen, but never reached.

But the whole bay is shining now, the islands, the city on its hills, the wooden houses and the towers, the green treetops, the flashing waves and wings, the glory that moves all things resplendent everywhere.

4. A Long Choosing

Though he has not moved, he has turned. *I must go now. If I am going to go, it is time.* On the verge of his journey, he is thinking about choice and chance, about the disappearance of chance into choice, though the choice be as blind as chance. That he is who he is and no one else is the result of a long choosing, chosen and chosen again. He thinks of the long dance of men and women behind him, most of whom he never knew, some he knew, two he yet knows, who, choosing one another, chose him. He thinks of the choices, too, by which he chose himself as he now is. How many choices, how much chance, how much error, how much hope have made that place and people that, in turn, made him? He does not know. He knows that some who might have left chose to stay, and that some who did leave chose to return, and he is one of them. Those choices have formed in time and place the pattern of a membership that chose him, yet left him free until he should choose it, which he did once, and now has done again.

Nancy Beechum had her father to keep house for and then nurse and then bury, and her brother to raise. Ben Feltner was her faithful and patient suitor for eleven years. They married in 1879, when she was thirty-four and he thirty-nine. They had four children, of whom Mat, after the perils of birth, accident, and epidemic, was the one survivor. Mat was the

first Feltner in his own line to leave Port William after the first ones had
come there at the beginning of the century, and by then it was the beginning of the next.

He did not go by his own choice. He went because he was sent; he was
fifteen, and the time had come to send him, if he was ever to go. He had
been the subject of discussion between his father and his mother, he
knew. And so he was discomforted but not surprised when one day,
instead of leaving the dinner table when he was finished, his father remained in his place and thought, and looked at Nancy, and looked at Mat.

"Mat, my boy, we think highly of you, you know, and so we must part
with you for a while."

They had arranged for him to attend a boarding school at Hargrave,
run by a couple named Lowstudder. Mat did not want to go. He had
never thought of going, and now that he had to think of it his reluctance
took the shape of a girl, Margaret Finley, whom he had never not known,
and whom, now that he thought of leaving her, he did not want to leave.

But when the time came he did leave her. Ben drove him to the landing and put him on the boat with a small trunk, and shook his hand and
gripped his shoulder and said nothing and left him. They raised the gangplank, the little steamboat backed into the channel, and Mat watched the
green water widen between him and his life as he knew it.

After three weeks Ben came to see him. Mat, summoned, found him
sitting on the stile block where he had hitched his horse. He was smiling.
He shook Mat's hand, and Mat sat down beside him.

"Do you like it here?"

"Nosir."

Ben, his hand flat on his beard, sat looking out at the big trees in the
yard in front of them.

"Have you learned anything?"

"Yessir. Some."

Again Ben looked away and considered.

"Do you cry any of a night, son?"

"Nosir."

"Are you lonesome for Margaret Finley?"

"I miss you all too."

Ben stroked his hand slowly down his face and beard, thinking of something that made him smile.

"You're a good boy, Mat. I think you'd better stay."

He stayed four years. And then — because he did well enough, because Ben and Nancy thought well of him still — he went to the state college at Lexington. After two years, because he knew his own mind by then, and knew Margaret's, he wrote at the end of one of his letters home: "Pa, when I come back this June, I am going to stay." And Ben replied:

My dear Mat,
You have grown to a man and a good one I think. I ask no more. Come ahead. Stay on. There is employment here for you as much as you can make yourself equal to. We are plowing as weather permits. We have two excellent mule foals from the gray mares. Your Ma is well and sends her love, as I do also.
Pa

It is early June of 1906, a sunny day. The little steamboat, *The Blue Wing*, has stopped, it seems to him, a hundred times, to unload a barrel of flour and a bolt of cloth at one landing, and at another, a mile downstream, to load a drove of hogs and two passengers, as unmindful of his haste as time itself.

At last he sees forming ahead of them, still blue with distance, the shape of the Port William hill, and then one of his father's open ridge-tops, and then the steeple pointing up over the trees, and then the old elm at the landing. As the boat sidles in out of the current, he looks up and sees standing on the porch of the store above the road Margaret, who has loved him all his life until then, and will love him all the rest of it. She has heard the whistle and walked down to meet him. He waves. She smiles and waves back, and an old longing, the size of himself, opens within him.

He is moving toward the gangplank, the end of which is already poised over the bank. The boat is coming in only to put him off; it will not stop long enough to tie up. He is ready to step onto the plank when an old man who has been watching him hooks him with his cane.

"You're Ben Feltner's boy."

"Yessir."

The old man shakes his white beard in self-congratulation. "I sometimes miss the dam. I never miss the sire."

"Yessir."

"And your mammy was a Beechum."

"Yessir."

"Well, you got some good stock in you," the old man says, feeling his shoulder and looking him over. Oh, taking his time!

"You been up there to that college, my boy?"

"Yessir."

"Well, you'll be going away now, I reckon, to make something out of yourself."

Mat is stepping onto the plank, free now. "Nosir, I reckon not."

Margaret is coming down the bank to meet him, her long skirt gathered in one hand to keep it out of the dew.

❦

"Now, here are your extra clothes. They're clean, and I've darned your socks. That sack's got your shaving things in it and some other odds and ends. And there's a check in there from your granddaddy for your wages, and I think maybe a little more."

Margaret has a list in her mind. Andy is going away to college, and she has been thinking, for days maybe, of what she must do and what she must say.

"Okay," he says. He would like to leave, for he knows that all these things signify her love for him, and he is going away, and she is sad, and he is.

"Now wait. I'm not finished. Inside that sack is a tin of cookies for you to take with you to school. Don't shake them and make crumbs out of them, and don't eat them before you get there. And when you do get there I want you to apply yourself and study hard, because I think you've got a good mind and it would be a shame to waste it. Your granddaddy thinks so too."

She pauses, thinking over the rest that she must say. Her eyes are on him, direct and grave behind her glasses. He cannot turn away or look away until she is ready for him to go. He is grinning but not, he knows, fooling her.

"Listen. There are some of us here who love you mighty well and respect you and think you're fine. There may be times when you'll need to think of that."

❧

He has two thousand miles to go, and if he is going he must begin. He thinks of how far he has come, how many miles, how many steps. Some who came here came by steps, across prairie and desert and mountain, past the whitened bones of starved oxen and horses and mules, the discarded furniture and wrecked wagons, the stone-mounded graves of those who had come earlier and come no farther. He thinks of flying. At what risk and cost do the fallen fly?

Preserve me, O Lord, until I return. Preserve those I am returning to until I return.

When he does remove his elbows from the parapet where he has been leaning, and turns, and steps away, a history turns around in his mind, as if some old westward migrant, who had reached the edge at last and seen the blue uninterruptible water reaching out around the far side of the world, had turned in his tracks and started eastward again.

He walks along the pier, past the backs of the intent fishermen and the concrete benches and back onto land again. There are swimmers in the harbor, early sightseers standing and walking about, and on the walks of Aquatic Park joggers trotting in pairs and talking. He makes his way among them, in the hold of a direction now, stepping, alone and among strangers, in the first steps of a long journey that, by nightfall, will bring him back where he cannot step but where he has stepped before, where people of his lineage and history have stepped for a hundred and seventy-five years or more in an indecipherable pattern of entrances, minds into minds, minds into place, places into minds: the worn and wasted, sorrow-salted ground, familiar to him as if both known and dreamed, that owns him in a membership that he did not make, but has chosen, and that is death and life and hope to him. He is hurrying.

"Hey, man!"

Andy stops, astonished, for it is clear to him that he is being addressed, though he does not yet see by whom. And then he sees the fringed and shaggy man hurrying toward him out of a side street, the rolled bandanna around his head, his hand in the air.

"Say, good brother, could you, like, spare me a buck for a light lunch?"

"Hold on, now," Andy says. "Isn't this the same day it was this morning when I gave you six dollars?"

"Ah!" the man says. "Indeed!" He steps back a pace and makes the low bow of a cavalier, sweeping the pavement with the edge of his hand. "Pass, friend."

"Thanks, friend," Andy says. He hurries on.

The city encloses him now, the bay out of sight behind him. The streets are all astir, thousands of directions and purposes shifting and turning, meeting and passing, each making its way in the midst of the rest, colliding, turning aside, failing, succeeding, so that a man without a direction would be lost there and carried away. Ahead of him, up Columbus Avenue, the Transamerica Pyramid points up into an empty sky, so blue it makes his eyes ache.

He is hurrying. He is walking up Columbus Avenue on his way to Port William, Kentucky, but he is moving too in the pattern of a succession of such returns. He is thinking of his father.

Wheeler is on a train in the mountains west of Charlottesville, thinking of his father. It is a late evening in early summer. The sun is down, its light still in the sky. Wheeler's valise is in the rack overhead, his small trunk in the baggage car. Tomorrow morning he will get home. Marce will be at the station to meet him. Ordinarily he would come in the buggy, but tomorrow, because of the trunk, he will have the team and wagon. Wheeler is thinking of his father, and of tomorrow when they will ride together on the spring seat of the wagon through the tree-shaded lanes, looking at the country and at the light sliding over the sleek hides of the mules — five miles from the station at Smallwood, through the sweet gap that Wheeler feels opened around him now between his past and his future, and then they will be home, and his mother will have dinner ready. His thoughts force Wheeler suddenly to breathe deeply as if to make room for his heart to beat. He has the whole night ahead of him.

Later, he will go to the dining car for supper, and afterwards sleep, if he *can* sleep. Sleep will shorten the time.

Andy has tried before this to imagine his father as a young man. And now, without any effort or even forethought of Andy's, his father has appeared to him: a young man, eight years younger than he would be at Andy's birth, sixteen years younger than Andy is now, his face pleasant, lighted by humor, and yet his mouth and jaw are already firmed by a resolution that will be familiar to anyone who will know him later, and in his eyes there is already the shadow of effort and hard thought.

Wheeler was an apt and ambitious student who, after college, had been invited by the about-to-be-elected congressman from his district, Forrest Franklin, to go to Washington with him as his secretary. Wheeler accepted, on the condition that he would be permitted to attend law school as well. Mr. Franklin agreed to that, perhaps supposing that Wheeler would soon find the double load too much and would quit law school. Wheeler did not quit either one, and he did well at both.

By the time Wheeler's graduation was in sight, Mr. Franklin, who had become his friend, undertook to help him find employment. Mr. Franklin assumed, along with virtually every teacher Wheeler had ever had, that Wheeler's destiny was to be that of thousands of gifted country boys since the dawn of the republic, and before: college and then a profession and then a job in the city. This was the path of victory, already trodden out and plain. But Wheeler, to Mr. Franklin's great surprise, hesitated and put off. And one day Mr. Franklin called him in. The job in question was one with a large packing house in Chicago.

"Wheeler, you're an able young man. You've got the world in front of you. You can grow and develop and go to the top. You can be something your folks never imagined. You've got the ability to do it, Wheeler. And nobody will be prouder or delight more in your success than I will."

Mr. Franklin put both feet on the floor and leaned forward. He propped his right forefinger on Wheeler's knee.

"Wheeler. Listen. Don't, damn it, throw this opportunity away."

"Thank you, Mr. Franklin," Wheeler said, "I understand. I'll think about it."

He did think about it. He sat down at his desk and he thought. He thought of his mother and father who had skimped and denied themselves to send him to school. He asked himself what they had imagined he might become or do as an educated man, and he knew that they had imagined him only as he was, a bright boy and then a bright young man, deserving, they thought, of such help as they could give; for their help they wanted only his honest thanks, and they did not ask even for that. He knew that he could become what they had never imagined, and what he had never imagined himself. And he asked finally, thinking of them, but of himself too, "Do I want to spend my life looking out a window onto tarred roofs, or do I want to see good pastures, and the cattle coming to the spring in the evening to drink?"

Elation filling him, he answered, "I want to see good pastures and cattle coming to the spring in the evening to drink." For suddenly he did imagine what he could be. He saw it all. A man with a law degree did not have to go to Chicago to practice. He could practice wherever in the whole nation there was a courthouse. He could practice in Hargrave. He could be with his own.

He got up then and went back to Mr. Franklin's office. "Mr. Franklin," he said, "I'm going home."

And Mr. Franklin said, "WHAT?"

❧

Andy knows how firmly ruled and how unendingly fascinated his father has been by that imagining of cattle on good grass. It was a vision, finally, given the terrain and nature of their place, of a community well founded and long lasting. Wheeler held himself answerable to that, he still holds himself answerable to it, and in choosing it he gave it to his children as a possible choice.

"It can inspire you, Andy," he said. "It can keep you awake at night. It doesn't matter whether you've got a manure fork in your hand or a library in your head, or both — you can love it all your life."

"Look," he says, for he has brought Andy where he has brought him many times before, to the grove of walnuts around the spring, and the cattle are coming to drink. The cattle crowd in to the little stone basin, hardly bigger than a washtub, that has never been dry, even in the terrible drouth of 1930; they drink in great slow swallows, their breath riffling the surface of the water, and then drift back out under the trees. Andy and Wheeler can hear the grass tearing as they graze.

"If that won't move a man, what will move him? It's like a woman. It'll keep you awake at night."

Andy is old enough to be told that loving a place is like loving a woman, but Wheeler does not trust him yet to know what he is seeing. He trusts it to come to him later, if he can get it into his mind.

"Look," he says. And as if to summon Andy's mind back from wherever it may be wandering, for Andy's mind can always be supposed to be wandering, Wheeler takes hold of his shoulder and grips it hard. "Look. See what it is, and you'll always remember."

What manner of wonder is this flesh that can carry in it for thirty years a vision that other flesh has carried, oh, forever, and handed down by touch?

Andy would like to know, for he is walking up Powell Street alone with the print of his father's hard-fingered, urgent hand as palpably on his shoulder as if the hand itself were still there. He is going past storefronts lined with fish, vegetables, and herbs, roasted ducks hanging by their necks in windows. He is hurrying among all the other hurriers, on his way to Port William.

Where is Port William? If he asked, who would know? But he knows.

He reaches the hotel and enters the lobby. It is all alight now with ordinary day. People are coming and going, standing around, sitting and talking. Reflected light from the passing traffic quivers and darts on the walls.

His room, once he has drawn the curtains back, is filled with ordinary daylight too, no longer the place of nightmare. His suffering of the night and early morning now has given way to a suffering of haste, distance, and mortality. He must get back before chance or death prevents him. He feels his frailty amid the stone and metal of the world crashing and roaring around him. He is praying to live until he can get home. To get there, he must pass a thousand ways to die. He has no time to waste. He bathes quickly, and shaves and combs his hair, looking at himself, it seems to him, for the first time in almost a year — a small, older, plainer man than he was before.

He puts on fresh underwear and shirt, and repacks his things into his suitcase. And then he thinks of the hook, tempted at first to leave it.

No. Get it. It is only a tool.

It is not a hand. It is not a substitute for a hand. It is a tool, only a tool. His hand is gone. Sometime, somewhere behind him, his hand has left him. It has died, and is at peace.

5. A Place Known and Dreamed

He pays his bill and goes out to wait on the curb for the airport limousine. He puts his bag between his feet and leans against a signpost as near the corner as he can get and yet be out of the way of the crowd. He is still now, gathered together, ready to go, and the city continues its coming and going around him.

He is a man fated to be charmed by cities. They frighten him and threaten to break his heart, but they charm him too. He came to them too late not to be charmed by them. The great cities that he has been to have exhilarated him by the mere thought of the abundance that is in them, not needing to be sent for.

Years ago, he resigned himself to living in cities. That was what his education was for, as his teachers all advised and he believed. Its purpose was to get him away from home, out of the country, to someplace where he could live up to his abilities. He needed an education, and the purpose of an education was to take him away.

He did not want to go, and he grieved at night over his forthcoming long and distant absence. But no one he met at the university offered him reprieve. He could amount to something, maybe; all he needed was an education, and a little polish.

"For Christ's sake, Catlett," one of his professors told him in his freshman year, "try to take on a little *polish* while you're at it. You don't have to go through the world *alarmed* because other people don't have cowshit on their shoes."

As it turned out, he did not take a very high polish. Polishing him was like polishing a clod of his native yellow clay; as soon as he began to shine, the whole glaze would flake off, leaving the job to be begun again.

After graduation he married, and went to San Francisco, where he worked as a journalist, a very minor journalist, covering minor rural and agricultural events. He learned a little of the way the agricultural world wagged, and, perhaps because he was so far from home and from what his father would have told him if he had asked, he assumed that the way it wagged was the way it was supposed to wag: that bigger was better and biggest was best; that people coming into a place to use it need ask only what they wanted, not what was there; that whatever in humanity or nature failed before the advance of this mechanical ambition deserved to fail; and that the answers were in the universities and the corporate and government offices, not in the land or the people. He was capable, in those days, of forgetting all that his own people had been. He loved them, he thought, but he had gone beyond them as the world had. He was a long way, then, from his father's ideal of good pasture, and from all that his old friend Elton Penn was and stood for and meant.

After three years in San Francisco, he went to Chicago to work for his university classmate and friend, Tommy Netherbough, who had become an editor of *Scientific Farming*. Tommy was from Indiana, a farmer's son, who openly despised what he called the "dungship" of his servitude, as a boy, to his father's antiquated methods. There were differences of attitude and affection between Tommy and Andy, but they lay dormant under Andy's assumption that Tommy was fundamentally right, and that his way was the way of the world. Tommy was a hard worker and he knew his business. As a student, he had known what he wanted to do, and once he was out in the world he began to do it, and to do well at it. Now, as an editor, he was better than ever. Andy liked him. They worked together for five years, and they got along. And then in the early spring of 1964 they had an argument that put them on opposite sides and changed Andy's life.

Andy went to Ohio to interview a farmer named Bill Meikelberger, who was to be featured in the magazine as that year's Premier Farmer. Meikelberger had caught Tommy Netherbough's eye because, like all the Premier Farmers before him, he was, as Tommy liked to put it, "one of the leaders of the shock troops of the scientific revolution in agriculture."

And Meikelberger was, in fact, out in front of almost everybody. He was a man, clearly, of exceptional intelligence, energy, and courage. He lived in the rich, broad land south of Columbus, where he farmed the two thousand acres he had acquired by patiently buying out his neighbors in the years since his graduation from the college of agriculture at Ohio State. He was the fulfillment of the dreams of his more progressive professors. On all the two thousand acres there was not a fence, not an animal, not a woodlot, not a tree, not a garden. The whole place was planted in corn, right up to the walls of the two or three unused barns that were still standing. Meikelberger owned a herd of machines. His grain bins covered acres. He had an office like a bank president's. The office was a carpeted room at the back of the house, expensively and tastefully furnished, as was the rest of the house, as far as Andy saw it. It was a brick ranch house with ten rooms and a garage, each room a page from *House Beautiful,* and it was deserted.

When Andy and Meikelberger had toured the farm and were going to the house for coffee, Meikelberger apologized for the absence of his wife.

"I'm sorry, too," Andy said. "Is she away on a trip?"

"She's in town at work."

"Oh, I see," Andy said, looking at Meikelberger.

"Every little bit helps," Meikelberger said.

There were only the two of them at home now. One of their children was a doctor in Seattle, one was in law school, one was married to a company executive in Moline.

The kitchen was large, modern, equipped with every available appliance, shiny, comfortable, and clean. Andy sat at the table while Meikelberger made coffee.

"Some kitchen," Andy said.

"Well, we don't use it much," Meikelberger said. "Helen went to work in town when our youngest child started school. With that and keeping the books here, she stays plenty busy. And I'm busy all the time. We don't do much housekeeping. We eat in town, mostly."

Andy sat with his notebook on the table in front of him, watching Meikelberger, and liking him, though Meikelberger was troubling him too. He kept making a few notes, knowing that he was not understanding everything yet.

Meikelberger was a heavy-shouldered, balding man, with a worried, humorous face. Andy had expected him to be proud of his farm, and he obviously was. He had recited readily, and with some pleasure, all the facts and figures Andy had asked for. But he also supplied, apparently with as much pleasure, a good many personal facts that were plainer and tawdrier than his production statistics.

Meikelberger poured their coffee and sat down. "There have been some changes here since my grandfather's time," he said. "He and my grandmother settled here on eighty acres, would you believe that? They raised six children. We tore down the old house to build this one. Helen couldn't stand it, and I saw what she meant. It was a barn."

And then, as if to see what Andy would think, he turned to the glass doors, which opened onto the small backyard, and, pointing, showed Andy the layout of the old farmstead: cellar and smokehouse, henhouse and garden, crib and granary, barn lot and barn, all now disappeared.

"They'd be amazed if they could see this, wouldn't they?" Meikelberger waved his hand at the outside, where the little lawn became, without transition, a cornfield. "They'd think they were in another world."

"I guess they would," Andy said.

Meikelberger finished his coffee, pushed back his cup, and inserted a large white tablet into his mouth, something that Andy had seen him do earlier.

"Are you sick, Mr. Meikelberger?"

"Ulcer acting up."

"I'm sorry. What's the cause of that?"

Again Meikelberger grinned. "You can't farm like this without having it on your *mind*."

"I'm sure you do have a lot to think about."

"Well, I've got hired help to keep track of, and machinery to keep running, and creditors to deal with, and so forth."

"You have creditors?"

"Hell yes! You know it as well as I do. Debt is a permanent part of an operation like this. Getting out of debt is just another old idea you have to junk. I'll never be out of debt. I never intend to be."

"I guess that's bound to keep your mind busy. But it sounds like your stomach would like some time off occasionally."

"You can't let your damned stomach get in your way. If you're going to get ahead, you've got to pay the price. You're going to need a few pills occasionally, like for your stomach, and sometimes to go to sleep. You're going to need a drugstore just like you're going to need a bank."

Andy did not learn anything from Meikelberger that surprised him, but he had not expected Meikelberger's frankness. He drove away with a notebook full of figures, and many quotations and observations written in his private language of abbreviations, and some things in his mind that he would have trouble writing down in the language of *Scientific Farming*. The obstacle that now lay in his way was his realization, which Meikelberger himself had left him no room to avoid, that there was nothing, simply nothing at all, that Meikelberger allowed to stand in his way: not a neighbor or a tree or even his own body. Meikelberger's ambition had made common cause with a technical power that proposed no limit to itself, that was, in fact, destroying Meikelberger, as it had already destroyed nearly all that was natural or human around him.

The extent and gravity of the impasse Andy had come to was not immediately clear to him. He did not immediately admit to himself that he could not write the article on Meikelberger, but he did not go to work on it that night in the motel in Columbus, as ordinarily he would have done, and he did not work on it the next morning. He had, as it turned out, a job for that day, but he did not yet know what it was.

That evening he was supposed to be in Pittsburgh, which left him a long half-day for work. But he did not work. He ate breakfast and then he started to drive. He drove eastward toward Pittsburgh, and as he did so it came clear to him that he did not want to get there in a hurry — that, in fact, he did not want to get there any sooner than necessary. He was in the hill country by then, and he began to ramble northward, taking the back roads. The character of the country had changed. The fields were smaller, the farmsteads were closer together, and there were many woodlands. He was meeting and passing buggies on the road. Presently he came to a grassed field between a woodland and a stream. Through the middle of the field a backfurrow had been freshly turned. It was a beautiful place, and as Andy slowed down to look at it a three-horse team appeared, coming around on the curve of the slope, drawing a plow. Andy pulled the car off the road and got out. The man riding the plow was bearded; he was dressed in black and wore a black broad-brimmed hat. Seeing Andy, he raised his hand. He drove on to the end of the furrow, raised the plow out of the ground, and stopped the team.

"Good morning!" he said, and his otherwise cheerful voice carried just a hint of a desire to know what Andy's business was.

Andy said, "You're not going to get anywhere very fast that way." And then he was sorry. It was what Meikelberger would have said.

But the man seemed not to mind. "Oh, they step right along," he said cheerfully. He had got off the plow and was now standing beside his furrow-horse with his hand on her neck. "They'll carry you over a lot of ground in a day." He smiled and looked at Andy. "But then, of course, you don't do more than you *ought* to."

There was something friendly and undisguised about the man. Though there was gray in his beard, his face was young. He was maybe ten years older than Andy. The openness and clarity of his countenance surprised Andy and yet seemed to offer some comfort to him. He realized that, without knowing this man at all, he trusted him. The team was made up of three large black mares. Andy wanted to be closer to them. He walked through the grass and dead weeds of the roadside to the fence.

"Do you breed your mares?"

"Those two have colts in the barn. This one"—the man patted the neck of the mare next to him—"she's the grandmother. She took the year off." And then, seeing that Andy would like to come nearer, he said, "If you want to, step over the fence there at the post. That'll be all right."

Andy did so, and spoke to the horses and came and stood beside them with the Amishman. He asked about each of the mares and the man told him her breeding and history. The mares were excellent, Andy saw that, and he felt their strength and their patience.

"When I was growing up, we worked horses at home," he said. "Some horses, but mostly mules."

The man looked at him and smiled. "Well, maybe you would like to try these a round or two."

"Maybe you oughtn't to trust me," Andy said. "You don't know me."

"Oh, I see that you've been around horses. And these are gentle. Almost anybody can drive them."

"Well, my name is Andrew Catlett. They call me Andy." He put his hand out and the man took it.

"My name is Isaac Troyer."

Andy got onto the seat of the plow and took the lines into his hands, surprised at how familiarly he received them back again. He spoke to the horses, Isaac watching him, and turned them, and the grandmother mare stepped into the furrow on the other side of the land.

As he drove the long curve of the plowland, watching the dark furrow open and turn, shining and fresh-smelling, beneath him, Andy could feel the good tilth of the ground all through his body. The gait of the team was steady and powerful, the three mares walked well together, and he could feel in his hands their readiness in their work. Except for the horses' muffled footfalls and the stutter of the plowshare in the roots of the sod, it was quiet. Andy heard the birds singing in the woods and along the creek. How long had it been since Meikelberger had heard the birds sing? Meikelberger had no birds, except for the English sparrows that lived from his wasted grain, and even if he had had them he could not have heard them over the noise of his machines.

"How do you like them?" Isaac asked, as Andy raised the share at the furrow's end.

"I like them," Andy said.

"Well, drive them another round, if you want."

Andy drove them another round. This time, more at ease, he remembered something that as a child he had heard about, but now saw:

Mat, his grandfather, as a little boy, was sitting on a board that Jack Beechum had nailed to his plowbeam to make him a seat. As Jack walked behind the plow, Mat sat on the beam, and they talked. They talked about the pair of mules that drew the plow, and about the plow and how it was running, but they talked too about everything that a small boy could think to ask about, who had nothing to do but look and think and ask, except maybe, up in the afternoon, go to the spring to bring back a fresh drink of water in the gourd.

Was that a school? It was a school.

Andy thought of his own young children, who had descended, in part, from that school on the plowbeam, and did not know it. The mares strode lightly with their burden, the birds sang, the furrow rolled off the plow in a long, fluent motion, and a thrill grew in Andy at the recognition of something he wanted that he had forgotten.

At the end of the round, this time, Isaac Troyer took back his team. Andy, feeling awkward, said, "Look, I have an interest in farming. I like what I see of your place. Would you mind if I stay around a while?"

"Oh, well," Isaac said. "Oh, sure."

"Well, I thought I might like to walk around a little bit."

"Oh, sure. That's all right."

It was March, the air a little chilly, but the sun was warm. Andy walked along the creek to the end of the field, and then up along the fence through the band of woods on the steeper ground, the sprawled shadows of bare branches and the earliest flowers, and came out again on an upland, where he could see Isaac's house and barn and outbuildings.

He saw that the buildings were painted and in good repair. He saw the garden, newly worked and partly planted behind the house. He saw the martin boxes by the garden, and the small orchard with beehives under the trees. He saw fifteen guernsey cows and two more black mares in a pasture. He saw a stallion in a paddock beside the barn, and behind the barn a pen from which he could hear the sounds of pigs. He saw hens scratching in a poultry yard. Now and then he could hear the voices of children. On neighboring farms, he could see other teams plowing. He walked as with his father's hand on his shoulder, and his father's voice in his ear, saying, "Look! Look!" He walked and looked and thought and wondered, and then he walked back down to the field that Isaac was plowing.

Isaac was unhitching the team. "Well, did you look around?"

"I did."

"Well, is this the kind of farm you're used to seeing?"

"It's not quite the kind I've been looking at. Would you mind if I asked you some questions about it?"

"Oh, I don't know." He spoke, as before, out of some good cheer, some satisfaction, some confidence that Andy was having trouble accounting for.

This was not one of the Premier Farmers that Tommy Netherbough held in such esteem. He was apparently less worried, for one thing. Andy thought of Meikelberger and his farm, a way of agriculture as abstract as a graph or a statute or an airport. And he thought of Isaac's place, which was, all of it, a home. It was a home to many lives, tame and wild, of which Isaac's was only one, and was so meant. There was something— Andy was trying for words—something cordial or congenial or convivial about it. Whatever it was, it said that a man could live with trees and animals and a bending little tree-lined stream; he could live with neighbors.

And with strangers who happened by, too, for Isaac had just said, "Would you want to come eat? We got plenty."

"I'd hate to impose on you."

Isaac smiled at him. "Maybe you won't like what we got. It'll be plain."

"Plain will be lovely," Andy said. "Thanks."

And so he left the car by the road and walked beside Isaac, behind the team, up through the woods to the barn, and on the way he questioned him.

"How much land do you have, Isaac?"

"Eighty acres."

"Eighty acres. Is that enough?"

"Enough for what?"

"To make a living."

"Well, we're living, aren't we?"

"How long have you been here?"

"Seventy-four years."

"But you're not seventy-four?"

"No," Isaac said, and laughed, "my father is seventy-four. We came here the year he was born."

Isaac and his wife had five children, three in school and two little ones still at home, and Isaac's father and mother lived in a small house of their own a few steps from Isaac's.

"Do you have work for everybody?"

"Oh, yes, plenty of work."

"For the old people and the little ones too?"

"Oh, yes, we need them all."

"You stay busy all the time?"

"We don't work on Sunday. Or after supper. Sometimes there's a wedding, or we go fishing."

Isaac watered his horses and fed them, and Andy went with him to the house. He met Anna, Isaac's wife, and Susan and Caleb, their two youngest children. He bowed his head with them over the food at the kitchen table. It was a clear, clean room. The food was good. A large maple tree stood near the back porch, visible from the kitchen windows, and the wind quivered in the new grass at its foot. Beyond were the white barn and outbuildings. It was a pretty place, its prettiness not so much made as allowed. It was a place of work, but a place too of order and rest, where work was done in a condition of acknowledged blessedness and of gratitude. As they ate, they talked, making themselves known to each other.

"Oh, *Scientific Farming*," Isaac said. "I've heard of that."

"No," Anna said. "You've seen it. Our neighbor gave us a copy once. I read it."

"Did it give you any advice that you could take?" Andy asked.

"Some, maybe." She laughed. "Not much."

After dinner, taking Susan and Caleb along, Isaac and Andy walked over the little farm together, Andy questioning and, with Isaac's permission, writing down many of the answers. He learned about the various enterprises of the farm, about the exchanges of work within the neighborhood, about the portioning of work within the family, about the economies of household and homestead from which the family principally lived. Putting together what he heard and what he saw with what he knew already, Andy began to see that these people lived very well on their eighty acres and with their neighbors, whose farms were all more or less the same size, and finally, uneasy but unable to resist, he asked point-blank, "Do you owe any money, Isaac?"

"Not for a while."

"Do you have any money saved?"

"Well, I'd better, hadn't I, with five children?"

"How much would you say you net in an average year?"

They looked at each other then, and both smiled in acknowledgment of the limit they were approaching.

"About half," Isaac said.

"Are all the Amish good farmers?"

"Some better than others. All the Amish are human."

By then Isaac was carrying Susan, who had gone to sleep as soon as he picked her up.

And then Andy told him about Meikelberger's farm. Had Isaac ever thought of buying more land — say, a neighbor's farm?

"Well, if I did I'd have to go in debt to buy it, and to farm it. It would take more time and help than I've got. And I'd lose my neighbor."

"You'd rather have your neighbor?"

"We're supposed to love our neighbors as ourselves. We try. If you need them, it helps."

"Have you ever thought of mechanizing the place you have?"

"What for? So my children can work in a factory?"

The horses were rested. It was time for Isaac to return to work and for Andy to be on his way. After taking the children to the house, they returned with the team to where they'd left the plow. They shook hands.

"Thanks," Andy said. "Thank you very much. I hope we'll meet again."

"That would be good," Isaac said. "Maybe we will. I'll be here."

In the middle of that afternoon, after Andy had been back on the main road a long time, all that he had learned in the last two days finally settled into place in his mind. He braked suddenly and again pulled over to the side of the road, for at last he had seen what was unmistakably the point: Twenty-five families like Isaac Troyer's could have farmed and thrived — could have made a healthy, comely, independent community — on the two thousand acres where Bill Meikelberger lived virtually alone with his ulcer, the best friend that the bank and the farm machinery business and the fertilizer business and the oil companies and the chemical companies ever had.

Andy sat for a long time then with his hands on top of the steering wheel and his head on his hands, and then he picked up a pad of paper from the seat beside him and outlined an article about Isaac Troyer. He would write it for his friend Rove Upperson, the only agricultural journalist he knew who would want to read it.

❧

"Did you *really* think we could publish this?" Tommy Netherbough asked. He was sitting with one foot on the corner of his desk, holding the Isaac Troyer article with two fingers as if it were covered with mayonnaise.

Andy was sitting in a chair on the other side of the desk. He had understood that the dividing of ways had come when he received Tommy's peremptory note: "See me." Once in Tommy's office, he got the feeling that he was supposed to remain standing, as one who was outside the perquisites of friendship, and so he sat down.

"We're interested in successful farmers, aren't we?"

"I sent you to write on a successful farmer. Where the hell is the Meikelberger article?"

"If I wrote the truth about Meikelberger, you wouldn't publish that either."

"Meikelberger's the future of American agriculture."

"Meikelberger's the end of American agriculture—the end of the future. He's a success by way of a monstrous debt and a stomach ulcer and insomnia and the disappearance of a neighborhood. Isaac Troyer's the successful one of the pair, by any standard I know."

"Isaac Troyer is over and done with. He's as obsolete as the outdoor toilet. His farm is history, Andy. It's a museum."

"You mean you're against it."

"I'm not against it or for it. I can see that it's finished. We're not going to farm that way."

"You mean you don't *want* anybody to farm that way."

"I mean I don't want anybody to farm that way. You're letting nostalgia overrule your judgment. You've lost your sense of reality. What do you want, a job with *The Draft Horse Gazette*?"

"*The Draft Horse Gazette*—I'll have to find out about that."

"You should."

"I will."

The dividing of ways had come, but Andy made no move to get up. He was not arguing for himself now.

"What is this magazine trying to do—improve farming and help farmers, or sell agri-industrial products?"

Tommy sat looking at him, slowly nodding his head. He was angry now, Andy saw, and he did not care. He was angry himself. He was going to go. He had known it ever since the afternoon after his visit with the Troyers. He knew he was going; he did not yet know where.

Tommy said, "What you are, you know, is some kind of anarchist."

And then Andy knew what he was. He was not an anarchist. He was a throwback to that hope and dream of membership that had held together his lineage of friends and kin from Ben Feltner to himself. He was not arguing for himself, and not just for Isaac and Anna Troyer. He was arguing his father's argument. He was arguing for the cattle coming to the spring in the cool of the day, for the man with his hand on his boy's shoulder, saying, "Look. See what it is. Always remember." He was arguing for his grandparents, for the Coulters and the Penns and the Rowanberrys. And now he had seen that hope and dream again in Isaac Troyer and his people, who had understood it better and longer, and had gauged the threat to it more accurately, than anybody in Port William.

"Well," he said, looking at Tommy, trying to make his voice steady, "you do have to take an interest in your subscription list, don't you? You will have to consider, won't you, that more Meikelbergers will mean fewer farmers?"

After he spoke, he could hear the pleading reasonableness of his voice, and he regretted it.

Tommy looked at him in silence, still angry, as Andy was glad to see, and he let his own anger sound again in his voice. "Don't you have subscribers, for God's sake, whose interest is finally the same as your own? Don't you have a responsibility to your clients?"

"To hell with the subscribers! Listen! Let me give you a little lesson in reality. I don't know where you've been hiding your head. It's not subscribers that support this business — as you know damned well. It's advertisers. Our 'clients' are not farmers. They're the corporations that make the products that they pay us to advertise. We're not thinking in terms of people here. We're thinking in terms of blocks of economic power. If there are fewer farmers, so what? The ones that are left will buy on a bigger scale. The economic power will stay the same. A lot of farmers will buy little machines; a few farmers will buy big machines. What's the difference?"

Andy wanted to hit him. They were not even in the same argument that Andy had thought they were in. It was not an argument about right and wrong ways of farming. It was an argument about the way things were going to be for the foreseeable future. And he was losing that argument. He was now on the side that was losing it, and he was furious. He felt his fury singling him out. And he was exultant. He stood, to discover that he was shaking.

For the foreseeable future, then, no argument would be effective against the blocks of economic power. Farmers were going to fail, taking the advice of Netherbough and his kind. And Netherbough and his kind were going to thrive, giving bad advice. And that was merely what was going to happen until the logical consequences of that course of success became intolerable. And then something else would happen. And who knew what?

But that an argument was losing did not mean that it should not be made. It had already been made and it would be made again, not because he would make it, but because it existed, it always had, and he belonged to it. He would stand up on it here, in Tommy Netherbough's office, in Tommy Netherbough's face. That it was losing did not mean it was beaten.

"We have a difference," he said. "You don't think Isaac Troyer represents anything that you and your readers ought even to consider?"

"I don't think he's even considerable."

"Do you know whose side I'm on, between you and Isaac Troyer?"

"I don't think you have such a choice."

"Well, I choose Isaac Troyer's side."

"Do you know what that choice will cost you?"

He knew. He was shaken, and shaking, but he knew. "It won't cost anything I can't pay."

He knew then where he was going. As he was leaving Tommy's office, it came to mind, all of a piece, a place familiar as if both dreamed and known: the stone house above the wooded bluff, the spring in its rocky cleft, the ridges, the patches of old woods, the smell of bruised bee balm in the heat of the day, the field sparrow's song spiraling suddenly up into the light on the ridgetop, the towhee calling "Sweet!" in the tangle.

He asked a secretary to get word to Flora that he had been called out of town and would be back tomorrow. And then he drove to the airport.

※

He is in the limousine, swinging in the curves of the freeway, heading south out of San Francisco toward the airport. His bag is under his feet, the other passengers are looking straight ahead, nobody has said a word. He is thinking of himself driving out of Chicago toward the airport, twelve years ago, his anger at Tommy Netherbough grown to a kind of elation, lifting his thoughts, and he was thinking of the Harford Place.

When they wanted to be very specific about it, they called it the Riley Harford Place. Riley Harford had died there in 1903, and his neighbor, Griffith Merchant, Ben Feltner's first cousin, had bought the hundred acres. In 1903 Griffith Merchant was on his last legs himself, but buying land was his habit, and when he got the chance he bought Riley Harford's. After Griffith's death in 1906, the Harford Place, along with the rest of the Merchant land, was jointly inherited by Roger, Griffith's son, and Griffith's daughter, Violet, who was living in Paducah. From 1906, the Harford Place, along with the rest of the Merchant land, declined until 1945 when Mat Feltner assumed guardianship of Roger, who had by then become *non compos mentis* by the agency of drink, silliness, idleness, and age. Mat kept it, at least, from declining any further until 1948 when Roger died and it fell into the managerial powers of a Louisville law firm hired by Violet, and then, after Violet's death, by her daughter, Angela, who lived in Memphis. And now Angela was dead, and her children had moved to sell the land, most of it to be divided for that purpose into its original tracts. Henry Catlett, Andy's brother, had been hired by the Louisville firm to oversee the sale of it.

Andy had known the place all his life. He had hunted over it many times, and had worked over it almost as many, for, in the 1950s, after the house had been vacated by its last tenants, Wheeler and Elton had rented it, plowed the whole arable surface of it, and sowed it all in alfalfa and bluegrass. They made hay and pastured cattle there for five or six years, until the heirs refused to rebuild the fence. After that, as far as Andy knew, the place had lain idle, growing weeds and bushes.

❧

By the time he flew to Cincinnati, rented a car, and drove to Hargrave, it was long past dark. He ate a sandwich in Hargrave, and then drove up through Port William and turned onto the Katy's Branch road. At the mouth of the lane going up Harford Run, he hesitated. It had been a long time, he imagined, since anybody had been up that lane with a tractor, let alone an automobile. But the momentum that had carried him out of Tommy Netherbough's office was still upon him, and he did not let the car come all the way to a stop. He turned, and as he entered the lane immediately saw that he could not see. The lane was choked with tree sprouts, the tall dead stems of last year's weeds, vines, raspberry briars, and, underneath the rest, a thatching of dead grass. The headlights penetrated the tangle to about the length of his arm, but they showed him at least the hill slope on the right-hand side, cut back to accommodate the little ledge of the road.

"Come on," he said to the car, accelerating a little to keep it boring in, while the brush rattled and scraped around it. He was just trusting the road to be there, and it kept on being there, approaching him as anxiety, passing beneath him as relief.

"Come on," he said. It seemed to him that the little car was surprised, not having been brought up to such work. And then he saw abruptly the trunk of a tree fallen across the lane at the height of the windshield, and he jammed the car to a stop.

He pushed in the light switch and killed the engine, and sat still while the violence of his entry subsided around him. He heard silence, and then the peepers shrilling along Harford Run. After a time he got out and began to walk.

He wished for a flashlight, but he had not brought one. He had brought nothing but himself. But there was light from the moon, and he knew the place. He knew it day and night, for he had walked and worked over it in the daytime, and had hunted over it at night with Elton and Burley Coulter and the Rowanberrys. He would be all right except for the briars, which he found only by walking into them; he would have to put up with that. He was hurrying. He wanted to see if the old house was still standing. He wanted to see if its roof still covered it.

He followed the lane up over a rise and then down again, and through the three little tree-ringed meadows that lay along Harford Run, the peepers falling silent as he passed. He could hear the creek tumbling in the riffles. The woods stood dark on the bluff above the creek. The meadows were weedy, but he could see his way, for the night shone and shone upon them. And then there was an opening among the trees on the bluff, and he followed the road up through it to where the road went level again. From there he could see the top of the great spreading white oak that stood by the house. And then he could see the house.

It was a low stone house, thick walled, with an ell — four rooms downstairs, and upstairs two low, dormered ones with sloped ceilings. He walked through the shadow of the tree and up onto the porch. The door, when he pressed it, did not resist at all, the latch broken. He went in and walked, feeling his way through the dark, damp, mouse-smelling air, to the back door and came out again. It was sound, he knew then; after all the years of use and misuse and abandonment, not a board had creaked.

He went and looked at the barn, which had swayed off its footings along one side, but was still roofed and probably salvageable. He walked into the driveway, smelling the must of old hay and manure, old use. He stood in the barn in the dark, looking out into the bright night through fallen-open doors at each end. Many had worked there, some he knew, some he had heard of, some he would never hear of. He had worked there himself — work that he had thought he had left behind him forever, and now saw ahead of him again.

He had begun to dream his life. As never before, he felt it ahead of him, not maybe, not surely, as it was going to be, but as it *might* be. He thought of it, longing for it, as he might have thought of a beloved woman, known and dreamed. He dreamed, waking, of a man entering a barn to feed his stock in the dark of a winter morning before breakfast. Outside, it was dark and bitter cold, the stars glittering. Inside, the animals were awaiting him, cattle getting up and stretching, sheep bleating, horses nickering. He could smell the breath and warmth of the animals; he could smell feed, hay, and manure. The man was himself.

He went out. He went past the house and under the tree again. Following only a path now through a fallen gate, he went farther along the slope, crossed a little draw, and slanted down through the still sheen of the moonlight to where a shadowed notch opened in the hillside beneath another white oak as large and spreading as the one by the house. Again feeling his way, he went into the shadow and up into the notch. When the shadow seemed to hover and close around him, he felt with his hands for the cleft in the rock, and found it, and felt the cold water flowing out and the flat stone edging the water. He knelt and drank.

His hurry was over then. He walked, taking his time, around the boundary of the hundred acres. After he had done that he went back to the car and put on his overcoat and got in under the steering wheel again and slept. As soon as it became light enough to see, he started the car and backed it out of the lane.

☘

When he walked into the house, his clothes fretted by briars, mud from the Harford Place still on his shoes, Flora was sewing.

"Flora," he said, suddenly frightened, as if he did not know her, as if he might have mistaken her entirely, "we're going home."

She looked at him with her mouth full of pins, and then she took them out. "Well, it's about time."

"Well, don't you think we should? I mean, don't you want to know what I'm talking about?"

"Sure."

6. Bridal

He passes through the Gate of Universal Suspicion and is reduced to one two-hundred-millionth of his nation, admitted according to the apparent harmlessness of his personal effects. Or it is an even smaller fraction that he is reduced to, for all the world is here, coming and going, parting and greeting, laden with bags and briefcases, milling around piles of baggage, hurrying through the perfect anonymity of their purposes. And none may be trusted, not one. Where one may be dangerous, and none is known, all must be mistrusted. All must submit to the minimization and the diaspora of total strangeness and universal suspicion. The gates of the metal detectors form the crowd momentarily into lines, and send it out again, particled, into the rush of the corridor. Adrift, he allows himself to be carried into that eddying, many-stranded current.

A man to the love of women born, no specialist, he feels his mind tugged this way and that by lovely women. They seem to be everywhere, beautiful women in summer dresses beautifully worn, flesh suggesting itself, as they move, in sweet pressures against cloth. He lets them disembody him, his mind on the loose and rambling, envisioning unexpectable results, impossible culminations. What pain of loneliness draws him to them! As though ghostly arms reach out of his body toward them, he yearns for some lost, unreachable communion. *You. And you. Oh, love!* Loving them apart from anything that he knows, or might know, he is disembodied by them: no man going nowhere, or anywhere, his mind as perfectly departed from his life as a lost ghost, dreaming of meetings of eyes, touches, claspings, words. He hears their music, each a siren on her isle, and deep in his own innards cello strings throb and strum in answer. He goes by them bound to his own direction. They flow past each other in their courses, countenances veiled, as though eternally divided, falling. They will not sing to him.

It seems to him that he is one among the living dead, their eyes fixed and lightless, their bodies graves, doomed to hurry forever through the abstraction of the unsensed nowhere of their mutual disregard, dead to one another.

This is happening to my soul. This is happening to the soul of all the world.

All in the crowd are masked, each withdrawn from the others and from all whereabouts. The light of their eyes, the regard of their consciousness and thought, their body heat — all turned inward. And the faces of the women are the most closed of all. For fear. Lost to men by fear of men in the Land of Universal Suspicion. The good level look of their eyes lost.

The more he sees of them in this place, the less he can imagine them. Who are they? What are their names? Where are they going? Who loves them? Whom do they love? They appear and pass, singly, each in the world alone, the solitary end result of the meetings of all the couples that have made her, each the final, single point of her own pedigree.

And where is the dance that would gather them up again in the immortal ring, the many-in-one?

He has heard the tread of his own people dancing in a ring, the fiddle measuring time to them, a voice calling them, through the steps of change and absence, home again, the dancers unaware of their steps, which only the music, older than memory, remembered. Now that dance is broken, dismembered in the Land of Universal Suspicion, where no face is open to another. Where any may be dangerous and none may be trusted, all must live in conflict, the fire of the world's death prefigured in every heart.

Shall we disappear with our longing, dismembered, in the annihilating flame?

Spare us, O Lord, the logical consequence of our folly.

Here is the eye of the whirlwind of directions. These gathered here today, tonight will be in Tokyo, Delhi, Paris, Lima, where? Dead, perhaps, on an unseen mountainside? Or dead in the world's death? The long corridor stretches out ahead of him, a noplace to which all places reach, beyond the last horizon of the world.

Where now is the great good land? Where now the house under the white oak? Oh, cut off, cut off!

A woman is walking ahead of him whose face he will never see. She is wearing a simple dress that leaves it to her to have the style. And she has it. How he would like to go up and walk beside her! How he would like to walk with his arm around her! He can imagine such a permission coming to him from her as would darken and stagger him as if blindfolded and turned round three times.

He will never see her again. He will never see her face. The dance that would bring her back again is broken. The hand that he would open to her is gone.

⚘

When he returned, bringing Flora and their children to live at the Harford Place, he returned to a country in visible decline. After his absence, he saw his native place as by a new birth of sight, and rejoiced in it as never before. But now he saw it also as a place of history — a place, in part, the result of history — and he began to see the costs that history had exacted: hillsides senselessly cropped, gullies in old thicket-covered fields that would not be healed in ten times the time of their ruin, woodlands destructively logged, farms in decline, the towns in decline, the people going to the cities to work or to live. It was a country, he saw, that he and his people had known how to use and abuse, but not how to preserve. In the coal counties, east and west, they were strip-mining without respect for the past or mercy to the future, and the reign of a compunctionless national economy was established everywhere. Andy began to foresee a time when everything in the country would be marketable and everything marketable would be sold, when not one freestanding tree or household or man or woman would remain. Such thoughts, when they came to him, shortened his breath and ached in the pit of his stomach. Something needed to be done, and he did not know what. He turned to his own place then—the Harford Place, as diminished by its history as any other—and began to ask what might be the best use of it. How might a family live there without reducing it?

He has come to the second gate now, that between earth and sky, where his plane is waiting. He goes into the waiting lounge and chooses a seat against the end wall where he can see everything. He is sure that he will see nothing that will be of any use to him, but he is an economizer of opportunities.

Directly across from him is a man in a Palm Beach suit, with rings on the ring fingers of both hands, hidden from the lap up behind a newspaper proclaiming: TRANSVESTITE's LIFE ENDS IN SHOOTING. Next there is a young couple—a young man in an army private's uniform, a young woman in T-shirt and jeans—who sit holding hands and do not speak. Beside them is a woman of perhaps sixty, in half-glasses, knitting a sweater, the yarn traveling upward in jerks from her large handbag. And beside her is a professional football player with his leg in a cast, chewing gum rapidly and reading a copy of *Keyhole* magazine. His showpiece lady is clinging to his arm, unattended. His injured leg propped on two pieces of leather luggage, the football player is wearing a warm-up suit with his team's famous name in block letters on the jacket. People recognize him and stare at him as they pass.

At the other end of the row, divided by an empty seat from the man with the newspaper, a woman in a tailored suit is sitting with a legal pad on her lap. She is talking to a tiny machine that she holds in her hand. She speaks, snaps off the machine to think, snaps it on again and speaks. She speaks almost inaudibly, but otherwise seems oblivious of the crowd around her. It is a wonder that she is of the same species and sex as the football player's lady, and yet both seem to have themselves in mind as types—symbols, perhaps, of historical epochs or phases of the moon. The businesswoman is austerely tailored and coiffured; her eyeglasses are severe. She lives, her looks imply, entirely by forethought, her beating heart nobody else's business. Her taste and bearing are splendid. She is impeccable.

And Andy would like to give her a little peck on her ear. His mind is calling out to her: "Hello, my Tinkerbelle, my winsome, weensy crocodile. Come out! Come out! I know you're in there somewhere."

He says to his mind, "Shut up, you dumb bastard!"

And yet he cannot take his mind or eyes from her, for she is very beautiful. And who is she? Where did she come from? Where is she going? He knows that he is looking at her across an abyss, that if all the world should burn, they would burn divided in its flames. She is wearing the veil of American success, lost in the public haze that has covered the land from sea to sea. He is lost there himself, divided and burning. How would they break the veil? How call out?

O exile, for want of you, what night is cold, what stream is dry, what tree unleaved?

※

"*Ladies* and gentlemen, thank you for waiting. Flight 661 *has* now been accessorized, and is ready *for* passenger boarding *through* the jetway *at* gate eleven. We *would* like first to preboard those passengers requiring assistance *in* boarding and those *with* young children."

There is a small stir now among the waiting passengers. The wingless are preparing to fly. Andy feels the first clench of the difference between earth and air. The woman knitting looks up and looks back down again. The football player hands his magazine to his lady without looking at her, and stands. She puts the magazine into her purse, hands him his crutches, and follows him to the door, carrying their bags. Even on crutches and hampered by the unwieldy cast, he moves gracefully. His grace and bearing and a certain neatness of conformation have deceived Andy about his size. It is only when noticed point by point, neck and shoulder and arm, that the mass of the man becomes evident. He weighs maybe two hundred and fifty pounds, and yet he moves and places himself with a light and easy precision. His hands too are precise, as if alert to catch a flying bird.

Presently, the voice in the air wishes the other passengers to begin boarding. It asks those in the back rows of the plane to be seated first.

The beautiful businesswoman puts her pad of paper and her recording machine back into her briefcase. The man with the newspaper refolds it and puts his glasses in his shirt pocket. The soldier and his weeping girl stand up and hold each other tightly.

As their rows are called, they get up stragglingly and join the line at the door. They do not look at one another, each remaining in a separate small capsule of air, observing scrupulously the etiquette of strangers, careful lest by accident they should touch. The uniformed stewardess taking their boarding passes gives them each a smile made for strangers. "Thank you!" she says. "Thank you! Thank you! Thank you!" As Andy passes and goes on down the quaking tunnel toward the plane, he can smell the stench of engine exhaust and spilled fuel. The line moves to the door of the plane in little nudging advances that begin at the front and move back along its length to the rear, as an earthworm moves. Andy enters the door in his turn, and the halting movement of the line continues, branching into the aisles of the huge plane. Many are already in their seats, some reading newspapers, some opening their briefcases to go to work.

He says to himself, as he always does, "It is like a bus or a train. People take it for granted, and are at ease in it. Millions of people do this without death or injury. It is safer than driving a car. It is an ordinary thing."

But, also as he always does, he begins to argue with his first proposition: "It is too big. It is like a lecture hall. It is preposterous. And it is *most* extraordinary that humans should fly. They have done so only recently, and they do so only clumsily, with a ludicrous hooferaw of noise and fire. Human flight, after all, is only a false and pathetic argument against gravity, which has the upper hand and is the greater fact. All will come down. And some will fall."

A stewardess stands leaning against a bulkhead with her hands behind her back, saying, "*Good* morning! *Good* morning!"

He can smell the chemical smell of the plane, the disinfected cleanness of something that, though not new, is meant always to seem new. It is not marked either by its makers or its users. It will not wear like stone or wood and grow more beautiful. It is purely the result of design, purely answerable to function. All its flaws are secret, lying in wait in the imperfect attention and responsibility of human beings, in the undiscovered wear or breakage of some bolt or bearing or little wire.

He finds his seat next to a window on the left side of the plane, sidles

in, and sits down. The aisles remain full of people coming in, finding
seats, stowing luggage. In the seat across from Andy, a businessman has
his opened briefcase on his lap. He is holding a sheaf of invoices in his
left hand, and with his right hand is working rapidly a small calculator, a
pencil crosswise in his mouth. And now a very pretty young lady, a very
pleasant, intelligent-looking lady, nicely made, stops beside Andy. She
opens the overhead compartment and lifts her suitcase. It is heavy, and
she struggles with it.

"Can I help you?" Andy says.

"No," she says. "But thanks."

She puts the bag into the compartment, and he is relieved. He did not
want her to see that he has lost his hand, a fact which he now disguises by
folding his arms, the stumped arm beneath the good one. She settles herself in the seat next to him, makes herself comfortable and orderly with
little attentions to her clothes. Like other women alone in such places,
she is enclosed within herself, not wary perhaps, but composed with a
composure that certainly includes the possibility of wariness. She takes
from her purse a book, *Beyond the Hundredth Meridian,* and opens it and
begins to read. It is a book that Andy knows, by a writer he loves, and he
almost speaks to her about it, but he does not. He does not want her to
be wary of him. It seems to him that he could not bear for her to be wary
specifically of him.

※

The travelers are all in their seats now. There is a click and an unlocatable
aerial voice says, *"Ladies* and gentlemen, our destination today *is* Cincinnati *and* Cincinnati *only. If* Cincinnati is not *your* destination, please *do*
deplane the aircraft." There is another click, and presently the sound of
the door closing, the outside noise suddenly excluded, the inside noise
suddenly contained, and they are sealed within the possibility of flight,
committed to the air.

We commit these bodies to the air, O Lord, and to Thy keeping.

The plane lurches and rolls back from the gate and turns, brakes,
lurches, and begins its trip out to the runway. The passengers all move as
it moves, lurch as it lurches, all enveloped now in the one power.

A stewardess stands at the head of the aisle, and another at the head
of the aisle on the other side of the plane, and as the disembodied voice

explains their movements, these two act out the ritual pantomime of survival in the breathless heavens, salvation in the midst of danger: how to fasten the seat belt, when to refrain from smoking, how to don the oxygen mask, how to find the exits.

"This voice is talking about *falling*," Andy thinks. "It is talking about breathing oxygen while we fall. It is talking about finding the exits after we have fallen. That is why the voice is from the air, disembodied."

The plane waits in the line of planes waiting to take off. It stops and starts, moving around slowly to the end of the runway. When its turn comes, it leaps forward, roaring, jolting, and shuddering with its sudden commitment to flight. It lifts and rises. Going up through the lower, warming layers of the air, it bucks and tosses like a little boat in waves. Andy braces his feet against the legs of the seat in front of him and holds tight to the arm of his seat, panicked, as always, to feel that there is nothing to hold to that is not in the air.

When the air becomes smooth, he can think again. He becomes aware, with a kind of wonder, of the unconcern around him. The people who were reading newspapers are still reading them. The young woman sitting next to Andy has not looked up from her book. He looks at the page she is reading and finds John Wesley Powell's sentence: "I feel satisfied that we can get over the danger immediately before us; what there may be below I know not."

Afloat in fickle air, laboring upward, the plane makes a wide turn out over the ocean, and heads inland. Andy can see the city with its bridges, the Marin peninsula, and, even farther below, the upper part of the bay, and then the marshes of the river delta. As they rise from it, the details of the ground diminish, draw together, and disappear. The land becomes a map of itself.

To Andy, the air is an element as dangerous to mind as to body. For wingless creatures, it is the element of abstraction: abstract distance and speed, abstract desire. Flight seems to him to involve some radical disassemblement, as if one may pass through it only as a loose suspension of particles, threatened with dispersal.

"Ladies and gentlemen, this is your captain speaking. We want to welcome you aboard, and thank you for flying with us. We're ascending now to our cruising altitude of 37,000 feet. Our route today will carry us approximately over Denver, Salina, Kansas, Springfield, Illinois, Indianapolis, and then on down to Cincinnati. Our flying time will be, oh, about three hours and fifty-three minutes. As soon as we have reached altitude, our cabin attendants will be around with complimentary beverages and lunch. So settle back, folks. Enjoy your flight."

Thirty-seven thousand feet is over seven miles. How long would it take to fall seven miles? He thinks of falling seven miles and knowing that one is falling. Flight has always returned him to the ancient desire to die at home. He does not want to die in some place of abstraction, or in a featureless heap in some place he has never seen. But he fears most his body's brutal fear of falling, of falling through the high and alien air and knowing it. He imagines the moment before the crash when the body, remembering its long familiarity with itself, would find it strange. His hand, that had imagined many things, had never imagined its absence.

He wonders, if they were going down, would the young woman sitting beside him be willing to hold his hand? He looks at her, covertly, wondering. Holding hands, they would go down through the miles of air and crash into their total absence from the earth forever. She catches him looking, lifts her chin a little, and tugs down the hem of her skirt.

"Now you've done it!" he thinks. "You'll have to crash by yourself."

They cross the patchwork of farmland in the valley, and then the foothills, golden under the dark green oaks. And then the forests begin, and the bright gray rock of the Sierra Nevada, snow on the higher summits. Yosemite Valley, under a flock of little clouds, opens deep in the stone. Andy thinks of the islands of wilderness, bypassed in settlement, now tramped by modern backpackers, starved for what has been destroyed elsewhere and what their economy is destroying everywhere. Over it all hangs the brown veil of the world's entrails lifted up and burned.

Spare us, O Lord, the logical consequence of our folly.

Out his window he can see the huge engine shuddering under the wing. The cabin is flooded with light. They are flying in the pure sky, corrupted only by their flight, and below that is the smutted sky, and below that the world, that cannot be helped except by love.

※

They are flying above white, flat-bottomed clouds sailing eastward, their shadows dark on the treeless red hills of Nevada. Among the hills there is a large lake, blue as the sky. The streams curve sweetly against the curves of the land. The older roads follow the streams, curving with them. The newer, larger roads are ruled according to the ideal of flight, deferring as little as possible to the shapes of the land. And above it all is the veil of the smog, and above the smog this little room in the air, on the long stem of its seven-miles-fallen shadow, depending for life on speed and fire, on the ability of an explosion to sustain itself for three hours and fifty-three minutes.

✳

Andy is one of the last to receive his lunch: a plastic tray containing a tossed salad, an empty coffee cup, a helping of roast beef with gravy, small carrots, and a potato, a piece of chocolate cake, a tiny paper carton of pepper and one of salt, a plastic envelope containing a knife, a fork, a spoon, and a napkin.

Andy tears the envelope of salad dressing with his teeth and squeezes the contents onto his salad, needing another hand for this operation, but finally succeeding approximately; and then he begins the struggle to liberate his silverware.

The stewardess, pausing in the aisle with a pot of coffee, watches him a moment with unseemly absorption — a one-handed man in the toils of supraterrestrial sanitation — and then, leaning solicitously toward him, asks, "Does everything seem to be all right, sir?"

"Well, as long as we are supposing, let us suppose so."

"I beg your pardon, sir?"

"I'm sorry," he says, "I was joking. Everything seems to be all right. Thank you."

She returns to her distance and her smile. "Enjoy your meal, sir."

They eat and drink, pretending to be groundlings who are pretending to fly, trays in front of them laden with food and drink that will leave a plastic residue to be thrown away in some place out of the sight of groundlings pretending to be clean, the country below them become a map, perhaps not even of itself.

What there may be below I know not.

There comes over Andy a longing never to travel again except on foot, to restore the country to its shape and distance, its smells and looks and feels and sounds.

Spare us, O Lord, the logical consequence of our ingratitude.

Remember not, Lord, our offences, nor the offences of our forefathers.

The stewardesses have taken the trays away. Utah is below them now, canyon country, eroded yellow and pinkish walls opening among sparsely forested slopes. Andy is thinking of the wagons laboring westward against the resistant shapes of the land, places supplanting places. Of the one-armed Powell and his men on the Colorado, living by intelligence and strength and will alone.

How many connecting strands are braided there in the passes and the fording places, to be dissolved out of mind and lost almost before the grass could grow again over the wheel tracks, almost before the rain could wash them away?

I should walk. I should redo every step. It is all to be learned again.

❧

"Andy, here's something you ought to see," Burley Coulter says, handing him a page, folded and worn, brown with age, the ink on it brown. Burley is sitting in his chair by the stove in the living room with a shoebox open on his lap.

Flora is there too, and Danny and Lyda Branch, their children playing among the chair legs, returning now and again to the large bowl of popcorn that Lyda is holding. Outside, the wind is blowing and it has started to snow. Andy and Flora have already said twice that they need to be going, but Burley has kept on taking things from the box and handing them to Andy, who has examined them and passed them on to Flora, who has passed them on in turn to Lyda and Danny. They do not remember what reminded Burley of the box. At some point in their conversation he remembered it, and went up the stairs to his room and got it. He set it on his lap, untied the heavy string that was around it, and began to probe into it with his crooked, big-knuckled forefinger. The box contains his keepsakes — the family's from long back, but his because after his mother's death he continued to keep them and to add to them the odd relics of his own life that he could not bring himself to part with. There were some photographs, a few letters, a gold watch, Spanish and French coins carried back along the footpaths from New Orleans in the pockets of Coulter men who had made the downward trip on flatboats or rafted logs. These had all been looked at and explained as far as Burley could explain them. And then from the very bottom of the box he brought up the folded brown page.

"Boys," he says, "your great-great-great-grandmother wrote that. She was married to the first Nathan Coulter. Way back yonder. She was a McGown. Letitia. Letitia McGown. Read it, Andy. My eyes have got so I can't make it out."

And so Andy reads the script, not much used since it was a schoolgirl's, of an old woman dead before the Civil War:

"Oh that I should ever forget We stood by the wagon saying goodbye or trying to & I seen it come over her how far they was a going & she must look at us to remember us forever & it come over her pap and me and the others We stood & looked & knowed it was all the time we had & from now on we must remember We must look now forever Then Will rech down to her from the seat & she clim up by the hub of the wheel & set beside him & he spoke to the team She had been Betsy Rowanberry two days who was bornd Betsy Coulter 21 May 1824 Will turnd the mules & they stepd into the road passd under the oak & soon was out of sight down the hill The last I seen was her hand still raisd still waving after wagon & all was out of sight Oh it was the last I seen of her that little hand Afterwards I would say to myself I could have gone with them as far as the foot of the hill & seen her that much longer I could have gone on as far as the river mouth & footed it back by dark But however far I finaly would have come to wher I would have to stand and see them go on that hand a waving God bless her I never knowd what become of her I will never see her in this world again"

⚜

They have passed the snowfields of the Rockies, Denver under its pall, and now in their orient flight are passing above a great floor covered with newly sheared fleeces shining in the sun, sight going down through it, where it thins, into shadow, the shadowed world, diminished, thirty-seven thousand feet below.

Now it comes back into his mind, that country, green and folding, that he knows as his tongue knows the inside of his mouth. It appears to him as if from the air, as in fact he remembers seeing it from the air, when a plane he was on happened to fly over it. He saw it then, he thought, as it might appear to the eye of Heaven, and afterwards was obliged to see himself and his life as small, almost invisible, within the countryside and the passage of time.

❄

He sees Elton's old truck rocking and jarring over the humps and holes of the Katy's Branch road on the way to the Harford Place early in the morning. He and Henry and Elton are in the cab. He is sitting between Elton and Henry. Elton is driving. He sees the countryside shadowy and dewy under the misty light; he sees the road and the truck and the three of them in the cab littered with tools, ropes, spare parts, and other odds and ends that they have grown used to or may need. Henry is holding the water jug on his lap to keep it from turning over. He has been telling about his date of the night before for the edification of Elton, who has been egging him on by protesting that *he* would never have thought of anything like that, not him.

Elton says, "What did you do last night, Andy?"

"I stayed at home."

"You run out of girls?"

"Yes."

"Well, you need to find one that's not too smart, old pup."

Henry says, "*Duh,* kiss me, old pup."

And Andy says, "Shut. Up."

Henry makes his hands quiver. "Sometimes. He causeth me. To tremble."

"I told you."

"He giveth me. Trembolosis. Of the lower. Bowell."

Elton is enjoying this, but he knows he won't enjoy it long. "I'll causeth you to tremble in a minute. *Both* of you shut up."

He sings with raucous sorrow two lines of "Blue Eyes" as a comment on Andy's girl-lessness, and gives a long raucous squall as a comment on yodeling. They laugh and go on up the lane, happy, the old truck creaking and rattling, the day brightening.

Andy can see the three of them jolting along over the bumps of the road—no blacktop on it then—overgrown with trees, a tunnel. It is as though he is standing in the air, watching, and at the same time an unseen fourth person in the cab. And he is moved with tenderness toward them and with love for them.

They come to the bright field, the stand of alfalfa nearly perfect on it, and Elton stops beside the two tractors where they left them the evening before. They fill the gas tanks and check the oil. They make the necessary small repairs on the mowing machines and grease them.

Elton says, "All right. You're ready to go. Be careful. If the hay you cut day before yesterday is dry enough by ten-thirty or eleven o'clock, Henry, you quit mowing and hitch to the rake. I'll be back to get you at dinnertime."

And then, looking up at Henry, who is standing on the truck bed, looking down at him, he says, "Get off of there now, damn it, and get started."

Henry takes three steps and does a handspring off the truck bed and lands standing up in front of Elton, who has to grin in spite of himself. "I wonder," he says. "Sometimes I wonder."

�֍

That was an island in time, between the horse and mule teams and the larger, more expensive machines that came later. They were not going to live again in a time like that.

The Harford Place appealed to Elton and touched his imagination, and he made them see it as he saw it.

"Listen," he said to Andy once—they had brought sandwiches with them that day and were eating in the shade by the spring—"do you see what this old place is? The right man could do something here. It's been worked half to death and mistreated every way, but there's good in it yet." He gestured up toward the house and barn. "That's still a sound, straight old house. The barn's not much, but it could be put right and made into something."

He had been thinking about it all morning, Andy knew, studying it as it was, foreseeing it as it might be, and now was telling him about it, because, though Elton knew that he would never make it over himself, he wanted *somebody* to do it.

"Listen, Andy," he said, "if you could find the right girl, a little smarter than you, and willing to work and take care of things, here's where you could get started and amount to something. Put some sheep here. A few cows. I'd help you, and the rest of them would, we'd neighbor with each other and get along."

And so Andy had the old place in mind, as it was and as it might be made, long before it ever occurred to him that he might be the one to live there and attempt to make it as it might be.

For that to happen required, in fact, the right girl, but also many miles, many happenings, and several years.

※

And it required trust. He sees it now. What he and Flora have made of the Harford Place has depended all on trust. They have not made it what it might be—how many lives will it require for that?—but they have made it far more than it was when they came to it. In twelve years they have given it a use and a life; a beauty has come to it that is its answer to their love for it and their work; and it has given them a life that belonged to them even before they knew they wanted it. And all has depended on trust. How could he have forgotten? How could he have failed to under- stand?

His life has never rested on anything he has known beforehand— none of it. He chose it before he knew it, and again afterwards. And then he failed his trust and his choice, and now has chosen again, again on trust. He has made again the choice he has made before, as blindly as before. How could he have thought that it would be different? How could he have imagined that he might ever know enough to choose? As Flora seems to have known and never doubted, as he sees, one cannot know enough to trust. To trust is simply to give oneself; the giving is for the future, for which there is no evidence. And once given, the self cannot be taken back, whatever the evidence.

He sees again the long room, the librarian at her desk, tall shelves of books all around the walls, the double row of heavy oak tables with shaded lamps — a place where two ways met. He sees as from the penumbra above the shelf tops the eight students at the table in the farthest corner of the room: Flora, Hal Jimson, Ted Callahan, Norm Leatherwood, himself, and three others. They are most of Professor Barton Jones's class in the history of the American Revolution. Professor Jones, known beyond his own earshot as Black Bart, is legendary for his freshman history classes, which terrorize even those freshmen who do not take them. The eight at the table are not freshmen, and they are not terrified; but the midterm examination is approaching, and they are properly intimidated. Professor Jones regards the teaching and learning of American history as a matter of desperate emergency. Day after day he has stood in his classroom in his portentous bulk, glowering upon them, thumbing his text with his great thumb, or beating with a pointer for emphasis upon a blackboard perfectly blank. That he loves the people he is teaching about, or some of them, only a little on the critical side of idolatry, and that he is capable of the most generous kindness to those whom he is teaching, they all know. And yet they are intimidated. For they know too the simple ferocity with which he regards their least proclivity to misunderstand or forget. They have been trying to make fluent their understanding of the development and the influence of the mind of Thomas Jefferson. They know that they are going to have to deal convincingly with that on the midterm, and again on the final.

It is late. The room is almost empty. The quiet in the room has begun to communicate with the quiet of the dark trees outside. One by one, Black Bart's little clutch of students disperses, having attained either confidence or resignation. Now only Andy and Flora remain, Andy at the foot of the table and Flora two chairs away. With each departure it has become harder for Andy to think about Thomas Jefferson, and now he is not thinking about Thomas Jefferson at all. He is thinking about Flora, who is still at work, bent over her book and notebook. Andy is not at work, though he is pretending to be. He is looking at his book and thinking about Flora, from time to time raising his eyes over the top of the book to look at her, to see if external reality lives up to the image in his mind, realizing, each time with a clench in his chest very like pain, that it does. For a college girl of the time, she is plainly dressed: a gray skirt, a white blouse with little buttons, open at the throat, a black unbuttoned cardigan. Except for perhaps a touch of lipstick, she wears no makeup, and needs none, and no jewelry, and needs none. Above her preoccupied face, her dark curls are rejoicing on their own.

He can see nothing wrong with her. She has closed entirely the little assayer's office that he runs in his mind. She seems perfect to him, and there is something about her, something beyond her looks, something that he calls "something about her," that has unsteadied whatever square yard of ground or floor he happens to be walking or standing on.

Such joy and pain are in him to be so near her, alone with her, permitted to look at her, that he can hardly breathe. It seems to him that apart from her he can no longer breathe. It seems to him that if he does not speak to her he will stop breathing. If he speaks, he knows, everything is going to change, into what he does not know.

He says, hardly above a whisper, his heart crowding so into his throat, "Flora, do you want to come here for just a while?"

She smiles and looks up at him with a look that she will give him again, amused a little, perhaps, but not surprised; it is a look that suggests to him, in his alarm, that she never has been surprised in her life.

❦

He cannot deny her. Her eyes as they were then are on him now, and as they were when he saw them last, hurt and angry, full of tears. He cannot meet her eyes. It has been a long time since that night when she first looked at him, her face open to him, her eyes unguarded. It has been twenty years. He knows their duality in those years, the imperfection of them both, the grief and longing of their imperfection. And yet it is her justice that he feels now. He cannot meet her eyes that give his eyes such pain he cannot raise or open them. He has been wrong. His anger, his loneliness, his selfish grief, all have been wrong. That she, entrusted to him, should ever have wept because of him is his sorrow and his wrong. He sits with his head down, his eyes burning, such fire of shame covering him that he can hardly hold himself in his seat.

He knows she is right. He must have her forgiveness. He must forgive himself. He must forgive the world and his own suffering in it.

Have mercy upon me, O God, after thy great goodness; according to the multitude of thy mercies do away mine offences.

He must have his own forgiveness and hers and the children's, and the forgiveness of everyone and every thing from which he has withheld himself.

Thou shalt make me hear of joy and gladness, that the bones which thou hast broken may rejoice.

Now she comes to him again. He can see her again: a bride, dressed all in white, as innocent as himself of the great power they were putting on, frightened and smiling—a gift to him such as he did not know, such as would not be known until the death that they would promise to meet together had been met, and so perhaps never to be known in this world.

The way is open to him now. Thanks, as if not his own, shower down upon him.

"Are you all right?"

It is the young woman in the seat next to him, who to his astonishment is patting his arm.

"Yes. I've been all right before, and I'm all right now."

7. The Hilltop

Returned from the sky, his shadow attached to him again, Andy unlocks the door of his old pickup, slides the suitcase in across the seat, and climbs again into the aura of his workdays: the combined essences of horse sweat, man sweat, sweated leather, manure, grease and oil, dirt. He opens the windows to let out the trapped hot air, starts the engine, which roars loudly through its leaky muffler, drives to the booth, pays the girl in the glass enclosure, and heads for the interstate, hurrying again, but being careful.

He passes through the swoop of the entrance ramp, and is at once hurtling along in four lanes of roaring traffic that seems to have been speeding there forever. He speeds along with it, being careful, eternity gaping all around him. He drives like a messenger entrusted with a message that at all costs he must deliver. The message, it seems, is only himself. When he arrives he will have some things to say, he will have to say some things, but he does not yet know what.

But he is not trying to think of words now. He is thinking about being careful, the bright crustaceans speeding all around him along the road, each enclosing its tender pulp of flesh, creatures of mud and light, each precious beyond telling for reasons never to be known to the others, already dead to one another in mutual indifference. If one of those particles erred in its flight, then an appalling innovation would occur, an entrance to another world mauled through the very air and light. He is praying to remain in time until what he owes is paid.

The eight lanes of the interstate become six and then four. The traffic thins. The city is behind him now, except for the road itself that is the city's hardened effluent, passing through its long gouge without respect for what was there before it or for what is now alongside it. The road reminds him, as it always has before, of the power of words far removed from what they mean. For the road is a word, conceived elsewhere and laid across the country in the wound prepared for it: a word made concrete and thrust among us.

He knows that he is not yet beyond the spell of the unpeopled language that emanates from conference rooms and classrooms and laboratories and offices and electronic receivers, day after day, all across the land, the deserted speech of a statistical greed, summoning intelligence and materials out of the land to turn them into blights, justifying by an unearthly accounting and speech what decency would never have considered in the first place. There is no place that is not within reach of it and under threat of it. That speech is in Port William too, coming out of the walls of the houses, saying that all is well, all is better than ever, while the life of the place itself frets and fritters away.

By the time Andy and Flora returned from Chicago, the Port William schoolhouse had become a "rest home," where the old, the useless, the helpless, and the unwanted sat like monuments, gaping into the otherworldly light of a television set. There, within two years of their return, Jarrat Coulter lay like a man carved on a tomb, only breathing, a forlorn contraption living on fluids needled into his veins. Andy would go from time to time, as the others did, and stand by his bed and gaze upon his wasting body, the derelict hands lying useless on the sheet. All of them went from time to time, duty bound, to stand beside him and watch him breathe indomitably on, and leave and never speak, to be troubled afterwards by what — whatever it was — they had not said.

Only Burley had the courage or the grace to make what seemed a visit. He did not stand by Jarrat and look. He went in and sat down as though invited to do so, and put his hat on his lap. And he talked. He talked without embarrassment either at his brother's silence or at the presence of anybody else who might be there. He spoke into the silence where Port William's children had studied and played, and into Jarrat's silence. Sometimes, he would tell things that nobody on earth but Jarrat would have understood, if Jarrat was understanding them.

After he had said whatever Jarrat might be interested in hearing, he would get up and put on his hat. "Well, I've got to go. But I'll be back." He would lay his hand that was still brown and hard on his brother's pale, softening one. "Don't worry. You don't have to worry about a thing. Just rest and be easy in your mind."

※

In the river valley Andy takes the slower Port William road, and the pickup begins to move with a different motion, approaching the shape of the country. It moves now more nearly as eyes or feet might move, curving along the bases of the hills, not like a pencil point along the edge of a ruler. And Andy's body begins to live again in the familiar sways and pressures of his approach to home. His own place becomes palpable to him. Those he loves, living and dead, are no longer mere thoughts or memories, but presences, approachable and near.

He turns up Katy's Branch, going ever slower now, following the road up along the creek in the shade of the overarching trees. He comes to his mailbox and turns into his own lane up Harford Run, the road hardly even a cut now but just a double track leveled along the valley side under the trees.

Now they are coming to him again, those who have brought him here and who remain—not in memory, but near to memory, in the place itself and in his flesh, ready always to be remembered—so that the place, the present life of it, resonates within time and within times, as it could not do if time were all that it is living in.

Now Mat runs up the bank toward Margaret, who is running to meet him with her arms open; they meet and hold each other at last.

Wheeler, standing on the bottom step of the coach as it sways and slows finally to a standstill at the station at Smallwood, puts his hand into his father's hand and steps down.

Andy pushes open the door of the old house, and steps in behind Flora. They stop and stand looking at the wallpaper hanging in droops and scrolls, at the broken windowpane, at the phoebe's nest on the mantelpiece, and Flora says, "Oh, good!"

※

When he has driven up the slope in front of the house, and back along-side the house into the barn lot, and stopped the pickup in front of the barn, Andy switches off the engine, and sits still while the five-and-a-half-hour, two-thousand-mile uproar of his approach loosens from him and begins to withdraw like a long swarm of bees. When it has gone away, and the evening quiet of the place has returned to it and to him, he opens the door and gets out. An old black and white Border collie who has been standing beside the truck, waiting for him, now walks up and lifts his head under Andy's hand.

"You here all by yourself?"

The dog wags his tail appreciatively, and Andy strokes his head.

"Where is everybody?"

The evening chores, he sees, are done. The two jersey cows are loaf-ing in the shade by the spring, their udders slack, and Flora's car is gone. He can hear the somnolent drumming of a woodpecker off in the woods, and from somewhere on the hillside above the barn the bleating of a sheep.

He takes his suitcase out of the cab and walks to the house and across the back porch, through the screen door, and into the kitchen, a pretty room, bright and quiet. He loves this quiet and he stands still in it, breath-ing it in. There is a note to him on the table; after looking at it for a minute or two, he goes over and reads it:

> You're back?
> Mart called. They have lots of beans.
> We've gone to pick and visit.
> Love,
> F.

With her note in his hand, standing in her place, in her absence, he feels the strong quietness with which she has cared for him and waited for him all through his grief and his anger. He feels her justice, her great dignity in her suffering of him. He feels around him a blessedness that he has lived in, in his anger, and did not know. He is walking now, from room to room, breathing in the smell of the life that the two of them have made, and that she has kept. He walks from room to room, enter-

ing each as for the first time, leaving it as if forever. And he is saying over
and over to himself, "I am blessed. I am blessed."

After a while he returns to the kitchen. He takes his suitcase to his and
Flora's bedroom and unpacks it and puts it away, and walks again. He can
no more sit down than if he has no knees. He does not know when Flora
and the children will be back, and he sees that he cannot wait for them in
the house. He puts on his work clothes and starts out the back door. And
then — the thought of mortality returning to him; he must take no
chance — he goes back to the kitchen table and beneath Flora's note
writes:

> Yes.
> I'm better now. Can you
> forgive me? I pray that you
> will forgive me.

❦

The cows are still at the spring, still in the leisure of their drinking. They
look at him and look away, knowing him. To them he is no one who has
been far away, but only himself, whom they know, who is here. He takes
a tin can from the ledge above the spring outlet and dips and drinks. And
then he walks out into the pasture on the hillside.

The air is cooling now, the shadows growing long. He is walking upward along the face of the slope, following the slanting sodded groove of
what was once a wagon road — before that perhaps a buffalo trace — that
went from Katy's Branch to Port William. Where the road enters the
woods, he opens a gate and goes through.

When he fenced the woods to keep the stock out, Elton asked him,
"Why did you do that?"

"For the flowers," Andy said, giving one of his reasons.

Elton looked at him to see if he meant it. "Well. All right," he said.

The almost-disappearing road slants on up along Harford Run,
through the woods, through the Harford Place and the others beyond,
for perhaps a mile, until finally it comes out of the woods again on a high
part of the upland near Port William.

The evening is quiet; there is no wind, and no sound from the stream that here, above the spring, is dry. The woods is filling with shadows. Everything seems expectant, waiting for nightfall, though the sky is still sunlit. Andy walks slowly upward along the road until he is among the larger trees and the woods has completely enclosed him. And here finally he comes to rest. He finds a level place at the foot of a large oak, and sits down, and then presently lies down. A heavy weariness has come over him. For a long time he has not slept a restful sleep, and he has journeyed a long way.

But the sleep that comes to him now is not restful. He has entered the dark, and it is such a darkness as he has never known. All that is around him and all that he is has disappeared into it. He sees nothing, remembers nothing, knows nothing except a hopeless longing for something he does not know, for which he does not know a name. Everything has been taken away, and the dark around him is full of the sounds of crying and of tearing asunder. If it is a sleep that he is in, he cannot awaken himself. Once he was nothing, and did not know it; and then, for a little while, it seems, he was something, to the sole effect that now he knows that he is nothing. And somewhere there is a lovely something, infinitely desirable, of which he cannot recall even the name. What he is, all that he is, amid the outcries in the dark and the rendings, is a nothing possessed of a terrible self-knowledge.

But now from outside his hopeless dark sleep a touch is laid upon his shoulder, a pressure like that of a hand grasping, and his form shivers and forks out into the darkness, and is shaped again in sense. Breath and light come into him. He feels his flesh enter into mind, mind into flesh. He turns, puts his knee under him, stands, and, though dark to himself, is whole.

He is where he was, in the valley, on the hillside under an oak, but the place is changed. It is almost morning and a gray light has made its way among the trees. The freshness of dew is on everything. And it is springtime, for the dry stream has begun to flow. The early flowers are in bloom, pale, at his feet. Everywhere, near and far away, there is birdsong. The birds sing a joy that is theirs and his, and neither theirs nor his.

When he has stood and looked around, he sees that a man, dark as shadow, is walking away from him up the hill road, not far ahead. Andy knows that, once, this man leaned and looked at him face-to-face and touched him, but now, walking ahead of him, is not going to look back.

He hurries to follow the dark man, who is almost out of sight and who he understands must be his guide, for the place, though it is familiar to him, is changed. Though he can see ahead to where his guide walks, the ground underfoot is dark, seeming not to exist until his foot touches it. He follows the dark man along the narrow ancient track in the almost dark, as when he was a boy he followed older hunters in the woods at night, Burley Coulter and Elton Penn and the Rowanberrys, men who knew the way, who *were* the way of the places they led him through.

The trees on the hillside are large and old, as if centuries have passed since Andy was last here. It is growing rapidly lighter. Daylight is in the sky now, and against it, still in shadow, Andy can see the small new foliage of the great trees, the white and yellow and blue of the flowers, and birdsong fills the sky over the woods with a joy that welcomes the light and is like light.

And now above and beyond the birds' song, Andy hears a more distant singing, whether of voices or instruments, sounds or words, he cannot tell. It is at first faint, and then stronger, filling the sky and touching the ground, and the birds answer it. He understands presently that he is hearing the light; he is hearing the sun, which now has risen, though from the valley it is not yet visible. The light's music resounds and shines in the air and over the countryside, drawing everything into the infinite, sensed but mysterious pattern of its harmony. From every tree and leaf, grass blade, stone, bird, and beast, it is answered and again answers. The creatures sing back their names. But more than their names. They sing their being. The world sings. The sky sings back. It is one song, the song of the many members of one love, the whole song sung and to be sung, resounding, in each of its moments. And it is light.

He would stop, he would stop to stand and listen, or to stay forever, for he knows now that he has entered the eternal place in which we live in time, but the dark man, the dark man giving light, does not stop. He steps on up the hill road, and he does not look back.

Though the climb is longer than Andy remembers, even in its strangeness it is familiar. They go up beneath the great-girthed outspreading trees beside the stream of water coming down, the light glancing and singing off the little falls. As they climb, the music grows steadily stronger and brighter around them. The sun has come over the hill and is shining into the valley now. The shiver that stretched out in Andy's body when the dark man touched him has stayed in it. He is full of joy and he is afraid. He expects to die, and yet he lives, stepping on and on over the dry leaves and the little trembling flowers.

Finally the road brings them up, out from under the trees, onto the high part of the upland. And here the dark man does stop, and Andy stops, nearer to him than he has been before, but still several steps behind.

The dark man points ahead of them; Andy looks and sees the town and the fields around it, Port William and its countryside as he never saw or dreamed them, the signs everywhere upon them of the care of a longer love than any who have lived there have ever imagined. The houses are clean and white, and great trees stand among them and spread over them. The fields lie around the town, divided by rows of such trees as stand in the town and in the woods, each field more beautiful than all the rest. Over town and fields the one great song sings, and is answered everywhere; every leaf and flower and grass blade sings. And in the fields and the town, walking, standing, or sitting under the trees, resting and talking together in the peace of a sabbath profound and bright, are people of such beauty that he weeps to see them. He sees that these are the membership of one another and of the place and of the song or light in which they live and move.

He sees that they are the dead, and they are alive. He sees that he lives in eternity as he lives in time, and nothing is lost. Among the people of that town, he sees men and women he remembers, and men and women remembered in memories he remembers, and they do not look as he ever saw or imagined them. The young are no longer young, nor the old old. They appear as children corrected and clarified; they have the luminous vividness of new grass after fire. And yet they are mature as ripe fruit. And yet they are flowers.

He would go to them, but another movement of his guide's hand shows him that he must not. He must go no closer. He is not to stay. Grieved as he may be to leave them, he must leave. He *wants* to leave. He must go back with his help, such as it is, and offer it.

He has come into the presence of these living by a change of sight, by which he has parted from them as they were and from himself as he was and is.

Now he prepares to leave them. Their names singing in his mind, he lifts toward them the restored right hand of his joy.

A World Lost

The dead rise and walk about
The timeless fields of thought.

1

It was early July, bright and hot; I was staying with my grandmother and grandfather Catlett. My brother, Henry — who might have been there with me; we often made our family visits together — was at home at our house down at Hargrave. For several good and selfish reasons, I did not regret his absence. When we were apart we did not fight, we did not have to decide who would get what we both wanted, we did not have to trump up disagreements just to keep from agreeing. The day would come when there would be harmony between us and we would be allies, but we had many a trifle to quarrel over before then.

Uncle Andrew, who often ate dinner at Grandma Catlett's, was at work up on the river at Stoneport, as he had been for a week already. He had refused to take me with him. This was in the summer of 1944, when I was nine, nearly ten. The war had made building materials scarce. My father and Uncle Andrew, along with Uncle Andrew's buddies, Yeager Stump and Buster Simms, had bought the buildings of a defunct lead mine at Stoneport with the idea of salvaging the lumber and sheet metal to build some barns. The work was heavy and somewhat dangerous; it was going to take a long time. I could not go because I was too short in the push-up. I felt a little blemished by Uncle Andrew's refusal, and I missed him. Now and again I experienced the tremor of my belief that the adventure of Stoneport had been subtracted from me forever. But I was reconciled. As I was well aware, there were advantages to my solitude.

No day at Grandma and Grandpa's was ever the same as any other, but there were certain usages that I tried to follow, especially when I was there alone. That afternoon, as soon as I could escape attention, I knew I would go across the field to Fred Brightleaf's. Fred and I would catch Rufus Brightleaf's past-work old draft horse, Prince, and ride him over to the pond for a swim. And after supper, when Grandma and Grandpa would be content just to sit on the front porch in the dark, and you could feel the place growing lonesome for other times, I would drift away down to the little house beside the woods where Dick Watson and Aunt Sarah Jane lived. While the light drained from the sky and night fell I would sit with Dick on the rock steps in front of the door and listen to him tell of the horses and mules and foxhounds he remembered, while Aunt Sarah Jane spoke biblical admonitions from the lamplit room behind us; to her, Judgment Day was as much a matter of fact, and as visible, as the Fourth of July.

I was comfortable with the two of them as I was with nobody else, and I am unsure why. It was not because, as a white child, I was free or privileged with them, for they expected and sometimes required decent behavior of me, like the other grown-ups I knew. They had not many possessions, and the simplicity in that may have appealed to me; they did not spend much time in anxiety about *things*. They had too a quietness that was not passive but profound. Dick especially had the gift of meditativeness. Because he was getting old, what he meditated on was the past. In his talk he dreamed us back into the presence of a supreme work mule named Fanny, a preeminent foxhound by the name of Strive, a long-running and uncatchable fox.

There had been, anyhow, only three of us at the table in Grandma's kitchen that noon: Grandma and Grandpa and me. After dinner, Grandpa got up and went straight back to the barn. I sat on at the table, liking the stillness that filled the old house at such times. The whole world seemed stopped and quiet, as if the sun stood still a moment between its rising up and its going down; you could hear the emptiness of the rooms where nobody was. And then Grandma set the dishpan on the stove and started scraping up our dishes. She had her mind on her work then, and I headed for the door.

"Where are you off to, Andy, old traveler?"

"Just out," I said.

She let me go without even a warning. The good old kitchen sounds were rising up around her. As I went out across the porch I heard her start humming "Rock of Ages." When she was young she had been a good singer, but her voice was cracked now and she could not sustain the notes.

I went down through the field we still called the Orchard, though only one old apple tree was left, and then into the Lower Field, across the part of it that had been cut for hay, and then followed the dusty two-track road around the edge of a field of corn. I saw the groundhog that I planned to shoot as soon as I got old enough to have a .22 rifle. Grandma always put dinner on the table at eleven-thirty, and so it was still close to noon. My shadow was almost underfoot, and I amused myself by stepping on its head as I went along. I was wearing a coarse-woven straw hat that Uncle Andrew had bought for me, calling it "a two-gallon hat, plenty good for a half-pint." The sun shone through holes in the brim in a few places, making little stars in the shadow. I walked fast, telling myself the story of myself: "The boy is walking across the farm. He is by himself. Nobody knows where he is going. It is a pretty day."

On the far side of the cornfield I went through a gate into the creek road and then through another gate into the lane that went up to the Brightleafs' house. There was a row of tall Lombardy poplars that somebody had planted along the little stream that flowed from the Chatham Spring. When I got into the shadow of the first poplar I stopped and called, "Oh, Fred!"

Nobody answered. All around it was quiet. I walked the stepping-stones across the stream and went up to the house, knowing already that nobody was home but not wanting to believe it. I went all the way up to the yard fence and called again. It was a fact. Nobody was there, except for Jess Brightleaf's old bird dog, Fern, who had a litter of pups under the front porch, and Mrs. Brightleaf's old hens who looked at me from their dust holes under the snowball bush and did not get up. It was hot and sweaty, the kind of afternoon that makes you think of water.

Everybody was gone, and for a minute or two I felt disappointed and lonesome. But then the quiet changed, and I ceased to mind. All at once the countryside felt big and easy around me, and I was glad to be alone in it.

I looked at the sugar pear tree, but no pears were ripe yet, and I went on down to the spring. Some of the Chathams had lived there once and had left their name with the good vein of water that flowed from the bedrock at the foot of the hill. But the Chathams probably had not called it the Chatham Spring; probably they had called it after somebody who had been there before — maybe after an Indian, I thought. People named springs after other people, not themselves.

The Chatham Spring was cunningly walled and roofed with rock. There was a wooden door that you opened into a little room, moist and dark, where the vein flowed out of the hill into a pool deep enough for the Brightleafs to dip their buckets. The water flowed out of the pool under a large foot-worn rock that was the threshold of the door. The Brightleafs carried all their household water from the spring.

I opened the door. When my eyes had accepted the dimness I could see the water striders' feet dimpling the surface of the pool and a green frog on a glistening ledge just above the water. I fastened the door and lay down outside at the place I liked best to drink, which was just below the threshold stone where the water was flowing and yet so smooth that it held a piece of the sky in it as still and bright as a set in a ring. The water was so clear you could look down through the reflection of the sky or your face and see maybe a crawfish. I took my hat off and drank big swallows, relishing the coldness of the water and the taste it carried up from the deep rock and the darkness inside the hill. As I drank, the light lay warm on my back like a hand, and I could smell the mint that grew along the stream. When I had drunk all I could hold I put my nose into the water, and then my whole face.

The Chatham Spring had never been dry, not even in the terrible summers of 1908 and 1930 and 1936. People spoke of it as "an everlasting spring." There was a line of such springs lying across that part of the country, and all of them had been cared for a long time and bore the names of families: Chatham and Beechum and Branch and Bower and Coulter. There were days, I knew, when my Grandfather Catlett would ride horseback from one to the other, arriving at each one thirsty, to drink, savor, and reflect on the different tastes of the different waters, those thirsts and quenchings, tastes and differences being signs of something he profoundly knew. And I, as I drank and wetted my face, thought of the springs and of him, my mind leaning back out of the light and into time.

❦

From the spring I went back to the creek road and across and through another gate and up the long slope of an unclipped pasture. I could see my grandfather's steers gone to shade in a grove of locust trees on up the creek. I walked a while through the ripened bluegrass stems and the clover and Queen Anne's lace, and then I came to a path that led up to a gate at the top of the ridge. There was a fairly fresh manure pile in the path, and I stopped to watch two tumblebugs at work. They shaped their ball, rolled it onto the path, and started down the hill with it, the one in front walking on its forelegs and tugging the ball along with its hind legs, the one in the back walking on its hind legs and pushing the ball with its forelegs. For a while I lost myself in poking around on my hands and knees, looking at the other small creatures who lived in the grass: the ants, the beetles, the worms, the butterflies who sought the manure piles or the flowers, the bees that were working in the clover. Snakes lived in the field too, and rabbits and mice and meadowlarks and sparrows and bobwhites, but I wasn't so likely to come upon those by crawling around and parting the grass with my hands.

After a while I went on up to the gate, and through it, and across the ridge to the pond. That field was the one we called the Pond Field. Grandpa said that when he took over the farm as a young man, that field had been ill used and there were many gullies in it. He had made the pond by working back and forth across a big sinkhole, first with a breaking plow, and then with a slip-scraper in which he hauled the loosened earth to the gullies and filled them. And thus he restored the field at the same time that he dug the pond. A breeze was moving over the pond, covering the surface with little shards and splinters of blue sky. I shucked off my sweaty clothes and laid them in the grass.

Fred Brightleaf and Henry and I were absolutely forbidden to swim in the pond, or anyplace else, without a grownup along. We were absolutely, absolutely forbidden to go swimming alone, without at least another boy on hand to tell where we had drowned. My poor mother, terrified by my transgressions, attempted to keep me alive until grown by a remedy known in our family as "peach tree tea"—a peach (or lilac) switch applied vigorously to the shanks of the legs. This caustic medication inflicted great suffering on me and on her, and produced not the slightest correction in my behavior. If she had been able to whip me *while* I was swimming, then the pain might have overridden the pleasure and destroyed my willfulness. But since her punishment was necessarily distant from my immersions, the pleasure outweighed the pain and lasted longer. Back there at the pond by myself I could maintain for at least a while the illusion that I was no more than myself, Andy Catlett, as ancestorless as the first creature, neither the son of Bess and Wheeler Catlett nor the grandson of Dorie and Marce Catlett and Mat and Margaret Feltner.

I crossed the rim of deep cattle tracks at the edge of the pond and waded in, feeling the muddy bottom grow soft and miry underfoot. When I was in knee-deep I launched myself flat out, smacked down, went under, came up, and swam my best overhand stroke out toward the middle. If Fred and Henry had been there we would have raced. Being alone, I took my time. When I got out to the deep place I sucked in a big breath and dived. Way down where the water was black and cold it was revealed to me that if I drowned before I lived to be grown I would be sorry, and I kicked and stroked at the dark, watching the water brighten until my head broke out into daylight and air again.

I swam back into shallow water. This partial concession to my mother's fears made me feel absolved without confession, forgiven without regret. I turned over on my back and floated for a long time. Looked at from so near the surface of the pond, the sky was huge, the world almost nothing at all, and I apparently absent altogether. The sky seemed a great gape of vision, without the complication of so much as an eye. Now and then a butterfly or a snake doctor or a bird would fly across and I would watch it. But what really fascinated and satisfied me were the birds high up that, after you had looked into the sky a while, just appeared or were just there: a hawk soaring, maybe, or a swift or a swallow darting about.

There were three joys of swimming. The first was going down out of the hot air into the cooling water. The second was being in the water. The third was coming out again. After I was cooled and quiet, a little tired, and had begun to dislike the way my fingertips had wrinkled, I waded out into the breeze that was chilly now on my wet skin. I stood in the grass and let the breeze dry me, shivering a little until I felt the warmth of the sun. And maybe the best joy of all, a fourth, was the familiar feeling of my clothes when I put them on again.

For a long time then I just sat in the grass, feeling clean and content, thinking perhaps of nothing at all. I was nine years old, going on ten; having never needed to ask, I knew exactly where I was; I did not want to be anyplace else.

2

What moved me finally was hunger. I thought of the bowl of cold biscuits that Grandma kept covered with a plate in the dish cabinet. If she was in the kitchen when I got there, she would butter me two and fill them with jam. If she was not in the kitchen, I would just take two or three from the bowl and eat them as they were, and that would be good enough.

When I came over the ridge behind the house and barns and started down toward the lot gate, I was pretending to be a show horse. Our father had taken Henry and me to the Shelby County Fair not long before. We had watched the horse show in the old round wooden arena, and I had brought home a program that I read over and over to savor the fine names of the horses. And often when I was out by myself I did the gaits.

It was not apparent to me how a two-legged creature could perform the slow gait or rack, but I could do very credible versions, I thought, of the walk, trot, and canter. And so I was a three-gaited horse, light sorrel, very fine in my conformation and motion and style. And I was the rider of the horse I was. And I was the announcer who said, "Ladies and gentlemen, please ask your horses to canter."

I saw my grandfather then. He was on Rose, his bay mare, coming around the corner of the barn toward the lot gate. He let himself through the gate and shut it again without dismounting, and started up the rise toward me. He was eighty that summer; his walking cane hung by its crook from his right forearm. He had the mare in a brisk running walk.

From where I watched, except for the cane, you would have thought him no older than my father. Afoot, he was clearly an old man; on horseback he recovered something of the force and grace of his younger days, and you could see what he had been. He rode as a man rides who has forgotten he is on a horse.

As we drew near to each other, I slowed to a walk and then changed to a trot, which I thought my best gait, wanting him to be pleased. But his countenance, set and stern as it often was, did not change. He reined the mare in only a little.

"Baby, go yonder to the house. Your daddy wants you."

"Why?" I knew he wouldn't tell me, but I asked anyhow.

"Ne' mind! He wants to talk to you."

He put his heel to the mare and went by and on up toward the ridgetop. He rode looking straight ahead. The wind carried the mare's tail out a little to the side and snatched puffs of dust from her footfalls. I watched until first the mare and then he went out of sight over the ridge.

I did not enjoy transactions that began "Your daddy wants to talk to you." I did not cherish the solemn precincts of the grown-up world in which such transactions took place. But I had no choice now, having heard, and I went on to the house. In my guilt I supposed my father had somehow learned of my trip to the pond.

There was nobody in the kitchen; it was quiet; a cloth was spread over the dishes on the table; the afternoon sunlight came into the room through the open pantry door. I went through the back hall to the front of the house. When I came into the living room I was surprised to see Cousin Thelma there, dressed up. She was Grandma's sister's child, about my father's age, forty-five or so. She and my father were sitting in rocking chairs, talking quietly. I do not know where my grandmother was.

When I opened the door my father and Cousin Thelma quit talking. Cousin Thelma smiled at me and said, "Hello, Andy, my sweet."

My father smiled at me too, but he did not say anything. He stood, held out his hand to me, and I took it. He led me out into the hall and up the stairs.

And I remember how terribly I did not want to go. I had come in out of the great free outdoor world of my childhood—the world in which, in my childish fantasies, I hoped someday to be a man. But my father, even more than my mother with her peach switch, was the messenger of another world, in which, as I unwillingly knew, I was already involved in expectation and obligation, difficulty and sorrow. It was as if I knew this even from my father's smile, from the very touch of his hand. Later I would understand how surely even then he had begun to lead me to some of the world's truest pleasures, but I was far from such understanding then.

We went back to the room over the dining room. My father shut the door soundlessly and sat down on the bed. I stood in front of him. He was still holding my hand, as though it were something he had picked up and forgotten to put down.

"Andy," he said, "Uncle Andrew was badly hurt this afternoon. A fellow shot him. I want you to understand. It may be he won't be able to live."

He was looking straight at me, and I saw something in his eyes I never had seen there before: fear—fear and grief. For what I felt then I had, and have, no name. It was something like embarrassment, as if I had blundered into knowledge that was forbidden to small boys. I knew the disturbance my father had felt in imparting it to me; this made me feel that something was required of me, and I did not know what. That Uncle Andrew was a man who could be shot had not occurred to me before, but I could not say that.

What I said sounded to me as odd and inane, probably, as anything else I might have said: "Where did he get shot?"

"Down at Stoneport."

"I mean where did he get hit?"

"Once above the belt and once below." And my father touched his own belly in the places of Uncle Andrew's wounds. Now, when I remember, it sometimes seems to me that he touched those places on my own belly—certainly, in the years to come, I would touch them myself—and perhaps he did. "Here," he said, "and here."

"Did you see him?"

"Yes. I've been to the hospital, and I saw him."

"What did he say?" I was trying, I think, to call him back, not from death, but from strangeness, the terrible distinction of his hurt, into which he was now withdrawn.

"He said a fellow shot him."

And I did then have at least the glimpse of a vision of Uncle Andrew lying on a bed, saying such words to my father who stood beside him.

What more we said and how we left that room I do not remember.

Now I know that my father led me away to keep me, in my first knowledge of what had happened, away from Grandma in her first knowledge of it — as if to reduce grief by dividing it. Also I think he was moved by a hopeless instinct to protect me, to shield me from the very thing he had to tell me, before which he was himself helpless and unprotected.

⚜

Somehow I got out of the house again. As I stepped around the corner of the back porch, Jarrat Coulter and Dick Watson drove up to the barn lot gate in Cousin Jarrat's scratched and dusty car. They had been to town to get Grandpa's broken hay rope spliced; there was hay to be put up the next day.

I ran to greet them. Both of them were my friends, and I was happy to see them. I needed something ordinary to happen.

They were looking out at me, smiling. Ordinarily Cousin Jarrat would have said, "Andy, how about opening the gate, old bud?"

But I violated my own wish for the ordinary by stepping up on the running board and announcing, "Uncle Andrew got shot."

They had already heard — I could see that they had — but in their confusion they pretended that they had not.

Dick said nothing, and Cousin Jarrat said, "Aw! Is that a fact? Well!"

And then the day seemed to collapse around me into what it had become. There was no place where what had happened had not happened.

⚜

Later, I remember, I was standing in the little pantry off the kitchen, watching my grandmother at work. In the pantry was the table covered by a broken marble dresser-top where she rolled out the dough for biscuits or pie crusts, and so she must have been making biscuits or a pie, though it is not clear to me why she should have been doing that at such a time. I suppose that, in her trouble, she had needed to put herself to work. Perhaps she thought she was distracting or comforting me. She knew at least how I loved to watch her at work there, especially when she made pies: rolling out the dough for the bottom crust and pressing it into the pan, pouring in the filling, crisscrossing the long strips of dough over the top, and then holding the pan on the fingertips of her left hand while she stroked a knife around the edge, cutting off the overhanging bits of dough.

The sun, getting low, shone in at the one window of the pantry, and everything it touched gleamed a rich reddish gold. I stood at her elbow, as I had done many times, and watched and we talked, about what I cannot imagine. My father must have been gone for some time. Cousin Thelma, if she was still there, was in the living room. My grandfather had not returned.

And then my other grandfather, Mat Feltner, rapped at the kitchen door and came in. He had come, he said, to take me home. I remember him and Grandma smiling, speaking pleasantly, looking down at me.

I followed my grandfather out to his car. We got in and started down toward Hargrave. We had gone maybe two miles when Granddaddy, who had driven so far in silence, laid his hand on my knee, as he would do sometimes, and said, "Hon, your uncle Andrew is dead. He died about five o'clock."

I did not reply, and he said no more. He was a comforting man to be with. Perhaps that was enough.

The sun was down by the time we got to Hargrave. Granddaddy pulled up in front of our house, and I got out. Where he went then, I do not know.

Henry and our friends Tim and Bubby Kentfield and Noah Burk were standing in the front yard. They gathered around me.

"Uncle Andrew got killed," Henry said.

I said I knew it. They were all looking at me, solemn-faced and excited at the same time.

"I know it," I said. "Granddaddy told me."

There we were, all of us together as we often were, and yet changed, and none of us knew what to do.

"Well. What are we going to do?" Henry said.

"The man that killed him's name's Carp Harmon," Noah Burk said. "He shot him with a .38 pistol."

"Carp Harmon," I said.

"They got him in the jail right now."

I went on into the house — looking, I suppose, for something that was the same as before. But neither of my parents was in the house. Nor were my sisters. The kitchen was full of women who had come to help or bring food. They were putting things away, sort of taking over, the way they would do.

"Hello, Andy hon," they said. They gave me hugs. They were treating me like somebody special, which made them seem strange. And their presence in the house without at least my mother there made *it* seem strange.

Miss Iris Flynn said, "Honey, I loved your uncle Andrew. We'll miss him, won't we?" She bit her underlip and looked away.

Some of the others said things too. It was a little as though they wanted to ensure that their love would last by telling it to somebody young.

I wanted to be able to think of something proper to say. It came to me that if I had been a grown man I probably could have thought of something. I would have comforted them.

"Well, good-bye," I said. "I reckon I'm going outdoors." And I went out.

"Come on," Henry said. He was the youngest one of us, but nobody held back to argue. We all went out to the street and started down into town.

I don't know where any of our grown-ups were. They were somewhere else, struck down or disappeared. The streets were empty. It was late in the evening, a weekday, and everybody was at home, eating supper maybe, or getting ready for bed, or sitting on porches or in backyards, cooling off. But to us, to me at least, it seemed that the life of the town had drawn back and hushed in wonder and sorrow that Uncle Andrew was dead. It was as if the people withdrew and hid themselves in deference to us boys who used to devil Uncle Andrew to take us swimming, which he had sometimes done. In the warm, slowly dimming twilight, nothing was abroad in the town except the pigeons clapping their wings about the courthouse tower and our little band walking bunched together to the jail. Nobody saw us. It seems to me that, for the time being, not even a car passed. The river flowed solemnly by as if strictly minding its own business.

The jail adjoined the back of the courthouse, its tall stone-barred facade set back a little behind an iron fence. When we got there we just stopped and looked at it, as though at that moment an immense reality, that we would not be done with for a long time, first laid hold on us. Uncle Andrew had been killed. Somewhere inside the jail, only a few feet from us, was the man who had killed him. For a long time there was nothing to be done but stand there in the large silence and the failing light, and know and know the thing we knew.

And then, filling his eight-year-old voice with a bravado that astonished me and perhaps astonished him, Henry called out at the front of the jail and its padlocked iron door: "Carp Harmon, you son of a bitch, come out of there!"

After dark that night somebody took Henry and me to Granny and Granddaddy Feltner's house up at Port William. I do not know which of the grown-ups had decided that we would be better off there, but I am sure they were right. On the way to Port William we stopped at Grandma and Grandpa Catlett's, I suppose to let me get my extra clothes and whatever else I had left.

While we were there one of the grown-ups said to me, "Don't you think you ought to go speak to your grandma?" It would have been like my father to say that, and he may have been there, but I don't remember. It could have been Aunt Lizzie, Grandma's sister. This was fifty years ago, and I have forgotten some things. But I must have been too filled with astonishment and alarm even to have noticed some things that I wish now I could remember.

I remember climbing the stairs again, by myself this time, and going into the bedroom where my grandmother was. She was in the dark, alone. I could barely see her lying motionless on the old iron bed. Her stillness touches me yet. She seemed to lie beneath the violence that had, in striking Uncle Andrew, struck her and struck us all, and now she merely submitted to it, signifying to herself by her stillness that there was nothing at all that could be done.

What had happened to us could only be suffered now, and we would be suffering it a long time; I knew that as soon as I entered the room. I had been sent perhaps with the hope that seeing me might be of some comfort to her, but I remember how swiftly I knew that she could not be comforted. Comfortlessness had come and occupied the house. She had been felled, struck down, and there she was, greatly needing comfort where there was no comfort. I walked over to the bed and stood beside it.

She must have recognized my footsteps, for she said in a voice that I would not have recognized as hers if it had not come from her, "Oh, honey, we'll never see your Uncle Andrew again. We never will see him anymore."

※

Perhaps it was the next day that Henry and I, dressed in our Sunday clothes this time, were taken back to Hargrave, stopping again at Grandma and Grandpa Catlett's, why I do not know. It was a sunny morning. The hushed old house was occupied by the usual population of neighbors come to do what they could. I remember only my Grandfather Catlett sitting in the swing on the back porch, wearing his straw hat as he was apt to do even in the house, forgetting to take it off, his hands clasped over the crook of his cane. Cousin Thelma was sitting beside him. She was smiling, speaking to him with a wonderful attentiveness. He was trying, I remember, to respond in kind, and yet he could not free himself of his thoughts; you could tell it by his eyes.

When we got to our house at Hargrave we did not see our father and we did not see Aunt Judith, Uncle Andrew's wife. The house was full of flowers and quiet people, who got even quieter when they saw us. Our mother, smiling, met us at the door and welcomed us, almost as if we were guests, into the front room, which had been utterly changed to make way for the coffin that stood on its trestle against the wall farthest from the door.

Our mother led us over to the coffin and stood with us while we looked. Lying in the coffin, dressed up, his eyes shut and his hands still with the stillness of death, was Uncle Andrew. And so I knew for sure.

Henry and I seemed to be like people walking in what had been a forest after a terrific storm. Our grown-ups, who until then had stood protectingly over us, had fallen, or they were diminished by the simple, sudden presence of calamity. We seemed all at once to have become tall; it was not a pleasant distinction.

❧

We stayed at Port William in the care of Nettie Banion, Granny Feltner's cook, while Granny and Granddaddy and our aunt Hannah went to Hargrave for Uncle Andrew's funeral. When we heard the car returning into the driveway, we went around the house to meet them. Granny and Granddaddy greeted us as if it were just an ordinary day and we were there on an ordinary visit. It was a kind pretense that became almost a reality, something they were good at.

But Hannah, who was young and not yet skilled in grief, could not belie the actual day that it was. Tears came into her eyes when she saw us. Forcing herself to smile, she said, "Boys, he looked just like he was asleep."

Hannah was married to our Uncle Virgil, who was away in the war. She was beautiful, I thought, and I imagined that someday I might marry a woman just like her. She was always nice to Henry and me, and it was not just because she loved Uncle Virgil who loved us; she was nice to us because she loved us herself. I was far from seeing any comfort in what she said to us about Uncle Andrew; I knew he was in no ordinary sleep. But it was good of her to say it, and I knew that as well.

When all this happened I was younger almost than I can imagine now. It is hard for me to recall exactly what I felt. I think that I did not grieve in the knowing and somewhat theoretical way of grown people, who say to themselves, for example, that a death of some sort awaits us all, and who may have understood in part how the order of time is shaped and held within the order of eternity. I had no way of generalizing or conceptualizing my feelings. It seems to me now that I had no sympathy for myself.

Only once do I remember attempting in any outward or verbal way to own my loss. I admired a girl named Marian Davis who was in my room at school. One afternoon in the fall of the year of Uncle Andrew's death, we were walking home in the crowd of boys and girls that straggled out along the street. Marian was walking slightly in front of me. All at once it came to me that I might enlarge myself in her eyes by attaching to myself the tragedy that had befallen my family. I stepped up beside her and said, "Marian, I reckon you heard about Uncle Andrew." Perhaps she had not heard—that did not occur to me. I thought that she had heard but was dumbfounded by my clumsy attempt to squander my feelings; perhaps she even sensed that I was falsifying them in order to squander them. She pretended not to hear. She did not look at me. In her silence a fierce shame came upon me that did not wear away for years. I did not try again to speak of Uncle Andrew's death to anyone until I was grown.

Perhaps I did not grieve in the usual sense at all. The world that I knew had changed into a world that I knew only in part; perhaps I understood that I would not be able ever again to think of it as a known world. My awareness of my loss must have been beyond summary. It must have been exactly commensurate with what I had lost, and what I had lost was Uncle Andrew as I had known him, my life with Uncle Andrew. I had lost what I remembered.

4

I was Uncle Andrew's namesake, and I had come to be his buddy. "My boy," he would call me when he was under the influence not only of the considerable tenderness that was in him but of what I now know to have been bourbon whiskey.

When I first remember him, Uncle Andrew and Aunt Judith were living in Columbia, South Carolina, where Uncle Andrew was a traveling salesman for a hardware company. They came home usually once in the summer and again at Christmas. They would come by train, and my father would take Henry and me and go to meet them. When Aunt Judith came early and Uncle Andrew made the trip alone, he would not always arrive on the train we met. I remember standing with Henry on the station platform while our father hurriedly searched through the train on which Uncle Andrew was supposed to have arrived. I remember our disappointment, and our father's too brief explanation that Uncle Andrew must have missed the train, leaving us to suppose that when he missed it Uncle Andrew had been breathlessly trying to catch it. In fact, he may have missed it by a very comfortable margin; he may have been in circumstances in which he did not remember that he had a train to catch.

His and Aunt Judith's arrival, anyhow, certainly made life more interesting for Henry and me. Aunt Judith, who was childless, was affectionate and indulgent—in need of our affection, as she was of everybody's, and willing to spoil us for it. Uncle Andrew was so unlike anybody else we knew as to seem a species of one. He was capable of adapting his speech and manners to present company if he wanted to, but he did not often want to. He talked to us boys as he talked to everybody else, and in that way he charmed us. To us, he seemed to exist always at the center of his own uproar, carrying on in a way that was restless, reckless, humorous, and loud. One Christmas — it must have been 1939 — Henry and I conceived the idea of giving him a cigarette tin filled with rusty nails. Our mother wrapped it prettily for us and put his name on it. A perfect actor, he received it with a large display first of gratitude and affection, and then, as he opened it, of curiosity, anticipation, surprise, indignation, and outrage. He administered a burlesque spanking and stomping to each of our "bee-hinds," as he called them, uttering throughout the performance a commentary of grunts, raspberries, and various profane exclamations. Thus he granted success to our trick.

At about that time his drinking seems to have become a problem again. My father, who could not rest in the presence of a problem — who in fact was possessed by visions of solutions — decided that Uncle Andrew should come home and farm. Borrowing the money, my father bought two farms, one that we continued to call the Mack Crayton Place about five miles from Hargrave, and another, the Will Bower Place, adjoining Grandma and Grandpa Catlett's place nearer to Port William. Uncle Andrew, according to the plan they made, would look after the farms while my father concentrated on his law practice. My father sent Uncle Andrew enough money to buy a 1940 Chevrolet, and Uncle Andrew and Aunt Judith came home. Uncle Andrew was then forty-five years old, five years older than my father.

That homecoming gave me a new calling and a new career. Uncle Andrew and Aunt Judith rented a small apartment in a house belonging to an old doctor in Hargrave. Uncle Andrew began his daily trips to the farms, and I began wanting to go with him. I was six years old, and going with him became virtually the ruling purpose of my life. When I was not in school or under some parental bondage, I was likely to be with him. On the days I went with him, the phone would ring at our house before anybody was up. I would run down the stairs, put the receiver to my ear, and Uncle Andrew's voice would say, "Come around, baby."

I would hang up without replying, get into my clothes as fast as I could, and hurry through the backstreets to the apartment, where Aunt Judith would have breakfast ready. She made wonderful plum jelly and she knew I liked it; often she would have it on the table for me. Uncle Andrew called coffee "java," and when Aunt Judith asked him how he wanted his eggs, he would say, "Two lookin' atcha!" singing it out, as he did all his jazzy slang.

To me, there was something exotic about the two of them and their apartment. I had never known anybody before who lived in an apartment; the idea had a flavor of urbanity that was new and strange to me. Uncle Andrew and Aunt Judith had lived in distant places, in cities, that they sometimes talked about. They had been to the South Carolina seashore, and Uncle Andrew had fished in Charleston Harbor. I had never seen the ocean and I loved to quiz them about it. Could you actually ride the waves? How did you do it? If you looked straight out over the ocean, how far could you see? I could not get enough of the thought that you could not see across it. Besides all that, Aunt Judith was the only woman I knew who smoked cigarettes, and this complicated the smell of her perfume in a way I rather liked.

We would eat breakfast and talk while the early morning brightened outside the kitchen window, and they would smoke, and Uncle Andrew would say, "Gimme one mo' cup of that java, Miss Judy-pooty."

Finally we would leave, and then began what always seemed to me the day's adventure; I knew more or less what to expect at breakfast, but when you were loose in the world with Uncle Andrew you did not know what to expect.

The Chevrolet was inclined to balk at the start, and Uncle Andrew would stomp the accelerator and stab the engine furiously with the choke. "That's right! Cough," he would say, stomping and stabbing, "you one-lunged son of a bitch!" And the car would buck out of the driveway and up the low rise like a young horse. He treated all machines as if they were recalcitrant and uncommonly stupid draft animals. When the car, under his abuse, finally learned its lesson and began to run smoothly, he would look over at me, screwing his face up and talking through his nose —in the style, probably, of some cabdriver he remembered: "Where to, college?"

"Oh," I would say, laughing, "up to the Crayton Place, I reckon."

Of the two farms, Uncle Andrew much preferred the Crayton Place, where Jake and Minnie Branch lived—and so, of course, I preferred it too. The Bower Place was perhaps a little too close to Grandpa Catlett's; also the tenant there, Jake Branch's brother, was a quiet, rather solitary man who thought mostly of keeping his two boys at work and of staying at work himself. But at the Crayton Place, what with Jake's children and Minnie's children and Jake's and Minnie's children and whichever two or three of Minnie's six brothers Jake had managed to lure in (or bail out of jail) as hired hands, together with the constant passing in and out of more distant relations, neighbors, and friends, there was always commotion, always the opportunity for talk and laughter and carrying on. Some rowdy joke or tale could get started there and go on for two or three days, retold and elaborated for every newcomer, restlessly egged on— over the noisy objections and denials of whoever was the butt of it—by pretended casual comments or questions asked in mock innocence. Minnie never knew the number she would feed at a meal. I have seen her put biscuits on the table in a wash pan, three dozen at a time.

❧

Perhaps Uncle Andrew had some affection for farming. He had, after all, been raised to it—or Grandpa, anyhow, had tried to raise him to it. But he was unlike his father and my father, for whom farming was a devotion and a longing; it was not a necessity of life to him. He saw to things, purchased harness and machine parts, did whatever was needed to keep men and teams and implements in working order, and helped out where help was needed. But what he really loved was company, talk, some kind of to-do, something to laugh at.

When our association began, I appointed myself his hired hand at a wage of a quarter a day. Since I was not big enough to do most of the jobs I wanted to do, I tended to spend the days in an uneasy search for something I could do to justify my pay. I served him mostly as a sort of page, running errands, carrying water, opening gates, handing him things. Occasionally he or Jake Branch would dignify me with a real job, sending me to the tobacco patch with a hoe or letting me drive a team on the hay-rake. But Uncle Andrew never let my wages become a settled issue. Sometimes he paid me willingly enough. Sometimes I would have to argue, beg, and bully to get him even to acknowledge that he had ever heard of the idea of paying me. When the subject came up in front of a third party, he would say, "It's worth a quarter a day just to have him with me." That confused me, for I treasured the compliment and yet felt that it devalued my "work."

One day when he and I were helping Jake Branch set tobacco on a stumpy hillside, a terrific downpour came upon us. R. T. and Ester Purlin, two of Minnie's children from her first marriage, and I were dropping the plants into previously marked rows, and the men were coming behind us, rapidly setting them in the rain-wet ground, all of us working barefoot to save our shoes. When the new hard shower suddenly began, we all ran to the shelter of the trees that grew along the hollow at the foot of the slope. Uncle Andrew and I stood beneath a sort of arbor made by a wild grapevine whose leaves had grown densely over the top of a small tree. For a while it was an almost perfect umbrella. And then, as the rain fell harder, the foliage began to leak. The day was chilly as well as wet, and Uncle Andrew was wearing a canvas hunting coat, which he now opened and spread like a hen's wing. "Here, baby," he said. I ducked under and he closed me in. For a long time I stood there, dark and dry in his warmth, in his mingled smell of sweat and pipe tobacco, while the rain fell hard around us and splattered on the ground at our feet.

In the winter when nightfall came early, he would often stop by our house as he was going home. He would come in and sit down. My father would lay aside the evening paper, and they would talk quietly and companionably, going over the stages of work on the farms, saying what had been done and what needed doing. Uncle Andrew would have on his winter clothes: an old felt hat, corduroys, the tan canvas hunting coat, and under that a lined suede jacket with a zipper. He would not take off his outdoor clothes because he was on his way to supper and did not intend to stay long. I would climb into his lap and make myself comfortable. Perhaps I appeared to be listening, but what I was really doing was smelling. There was the smell of Uncle Andrew himself, which was a constant and always both comforting and exciting, but on those evenings his clothes gave off also the cold smells of barns and animals, hay and tobacco, ground grain, wood smoke. Those smells charmed me utterly and saddened me, for they told me what I had missed by being in school.

"Take me with you in the morning," I would say.

And he would say, "Can't do it, college." Or, in another mood, he would give me a hug and a pat. "I wish I could, baby, but you got to go to school."

For children his term of endearment, which also was Grandpa's, was "baby." He called me that when he felt tender toward me, as he often did, nearly always when he was drinking but often too when he was not.

He might have wanted a boy of his own, I sometimes thought, and maybe I was the kind of boy he wanted. At school I took to signing myself "Andrew Catlett, Jr." Sometimes it seemed unfair to me that I was not his son. I wanted to be a man just like him.

I liked his rough way of joking and carrying on. Often when I showed up at his apartment, he would say in his nasal slang, "Hello, bozo! Gimme five!" And we would do a big handshake.

His term of emphatic agreement was "Yowza!" Or he would say, "Aw yeah!"—pronounced as one word: "Aw'eah!"—which was both affirmative and derisive. He could make one word perform lots of functions.

Anybody dead and buried, especially any of Aunt Judith's relatives, was "planted in the skull orchard."

Anybody licked or done in had been "nailed to the cross."

His threats to Henry and me, even when somewhat meant, were delivered with a burlesque of ferocity that made us laugh: "I'm going to stomp your bee-hind!" he would say. "I'm going to rap on your ding-dong! I'm going to cloud up and rain all over you! I'm going to get you down and work on you!"

He would sometimes put on Henry's or my straw hat, much too small for him, insert an old magnifying lens in his eye as a monocle, look at us, and say, "Redwood fer dittos, college!" What that meant I do not know; I don't know even if those are the right words. That was what it sounded like. Wearing the "monocle" and tiny-looking hat, speaking sentences imitated, I suppose, from somebody he had run across somewhere away, he could transform himself, sometimes a little scarily, into somebody we had never seen before. Leering and mouthing, carrying on an outrageous blather of profanity and nonsense, he could make us laugh until we were lying on the floor, purged, exhausted, aching, and still laughing.

We had a mongrel bull terrier bitch named Nosey that he did not especially care for. Somebody told us we ought to bob her tail. As we did with all out-of-the-way propositions, we laid this one before Uncle Andrew.

"Uncle Andrew, do you know how to cut off Nosey's tail?"

"Why, hell *yes!*" he said, opening his pocketknife, "I'll cut it off right behind her ears."

And then he mimed the whole procedure, whooping and making raspberries, laughing at himself, until it was funny even to us.

❧

Sometimes, for reasons unclear to us then, he would feel bad and need to sleep. In Jake Branch's yard under the big white oak, or in the woods at the Bower Place, or on the shady side of one or another of the barns, he would open both doors of the car, stretch out on the front seat, and sleep an hour or two, or all afternoon. I would be utterly mystified and even offended. How could anybody sleep when there were so many things to do?

Or Henry and I would bring Bubby Kentfield and Noah Burk and maybe two or three more around to the apartment on a Sunday afternoon and find him asleep on the couch.

We would tramp into the room in a body, like a delegation, assuming that if he was not in a good mood, we could get him into one. We believed that there was strength in numbers.

"Uncle Andrew, we was wondering if you'd take us swimming."

"Yeah, Uncle Andrew, we want to go to the quarry."

He would turn his head reluctantly and look at us. "Aw God, boys, you all don't need to go swimming."

"Yes, we do. It's hot."

"Well, go on then!"

"Well, we need you to go with us."

"No, you don't."

"Yes, we do. Mother said if you went, we could go."

"Suppose you drown."

"She thinks you won't let us drown."

"The hell I won't!"

"Well, are you coming?"

"Go on, now, damn it! Get out of here! Go do something else."

He would fold his hands and shut his eyes, the picture of hope defeated.

Sometimes he would be quiet and sad-seeming. Always at those times he sang the same song:

> Missed the Saturday dance
> Heard they crowded the floor
> Couldn't bear it without you
> Don't get around much anymore.

Was there, somewhere, a woman he missed, or was he mindful that he was getting older, or did he just like the song? He had a good voice, and he sang well.

※

For fifty years and more I have been asking myself, What was he? What manner of a man? For I have never been sure. There are things that I remember, things that I have heard, and things that I am able (a little) to imagine. But what he was seems always to be disappearing a step or two beyond my thoughts.

He was, for one thing, a man of extraordinary good looks. He had style, not as people of fashion have it (though he had the style of fashion when he wanted it), but as, for example, certain horses have it: a self-awareness so complete as to be almost perfectly unconscious, realized in acts rather than thoughts. He wore his clothes with that kind of style. He looked as good in work clothes, I thought, as he did dressed up. Clothes did not matter much to me, and yet I remember being proud to be with him when he was dressed up—in a light summer suit, say, and a straw boater—for I thought he looked better than anybody. He was a big man, six feet two inches tall and weighing a hundred and eighty pounds. He had a handsome, large-featured face with a certain fineness or sensitivity that suggested possibilities in him that he mainly ignored. His eyes, as Grandma loved to say, were "hazel," and they were very expressive, as responsive to thought as to sight. He loved ribaldry, raillery, impudence. He spoke at times a kind of poetry of vulgarity.

And yet there was something dark or troubled in him also, as though he foresaw his fate; I felt it even then. I have a memory of him with a certain set to his mouth and distance in his eyes, an expression of difficult acceptance, as if he were resigned to being himself, as if perhaps he saw what it would lead to. His silences, though never long, were sometimes solemn and preoccupied. When he was still in his twenties, his hair had begun to turn gray.

For another thing, he was as wild, probably, as any human I have ever known. He was a man, I think, who was responsive mainly to impulses: desire, affection, amusement, self-abandon, sometimes anger.

When he felt good, he would be laughing, joking, mocking, mimicking, singing, mouthing a whole repertory of subverbal noises. He would say — and as Yeager Stump later told me, he would do — anything he thought of. He would lounge, grinning, in his easy chair and talk outrageously, as if merely curious to hear what he might say.

I was in the third grade when the teachers at our school asked the students to ask their fathers to volunteer to build some seesaws on the playground. Henry and I, knowing our father would not spare the time, brought the matter before Uncle Andrew.

"Well, college," he said, "I'll take it under consideration. Tell all the women teachers to line up out by the road, and I'll drive by and look 'em over. It might be I could give 'em a little lift."

He had, I am sure, no intention of helping with the seesaws; he never had been interested in a school. But Henry, who was in the second grade, dutifully relayed the message to his teacher. I remember well the difficulty of hearing Henry's teacher repeat to my teacher Uncle Andrew's instructions. As I perfectly understood, our teachers' outrage was not necessarily contingent upon Henry's indiscretion; Uncle Andrew would have delivered his suggestion in person if the circumstances had been different and it had occurred to him to do so.

At times he seemed to be all energy, intolerant of restraint, unpredictable. His presence, for so small a boy as I was, was like that of some large male animal who might behave as expected one moment and the next do something completely unforeseen and astonishing.

One morning we went to the Bower Place only to find Charlie Branch stalled for want of a mowing machine part. We started back to Hargrave to get the part, Uncle Andrew driving complacently along at the wartime speed limit, and I chinning the dashboard as usual. We got to a place where the road went down through a shallow cut with steep banks on both sides, and all of a sudden Chumpy and Grover Corvin stepped into the road in front of us. Chumpy and Grover were just big teenage boys then, but they were already known as outlaws and bullies; a lot of people were afraid of them. They wanted a ride, and by stepping into the road they meant to force Uncle Andrew to stop. What he did was clap the accelerator to the floor and drive straight at them. His response was as instantaneous and all-out as that of a kicking horse. He ran them out of the road and up the bank, cutting away at the last split second. We drove on as before. He did not say a word.

5

While Uncle Andrew farmed and did whatever else he did, Aunt Judith and her mother busied themselves with the care and maintenance of the Hargrave upper crust. Aunt Judith's mother had been born a Hargrave, a descendant of the Hargrave for whom the town was named, and so Aunt Judith was virtually a Hargrave herself. By blood she was only a quarter Hargrave, but by disposition and indoctrination she was 100 percent, as her mother expected and perhaps required. The two of them belonged to the tightly drawn little circle (almost a knot) of the female scions of the first families of Hargrave — a complex cousinship that preserved and commended itself in an endless succession of afternoon bridge parties. At these functions everybody was "cud'n" somebody: Cud'n Anne, Cud'n Nancy, Cud'n Charlotte, Cud'n Phoebe, and so on. Theirs was an exclusive small enclosure that one could not enter or leave except by birth and death. My mother, for example, was excluded for the original sin of having been born in Port William — an exclusion which I believe she understood as an escape.

This feminine inner circle had of course a masculine outer circle to which Uncle Andrew pertained by marriage and in which he participated (being incapable of silence, let alone deference) by snorts, hoots, spoofs, jokes, and other blasphemies. He was particularly intrigued by the fervent cousinship of the little class that he had wedded, and he loved to enlarge it by addressing as "cud'n" or "cuz" any bootblack, barfly, yardman, panhandler, dishwasher, porter, or janitor he happened to encounter in the presence of his wife and mother-in-law. His favorite name for Aunt Judith was "Miss Judy-pooty," but he also called her "Cud'n Pud'n." Her mother he named "Miz Gotrocks" in mockery of her love of elaborate costume jewelry and big hats, and her little pair of pinch-nose glasses on a silver chain. But he also called her, as occasion required, "Cud'n Mothah" and "Momma-pie." The latter name, because we children picked it up from him, was what everybody in our family came to call her.

Aunt Judith, as I judge from a set of photographs that used to hang in Momma-pie's bedroom, had been a pretty girl. She was an only child, raised by her divorced mother, who had been an only daughter. Aunt Judith and Momma-pie were a better matched pair than Aunt Judith and Uncle Andrew. Aunt Judith had grown up in the protective enclosure prescribed by Momma-pie's status and character; Uncle Andrew had grown up in no enclosure that he could get out of. That the two of them married young and in error is plain fact. Why they got married — or, rather, why Uncle Andrew married Aunt Judith — is a question my father puzzled over in considerable exasperation for the rest of his life. He always reverted to the same theory: that Momma-pie had insidiously contrived it. A mantrap had been cunningly set and baited with the perhaps tempting virginity of Aunt Judith — and Uncle Andrew, his mind diverted to other territory, had obliged by inserting his foot. Maybe so.

Maybe so. If the theory was ever provable — and my father had no proof — the chance is long gone by now. But a story that Mary Penn told me, after I had grown up, suggests at least that Uncle Andrew was not an ecstatic bridegroom. One of Mary's cousins, a schoolmate of Uncle Andrew's, told her that on the night before his wedding Uncle Andrew got drunk and fell into a road ditch. His friends gathered around, trying to help him up.

"Aw, boys," he said, "just leave me be. When I think of what I've got to lay with tomorrow night, I'd just as soon lay here in this ditch."

He had seen his fate, and named it, and yet accepted it. Why?

However their marriage began, whatever its explanation, their unlikenesses were profound. The second mystery of their union was set forth as follows by my mother: "Did your Aunt Judith have so many health problems because your Uncle Andrew drank and ran around with other women, or did your Uncle Andrew drink and run around with other women because your Aunt Judith had so many health problems?" The answer to that question too, assuming that anybody ever knew it, has been long in the grave.

The question, anyhow, states their condition accurately enough. Aunt Judith did have a lot of health problems, some of which were very painful. Since no doctor ever found a cause or a remedy for most of them, it seems that the cause must have been in her mind, which is to say in her marriage. And perhaps also in her relationship to Momma-pie. My mother remembers that Aunt Judith never said anything without looking at Momma-pie to see if it was all right. But if Aunt Judith lived in some fear of Momma-pie, I am sure that she lived also in surprise, bewilderment, and dismay at Uncle Andrew, whom she nevertheless adored.

Sometimes Uncle Andrew could be sympathetic and tender with Aunt Judith, sorry for her sufferings, worried about her, anxious to help her solve her problems. Sometimes, unable to meet her demands for attention or sympathy with the required response, he met them instead with derision. Sometimes, I imagine, he was contrite about his offenses against her and wished to do better. But as they both surely had learned beyond unlearning or pretense, the time would invariably come when, under the spell of an impulse, he would fling her away. He would fling her away as a flying swallow flings away its shadow.

Aunt Judith always asked you for affection before you could give it. For that reason she always needed more affection than she got. She would drain the world of affection, and then, fearing that it had been given only because she had asked for it, she would have to ask for more.

"Sugah," she would say to whichever of us children had come in sight, "come here and kiss yo' Aunt Judith!" And she was capable of issuing this invitation with the broad hint that, because of her frail health, the grave might claim her before we would have a chance to kiss her again. I am glad to remember that, in spite of everything, I felt a genuine affection for her, especially in the time before Uncle Andrew's death — before fate authenticated her predisposition to woe. In those days she could be a pleasant companion for a small boy, and I remember afternoons when we sat together while she read to me from the evening paper a reporter's serialized account of the movement of a group of soldiers from training camp to troopship to battle. We both became deeply interested in those articles and looked forward to them. I remember how our reading fitted together our interest in the story of the soldiers, our sense of great history unfolding, and our mutual affection and pleasure. And yet when she turned toward me with her need, as sooner or later she always did, it was hard to provide a response satisfactory to either of us. It is hard to give the final kiss of this earthly life over and over again. Mostly I submitted silently to her hugs, kisses, and other attentions, profiting the best I could from that exotic smell of cigarette smoke and perfume that hung about her.

Her tone of self-reference almost always carried an overtone of self-pity. She asked for pity as she asked for affection—and her demand, as was inevitable in that hopeless emotional economy of hers, always outran the available supply. As she strove forward with her various claims on other people, she more and more destroyed the possibility of a genuine mutuality with anybody. Her need for love isolated and estranged her from everybody who might have loved her, and from everybody who did.

In her self-centeredness and her constant appeal to others to fulfill her unfulfillable needs, she was like Momma-pie. Both of them, I think, belonged to a lineage of spoiled women. From the time of her divorce, Momma-pie had lived with her expansive pretensions in a small room at the Broadfield Hotel on the income from a moderately good farm that she had never seen except from the road. During her life at the hotel she did nothing for herself except for the light and polite housekeeping of her room. Aunt Judith was a fastidious housekeeper and a good cook—she and Uncle Andrew had never had the money for household help—but her work always bore the implication of her poor health, and hints were often passed between her and Momma-pie that whatever she did she was not quite able to do.

The would-be aristocracy of the Hargrave upper crust was, after all, I think, a cruel burden for Aunt Judith and Momma-pie. According to the terms that they accepted and lived by, they were important because they were who they were. That was their axiom. And so there they were, suspended in the ethereal element of their pretension, utterly estranged from the farms and the work from which they lived, hard put to demonstrate their usefulness to much of anybody, and forced to bear the repeated proofs that Uncle Andrew assumed almost nothing that they assumed.

It is pleasant and useless to wonder what might have become of Aunt

Judith if she had married a milder, more tractable man, just as it is pleasant and useless to wonder what might have become of Uncle Andrew if
he had married a more robust and self-sustaining woman. Such might-
have-beens only renew the notice that Aunt Judith and Uncle Andrew
married each other, and in doing so joined snow and fire.

Uncle Andrew, except that he possessed "aristocratic good looks,"
could not have been anyone that Aunt Judith ever saw in her girlhood
dreams. She must have seen him simply as she wanted to see him: a young
man handsome as a prince, who would make her the envy of other girls.
She must have imagined herself and him as "a beautiful couple." To
Momma-pie — assuming that my father's theory of artful entrapment
was correct — he must have seemed "an excellent prospect," good raw
material in need of polish. If in fact they captured him, then they captured a bull in a henhouse. He was, as undoubtedly he already knew or
soon found out, the very reality that their not-altogether-pretended feminine delicacy was least disposed to recognize. And now they were
obliged to try to contain him in an enclosure prepared for another kind
of creature. He was, whatever else he was, a man of his own time and
place. He honored to some extent the conventions of his capture; he was
capable of affection, sympathy, and regret. Though his confinement did
not exist except when he submitted to it, sometimes he submitted to it.
But he could not be held. It was not so much that he resisted or defied or
rebelled against his bondage; he simply overflowed it. When he filled to
his own fullness, he overflowed his confines as a rising river overflows its
banks, making nothing of the boundaries and barriers that stand in its
way.

The three of them made their daily lives, formed and followed their
routines, made things ordinary and bearable for themselves. Their
strange convergence was not a perpetual crisis. But it was nonetheless
hopeless. They were two almost forceless women entangled past untan-
gling with an almost ungentled man. He of course was as spoiled in his
way as they were in theirs. They had been spoiled by generations of men
who had indulged and promoted their helplessness; he had been spoiled
by women who had allowed him to charm them into acceptance of his
inborn unstoppability. Aunt Judith and Momma-pie had spoiled him
themselves, as I think all the women in his life had done. They were under

his spell, as much caught by him as he by them. They could not contain him, but they could not expel him either.

The best friend he had, I am certain, was my father, who loved him completely. But my father, purposeful and tireless, sober and passionate, in love with his family and his work, true to his obligations, could not have been Uncle Andrew's crony. They could be friends within the terms of brotherhood and partnership, but partly perhaps because he was Uncle Andrew's brother, my father was not wild; the whole budget of Catlett wildness in that generation had been allotted to Uncle Andrew. For cronies, Uncle Andrew had Buster Simms and Yeager Stump.

In his look and laugh and way of talking, Buster Simms gleefully acknowledged the world's lewdness. He was a freckled, smallish, quick-eyed man whose conversation tended to be all in tones of joking, from aggressive to kind. He called Uncle Andrew "Duke." Yeager Stump was a tall, good-looking man of somewhat the same style as Uncle Andrew. Of the three, he was the quietest. You could see in the wrinkly corners of his eyes that he was always waiting to be amused, and was being amused while he waited. Of the three, he was the only one who lived to be old.

All three felt themselves too straitly confined in marriage, and they escaped into each other's company. Or rather, each other's company was their freedom that, spent or hung over, they allowed themselves to be recaptured out of, as Samson allowed himself to be bound with seven green withes that were never dried.

"We did everything we thought of," Yeager Stump would say later. "Our only limit was our imagination."

They called each other "Cud'n Andrew" and "Cud'n Bustah" and "Cud'n Yeagah"—for ordinary use abbreviated to "Cuz"—in endless parody of the female cousinship of Hargrave.

When they met in their daily comings and goings, they would greet one another with a broad show of camaraderie and affection:

"Hello, Cuz!"

"Hello, Cuz!"

And then they would laugh. Sometimes they started laughing before they had said anything.

6

The first apartment that Uncle Andrew and Aunt Judith lived in after they moved to Hargrave had no bathtub. Uncle Andrew loved a bathtub, and so he would sometimes come around to our house after supper to have a soak. That was one of the times when he and I would visit. I would perch on the lid of the thunder jug, as he liked to call it, and he would lie in hot water up to his chin, and we would talk. Or I would just sit and watch him, for in everything he did he fascinated me. Unlike my father, who was in all things thrifty and careful and neat and who bathed vigorously like a man grooming a horse, Uncle Andrew filled the tub full and bathed expansively, as if the tub were an ocean and he a whale. He would bask at length in the hot water, and then he would soap and rinse with a great heaving and sloshing and blowing and making of suds.

On one such evening, when I must have been about six or seven, I confided to him that I had fallen in love with the older sister of one of my friends. I said that I wanted to get her off by herself somewhere — a lonely back road, say — where we could be unobserved. I was going to say that I would then declare my love. I had given a lot of thought and effort to the planning of this event, but I lacked confidence; I wanted the counsel of experience. But I got no further than that detail about the lonely back road. For a while it looked as though Uncle Andrew might drown in the extremity of his glee.

"Aw'eah! *Aw'eah!*" he said as he laughed and whooped and splashed.

"*Now* you're getting right, college! *Now* you're cooking with gas! You got your mind properly on your *business*! You going out *among* 'em!"

It astonishes me a little yet to realize how characteristically he did not qualify himself. I had spoken as a small boy, and he had responded unreservedly as a man, as himself. I must have loved him almost absolutely to have so confided in him. And was I hurt or disappointed when he received my confidence with such rowdy approval, infusing my shy daydream with a glandular intensity from another vision entirely? Not in the least, as far as I remember. I was bewildered, certainly, but was happy as always to have pleased him and to be carried away on the big stream of his laughter. And now, of course, I am delighted.

Later, he would quote me to his cronies. Buster Simms would lean to glance in at me where I sat beside Uncle Andrew in the car. "Duke, is he looking at the girls yet? Is he transacting any private business?"

And Uncle Andrew would declare solemnly, without looking at me, "Why, he's *got* a girl! And he tells me that his business with her calls for the strictest privacy." And he would go on. Wishing he would stop, I yet listened in fascination, understanding vaguely that they spoke of a destination at which I had not arrived but to which my fare was already paid.

Thus, though I was as innocent as Adam alone, I became aware of the sexual aura that surrounded Uncle Andrew.

He was never apart from it. He was always playing to whatever woman was at hand, whether it was Minnie Branch, wearing a pair of Jake's castoff work shoes and with her brood in tow, or Miss Iris Flynn, who was in fact Yeager Stump's girlfriend, or Aunt Roxanna, Grandma's tall and lean oldest sister—anybody, so long as she was a woman. Or rather, he did not play to them; he lived to them, acknowledging them, requiring them to acknowledge him, as inhabitants of the same exuberantly physical and sexual world. How they responded he did not care, so long as they responded, which they invariably did. They scolded, scoffed, huffed, smiled; they reached out to him; they looked straight into his eyes and laughed. Of particular interest to me then, and still, was Uncle Andrew's friendship with Minnie Branch, for of all the people in that overflowing household on the Crayton Place, I think he liked Minnie best. For him, maybe, the female world turned on an axis held at one pole by Aunt Judith and at the other by Minnie Branch—Aunt Judith, with her bred-in dependency, her sometimes helplessness, ill with fright and self-regard, childless and forever needy; and Minnie, who was fearless, capable, hardy, fecund, unabashed, without apology or appeal. Minnie could cook and keep house for what amounted to a small hotel, split firewood, butcher a hog, raise a garden, work in the field, shoot a fox, set a hen or wring her neck. She was a large, muscular, humorous, plain-faced woman who wore a pair of steel-rimmed glasses. You could hear her laugh halfway to the back of the farm. I can see her yet with her white hens clustered at her feet, picking up shelled corn; she is leaning back against the weight of the child in her womb, fists on hips, talking and laughing.

She conceived and birthed as faithfully as a good brood cow, welcomed each newcomer without fuss, prepared without complaint for the next. There was a running joke on this subject that Uncle Andrew carried on with Minnie and Jake.

"Well, by God, Jake's been at it again! He's as hot as a boy dog!"

Minnie would throw back her head and laugh: "Haw! Haw!"

And Jake would grin and shake his head in wonder at himself. "They going to have to *do* something about me."

And when Minnie lay down on the bed, in the big, starkly furnished bedroom next to the kitchen, to suffer yet another birth, who would be there, anxiously hovering about, dispensing clean towels and hot water, eagerly bathing the infant who pretty soon appeared, but Aunt Judith and Momma-pie? They had no more to do with Minnie Branch in the ordinary course of their lives than they had to do with the farm. But Minnie's birth pangs drew them like some undeniable music, and their conversation afterward was full of the news of their participation.

Beyond the obvious reasons, Uncle Andrew liked Minnie, I think, because she made nothing special of him; she did not see him as anything unexpected. She liked him wholly and asked for nothing. He was comfortable with her.

One overcast afternoon, I remember, Uncle Andrew and I were sitting in Minnie Branch's kitchen, talking with Minnie and another woman I knew only as Mrs. Partlet. The older children and the hands, one of whom at that time was Jockey Partlet, Mrs. Partlet's husband, had been fed their dinner long ago and had gone back to the field. The firebox of the cooking range was almost cold. Uncle Andrew and I were there per-

haps just because Uncle Andrew enjoyed being there and did not particularly need to be anyplace else.

Minnie sat in a big rocking chair between the stove and the door
into the next room. She was rocking slowly back and forth, with Coreen,
her then-youngest, lying asleep in the crook of her arm. The second
youngest, Beureen, was asleep in a crib just beyond the door. Angeleen,
the third youngest, was standing quietly at Minnie's knee, looking as
though she would like to climb into her lap. At the moment, Minnie was
ignoring other people's wants. She had a chew of tobacco tucked into her
cheek and was taking her usual big part in the conversation. Now and
then she would turn her head and spit several feet into the ash bucket
behind the stove. Mrs. Partlet, a plump, pretty woman, sat in a straight
chair by the window. Her hands lay in her lap, and as the talk went on she
fiddled with her fingers. I sat at the end of the table nearest the stove in
one of the dozen or so straight chairs, no two of which were the same.
Uncle Andrew sat at the other end, by the back door, his chair tilted onto
its hind legs, his left arm lying along the edge of the table, his right hand
in his pocket. Between the stove and the window where Mrs. Partlet was
sitting, a large washtub full of soaking diapers sat on the floor.

The conversation went on casually enough for a while, and then it became humorous, and finally hilarious, carrying a sexual allusiveness that
was grown-up and powerful; even I could recognize it. They paid no more
attention to me than if I had been yet another infant too young to talk.

The laughter itself seemed to draw Uncle Andrew and Mrs. Partlet to
their feet. He extended his left hand; she granted her right. He placed his
right hand on her back and waltzed her around the room to a tune that
they both appeared to have in mind, the two of them laughing and Minnie laughing from her chair. Uncle Andrew danced Mrs. Partlet backward to the tub of soaking diapers, where to keep from falling in she had
to push against him, and she did. And then she whooped and ducked
away, still laughing, under his arm.

He looked at me. "Come on," he said. "Let's go."

The women still laughing behind us, we went out the back door and
past the well pump and the cellar wall.

And then Mrs. Partlet followed us out. "Andrew," she said.

When I looked back, Mrs. Partlet was standing in front of Uncle

Andrew, all flushed and flustered, her hands on his forearms, saying something to him that I was not supposed to hear.

He turned away, attempting to return to the hilarity of the moments before, but failing, and knowing it. "I got all the women I can take care of already."

His face as he came away was solemn-looking, as it was sometimes when he was quiet.

To him, I think, the idea of consequence was always an afterthought. He did not expect consequences; he discovered them. When he could, he laughed them away. When they pressed in through his laughter, he shut his mouth and bore them. What he had done was his fate, and so he bore it.

❦

The second apartment that Uncle Andrew and Aunt Judith rented after they moved to Hargrave was the upstairs — three rather low-ceilinged rooms and a kitchen — of a small frame house not far from their first apartment. The new one had a bathtub. It also had two bedrooms, and so Momma-pie left her room in the Broadfield Hotel and moved in with her daughter and son-in-law. After that Uncle Andrew had to laugh more than ever to keep the consequences at bay. His home life now required him to deal constantly with two women whose dignity and self-esteem depended upon illnesses that were frequent, dramatic, and potentially fatal and that Uncle Andrew was therefore obliged to take lightly whenever he could. I remember Momma-pie's patient and saintly smile, which told the world how much she had borne and how much she was resigned to bear. For if Uncle Andrew's instinct for the outrageous was unfailing, so was Momma-pie's instinct for the vengeance of patient endurance.

One of Uncle Andrew's favorite loitering places was the Rosebud Café just off the courthouse square in Hargrave. The Rosebud sold beer, and my parents did not allow me to go there; it seemed even to me to be no place for children. I never went there alone or with my schoolmates. But in those days I went there often with Uncle Andrew. The Rosebud was owned and run by Miss Iris Flynn, who always had three or four nice young women working for her. It was a good-humored, interesting-smelling place, full of light from the big front windows in the daytime, and at night dim, lit mainly by neon — as I knew from standing on the walk in front and peeking in. Uncle Andrew loved to go there in the lulls that came in the late morning and the middle of the afternoon. Often, then, we would be the only customers. Uncle Andrew would order soft drinks for us, and then he would sit, tilted back in his chair, talking and cutting up with Miss Iris and the other women. They would gather round, or stop in passing, to join in the talk and the carrying on. These interludes were intensely interesting to me, and I devoted a lot of study to them.

One night when I was eating supper with Aunt Judith and Uncle Andrew and Momma-pie at the little table in Aunt Judith's kitchen, I said, "Uncle Andrew, how come you spend so much time talking to those women down at the Rosebud?"

Momma-pie assumed her smile of sweet patience.

Uncle Andrew looked at me and said, "Well, I'll be goddamned!"

But he was already laughing. He either was embarrassed or knew he ought to be, and his embarrassment tickled him. For there I sat, the would-be friend of his bosom, his trusty hired hand, and I had betrayed him.

Burlesquing indignation to disguise whatever she felt — and maybe amused at me too; she could have been — Aunt Judith said, "Well! The next thing I know, Uncle Andrew'll be out in my car with one of those Rosebud girls!"

Uncle Andrew said, "Aw'eah! *Stretched* out in it!"

The big flow of his laughter poured out, and all of us, in our various styles, went bobbing away.

7

My memories of Uncle Andrew are thus an accumulation of little pictures and episodes, isolated from one another, unbegun and unended. They are vividly colored, clear in outline, and spare, as if they belong to an early age of the world when there were not too many details. Each is like the illuminated capital of a page I cannot read, for in my memory there is no tissue of connection or interpretation. As a child, I either was interested or I was not; I either understood or I did not. Mostly, even when I was interested, I did not understand. I had perhaps no inclination to explain my elders to myself. I did not say to myself, "Uncle Andrew is wild," or "Uncle Andrew does not think beforehand," or "Uncle Andrew does whatever he thinks of." Perhaps it was from thinking about him after his death, discovering how much I remembered and how little I knew, that I learned that all human stories in this world contain many lost or unwritten or unreadable or unwritable pages and that the truth about us, though it must exist, though it must lie all around us every day, is mostly hidden from us, like birds' nests in the woods.

For a long time after Uncle Andrew's death, when the phone would ring early in the morning, I would be out of bed and halfway down the stairs before I remembered his absence and felt the day suddenly change around me, withdrawing forever from what it might have been.

That was the way it went for I cannot remember how long. Uncle Andrew was right at the center of the idea I had formed of myself. I was his hand, his boy, his buddy, who was either always going with him or always wanting to go with him. I had wanted to be like him. It had not occurred to me to want to be like anybody else. That he was no longer present was a fact I kept discovering. It puzzled me that I did not cry; perhaps I would have, had I been able to name to myself what I had experienced and what I felt. Uncle Andrew had been a surprising man; often you did not know what he was going to do, and this was because he often did not know what he was going to do himself. But his death was a bigger surprise to me than anything I had seen him do while he was living. That he had been killed on purpose by another man, for a reason that was never adequately explained to me, made his death as much a mystery as it was a surprise. It was therefore a problem to me as much as it was a grief; I thought about it almost incessantly.

For my sake, I suppose, not much was said about Uncle Andrew or his death in my presence. Or maybe it was not for my sake. How easy, after all, would it have been to find the words? What could have been said that would have been adequate or fitting to a calamity so great and so new? The grown-ups' grief, especially my father's, stood silently around the life and death of Uncle Andrew like a wall or a guardian grove. I could no more have spoken of him or asked about the manner of his death than I could have doubted that he was dead.

Somebody told me merely that Carp Harmon had killed Uncle Andrew because Uncle Andrew had failed to cover a well near the lead mine, as he had promised he would do. I asked for no details, accepting the story as the truth, which it partly may have been, though I came to doubt it.

❧

We had an upright piano at our house, and sometimes in the evening my father would play. I had no gift for music, but I liked to hear him and to watch him. He played hymns and popular tunes, sitting very straight at the keyboard, playing with precision and strong rhythm. What I best remember him playing, sometimes singing as he played, was "Bell-Bottom Trousers," a sprightly, morale-boosting song that was popular for a while during the war, and another, a love song, "One Dozen Roses." After Uncle Andrew's death, my father never played the piano again. This was to me the most powerful of all the signs of the change that had come.

He went on with his law practice, of course, but now he also resumed the care of the farms. By then, he had to look after Grandpa Catlett's farm, which we called the Home Place, in addition to the Crayton and Bower Places, because after Uncle Andrew's death Grandpa was less and less able to see to it himself. All this, however great the burden or regrettable the cause, was one of the blessings of his life. Unlike Uncle Andrew, my father had a genuine calling to be a farmer. Farming was his passion, as the law was; in him the two really were inseparable. As a lawyer, he had served mostly farmers. His love of farming and of farming people had led him into the politics of agriculture and a lifelong effort to preserve the economy of the small farms. In my father's assortment of passions — his family, the law, bird hunting, and farming — farming was the fundamental one; from farming he derived the terms and conditions of his being. It was farming that excited him until he could not sleep: "Like a woman!" he would say in his old age, amazed and delighted that it could have moved him so. When he could, he would take a day off from the office to farm: Maybe he would work all day with the cattle or sheep; I remember days too when he would get everybody together to harness and drive for the first time the new teams of two-year-old mules. He made the rounds of the farms every evening, after the office was shut, to see to his livestock, to learn what had been done, to find out what needed doing, or just to drive his car through the fields and look. Or he would stop and sit, and let the world grow still around him. Often he would be out on one of the places, driving and thinking and looking, talking to Jake or Charlie Branch or one of the Brightleafs, before office hours in the morning.

Sometimes he would be late getting back.

"Where's Wheeler?" some would-be client, glancing in at my father's still-empty chair, would ask his secretary.

Miss Julia Vye would raise her hands in a gesture of helplessness and take a noisy little sip of air over the end of her tongue. "Heaven *knows* where! Out somewhere in a *field*, I *suppose!*"

One day as I walked past my father's car, parked on the street in front of his office, I saw a large grasshopper sitting on top of the steering wheel.

By the time my father had owned a car for a year or so, the paint was thoroughly scratched by bushes and briars, and the radiator was choked with seeds.

On Sunday afternoons, after church and dinner, he would be at farming again—he couldn't keep away from it—making the rounds that day with Grandpa, as long as he was able, or with Elton Penn or Nathan Coulter or Henry or me, or sometimes with all of us, Henry and I along to open the gates, to be teased and admonished, to listen. My father would drive slowly and alertly, turning the car abruptly this way or that to show an animal or a field to the best advantage.

When he could not go to the farms himself, he often sent Henry or me or both of us to do some piece of work he wanted done. He almost routinely overtaxed our abilities—as on the day he sent us, when we were still small boys, to separate the bull from the herd of cows on the Crayton Place and drive him to the Home Place; we saw a lot of the country on that trip, for the bull went into every side road and through every open gate he came to. Or else our father sent us to have some pleasure that he was too busy to have himself but that he imagined we could have if only he appointed us to have it and described it suggestively enough: He knew where we could catch a mess of fish or find a covey of birds, and he would tell us not only how to conduct the adventure he had in mind but also how to enjoy it.

Sometimes, later, he would say, as if thinking aloud, how much his interest and enthusiasm had been damaged by Uncle Andrew's death, how that had baffled and delayed him, and I knew that this was so. He regretted bitterly and always the loss of Uncle Andrew, and of that part of his own life that he felt had gone with Uncle Andrew to the grave. But if he was damaged, he was not destroyed; he still had more than half his life to live, and he was a farmer to the end.

Now, looking back after all my years of thinking about the two of them, I cannot help wondering how satisfactorily their partnership might have continued if Uncle Andrew had lived. I know that my father knew that Uncle Andrew was wild—I am pretty sure that he knew the extent of his wildness and what it involved—and yet my father spoke even less of that than of his grief. At the time of Uncle Andrew's death, he and my father had been partners for something like four years. As far as I know, it had gone well enough. Perhaps Uncle Andrew would have proved responsible enough and my father patient enough for their partnership to have endured—who could know? I know only that after Uncle Andrew's death my father suffered not only a lost reality but also a damaged dream. It was a dream bound to sustain damage and to cause pain, and yet he never gave it up, and he passed it on. He dreamed, simply, of a world intact, the family together, the place cared for, and all well.

🜎

Perhaps without much awareness that he was doing it, or why, he transferred his dream of partnership to Henry and me. Because he needed so much for us to share his interests, his demands on us were often burdening and overburdening, though they taught us much that we needed to know. In spite of his impatience and his sometimes immense exasperation at our shortcomings, he gave us also his love for the ordinary excellences of farming and of life outdoors, and his extraordinary pleasure in them. He could be absorbed and exalted in watching a herd of cattle graze or a red fox crossing a field.

In his eagerness to have us learn and to fill us with experience, he put us into the hands of other teachers. Often, in the summer or on weekends, he would take us with him on his morning rounds and just leave us wherever work was going on.

"Here," he would say to Jake Branch, for often it would be Jake with whom he left us. "Put 'em to work."

And to us he would say, "I want you to work and I want you to mind. Listen to Jake and do what he tells you."

"Jake," he would say, "make 'em do. Make 'em mind."

And Jake would say, "Aw, Mr. Wheeler, don't you worry about *them* boys. *Them* boys is all right. Me and *them* boys get along."

My father would touch the accelerator then, and be on his way.

🜎

Everything was different at Jake's and Minnie's without Uncle Andrew. It was quieter and plainer than it had been, and it was sad. As elsewhere, little was said about Uncle Andrew in his absence. Even Minnie, who talked easily about anything, would speak his name with care, as if both eager and reluctant to remember him. But it was Minnie who told me the little that I knew for many years about Uncle Andrew's last day.

"Andrew," she said, as if announcing her topic, "he come here that morning to bring Ab home. Ab got his hand cut, it was a bad cut, Andrew taken him to the doctor and then brought him here. And I'm here to tell you, Andrew knowed *then* that something was going to happen to him. He knowed it. He said he felt bad, and could he have a drink of water. I drawed a fresh bucket and give him a drink.

"We about had dinner ready and I said, 'Here, Andrew, set down and eat before you go back.'

"And then he started out the back door; he come in at the front door, bringing Ab in. I said, 'Andrew, it's bad luck to go in one door and out the other.'

"He said, 'It don't matter. It don't make any difference.'

"He went on out the back door. And it weren't but a little while then till he was dead.

"He knowed something was going to happen, I'm atelling you. He knowed it as sure as I'm setting here."

I believed her. Her story seemed to me to show that Uncle Andrew's death had been fated. Whether he entered into the course of his fate by coming in and going out by different doors, as at birth and death, or by some other way, I did not know. But I felt that on the day of his death he had been fated to die, and that he knew it.

Her story made me see him as he had been when he came into the kitchen with death's shadow over him and asked her for a drink of water, and drank, and set down the glass. I heard him say, "It don't matter. It don't make any difference." I can hear him yet. I can see the expression on his face as he says it. The shadow of his death is already on him. He speaks in eternity even as he is speaking in time.

And yet Miss Iris Flynn told me many years later that on that morning, having left Ab with the doctor, Uncle Andrew stuck his head into the door of the Rosebud, gave her a grin, and said, "Hi, babe!"

But of those two glimpses of him on that day, Minnie Branch's is the most powerful. I still raise with myself the question whether it is bad

luck to come in by one door and go out by another, which I still associate
with that old darkness of fate and calamity. And when I have it on my
mind, I still go out by the same door I came in.

※

Only once was I ever admitted into the unqualified presence of the family's grief. One night in the late fall of the year of Uncle Andrew's death,
I went with my father on his farm rounds after he had left the office for
the day. In the dusk of the early evening we stopped to see Grandma and
Grandpa Catlett. Grandma asked us and we stayed for supper. This was
something my father had always done from time to time, but perhaps he
had not done so since Uncle Andrew's death.

Grandma's kitchen was not so harshly utilitarian as Minnie Branch's —
it was neater, and the chairs at the table matched — but in its furnishings
and aspect it was nonetheless a room mainly to be used. It had no fuss
about it, nothing decorative except a calendar. It was a fairly large room,
containing in addition to the table and chairs an iron cooking stove, a
small coal oil stove sometimes used in hot weather, a wood box, a flour
box, a dish cabinet, and by the back door a small wash table with water
bucket and pan and a towel made of a flour sack hanging on a nail, the nail
protruding through a carefully worked buttonhole. By then, I believe,
there would also have been a small refrigerator. The table and chairs were
old, covered with many coats of paint, the old coats chipped and cracked
beneath the new. I remember from about that time a dishpan that had a
leak and was slightly rounded on the bottom; when Grandma set it on
the hot stove it was continuously rocked by little explosions of steam. Her
fine things consisted of a set of silver teaspoons, a beautiful old painted
pitcher, and a cut-glass bowl.

The table, covered with an oilcloth, stood under the windows on the
north wall. Cellar, smokehouse, henhouse, and garden were still live
institutions in those days. There would have been a crock of fresh milk;
Grandma would have fried a stack of corn batter cakes on the griddle;
she might have had a baked ham or a hen; the only sign of the war would
have been a scarcity of sugar.

While we ate nobody said anything that was not necessary. I was left
out of consideration almost as much as I had been in Minnie Branch's

kitchen on the day of Uncle Andrew's dance with Mrs. Partlet, and that was unusual.

When the meal was over, we went through the cold hall to the living room and sat down. Grandpa and my father sat on opposite sides of the stove, in which there was a fire. Grandma sat in her little spindle-backed rocker. I sat off to myself by the stand table on which was Grandma's small brown radio. Perhaps, feeling the sorrow in the room, I wanted to turn on the radio, but I did not turn it on. I could not have turned it on, or asked to do so. As several times before in the months since Uncle Andrew's death, I felt as if I had just happened into a world that I had not imagined, in which I found no comfort. I had an obscure feeling that it would be politest to be somewhere else but that there would be no polite way to leave. The grown-ups sat in their chairs for a while, not speaking, and then they started to cry — all three of them. They wept without moving or speaking, each as if alone. And then they ceased. My father and Grandma removed their glasses and wiped away their tears, my father with his handkerchief, my grandmother with a corner of her apron. Grandpa simply raised his right hand and passed his forefinger under his eyes.

No more was said in the car that night as my father and I drove home. I can imagine now that he was searching his mind for something to say to me. He would have been aware of the difficulty for me of what I had witnessed, for he was not unaware of much. Demanding as he could be at times, when sympathy was needed he was generous, and he was good at finding the words. But I cannot imagine what he could have said to ease or mitigate the grief that had shown itself so nakedly to me. I was glad he said nothing.

❧

Carp Harmon was tried and sentenced to two years in the penitentiary. This also was never explained to me, though I knew that my elders resented the lightness of the punishment. I learned of the trial itself only from Jess Brightleaf, who told me that my father had asked him not to attend. If Jess had gone to the trial, then my grandfather would have wanted to go too. The reason for that I understood without being told. Given my grandfather's character, his age, his grief and anger, he would not have considered himself subject to the restraints of the court, and my father did not want him raging there.

Later, after I knew that his sentence had expired, I spent a lot of time wondering what would happen if Carp Harmon gave me a ride while I was hitchhiking. Hitchhiking was another thing Henry and I did that we were absolutely forbidden to do. Our mother had read of many horrible things that had happened to hitchhikers, none of which I thought would happen to me. As I knew from experience, people I did not know who picked me up on the road I traveled, the Port William road, were likely to greet me by asking, "Ain't you one of Wheeler Catlett's boys?" or "I don't reckon you'd be a Catlett, would you?" What I worried about was getting picked up by Carp Harmon. Though I had not knowingly ever seen him, I had no doubt that I would recognize him. And I knew that I would need great courage, greater courage than I was sure I had, to speak the necessary words, which I had rehearsed: "Carp Harmon, you son of a bitch, you killed my uncle." And then perhaps he would pull out his .38 pistol and shoot me?

But he never gave me a ride; as far as I know, I never laid eyes on him in his life.

Another encounter that I grew to expect, as I grew into understanding of what I remembered of Uncle Andrew, was with a first cousin, some strange boy or young man, as I put it to myself, whom I would recognize because he would look something like Uncle Andrew, or even something like me. But if he exists, he has not come forward. As far as I know, I have not laid eyes on him either.

8

Widowhood gave new impetus to Aunt Judith's role as a sufferer. In the eighteen years that remained to her, she needed more sympathy than ever, and now more than ever she was persistent in asking or hinting for it, and was more than ever unappeasable. It was as though every calamity that Momma-pie had forestalled or denied by her masks of superiority had fallen on Aunt Judith, who was as naked to them as a shorn lamb. Whatever her faults, Aunt Judith lacked her mother's arrogance.

Yet as her afflictions grew she seemed to become increasingly self-concerned. Her sufferings finally were not at all conditioned by the understanding that others also suffered; she suffered in an almost pristine innocence, as if she were the world's unique sufferer and the world waited curiously to hear of her pains. She was so prompt and extravagent in pitying herself that she drove away all competitors.

She called Grandma Catlett on every anniversary of Uncle Andrew's birth and death, and on every other anniversary or holiday that reminded her of her loss and her suffering. She kept this up year after year, speaking of "our Andrew." Grandma said that she was grateful for these attentions, but they cannot have been easy for her.

Nor was Aunt Judith an easy burden for my father, who, in Uncle Andrew's absence, became her adviser and protector. He fulfilled his duties faithfully, but without, I think, ever having the satisfaction of feeling that she was satisfied.

When Momma-pie died, my father had the duty, among others, of taking Aunt Judith to the undertaker's to pick out a coffin. He got me to go along, but both of us together were as unequal to the occasion as he would have been alone. We knew that Aunt Judith had been dependent on Momma-pie for many things. We knew that Momma-pie's death would leave Aunt Judith much lonelier than before. But our sympathy was so much a surplus as to be hardly noticeable.

Handkerchief in hand, chin quivering, Aunt Judith said many times that she was going to be awfully lonely now. Many times she said she did not know what she was going to do. She gazed lingeringly into every one of the coffins, of which there was a roomful, and every one of them reminded her of her loss and renewed her grief. Every one of the coffins had something about it that Momma-pie would have liked, and at these reminders of Momma-pie's tastes and preferences Aunt Judith's voice would become a whisper and she would dab at her eyes. She was using her grief to invite sympathy, and in doing so falsified her grief, and in falsifying her grief made it impossible to sympathize with her. And she compounded the difficulty by the innocence of perfect self-deception; she had, I feel sure, no idea what she was doing. And what was one to say? I could find in myself not the least aptitude for the occasion. I longed to exchange places with the wallpaper or the rug. My father, having assured Aunt Judith that he would do all he could for her, had almost as little to say as I did. She placed and left us in our embarrassment as she would have seated us at a table.

※

For some years she worked as a typist in one of the offices in Hargrave. Later, she contracted glaucoma and became virtually blind. She made her way about the town then truly alone, avoided under cover of her blindness by people who could no longer bear her importunities for sympathy and her endless recitation of her ills.

My last clear, unshakable memory of her is from the summer of 1949, when I was fifteen. One afternoon as I was walking in front of the courthouse, I called out to one of my friends, and in the same instant looked across the street and saw Aunt Judith. She had recognized my voice, and she turned to stare sightlessly toward me. I did not want to go to her; I was just empty of the willingness to do so. I went on as I intended to go, pretending under her following blind gaze that it was not my voice that she had heard and that I was not myself.

For want of compassion—aware that I would inevitably fail to be compassionate enough, but also for want of enough compassion—I denied that I was who I was, and so made myself less than I was. This was my first conscious experience of a shame that was irremediable and hopeless—a shame, as I now suppose, that Uncle Andrew may have met in himself, in her presence, many a time.

This surely was the punishment that she dealt out, wittingly or not, willingly or not, to him and to the rest of us. And if at times in the past I could abandon her to the self-martyrdom of the self-absorbed, and though I see now better than then how impossible she was, still I am sorry. For I can no longer forget that loss and illness and trouble, however a person may exploit them, cannot be exploited without being suffered. Aunt Judith exploited them and suffered them, and suffered her exploitation of them. She suffered and she was alone.

And so she is inescapable. In my mind I will always see her standing there in the street, her head tilted stiffly up, hopelessly hoping for some earthly pity greater than her pity for herself.

9

The house that Uncle Andrew seemed most to be gone from was not, for me, the one where he had lived in rented rooms with Aunt Judith and Momma-pie. Nor was it my own house at Hargrave, or Jake and Minnie's at the Crayton Place. Where I most often met his absence and was obliged to deal with it was at Grandma and Grandpa Catlett's.

Grandpa had been born in an earlier house on that site, the last of five children, about a year before the end of the Civil War. That house burned when he was six, and the present house was built on the old foundation. In the second winter after Uncle Andrew's death, Grandpa took sick, went to bed, and did not get up again.

All his life he had gone to the barn at bedtime to see to his animals and make sure that all was well. That winter, staying at night with Grandpa, my father went to the barn at bedtime and returned to say that all was well. "And then," my father said, "he would be pleased."

"The day after I die," Grandpa told my father, "get up and go to work." He died where he was born, in the same corner of the same room, though in a different house. And on a raw day in the late winter we carried him, dressed up, to Port William and left him there in the hill under the falling rain.

The year and a half and a little more between the day of Uncle Andrew's death and the day of Grandpa's funeral seems to me now to have been a time of ending, not just of lives but of a kind of life and a kind of world. I did not recognize that ending as consciously then as I do now, but I felt its shadow. Uncle Andrew had not belonged to the older life; though he had grown up in it, he had lived away from it. He belonged to the self-consciously larger life that came into being with the First World War, and that was now rapidly establishing itself by means of another war, industrial machinery, and electric wires. But though that new world was undeniably present on the roads, the life of our fields still depended on the bodily strength and skill of people and horses and mules. In the minds of my grandfather and Dick Watson, the Brightleafs, and the Branches, the fundamental realities and interests and pleasures were the same as they had been in the minds of the people who had worked in the same fields before the Civil War.

The first death after Uncle Andrew's had been Dick Watson's, and Dick, like my grandfather, belonged to that older world. That the two of them belonged also to two different and in some ways opposite races did not keep them from belonging in common to a kind of humanity. They were farming people. What distinguished them from ever-enlarging numbers of people in succeeding generations was that they had never thought of being anything else. This gave them a kind of integrity and a kind of con- centration. They did their work with undivided minds, intent upon its demands and pleasures, reconciled to its hardships, not complaining, never believing that they might have been doing something better.

Dick and Aunt Sarah Jane's two-room house at the edge of the woods, down the hill from the barns, was a part of the Home Place, but it was also a place unto itself, with its own garden and henhouse and woodpile. Aunt Sarah Jane did not work "out." She kept house and gardened and cared for a small flock of chickens and foraged in the fields and woods and sewed and mended and read her Bible. In the mornings and the evenings and in odd times spared from the farmwork, Dick kept their house sup- plied with water and milk, meat and firewood. I remember their pleasure in all the items of their small abundance: buckets of milk from Dick's cow, cured joints and middlings from their hogs, vegetables from Aunt Sarah Jane's garden, the herbs and greens and mushrooms she gathered on her walks.

In those years when I could not be with Uncle Andrew, I loved almost as much to be with Dick, though the two of them could hardly have been less alike. Dick was as gentle and quiet as Uncle Andrew was brash and uproarious. And whereas Uncle Andrew's great aim in life was to "get out among 'em," Dick, when I knew him, anyhow, was mostly content to stay put. With Uncle Andrew, you were always on a trajectory that was going to take you back to the road and on to someplace else. With Dick, when he wasn't behind a team or on horseback, you traveled on foot, going not away but deeper in. Dick could sit still. He could sit on his rock doorstep after supper, smoke his pipe, and talk slowly and thoughtfully until bedtime. In my memories of Uncle Andrew, I am often behind him or off to the side, watching him, feeding my curiosity as to what manner of man he was. In my memories of Dick Watson, I am often beside him, holding his hand. From Dick I learned that the countryside was inhabited not just by things we ordinarily see but also by things we ordinarily do not see — such as foxes. That it was haunted by old memories I already knew.

Foxhunting with Dick, he on my grandfather's mare and I on Beauty the pony, I first came into the presence of the countryside at night, and learned to think of it as the hunters knew it, and learned there were foxes abroad in it who knew it as no human ever would. There would be an occasional dog fox, Dick said, who would venture up almost to the yard fence to invite the hounds to run, and who, when the hounds accepted the challenge, knew how to baffle them by running in a creek or along the top of a rock fence. I had from Dick a vision of a brilliant fox running gaily through the dark over the ridges and along the hollows, followed by hounds in beautiful outcry, and this to me was a sort of doctrineless mystery and grace.

But what I remember most, and most gratefully, is Dick's own presence, for he was a man fully present in the place and its yearly round of work that connected hayfield and grainfield and feed barn and hog lot, woods and woodpile and the wood box behind the kitchen stove, well and water trough. When the work was to be done, he was there to do it. He did it well and without haste; when it was done he took his ease and did not complain. Years later, when I was looking for the way home, his was one of the minds that guided me.

After he and then Grandpa were dead, the farm, in spite of my father's long caring for it, lacked a coherence that it had had before. It needed not just attention and work but lives that made it a world and lived from it.

For several years after those deaths, I stayed with Grandma for months at a time. She started coming to Hargrave to spend the winters in a room at the Broadfield Hotel. And then on a Saturday morning in March or April, with spring bright in the air, Elton Penn would come with his truck, and we would load Grandma's spool bed, her comfortable rocker, her clothes and linens, and take her home.

I would move in then to stay with her until she returned to town late the following fall. For me, this was freedom, more freedom probably than I was entitled to, but not more than I wanted and even needed. At Grandma's, I was the man of the house. I had as my own room the little hallway behind Grandma's bedroom, and I had, as it seemed to me, the whole country to range in, on foot or horseback, beyond sight or call of any grown-up. For grown-up company, when I wanted it, I had Grandma, and after 1945 Elton and Mary Penn on the Beechum Place, and Jess and Rufus Brightleaf and their wives. For a playmate, I had Fred Brightleaf. When my father took me or sent me to work for Jake Branch, I had the company of that large and various household. Hargrave, when I returned to it, took some getting used to. I decided to stay out of it if I could.

To get to school, I rode the bus or hitchhiked down to Hargrave in the morning and back again in the afternoon. I attended school by require-ment only. I did not think of it when I was not in it. I did not establish a great reputation as a student.

Once Grandma and I had moved in, we revived the old house around us. I thought it a great adventure to build a fire again in the kitchen range and to help Grandma get together the makings of our first meal. On the colder mornings we would get up and hurry down to the kitchen to renew the fire. Charmed by the elemental pleasure of needing to be warm and then getting warm, I watched the day grow bright outside the windows while Grandma cooked our breakfast. As we ate, the sun came up beyond the still-living oak snag at the corner of the woods.

This was a homecoming for me as much as for Grandma. I had lived there with my parents during my first two years. I had come newborn to that house. It was the first house of my memory and consciousness. Sleeping there in my crib beside my parents' bed, I had dreamed the sounds of the wind that drew its long breaths over the house at night. And I remembered waking there as if to a world entirely new, to see the sun shining on the wet grass and the white barns.

By the time I was born into it, the history of that place had become old. The sign of its age was much forgetfulness. Much had happened to us there that we did not remember. We had suffered and rejoiced there more than we knew. I acquired experiences there that never had happened to me at all. All my life I have recalled a sort of dream image of a man putting on his coat at the back door, speaking over his shoulder to a woman inside the house. A freed slave going away? One of our family going west? Or simply somebody going to the field? I cannot see his face; I do not know.

I had known, it seemed to me always, that when Grandpa was "just a little bit of a baby laying up yonder in the bed," some soldiers had come at night and taken his father. They were a small band of Union horsemen who had come to "recruit" my great-grandfather, who would have been in his early forties at the time. They did this, I suppose, with a pleasant sense of justice, because he owned a few slaves and for that and other reasons would not have been sympathetic to their cause. Forcing him to mount behind one of them, they carried him to their encampment on the top of the next hill. Still in her nightgown and barefooted, my great-grandmother, Lucy, followed them. By force of argument or character or both, she "made them give him back." According to the story as I heard it, Lucy "ran after them," and so in my mind, as if from my own birth, I have had the image of that distraught and determined woman running up the dark road.

And I have had in mind always the fire that burned the old house when Grandpa was six. It is a pod of fierce light that opens greatly in the dark. In that light Grandpa is a small boy suddenly filled with terrible knowledge. He stands holding his saddle, his most precious possession, which he has retrieved from under his bed. They bring to him a small Negro girl, the cook's daughter, a year younger than he. She is hysterical, wanting to run back into the burning house. And they tell him, "Hold her! Hold her tight!" And he holds her, while the grown-ups continue their effort to save things from the house, and then finally give up and watch it burn.

The new house had grown old too by the time I knew it, and had about it memories and reminders and intimations of unremembered things. The house itself was tall and finely outlined. Its high-ceilinged rooms, cool in summer, were lovely when filled with morning light. But its furnishings were meager and rather graceless. The best room, the parlor, in which we sat only on the most special occasions, contained an upright piano with a stool, a matching sofa and easy chair covered with rose and beige brocade, a glass-fronted bookcase, a small table, and two or three more chairs, not necessarily comfortable. The other rather formal room was the dining room, likewise seldom used. It was a north room, cool in summer, cold in winter, heated, like the parlor, only by a fireplace. I liked to go into that room for its strangeness and its cold smells of cloves and brown sugar.

The kitchen, living room, and three bedrooms upstairs — the rooms that were to varying degrees lived in — were furnished with not much of an eye for decoration or harmony. The furniture was inherited or haphazardly bought or come by; nearly all of it was old and well worn, some of it damaged or much repaired. The rugs were threadbare in spots, and where the travel was heaviest the finish was worn off the kitchen linoleum. It was a house that for a long time had been occupied by people struggling to hold themselves in place, who had not had much time for comfort or the means for luxuries. I understood this only much later; then it was merely familiar. The house had had a telephone for a good many years and electricity for four or five, but nothing else had changed, and it seemed somehow surprised by these amenities. It still had no running water. We used the privy down in a corner of the backyard, and carried water in buckets from the well.

There were a few framed photographs on the living room wall — pictures of Uncle Andrew and my father, and of us children. There was also a small tintype of Grandpa when he was a young boy; his mother had had to whip him, he said, to make him sit still for it. Upstairs there were larger photographic portraits of Uncle Andrew and my father as children, and of my great-grandfathers Catlett and Wheeler. Grandma's decorations consisted mainly of a few crocheted doilies and table scarves. Her yearning for nice things was revealed by her attachment to ornamented candy boxes with hinged lids; the few of these that she had received she kept and filled with photographs, letters, and the pretty greeting cards that came on holidays. The most beautiful thing in the house, I thought, was a sampler made by my mother. I read it often, fascinated by the close rhymes. It said:

> HOURS FLY
> FLOWERS DIE
> NEW DAYS
> NEW WAYS
> PASS BY
> LOVE STAYS

Between us, Grandma and I carried on the best we could the old kitchen economy of milk cow and hen flock and garden. I helped her care for the hens, and I did the milking and sometimes the churning.

To amuse myself while I milked the cows I would sometimes take aim at the flies that lit on the rim of the bucket and squirt them down into the foam. Grandma, seeing them in the strainer, would say, "Lord, the *flies*! Did anybody ever *see* the like!"

When I churned, sitting on the back porch with the stone churn between my knees, I could make buttermilk fly up through the dasher hole and hit the ceiling. And then Grandma would say, "Well, if you ain't the limit!"

When I would catch a nice mess of little sunfish at the pond, or a turtle, or anything wild and good to eat, she would say, "Well, *did* you ever!"

One bright day after rain, when I had waded along the risen branch picking raspberries with Elton Penn, who wore a pair of gum boots and was going directly ahead as usual, Grandma ignored the cap full of berries I held out to her and looked at my sopping shoes and pants legs. "Andy Catlett, I reckon you haven't got a lick of sense!"

I loved to stay with her, partly because she spoiled me, partly because she left me pretty free to live the life available in that place, which was the life I wanted. In the long summer mornings and afternoons I went alone on foot or horseback among the fields and woods and ponds and streams. Or I swam or quested about with Fred Brightleaf. Or I worked, if I could and if allowed, with the Brightleafs or Elton Penn or Jake Branch.

At mealtimes, and while we went about our chores, and at night,

Grandma and I talked. Mainly she talked; I questioned and listened. She talked of things that had happened and of things that had been said, things that she remembered and things that she remembered that other people had remembered. At night it was best. After the supper dishes were put away, the long light and heat of the day now past, we would darken the house and go out to sit on the front porch. Or if the breeze was better out in the yard we would carry chairs out and sit at the foot of a big old cedar tree that stood there then. While the lightning bugs carried their little winking lamps up out of the grass, and the katydids sang in the late summer foliage, and heat lightning shimmered on the horizon, we sat invisible to each other, just two voices talking, until bedtime.

She told of the roads and distances of the old days, of the time when the little patch of woods by Dick Watson's house had been part of a bigger woods that went on and on. She told of slavery times, when my great-grandmother, resting after dinner in the room over the kitchen, heard Molly, the cook, tell the cat, "Old Lucy's asleep now, and I'm going to beat the hell out of you." She told of the end of slavery, when all the slaves went away, and Molly returned and was sent away. "You have your freedom now," Lucy told her, "and you must go."

She told and retold, because I wanted to hear, of the night the soldiers came, and of the burning house.

She talked of Grandpa. There had been serious estrangements and difficulties between them, for both of them were strong-willed people, and they had not always willed the same things. But now in his absence that we both felt, she took pleasure in remembering him in his youth and his pride. She said, "He was the finest-looking man on the back of a horse that ever I saw." She said he was a beautiful whistler. She had loved to hear him, off somewhere in the distance, calling his cattle. She knew what hard times and failures and disappointments had cost him, and she sorrowed for him as she sorrowed for herself when she had been young and proud, paying the same costs. There had been times when they had barely made it.

As a young wife she had lived with her mother-in-law, about whom I never heard her complain, and she remembered much that Lucy had remembered: what the cook had said to the cat, for example, or an exchange of letters between Lucy and her brother, James. James,

Grandma said, was elected to the state legislature. When he was to be sworn in, he invited Lucy to attend the ceremony. She wrote back, "I have nothing suitable to wear." And James replied, "Wear the simplest thing you have, and let your manners correspond."

One of my favorite people in Grandma's stories was Grandpa's older brother, Will, indolent and vagrant, careless and fearless, a comedian drunk or sober, a disappointment and an aggravation to everybody, and yet dear.

"Will," Grandma asked him once, "were you ever in love with Sally Skaggs?"

"Yes, Dorie," he said, "I loved her a little once."

It was Uncle Will who cut off Uncle Andrew's long golden curls "to turn him into a boy," and broke Grandma's heart.

She told also, troubled and yet amused, of her own younger brother, Leonidas, whom we all called "Uncle Peach," who would get drunk and say to her, "Sing 'Yellow Rose o' Texas' to me, madam."

And it was Uncle Peach who had allowed Uncle Andrew to fall into the fire when he had just begun to walk, leaving what I thought a most attractive set of small scars across the backs of the fingers of Uncle Andrew's right hand.

Grandma recalled a Negro farmhand, Uncle Mint Wade, who argued, "You will read in the Bible whereupon it say, 'The bottom rail shall be the rider.'"

And she remembered Uncle Eb Markman, who pronounced, "The world is squar' and got four cawners to it."

From her reading she had culled a few phrases that she liked to repeat. It pleased her to speak of sleep as "nature's sweet restorer." Her speech had touches of self-conscious elegance that she used in tribute. Of dancing she would say, "It's a lovely thing, stepping to the music."

Our most frequent and fearful topic was the weather. Both of us were afraid of storms, which seemed to be uncommonly frequent in those days. Grandma would tell about storms that she remembered, and we would discuss the problem of where to be safe in case of a windstorm.

Before a thunderstorm, she would put a pillow over the telephone, theorizing that the feathers made good insulation and would prevent the lightning from coming into the house along the wire. And having affixed the pillow to the wall so that it covered the phone, she would always quote Uncle Will: "I believed that too, Dorie, till I saw lightning strike a goose."

When a cold spell would come late in the spring, causing us to feel that some fundamental disorder was at hand, she would quote from a source I have never found: "The time will come when we'll not know the winter from the summer but by the budding of the trees." And though that time has never come, I believed then that it would come, and I believe it still.

Like many country people of her time, she did not have a very secure belief in progress. She believed that hard times did not go away forever, but returned. She had known hard times, and she did not forget them. There had been a winter, when my father was about seven years old, when Grandpa's tobacco crop had not brought enough to pay the commission on its own sale. Grandma could not have forgotten that if she had lived a thousand years. My father's lifelong devotion to the cause of the small farmers of our part of the country dates from that memory, and it holds its power still over Henry and me.

It seemed to have gone by Uncle Andrew without touching him. Uncle Andrew was sometimes burdened and was sometimes a burden to himself, but he also had the gift of taking things lightly. Grandma would quote, with disapproval and with a laugh, his reply to Grandpa, who was worrying about a field infested with wild onions: "The cows'll eat 'em, and I don't have to sleep with the cows."

Grandma was thirteen when her mother died. Her father never remarried. She and her sisters grew up keeping house for themselves and their father and attempting with less than success to give a proper upbringing to Uncle Peach. For Grandma and her sisters, somehow, a mark of respectability and even gentility had been set. They cherished the schooling they got from the Bird's Branch School and *McGuffey's Eclectic Readers,* one through eight. All her life Grandma had struggled and aspired, and her ambition had been confronted and affronted at every turn by the likes of Uncle Will and Uncle Peach and Uncle Andrew, too wayward to be approved, too close and dear to be denied.

Uncle Andrew and Uncle Will and Uncle Peach passed and returned in her thoughts and her talk like orbiting planets. They divided her mind; they troubled her without end. She could see plainly what a relief it would have been if she could have talked some sense into their heads and straightened them out. It would have been a relief too if she could have waved them away and forgotten them. In fact, she could do neither. They were incorrigible, and they were her own. In their various ways and styles, they had worried and vexed and grieved her "nearly into the grave," as she would sometimes say. And they also charmed and amused and moved her. They were not correctable because of the way they were; they were not dismissable because of the way she was. She loved them not even in spite of the way they were, but just because she did. With them she enacted, as many mothers have done, and many fathers too, the parable of the lost sheep, who is to be sought and brought back without end, brought back into mind and into love without end, death no deterrent, futility no bar.

And so she suffered. She looked upon the human condition, I think, as not satisfactory — as unacceptable, notwithstanding that we are in it whether we accept it or not. She was a professed Christian and loved her little weatherboarded church, but I think that it was not easy, and may have been impossible, for her to make peace with our experience of mortality and error, of owning what we cannot correct or save, of losing what we love.

Grandma was fiercely, fiercely loyal to her own, and just as fiercely exclusive in electing her own. Within the small circle of her own, she was capable of profound charity; outside it, she could be relentless and unforgiving. And the boundary was not impermeable. Sometimes Uncle Andrew, for one, had been safely inside it, and sometimes he had been outside. When you were outside, as I knew from my own experience, her anger was direct and her tongue sharp.

Her term of execration was "Hmh!" which she could deliver as concussively as a blow and in tones varying from polite disbelief (for the benefit of guests) to absolute rejection. Her term of contempt was "Psht!" With it she could slice you off like the top of a radish.

Uncle Andrew had crossed the boundary into and out of her good graces many times. The nights of those years after his death, as we sat and talked, she was forever picking apart the divergent strands of her feeling for him. She would be pleased or amused or appalled, or amused and appalled both at once. And always she grieved.

When he was little, with that head covered with golden curls that she could not forget, he was beautiful. He could sing like an angel. And yet he was difficult and mischievous and never still. From the womb, virtually, he lived always a little beyond anyone's anticipation. Even before he could walk, she would have to restrain him by pinning his dresstail under the leg of the bed. He had hardly learned to walk when he flung her good blue pitcher onto the flagstones by the porch step. When he was old enough to receive as a gift his own little hatchet, he chopped one of the rungs out of the banister. She would say regretfully and a little proudly that after he started to school he had become a good fighter. Proudly and a little doubtfully she would say that there never had been anything like the way he could dance.

When he was ready for college, Grandma and Grandpa sent him to the University of Kentucky in a blue blazer — as handsome a young man, they thought, as they had ever laid eyes on — and to do so they spent all they had; Grandpa went without underwear that winter. When he went to Lexington to see his son, he looked everywhere and could not find him, for Uncle Andrew's adventures had begun. His fame as a dancer apparently began during his brief stay at the university.

Grandpa failed in Uncle Andrew, as he succeeded in my father, and it was a bitter failure. Except for the energy that both of them possessed in abundance, Grandpa and Uncle Andrew were as unlike as a tree and a bird. Grandpa could not tolerate, he could not understand, Uncle Andrew's waste of daylight. For him, Andrew was the name of whatever was careless. "Sit up!" he used to say to me as I went by on the pony. "You ride like your Uncle Andrew." It was not that Uncle Andrew rode badly but that he rode carelessly, his mind elsewhere, and Grandpa believed, and said, that "a man ought to keep his mind on his business"— he meant busy-ness, whatever you were doing. Uncle Andrew was Grandma's failure too, of course. It was a mutual property, that failure; it bound them in mutual suffering and even mutual sympathy, and yet I think it stood between them like a heap of thorns. I imagine that their ways of regret were different. Perhaps Grandpa only saw what had happened and named it and bore it, whereas Grandma saw before her always the beautiful child and forgave and hoped. Perhaps. I do not know.

When Grandma and I looked through her collection of photographs that had come with letters from various family members, we would come to a picture of several men in army uniforms squatting in a circle, shooting craps. One of them unmistakably was Uncle Andrew, who had sent the picture, and she would always say "Hmh!" and she would laugh. The laugh seemed both to acknowledge her embarrassment and confess her delight. She delighted in him though he had grieved her nearly into the grave.

He was on her mind forever, and as the evening wore on toward bedtime she would begin again to grieve for him. And always as we approached her grief, we were divided. My loss was nothing like hers. My loss had occurred within the terms of my childhood; it was answered, beyond anything I felt or willed, by my youth and unbidden happiness and all the time I had to live. Her loss would be unrelieved to the end of her life, never mind that she would live on until I was grown and married; her loss was what she had lived to at last and would not live beyond. I could feel that she had come to loss beyond life, unfathomable and inconsolable, as dimensionless as the dark that surrounded the old house and filled it as we talked.

He was on my mind forever too, as I now see. But I was a child; for me, every day was new. I lived beyond my loss even as I suffered it, and without any particular sympathy for myself. And what I have grown into is not sympathy for myself as I was but sympathy for Grandma and Grandpa as they were. I see how time had brought them, once, their years of strength and hope, energy to look forward and build and dream, as we must; and I see how Uncle Andrew took all they had vested in him, their precious one life and time given over in helpless love and hope into the one life and time that he possessed, and how he carried it away on the high flood of his recklessness, his willingness to do whatever he thought of.

I see now what perhaps I have known for a long time that I would see, if I looked: He was a child who wanted only to be free, as I myself had been free back at the pond that afternoon of his death. He was a big, supremely willful child whom Grandma and Grandpa and Aunt Judith could not confine, and who could be balked by no requirement or demand. And yet, hating confinement, he had been confined—in a hapless marriage, in bad jobs, sometimes in self-reproach, and finally in a grave with which he had made no terms. He had been confined because he had confined himself, as only he could have done, because he was the way he was and would not change, or could not. It was knowledge of his confinement, I think, that so surrounded us with pain and made us grieve so long.

When bedtime came, I would go up the stairs first and get into my bed in the little back hall, leaving the door open to the room where Grandma slept. I would hear her stirring in the rooms below, setting things to rights, making sure she had forgotten nothing. Assuming perhaps that I was asleep, she would have begun to talk aloud to herself. "Mm-*hmh!*" she would say as she shut a door or lowered a sash, "Mm-*hmh!*" as she turned off the lights.

And then I would hear her coming slowly up the stairs, the banister creaking under her hand as though now, alone with her thoughts, she bore the whole accumulated weight of time and loss. As she came up, she would be saying to herself always the same thing: "Oh, my poor boy! Oh, my poor, poor boy!"

I would hear her muttering still as she went about her room, preparing for bed: "May God have mercy on my poor boy!"

And then it would be dark. And then it would be morning.

10

The time had to come, of course, when what I knew no longer satisfied me. I had been told almost nothing about the circumstances of Uncle Andrew's murder, I had asked nothing, and yet I wanted to know. That death had remained in the forefront of my mind, as I knew it had in my grandmother's and my father's and Aunt Judith's. I knew too that for other people it had receded and diminished as it had mingled with other concerns. I could not have asked those whom my questions would have pained the most. With others, the subject did not come up. I did not want my curiosity about it to be known.

But finally when I was maybe in my last year of high school, I became conscious that there were such things as court records. The county court clerk at that time was Charlie Hardy, as dear a friend, I suppose, as my father had; they bird-hunted together. I made up my mind to ask Mr. Hardy to show me the records of Carp Harmon's trial, expecting to see transcripts of the lawyers' arguments and the testimony of witnesses; I imagined that there would be a great pile of papers that I could sit down somewhere and read, and at last know everything I wanted to know.

I watched for a time when Mr. Hardy was in his office alone. I did not want anybody but him to hear my request. Above all, I did not want my father to know what I was doing. What I intended to do was unbandage a wound. It was in part my own wound, but I felt it was my father's more than mine, and maybe I had no right to know more than he had told me.

Though I was determined to see those papers, I was also more than a little ashamed.

"Son, I'll show you," Mr. Hardy said when I finally walked in and asked him. "I'll show you what there is, I'll *show* you, son, but there ain't much."

Already I was sorry I had come, for I saw that he knew exactly what I wanted and that he too was thinking of my father. Spitting fragments of tobacco bitten from the cold stump of his cigar, he climbed a ladder up a large wall of file boxes ranked on shelves, selected one of the boxes, and brought it to me.

"See," he said, "there's not a hell of a lot here that would be of interest to you, son." He showed me the warrant for Carp Harmon's arrest, his indictment, several pleadings, all technical documents no more informative than they were required to be.

"I thought there would be a record of what was said at the trial."

"Naw, son," he said. "Nawsir, son, no such record was ever made. What was said at that trial is a long time gone."

He explained that there had been no appeal. There would have been a transcript only if there had been an appeal. By then I was relieved that there was no record. Mr. Hardy was putting the papers back into their box. "Nawsir, son, that record you want to see, it never did exist." He removed the cigar from his mouth, spat toward the wastebasket, and then looked at me. "Son," he said, "I'm sorry."

And still we both were embarrassed, for even though the record I sought did not exist, the fact remained that Charlie Hardy knew what had happened at that trial. I knew he could imagine my saying, "Well, Mr. Hardy, why don't you *tell* me what happened?" And I knew — I know much more certainly now — that he would have given years off his life to be spared the question.

"Well, thank you, Mr. Hardy," I said.

"Any time, son," he said. "Any time." He waved to me with the hand holding the cigar as if I were already out of the building and across the street. "By God, son, come back! *Any* time!"

But as time went on I did learn some things. Things that I did not know to ask for came to me on their own.

One day after the ewes were sheared, when Elton Penn and Henry and

I hauled the bagged wool to market, we ran into Yeager Stump. Something was said about dancing. Maybe Elton mentioned that Henry and I were going to a dance, or had been to one; maybe he was complaining, as he sometimes did, joking, but only half joking, that when we danced late into the night we were no account in the daytime. Whatever was said, it reminded Mr. Stump of Uncle Andrew.

"Boys," he said, and there was laughter in his eyes though he did not laugh aloud, "I've seen your uncle Andrew too drunk to walk, but I never saw him too drunk to dance."

Later it was Mr. Stump, leaning to talk to me through a car window, his eyes filled with that same quiet, reminiscent, almost tender unuttered laughter, who told me two little bits of Uncle Andrew's poetry. "Your uncle Andrew said that when he was with a woman and that old extremity came to him, every hair in his bee-hind was a jew's harp playing a different tune." Mr. Stump's voice recovered exactly Uncle Andrew's jazzy intonation. "He said a big covey of quail flew out his bunghole one bird at a time."

And then Mr. Stump did laugh aloud, briefly. He clapped his hand onto the metal windowsill and straightened up. "Well, he was something. There never was another one like him."

When I went away to Lexington to the university, forty years after Uncle Andrew's failed expedition there, I continued my checking account at the Independent Farmers Bank at Port William. A number of times when I wrote out a check for a woman salesclerk, the lady would look at my signature and the name of the town, and she would say—it was invariably the same sentence—"I knew an Andrew Catlett once."

"He was my uncle," I would say.

And then she would say, "He was *such* a dancer!" Or "Oh, *how* that man could dance!" Or "I just *loved* to dance with him! He was so handsome."

They always spoke of him as a dancer. They always smiled in remembering him. Speaking of him, they always sounded younger than they were, and a little dreamy.

One day in Lexington I cashed a check at Scoop Rawl's Ice Cream Parlor. Scoop himself was at the cash register. He looked at my signature. "Andrew Catlett," he said. "Port William. I knew an Andrew Catlett from down there."

"Yessir," I said. "He was my uncle."

He looked at me over his glasses. "Your uncle. God almighty, we had some times!"

I said, "Yessir," hoping he would say more, and he did, a little. He had known Uncle Andrew, apparently, not during his brief visit to Lexington as a student, but after his marriage, when he was traveling for a distillery.

"Andrew had a girl he called Sweetie Pie. He'd squall for her when he was drunk and you could hear him half a mile: 'Sweetie *Pie!*'"

I *knew* how he sounded. I could hear that raucous mating call rising in the midst of the late-night fracas and hilarity of some Lexington blind tiger as Uncle Andrew hooked cute little Sweetie Pie with his right arm and pulled her into his lap. During my college years also I encountered a woman who had lived near us in Hargrave when I was a child. She had been beautiful when she was young and had been married to an old man. Uncle Andrew, she told me, laughing, had said to her, "When that old son of a bitch is dead, I'm going to stomp on his grave until he's in there good and tight, and then I'm going to get straight into bed with you."

She told me too of the midnight when Uncle Andrew and his cronies in their mating plumage, transcendently drunk, burst into Momma-pie's bedroom, and Uncle Andrew snapped on the light. "Wake up, Momma-pie! We've bred all the women, cows, yo sheep, mares, and mare mules — and now, by God, we're going to breed you!"

In spite of Yeager Stump's later claim that they did whatever they thought of, I do not believe that this actually happened; if it had, Uncle Andrew's moments of retrospective self-knowledge and regret would have forbidden him to talk about it, but it was a story that was known because he had told it.

I can imagine a night of hilarity, Uncle Andrew and Buster Simms and Yeager Stump out among 'em, women and whiskey on hand, Uncle Andrew talking, the others laughing and egging him on. He is conjuring up the most outrageous scene he can think of: he and his buddies crowding into that chastely fragrant room like a nightmare, the sudden light revealing Momma-pie in her nightcap, sans teeth, sitting up in bed, clutching the bedclothes to her bosom. I can imagine the tale repeated and improved at every opportunity as if it had actually happened, the work of alcoholic incandescence and a refined sense of impropriety.

But I know too that Mr. Stump was right: A lot of the things they thought of, they did. Their taste in women ran simply to the available; their pleasures were restricted only by the possible. In his times of breaking out, which apparently were the times he lived for, Uncle Andrew granted an uncomplicated obedience to impulses that men of faith and loyalty like my father struggle against all their lives. Men who obey those impulses surely invite their own destruction, and I think there were moments when Uncle Andrew knew this.

But obviously not all are destroyed. Yeager Stump, for one, enjoyed life far beyond the conventional three score years and ten. Even at the end, when he was housebound, he continued to enjoy life. Miss Iris Flynn, devoted as always, kept him supplied with good bourbon. On one of her visits, she handed him the anticipated bottle and exclaimed about its lately increased cost. "Yes," said Mr. Stump, "maybe they'll finally charge what it's worth."

Whether or not Uncle Andrew invited the destruction he in fact received is at least a disturbed question, and perhaps an unanswerable one. But I did not even know it was a question until one day — I was grown by then — I said point-blank to Elton Penn: "Why did Carp Harmon kill Uncle Andrew?"

Probably Elton was no more comfortable with my curiosity than Mr. Hardy had been, but he gave me a straight answer. "Well, the way I heard it, your Uncle Andrew propositioned Harmon's daughter there in the store where the ones that were tearing down those buildings would go for lunch."

It was not as though Elton and I were two people merely interested in the pursuit of truth; we both knew the hardship that that story would have presented to my family. We did not pursue the subject further, partly because of the pain that surrounded it, partly because I thought the explanation credible and had no more questions to ask. I believed that if he had thought of doing so, Uncle Andrew would have propositioned Carp Harmon's daughter in the store, devil take the witnesses. He would have done it because he thought of doing it and because he enjoyed the outrageousness of it and because he relished the self-abandonment of it. From there, I supposed, the story had gone on to its conclusion according to the logic of anger.

∻

The year following my grandmother Catlett's death, I returned with my wife and baby daughter to live through the summer in the old house. Grandma's things were still there, put away in their places, just as she had left them, and it fell to me to dispose of them. Because she had known no extravagance in her life, she had saved everything salvageable: string, pieces of cloth, buttons and buckles, canceled checks and notes, bits of paper covered with now meaningless computations and lists, letters and cards, clippings from newspapers — anything that, within the terms and hopes of her life, had seemed valuable or potentially useful or in some way dear.

Among all else she saved were twenty or so letters from Uncle Andrew. Most of these were written on the stationery of hotels in southern states, mostly in South Carolina. All of them show a wish to be a good son, and I have no doubt that this was a wish that he felt genuinely enough when he felt it; I do not think that he felt it all the time. The letters always intend to assure Grandma and Grandpa that he is doing better, or is now all right, or has resolved to lead a cleaner life. He clearly did not like the thought that they were worried about him. And yet there are, even in this small and perhaps selective sheaf that Grandma saved, too many letters of that sort. It is impossible not to suspect that he was trying, as if by incantation, to lay to rest the more obvious consequences of failings that he could not help, or that he did not much want to help. It is almost as if he felt that if he could just stop Grandma and Grandpa, especially Grandma, from worrying, there would be nothing to worry about.

And yet they are troubled letters, and they are troubling. One of them in particular has occupied all alone a large place in my mind since I first read it. It was written a few months after I was born and given his name. According to the letter, he has been "out"—certainly out of a job and perhaps also drunk. But now, he says, "While not making any money am better off than I was, some, and believe in six months will be much better. First want to tell you and ask that you not worry one bit." He is evidently ready to begin work as a salesman for a liquor company. His associates, he says, are "the cleanest bunch of men you ever saw," and they do not drink. But if Grandma wishes, he will try to get another kind of job, which he does not believe would be hard for him to do. He thanks the family for their kindness and consideration of his feelings while he was "out." My mother in particular, he says, has been sweet and thoughtful. They all have shown him such love and affection that he could do nothing that would hurt them or shake their confidence.

And then he writes the sentence — troubled, tender, hopeful, and, as I know, hopeless — that binds me to him closer than my name: "And little Andrew, bless his heart — if for nothing else, I would be a man for him."

11

After I found the letters and read them and put them away again, I assumed that I knew as much about Uncle Andrew as I was ever going to know. I continued to remember him and to think and wonder about him, but I asked no more questions.

And then, thirty years later, after my father died, I found among his papers his file of bills, receipts, and other documents having to do with the settlement of Uncle Andrew's estate. Folded up in that file was a copy of the Hargrave *Weekly Express*, giving an account of the examining trial of Carp Harmon. Why I had not thought before to examine the back issues of the *Weekly Express* I am not sure; I had believed the little I had heard, and perhaps that had satisfied me, but perhaps I also had felt that the truth about Uncle Andrew's death, as long as my father was alive, was his belonging, not mine.

But now, that paper having come to me from my father's very hands, which had folded it and put it away so long ago, I opened it and read the article as eagerly, I think, as I have ever read anything. Much of the article deals with technicalities, but two paragraphs are given to the story of the murder:

"P. R. Gadwell, merchant at Stoneport, testified that Catlett and a group of workers at the lead mine, where buildings were being dismantled, came to the store for lunch and soft drinks. He said Harmon's daughter came in the store and gave her father some change. Gadwell then heard a noise and next saw Catlett getting up after being knocked down by Harmon. Harmon had hit him with an oilcan. He said he heard Catlett apologizing to Harmon, stating he did not know the girl was his daughter. Gadwell said he got Catlett and the other men out of the store but Harmon remained 10 or 15 minutes.

"Jake Branch of near Hargrave, who was assisting Catlett in the dismantling job, said he was 3 or 4 feet from Catlett when the accused hit him with the oilcan. He testified that the group went back to their work and about an hour had elapsed when Harmon suddenly came up to Catlett and said he was going to kill him and pulled a gun. He stated Catlett pleaded that it was 'my mistake' and 'don't shoot me.' Branch said Harmon fired two shots and the workmen rushed Catlett to the hospital.

"R. T. Purlin, 16-year-old stepson of Branch, with the group at the mine, said he yelled to Catlett when he saw Harmon slipping through the weeds but believes Catlett did not hear him."

R. T. Purlin, older than I by six years, had been a hero to Henry and me when we were boys, working and playing together on the Crayton Place, for even at the age of fourteen he was already in body a grown man with an arm like one of Homer's spear throwers, and he never tired of entertaining us with feats of strength. He had a truly clear and generous heart and was never condescending in his friendship to us smaller boys. R. T. was the last living witness to Uncle Andrew's murder. I had not seen him in a long time.

When I called him up and asked if I could come and talk with him, he said, "Yessir! You come right on over here."

🌿

The old house that R. T. was living in had no front porch, but a wide back porch ran the length of the ell. Good hounds were chained to their houses under the trees out back.

R. T. came out onto the porch to meet me. "What you been doing all these years?" He talked loudly, like his mother, and had her turns of speech, sounding both like her and like himself.

We went in and sat down at the table in the kitchen where his wife was at work. I complimented his dogs, and we talked a little about coon hunting. R. T. spoke of a tree so full of coons that when their eyes shone back in the beam of his light, the tree looked like a Christmas tree.

We remembered things that had happened on the Crayton Place in the old days. We spoke of his brothers and sisters, whole and half, and of his stepsisters, Jake Branch's daughters by his first wife, and we named and remembered Minnie's six brothers and all the hands who at one time or another had worked for Jake. We spoke of Grandpa Catlett's saddle mare, old Rose, and of Tige and Red, Jake Branch's good team of mules.

Finally I spoke the question I had come to ask: "What happened down there at the lead mine when Carp Harmon shot Uncle Andrew?"

It was hot, R. T. said, when they went back to work in the afternoon, and they were hard at it — all four of them, he and Col Oaks, one of Jake's sons-in-law, Jake himself, and Uncle Andrew. There was a spring of fine cold water down near the road, and after a while Uncle Andrew said, "Jake, let's go get us a drink and leave it with the boys for a while."

The two of them went down to where Uncle Andrew had left his car, just pulled in off the road, to get the top off Uncle Andrew's thermos jug to use as a drinking cup. And then R. T. saw Carp Harmon coming up the road. He ran from one tree or bush to another, trying to stay hidden. When he got near the men at the car, he shot Uncle Andrew, threatened Jake, and ran away down the road again, stopping now and then to look back, R. T. said, "like a sheep-killing dog."

I asked if Uncle Andrew had given some insult to Carp Harmon's daughter when they were down at the store.

R. T. said emphatically, "Nawsir! Andrew never said *nothing* to that girl."

⚘

On my way home, I stopped to see my mother. She was sitting in her chair, reading, as she usually is when I come by in the afternoon. And as usual she did not hear me until I rapped loudly on the door of the room where she was sitting. I always expect her to be frightened when I do that, but she never is, being far more reconciled to the unexpected than I am. And so she instructs me.

She looked up, smiled, and said, "Hello! Come in!"

I came in and sat down on the end of the sofa nearest her chair.

"Well, where have you been?"

"I've been to see R. T. Purlin."

"Oh, R. T.!" she said. "What for?"

"To talk," I said.

And then, surprising myself, broaching the issue with her for the first time in my life, I said, "R. T. says that Uncle Andrew didn't say anything sexual at all to Carp Harmon's daughter."

That I could have introduced this subject so abruptly made me aware that we were speaking of Uncle Andrew's death in my father's absence, in the absence of his grief, free of it at last, as I know we both believed that my father was now at last free of it.

"No," my mother said. "He didn't."

The whole business of the sexual insult to the girl, she said, was the defense attorney's lie. Years later, in fact, somebody had told my father that the defense attorney had admitted to the lie. He said that he did not blame my father for disliking him, for he had made the story up.

Thus, suddenly, I was involved in a way I had not expected to be. If the story of the proposition to Carp Harmon's daughter was a lie, then I was implicated in the lie, because for many years I had believed it. But I needed to consider also the possibility that it was *not* true that the defense attorney had lied. If his story was true and our people had falsely denied it, I assumed that this would not have been a deliberate or malicious lie but one that came about simply because those who loved Uncle Andrew, including R. T., could not bear to believe otherwise. And if this belief in Uncle Andrew's innocence was a lie, then I was implicated there also, for I was grateful for whatever comfort it had given to those who had believed it.

Unable now to put it off any longer, I went to the office of the *Weekly Express* and searched out the account of Carp Harmon's trial. According to the article I had already seen, the trial had been set for the September term, but I found that it had been moved to the January term because in September the jurymen had needed to be at home, harvesting their tobacco. In January the jury heard the case and gave their verdict. Carp Harmon received his sentence of two years in the penitentiary. The article in the *Weekly Express* seems meant only to explain the brevity of the sentence. These are the relevant paragraphs:

"During their lunch hour, according to Harmon, Catlett made a remark to Harmon's daughter and Harmon knocked him down. Catlett apologized. Later in the afternoon Harmon went to the scene of work where Catlett and his helpers were and he shot Catlett when Catlett reached for a 2 x 4, following some words between them.

"Harmon testified that he went back to the scene of work to nail a covering over a well. He said Catlett told him to get off the premises along with a remark about his daughter, whom he included in the order to stay away. Harmon said that he fired when Catlett reached for the piece of timber.

"When questioned as to why he had a gun on his person, Harmon said he had been told that someone had run his trotlines."

The jury obviously believed the story of the "remark" to Carp Harmon's daughter — as did the reporter for the *Weekly Express*. If it was a lie, it was the work of a good liar, who could make his story both plausible and consonant with Uncle Andrew's character, which would have been pretty generally known.

The *Weekly Express* writer evidently had believed the story also when it was told six months earlier at the examining trial. What seems significantly different between the two accounts is the appearance in the second of the two-by-four, which was not mentioned in the first.

If the story of the "remark" is true, and if it is true that Carp Harmon's lawyer later admitted that he had told a lie, then the lie may have been this business of the two-by-four, for it is the only reported detail that would have supported an argument of self-defense.

At any rate, I now had learned the basis of the story about the well cover that I had heard when I was a child.

Why, as I got older, did I not ask my father for his version of these events? Now that he is dead, it is easy to wish that I had asked. And yet I know why I did not. I did not want to live again in the great pain I had felt in the old house that night when he had wept so helplessly with Grandma and Grandpa. I did not want to be with him in the presence of that pain where only it and we existed. If I were to speak to his ghost, perhaps I still could not bring myself to ask. When I am a ghost myself, perhaps we will talk of it.

12

If you go toward Stoneport from the high ground instead of along the river, you go at first through a country of excellent broad ridges, farmland greatly respected for its depth and warmth. And then the upland becomes more broken, the ridges narrower, the hollows steeper, the soil thin and rocky. The road to the lead mine turns off one of the ridges and follows a creek bed, usually dry in summer, down into a narrow, wooded hollow. Much of that country is now wooded and has been so for a long time. The farming on those slopes was done in clearings that moved about in place and time as the trees were succeeded by crops, which were succeeded after a short time by a new growth of trees. Now, after its inevitable diminishment by such cropping, the land has been almost entirely given back to the trees.

After it has brought you down nearly to Stoneport on the river, the road passes the site of the old lead mine, which lies off to the right on the far side of the creek. There is still a weedy clearing, originally a hole in the woods to accommodate a hole in the ground. The clearing has remained open because the floor of the hollow has been leveled and covered with tailings from the mine. A squatter has recently lived there in an old bus, which is now abandoned and surrounded by weeds and junk. The main building of the mine, which housed its heavy machinery, was up on the slope. Its foundation, now bare and weathered, straddles the creek, which was used to bear away some of the waste from the extraction of the ore. Behind it, the deep well that Carp Harmon was so anxious to protect is still without a cover; the surface of the water, twenty feet down, is covered with a floating crust of plastic jugs and bottles. Somebody has tried to "improve" the spring of good water down by the road by digging a deep trench into it with a backhoe. The nature of the place seems more insulted by the ordinary acts and artifacts of the present than by the mining of half a century ago.

I went there once with my father when he and Uncle Andrew and the others were in the process of buying the buildings, and I had never been back. I did not even know how to get there until R. T. Purlin went there with me on a hot August afternoon not long after I had hunted up the story of Carp Harmon's trial in the *Weekly Express*.

We pulled off the road, now blacktopped but still just a narrow track coming down through the trees. While we walked over the valley floor and then climbed up over the old foundations into the returning woods, R. T. gave me the story again as the place brought it back to mind.

"Andrew parked his car yonder where you left your truck. Just pulled in off of the road, the way he did every day. Him and Jake went there to get the top off of Andrew's jug on their way to the spring. That fellow stepped out of the bushes must have been right there. Maybe he had stood there a little while, watching them."

He pointed into the air over the foundation of the main building. "Me and Col, we never seen him. We was way up maybe thirty feet in the framework of that building—*big* timbers!—tearing it down. And we heard the shots: *Bam! Bam!*

"I said, 'What the hell was that?'

"And Col said, 'I think that guy has shot Andrew.'

"And down we come."

"Did Uncle Andrew say anything after he was shot?"

"Naw. He went to hurting then. He never said anything."

"And Carp Harmon threatened Jake and ran off?"

"He run right back down the road," R. T. said, and he acted out Carp Harmon's flight, running and then stopping to look back, running and looking back.

"And then you all loaded Uncle Andrew into the car and started for the hospital."

"Yeah."

"And you drove?"

"I was the only one that *could* drive. Jake and Col didn't know how. Andrew had let me drive around a little on the farm. I never had drove on the road. I done pretty good that day till we got up to the top of the lane and onto the blacktop and I started trying to go fast. I had a hard time then to keep in the road. And Andrew was just kicking the car to pieces. We was lucky to make it."

What a ride that must have been for a sixteen-year-old boy who could barely drive, was badly frightened, and who loved the hurt man kicking in pain! In only a few seconds they had been carried from their ordinary work into a moment impossible to be ready for: Uncle Andrew fallen, holding his belly with bloody fingers, Carp Harmon's footsteps going away down the gravel road, nothing now in sight or memory that was quite believable, Uncle Andrew's car sitting there without a driver.

It started to come to me. I began to imagine it, as I knew my father had done, time and again, seeing it as it must have happened and as he could not help seeing it.

And now I too saw them there. I knew how it had been, as if this imagining had suddenly descended to me from my father. I saw them as they lifted Uncle Andrew and got him into the car and as Jake and Col got in, leaving the driver's seat empty.

I heard R. T., not just excited but scared now as well: "Who's going to drive?"

I heard Jake — helpless, angry, bewildered, in a hurry, and yet necessarily resigned: "You are, I reckon."

I saw the black car lurch backward into the road, and then lurch forward, gravel flying from under its wheels as it started up the hill.

And all this happened while I was swimming in the pond, for the moment safe.

❧

R. T. and I loitered around the place a while longer, trying without success to find a rock that R. T. could identify positively as lead ore. He was sure that there had been many such rocks lying around when they had been working down there, but we could find none. Giving up at last, we got into my pickup and started on down toward Stoneport, less than half a mile away.

"And you say Uncle Andrew didn't make a pass at Carp Harmon's daughter?"

"Nawsir. He never," R. T. said. "It was me that girl was talking to.

"I'll show you," he said. We were coming into Stoneport, just a few houses and other buildings scattered around a white weatherboarded church. R. T. showed me the small house where Carp Harmon had lived. He showed me the empty place where fifty years ago had stood the store belonging to P. R. Gadwell. He showed me the place on the roadside opposite where Uncle Andrew had parked his car under the trees.

"I was sitting in the car," R. T. said, "and the girl was leaning against it, talking to me. That fellow could stand in his yard and look right down the road at Andrew's car and see her there. That's how it all got started."

It is a wide street, the view unobstructed from the yard of the house that was Carp Harmon's down to Uncle Andrew's parking spot, a distance of three or four hundred feet. And so R. T.'s version of the story had the plausibility of a true line of sight. It could have happened the way he told it. He could have been himself the bait of a trap that had caught Uncle Andrew.

And yet R. T.'s memory, as I knew by then, was not safe from his imagination. He had told me, on two different days, both that he had and that he had not seen Carp Harmon as he came up the road before the shooting. And on that very day he had told me two versions of his and Col Oaks's hearing the shots; in the first version, R. T. had said, "What the hell was that?" and in the second, Col Oaks had said it. If he had seen the shooting, which he must have done if he had seen Carp Harmon's approach and had tried to warn Uncle Andrew, he apparently had found it too painful to remember. I don't think that these were falsehoods in the usual sense but rather that R. T., in brooding over the story for so many years, had imagined it from shifting points of view, had imagined what he had not seen, had seen what he had not remembered. There is no assurance that he had not imagined also things that had not happened.

If Uncle Andrew had not, in fact, made the "remark" to Carp Harmon's daughter, then why did both P. R. Gadwell and Jake Branch testify that Uncle Andrew apologized to Harmon?

The defense lawyer's story, true or untrue, depended for credibility on the general knowledge of Uncle Andrew's character. I was not the only one who assumed that if he had thought of it, Uncle Andrew would have openly propositioned a girl in a public place. According to that story, as I suppose the jury heard it, a man who lives by impulse invites his own destruction; if he is destroyed as a result of one of his impulsive acts, then a kind of justice has been done. Character is fate, and Carp Harmon was no more than the virtually innocent agent of the appointed fate.

If that story is false, if it *was* R. T. the girl was talking to, then Uncle Andrew's fate had nothing to do with his character and everything to do with chance and the character of Carp Harmon.

But R. T. told me something else that I cannot forget, though perhaps it leads nowhere. He said he had heard that Carp Harmon had been wanting to kill somebody for a long time. "People down there shied him," R. T. said. "He'd been carrying his pistol hid under a rag in the bottom of a ten-quart bucket. He wanted to kill somebody and make a big name for himself. He thought he could kill an outsider and lie his way out of it — which is about what he done."

This story has the standing merely of gossip, but some gossip is true, and Carp Harmon would hardly have been the first of his kind who went about with a hidden gun, looking for somebody to kill. If the piece of gossip *is* true, then the other explanations are not explanations but merely excuses. But a man looking for somebody to kill can presumably find reasons and candidates everywhere, the human race being what it is. If Carp Harmon was in fact such a man, then why did he choose Uncle Andrew, who was not even the only available outsider?

Well, I know too that Carp Harmon was a widower, raising his daughter by himself, undoubtedly afraid for her and afraid for that considerable part of his own self-respect that was at her disposal. And he believed, as he told the court, that somebody was running his trotlines; he was prepared to shoot whoever it was. He was exceptional in none of this — neither in his fear nor in his suspicion nor in his violence.

Nor in his carelessness. Murder, I suppose, is the ultimate carelessness. But Carp Harmon's seems to have been a fearful carelessness, the carelessness of a man who fears that he is small or that he is being held in contempt. And in Uncle Andrew, at least before their violent encounter in

Gadwell's store, he saw a man who must have seemed fearlessly careless, a man completely unabashed, carrying on as he pleased without regard to the possibility that somebody might mind. To a man fearing to be held in contempt, Uncle Andrew would have appeared to be the very holder-in-contempt he had been expecting, whose every gesture identified him as a lifter of skirts and trotlines, a man insufferably sure of himself.

If that is true, then I return again to the thought that Uncle Andrew's character was his fate, and Carp Harmon the agent of it.

But if murder is the ultimate carelessness, it is also the ultimate over-simplifier. It is the paramount act (there are others) by which we reduce a human being to the dimension of one thought. I knew the utterly reckless and fearless, unasking and unanswering Andrew Catlett that Carp Harmon saw. But if Uncle Andrew sometimes possessed a sort of invulnerability of exuberance and regardlessness, he was no longer regardless when he apologized to Carp Harmon. Then he had become pathetic, because, as events would soon prove, it was too late. Carp Harmon cannot have known the quietness and the look by which I knew that Uncle Andrew sometimes bore his life and fate as suffering. Carp Harmon cannot have known, as I know, that for Uncle Andrew there was always a time or a timelessness after (and before) the fact when he wanted to be a better man — if for nothing else, for me.

And all along I have had to wonder what difference I might have made if Uncle Andrew had let me go to Stoneport with him, as I wanted to. Might my presence somehow have unlocked the pattern of the events of that day? Might a small boy, just by being there, have altered the behavior of two reckless men by the tiny shift that might have been needed to change all our lives? Might it be that Uncle Andrew's great mistake was so small a thing as ignoring my advice that I should be taken along? Who can know? Who can know even that the difference, if it had been made, would have been for the better? It might be that if I had gone I would merely have witnessed the shooting. In which case I would not have needed to ask certain questions.

Finally grief has no case to make. All its questions reach beyond the world. And now I am done. The questions remain; the asking is finished. This gathering of fifty-year-old memories, those few brown and brittle pages of newsprint, all those years stand between me and the actual event as irremediably as the end of the world.

Finally you must believe as your heart instructs. If you are a gossip or a cynic or an apostle of realism, you believe the worst you can imagine. If you follow the other way, accepting the bonds of faith and affection, you believe the best you can imagine in the face of the evidence. And so at last, like R. T., I must believe as I imagine and as I therefore choose. I choose not to argue with the story of the "remark" to Carp Harmon's daughter, because it seems both likely and unlikely, and now it makes no difference. I choose not to believe the argument of self-defense; why would even a reckless man with only a two-by-four attack a man with a pistol? I choose to believe that Uncle Andrew said, "Don't shoot me," for it is too plain and sad to be a lie.

And so at last I can imagine it as it might have been.

❦

It is early in the afternoon. The sun is still shining nearly straight down into the tight little valley where Uncle Andrew, Jake Branch, Col Oaks, and R. T. Purlin are dismantling the framework of the main building of the lead mine. The two younger men are at work high up on the heavy timbers, which they are prying loose and letting fall. Uncle Andrew and Jake stand back as the timbers drop, and then move them out of the way and begin pulling out the nails. It is strenuous, dirty, and dangerous work (Uncle Andrew was right not to let me come along). In the small clearing there are stacks of timbers, sorted according to dimension, and piles of corrugated tin. The sun strikes all surfaces with relentless brilliance. Metal objects, including the tools the men are using, if laid down for long, become painful to pick up. There is no breeze; the air is humid, heavy, and still.

Uncle Andrew's sleeves are rolled above his elbows. His arms are shining with sweat and flecked with dirt. His shirt is soaked. And yet he wears his soiled and rumpled clothing and his narrow-brimmed straw hat with a kind of style. He is quick to take part in the talk that comes and goes or to pick up a joke; otherwise his face resumes the expression it has when he is enduring what must be endured. The noontime events down at the store have remained with him. He was knocked down (with an unopened quart can of oil, R. T. said), and he apologized. These facts lie in his belly like something indigestible. What has been done needs undoing, and cannot be undone. As many times before, it is not the present that surprises him but the past, the present slipped away into irrevocability. As many times before, he would like to turn away, find an opening, get out. He feels his own history crowding him, as near to him in that heat as his clinging shirt, as his flesh itself. He feels the weight of the history of flesh. He feels tired. He thinks, "I am already forty-nine years old." He has not drunk since they returned to work, and he is thirsty.

"Jake," he says, "let's go get us a drink, and leave it with the boys for a while."

The two of them put down their tools. They go to the car where Uncle Andrew left his thermos jug, the water in it by then too warm to drink. Off in the shade they can see the spring flowing out beneath its mossy ledge.

And then Carp Harmon steps from behind the trees, already close, and he has a pistol in his hand. Two men, both drawn to that giddy edge where people do what they think of doing, have come face-to-face, and one holds a pistol, and one does not.

"I'm going to kill you," Carp Harmon says, and Uncle Andrew knows he means it.

This, I imagine, was his second direct confrontation with his fate, the first having occurred in the road ditch on the night before his wedding. And I imagine that in this latter moment he knew clearly at last what he was: a man dearly beloved, in spite of his faults.

"Don't shoot me," he says. He is praying, not to Carp Harmon, but to another possibility, his own sudden vision of what he means to the rest of us — of what we all had meant and the much more that we might have meant to one another.

"Don't shoot me."

And Carp Harmon fires forever his two shots.

13

Except for his silent whirl with Mrs. Partlet that afternoon in Minnie Branch's kitchen, I never saw Uncle Andrew dance, but prompted by so many who did see and who remembered, I have often imagined him dancing.

He went into the music, I imagine, alert and aware and yet abandoned, as one might go running into the dark. Invested with the power that women granted him, he would be wholly given over to the music, almost gravely submitted to that which moved him, and yet elated, in reckless exuberance carried away.

I imagine a ballroom in some hotel — in Lexington or Louisville, or Columbia or Charleston — a large room dimly lit, a band on a dais at one end. The room smells of flowers, perfume, tobacco smoke. There is loud talking and laughter, Uncle Andrew in the thick of it, a little drunk. There is a sort of aura of careless delight about him, a suppressed extravagance of physical elation, as though he might at any moment do something that will draw the attention of the whole room to him. He seems himself to be unaware of this.

He is aware of the woman sitting beside him. (Who is she? She is, let us say, Aphrodite herself, for the while. Custom cannot stale her infinite variety.) For the while his being is directed toward her like the beam of a lamp, and she knows it. She casts back his light, granting him love — as I did, as we all did, because he had the power of attracting it; not ever asking for it, he called it forth.

The band members shift in their seats, take up their instruments, and begin another song. They play "Don't Get Around Much Anymore," a song elegant and inconsolable. (It may have come too late for him to have danced to it, but it is the one song I can remember hearing him sing, and so I imagine him dancing to it.) He reaches out without a word; the woman gives him her hand. They rise and walk onto the floor, dancing even before they dance. They step into the music. The woman's weight on his arm, given to him, he forgets his feet. The two of them ask and answer one another, motion for motion. He holds her with an assurance that is almost forgetfulness, and yet is entirely attentive to her and to the song that moves them:

> *Darling I guess*
> *My mind's more at ease*
> *But nevertheless*
> *Why stir up memories*
>
> *Been invited on dates*
> *Might have gone but what for*
> *Awf'lly diff'rent without you*
> *Don't get around much anymore.*

A trumpet solo sways, gleaming, in the air. Under it the man and woman turn and soar. The woman rests upon his arm, leaning back, at one with him in their now weightless flight. The little while it lasts, he does not know where he is.

14

One day maybe forty years ago my father told Elton Penn, "I almost did something once that I would have been awfully sorry for."

Elton told Henry and me not long afterward. We had been at work and were resting, as it happened, in the shade of some locust trees beside the tobacco barn that had been built of our share of the materials salvaged from the lead mine. Henry and I were grown boys then, eligible to be told things that Elton found it lonely to know by himself.

"I wonder what he meant," Elton said. "I couldn't ask him."

The two of them had been in my father's car, driving through the fields, looking at the condition of everything and talking, as they often did. My father, for some reason, reached over and opened the glove compartment. When he did so, Elton saw a small nickel-plated .32 revolver lying among the papers and other things my father kept there.

"What are you carrying that for, Wheeler?" Elton asked.

I no longer remember the reason. Probably he was on the lookout for stray dogs. He had sheep in those days, and dogs were always a worry.

Elton asked him if he had bought the pistol in fear that he might need to defend himself. We all knew that my father had once defended a man in a murder trial, at the end of which the acquitted defendant had been shot and killed by the victim's brother. Elton wanted to hear about that. But my father only shook his head and said that once he had almost done something he would have been sorry for.

Sitting under the locusts, we tried to think what it might have been. We decided, with the barn there to remind us, that it must have had something to do with Carp Harmon, though we did not know for sure.

Of course, we did not know at all. I don't remember that any of us ever brought up the subject again, though we were all much interested in my father and we talked about him interminably.

He fascinated us, I think, because he was so completely alive and passionate and intelligent, so precisely intent upon the things he loved, so eager to get work done, so fiercely demanding of us, and yet so tender toward us. We would be angry at him often enough, and yet he delighted us, and we were proud of him. Elton loved to mimic my father's way of driving up in his car in a hurry, rolling the window down, patting the accelerator with his foot while he talked to you, and then — bzzzt! — taking off again, sometimes in the midst of your answer to what he had just asked you. He could use the telephone the same way, hanging up the instant he found out what he had called to learn, leaving you talking to the dead receiver. But sometimes when you were out at work he would seem just to ease up out of nowhere; you would look up and there he would be, sitting in the car, watching you and smiling, glad to have found you, glad to be there with you. Wonderful conversations sometimes happened at those times.

One day in the early spring Elton was disking ground a long way from the house. The day turned cold, and he had not worn enough clothes. Gradually the chill sank into him until his bones ached. And then, as he came to the end of one of his rounds, he saw my father driving up. Elton left the tractor and got into the car. My father turned up the heater and the two of them sat there and talked of the coming year while Elton quit shivering and got warm. Finally, having only a little left to do, Elton returned to the tractor and my father went on wherever he was going.

In such wanderings and encounters, my father enacted his belonging to his country and his people. He could be as peremptory and harsh as a saw — we younger ones all had felt his edge — but he knew how to be a friend. One night when he was old, he named over to me all those of the dead who had been his friends. He said, "If they are there, Paradise is Paradise indeed."

He had a horseman's back, like his father, and would often sit on a chair as if it were a stool. He was wide awake and on watch, as if he expected a fly ball to be hit to him at any moment. He rarely loitered or ambled. Until he began to fail, when he was well into his eighties, he moved with great energy, a certain lightness, and the resolution sometimes of a natural force.

Even his gaiety was resolute. Or his gaiety came of a sort of freedom within his resolution. He was determined to do what he had to do; he would look for no escape; he was free. I always loved to watch him dress for the office, for often at that time he would be in a high good humor, dancing as he buttoned his shirt and knotted his tie, sometimes already wearing his hat before he put on his pants. He had things he wanted to do, and he could hardly wait.

I sat many a time, waiting for him, in the outer office where Miss Julia sat, typing, at her desk. I would know he was coming when I heard the street door open suddenly and almost in the same moment slam shut, rattling the glass, and then I would hear his footsteps light and rapid on the stairs, for characteristically he would be running. At the top, there would be two hard footfalls to check his speed, and he would hit the door, turning the knob, and the door would open as by the force of an explosion in the hallway, admitting my father, who would say all in one sentence: "Hello Andy Miss Julia what did we do with that Buttermore file?"

It would be the same when he came home: swift footfalls on the porch steps, three long strides across the porch followed by the implosion of the door—and there would be my father going full tilt to hang up his hat.

One day not long after Carp Harmon had been released from the penitentiary, my mother heard that pattern of sounds when she should not have heard it: in the middle of the morning. Nobody but my father came into the house that way, and she went to see what had brought him home. All this she told me after he was dead.

When she came into the front of the house, he was taking that little nickel-plated pistol from the top of the corner cupboard in the dining room.

"What are you doing?" she said.

It measures the strength of his love for her that he answered her straight. He said that he had seen Carp Harmon in town, and he was going to kill him.

I know well the look that anger put into my father's eyes; I can guess the size of the job my mother had on her hands.

She put herself in his way. She told him that killing Carp Harmon would not bring Uncle Andrew back. She told him he had more to think about than just Uncle Andrew. Or just himself. He had to think of his children, who would have to live with what he did.

He had to think of her.

It took her a long time, but she talked him out of it. He put the gun away.

She had spoken the simple truth: He could not bring Uncle Andrew back; he could not make justice by his own hand, according to his own will. She knew he was almost defeated, fallen under the weight of mortality and affliction and his own inclination toward the evil that afflicted him; he was nearly lost. And she called him back to his life and to us.

He told her one day that now he had nothing to live for.

"And then," she told me, "I let him have it. I felt for him as much as one human ever felt for another, but I let him have it. And it *did good!*"

In that time of grief and discouragement and defeat — it comes clear to me now — all that my father was and would ever be depended on my mother. I can see how near he came to turning loose all that he held together, and how, in holding it together, with my mother's help, he preserved the possibility of our life here; he quieted himself, lived, stayed on, bore what he had to bear. With my mother's help, he kept alive in his life our lives as they would be.

15

In the summer that I turned ten, the summer of Uncle Andrew's death, all the tobacco and corn on the Crayton Place was grown in the same field in the middle of the farm. The field was divided in two by a road, just a dirt track, by which we went from the gate on one side to the gate on the other. To the left of the road, going back, was a long, broad ridge, sloping gently to the fences on either side. To the right of the road and on the far side of the ridge, the slope was broken by hollows and was somewhat steeper. The field was beautifully laid out, so that all the rows followed the contours of the ridge. This was particularly noticeable in that far right-hand corner where the plowlands were smaller and were divided by grassed drains. The design of the field would have been my father's work: a human form laid lovingly upon the natural conformation of the place.

There came a morning when I stood in the dust of the road with a hoe in my hands, looking at the field, and was overcome by sudden comprehension of what was happening there. The corn was a little above knee-high, the tobacco plants about the size of a man's hat, both crops green and flourishing. R. T. and I were hoeing the tobacco. I could see Jake Branch plowing corn with a riding cultivator drawn by a good pair of black, white-nosed mules named Jack and Pete. Somewhere beyond the ridgetop, Col Oaks was plowing tobacco with a single mule, old Red, and a walking plow. The air smelled of vegetation and stirred earth. Beside

me, R. T. was filing his hoe. Standing there in the brilliance with my ears
sticking out under the brim of my straw hat and my mouth probably
hanging open (somebody was always telling me, "Shut your mouth,
Andy!"), I saw how beautiful the field was, how beautiful our work was.
And it came to me all in a feeling how everything fitted together, the place
and ourselves and the animals and the tools, and how the sky held us. I
saw how sweetly we were enabled by the land and the animals and our
few simple tools.

My moment of vision cannot have lasted long. It ended, I imagine,
when R. T. finished sharpening his hoe and nudged me with the file and
handed it to me. It was a powerful moment, a powerful vision nonetheless. I have lived under its influence ever since.

Its immediate result was that I became frantic to own a mule. I saw
how, owning a mule, a boy could become a man, an economic entity, dig-
nified and self-sustaining, capable of lovely work. I fixed my mind on
Pete, who was a little the tallest and a little the most stylish of the pair
Jake Branch was working that day in the corn rows. My conversations
with Uncle Andrew were all dominated by my obsessive importunings
and proposals for the purchase of the mule. I wanted to buy him on
credit, giving Uncle Andrew and my father my note for the full amount,
and pay for him by my work — which, given my irregular employment at
a quarter a day, would have taken quite a while.

It was a boy's dream, sufficiently absurd, and yet the passion that
attached to it I am still inclined to respect, for I still feel it. But Uncle
Andrew thought my obsession was funny, when he did not think it a nuisance. This was my first inkling that, as much as I wanted to be like him,
we were not alike. It was not a difference that I rationalized or made much
of, but I remember that it troubled me; something in the way I was had
set me apart from him, and I could not help but feel it. Though I know
more fully now than then how much I loved him, and though I love him
still, that is still a memory that troubles me.

After his death, anyhow, I went on to teachers who were more exacting: to Elton Penn, for one, and through Elton, to my father. Elton, whose
father had died when Elton was only a little boy, had made himself a student to my grandfather Catlett and to my father. My father thus spoke to
me through Elton before I learned to listen to him in his own right. And

so from the influence of Uncle Andrew I came at last under the influence
of my father, as perhaps I was destined to do from the first.

Elton and my father were alike in their love for farming and for work
well done. They loved the application of intelligence to problems. They
saw visions of things that could be done, and they drew great excitement
both from the visions themselves and from their practical results. I loved
those qualities in them, and longed to find or make the same qualities in
myself.

꙯

My father could be gentle to the point of tenderness, but he was not
invariably so. In certain moods, he had a way of landing on you like a
hawk on a rabbit. He could be wondrously impatient; whatever needed
doing he wanted already done by the time he thought of it, which would
have been going some. Or he could be fiercely put out because you did
not already know whatever he was trying to teach you. Sometimes this
amused Elton—he enjoyed mimicking my father in such moods—but
he suffered from it too, and so I could expect a certain amount of sympathy from him.

One day when I was angry at my father and needed somebody to
complain to, I found Elton out by his garden, sharpening bean poles. He
was kneeling on the ground in front of a small chopping block. He would
take a pole from the pile on his left, stand it on the block, point it with
three or four light licks of his hatchet, and lay it in the pile on his right.
I sat down, not offering to help, and began my complaint. Elton listened
to me, working steadily with his head down. For a long time he said
nothing.

Finally he said, "Well, you've got responsibilities, you know, that he's
trying to get you ready for."

I had known for a while what my answer to that would be, and I liked
the way it was going to sound: "My responsibilities can go to hell."

Elton stopped with the hatchet still in the air and looked at me with a
look that seemed to originate somewhere way back in his head. He
started to grin.

He said, "You don't know tumblebug language, do you?"

"No," I said.

He was wearing a leather glove on his right hand and he pulled it off. He held up two fingers in a V to represent the tumblebug's feelers. He wiggled the right-hand finger: "Roll it to the right!" He wiggled the left-hand finger: "Roll it to the left!" He wiggled both fingers: "Stop that shit!"

He wiggled both fingers at me with that look in his eyes and grinned, and the grin kept getting bigger.

I did not stop it that day, of course, for I had a long way still to go to be a grown man; sometimes I see that I have not altogether stopped it yet. But I had received the sign I was looking for.

16

I remember a later day — I was in college by then — when I went to my father's office to tell him of a certain very rough hill farm I wanted to buy in partnership with Elton Penn. It was a cool, bright day at the end of summer, the tobacco crop was in the barn, and Elton and I had been on the back of his place, disking the harvested field and drilling it in wheat.

We finished early in the afternoon, and dipped the last of the unplanted seed out of the drill. The Markman Place, adjoining Elton's at the back, had been put up for sale, and we stood leaning on the drill box in the satisfaction of the field replanted and safe for the winter, wondering who the buyer would be. The farm had been owned by an old couple, like many others, whose children had grown up and scattered to the towns. The husband had died on the place a good many years ago, and then, that spring, the wife had died at a nursing home down at Hargrave. Who the new owner would be was a mystery that troubled Elton, for it was unlikely that anybody would buy such a farm — small and off the road and now run down — as a place to live.

He stood silently looking over the fence a moment, and then he said, "Let's go over there and look at it."

And so we did. We climbed over the fence and started across a weedy field toward the house and outbuildings. Beyond the line fence the ridges grew narrower and dropped away toward the wooded hollows. Since the onset of Amster Markman's last illness, the farm had been cropped by a neighbor and otherwise unused. Briars and sumacs and young sassafras trees had begun to colonize in patches the pasture we were walking through.

We jumped a rabbit, and Elton mimed a shot, snapping an imaginary gun to his shoulder. I knew his mood. He was feeling free and excited; the most anxious stage of the year's work was behind him.

We went first to the house and walked around it, through the overgrown yard, to the front porch. We had in mind to look in through the windows — at least I did — but when we had climbed the steps we went no further. Miss Gladys Markman's ruffled curtains were still hanging in the windows. The porch swing still swung from its rusty hooks.

At the edge of the porch we stood and looked out past the sugar maple in the yard and over the tops of the trees on the bluff into the Bird's Branch valley. You could not help but imagine Gladys and Amster Markman, old and alone, sitting there in the cool of the evening.

"It's a fine place for a house," Elton said.

"It is," I said, moved by possibility.

"And it's a good house, too," Elton said. "It's been kept up. Nothing wrong with it at all." He looked at me and grinned, knowing that I had a girl I was serious about down at Hargrave.

We went on around the other side of the house and drew a drink from the well by the kitchen door. Elton stood with his hand still on the pump handle, looking at the weed-covered garden plot and the lots out by the barns. "Nobody going out to milk here *this* evening," he said.

The old tobacco barn was twisted and leaning as though about to collapse under the weight of its roof. The small feed barn was still straight, square, level, and plumb; we went in through the half-open door. The field we had walked across had been unscarred beneath the weed growth, and now we saw that Amster Markman had planted flagstones edge-up beneath the stall partitions and thus kept the manure from rotting the wood.

"He was a good farmer," Elton said. "He had that name."

There were stalls for four horses on one side of the driveway. On the other side there was a little feed room and two large pens, one with tie chains and troughs for five cows. A set of old harness still hung from pegs in front of two of the stalls. All the doors had neat wooden latches. There was still hay in the loft.

When we stepped out again into the daylight, Elton said, "Let's you and me buy this old place and set it to rights."

He was watching me, grinning again, to see how the thought would hit me. Remembering it now, I cannot be sure how serious he was. It was at least a thought that he could not resist thinking. And he was grinning, I suppose, because he knew that I could not resist it either.

"But how would I get the money?" I said.

"I don't know." He was still looking at me, grinning, poking in his shirt pocket for his cigarettes. "Maybe Wheeler would help you. You ought to ask him."

The possibility then seemed to descend upon us and envelop us, like a sudden change of weather. It changed everything: our minds, the day, the place.

We went into the careening tobacco barn.

"The framing and innards are all sound," Elton said. "It could be straightened up."

We spent a quarter of an hour dreaming aloud of what could be done. And then we walked in the other ridgetop fields, down into the woods, and back up by the lane that went out to the road.

"Here's a place where a young fellow could get started and go on," Elton said.

I knew it was. The thought of it had already gone all through me. It aches in me yet, though the Markman Place never became a real farm again and the house was vandalized and finally burned by hunters.

By the time we crossed the line fence again we knew the layout of the place, and we had thought of a way to farm it.

And so, late that afternoon, I climbed up the sounding well of my father's office stairs, the noises of the street shut out behind me so that I rose up within the sound of my own steps. At the top of the stairs I took the two further steps to the office door and opened it into the waiting room, now empty, where Miss Julia Vye's typewriter sat beneath its gray cover. The room was full of the level-lying late sunlight that entered through the back windows. I shut the door quietly and took another couple of steps to see if my father was at his desk.

He had already swiveled his chair around. He was smiling. He said, "Come in, Andy."

He was in one of his beautiful times. I knew of the times when he would quietly enter the shade where his cattle were resting, and sit down. I knew too that he loved the seldom-occurring times late in the afternoons when he sat on at his desk after the office had emptied, when he could be as quiet as the room, ordering his thoughts. It was a time when time seemed to have stopped and his work itself was at rest.

Sometimes when I interrupted him at work in the press of a day's events, he could be short enough, but now he welcomed me into his ease.

"Sit down. I'm glad to see you."

He positioned a chair for me and I sat down. He laid his writing pad on top of one of the neat stacks of books and papers on his desk. He screwed the top back onto his fountain pen, took off his glasses and rubbed his eyes, and then he looked at me.

"What have you got on your mind?"

I told him. Though I guessed that he already knew the Markman Place, I described it to him as Elton and I had seen it, walking over it. I told him the possibilities we had seen.

My father's attention, when he freely turned it to you, was a benevolent atmosphere. His hearing was the native element of my tale. He knew what I had seen; he had imagined such restorations as I had imagined; he had felt my excitement and my longing. The possibility I was trying to find voice for — an old place renewed and carried on — had kept him a farmer, though he was also a lawyer; it had sent him into endless struggles. Now, having lived to the age he was then and past it, and thinking of my own children, I know how stirred he was, listening to me, for he was hearing his own passion uttered to him by his son.

And yet he talked me out of it.

"Wait," he said. "You've got more directions in you than you know."

He wanted me to be free for a while longer. Perhaps he felt free to keep me free because he saw that I was already securely bound; my wish of that day would not leave me, though I had yet to drift far from it and return. In talking me out of my hope, he accorded it a gentleness that enabled me to keep it always.

17

Now that I have told virtually all I know of the story of Uncle Andrew and of his death and how we fared afterward, I see that I must return to my old question — What manner of man was he? — and make peace with it, for I am by no means certain of the answer. A story, I see, is not a life. A story must follow a line; the telling must begin and end. A life, on the contrary, would be impossible to fix in time, for it does not begin within itself, and it does not end.

Within limits we can know. Within somewhat wider limits we can imagine. We can extend compassion to the limit of imagination. We can love, it seems, beyond imagining. But how little we can understand!

Whatever he was, Uncle Andrew was more than I know. In drawing him toward me again after so long a time, I seem to have summoned, not into view or into thought, but just within the outmost reach of love, Uncle Andrew in the plenitude of his being—the man he would have been for my sake, and for love of us all, had he been capable. In recalling him as I knew him in mortal time, I have felt his presence as a living soul.

However we may miss and mourn the dead, we really give little deference to death. "Death," a friend of mine said as he approached it himself, "is a convention . . . not binding upon anyone but the keepers of graveyard records." The dead remain in thought as much alive as they ever were, and yet increased in stature and grown remarkably near. The older I have got and the better acquainted among the dead, the plainer it has become to me that I live in the company of immortals.

�֎

One by one, the sharers in this mortal damage have borne its burden out of the present world: Uncle Andrew, Grandpa Catlett, Grandma, Momma-pie, Aunt Judith, my father, and many more. At times perhaps I could wish them merely oblivious, and the whole groaning and travailing world at rest in their oblivion. But how can I deny that in my belief they are risen?

I imagine the dead waking, dazed, into a shadowless light in which they know themselves altogether for the first time. It is a light that is merciless until they can accept its mercy; by it they are at once condemned and redeemed. It is Hell until it is Heaven. Seeing themselves in that light, if they are willing, they see how far they have failed the only justice of loving one another; it punishes them by their own judgment. And yet, in suffering that light's awful clarity, in seeing themselves within it, they see its forgiveness and its beauty, and are consoled. In it they are loved completely, even as they have been, and so are changed into what they could not have been but what, if they could have imagined it, they would have wished to be.

That light can come into this world only as love, and love can enter only by suffering. Not enough light has ever reached us here among the shadows, and yet I think it has never been entirely absent.

Remembering, I suppose, the best days of my childhood, I used to think I wanted most of all to be happy — by which I meant to be here and to be undistracted. If I were here and undistracted, I thought, I would be at home.

But now I have been here a fair amount of time, and slowly I have learned that my true home is not just this place but is also that company of immortals with whom I have lived here day by day. I live in their love, and I know something of the cost. Sometimes in the darkness of my own shadow I know that I could not see at all were it not for this old injury of love and grief, this little flickering lamp that I have watched beside for all these years.